All
You Need
is
Love

Also by Carole Matthews and available from Headline Review

Let's Meet on Platform 8
A Whiff of Scandal
More to Life than This
For Better, For Worse
A Minor Indiscretion
A Compromising Position
The Sweetest Taboo
With or Without You
You Drive Me Crazy
Welcome to the Real World
The Chocolate Lovers' Club
The Chocolate Lovers' Diet
It's a Kind of Magic

All
You Need
is
Love

CAROLE
MATTHEWS

headline
review

First published in 2008 by Headline Review
An imprint of HEADLINE PUBLISHING GROUP

1

Cataloguing in Publication Data is available from the British Library

Hardback ISBN 978 0 7553 4575 5
Trade paperback ISBN 978 0 7553 4576 2

Typeset in Bembo by
Palimpsest Book Production Limited, Grangemouth, Stirlingshire

Printed and bound in the UK by
CPI Mackays, Chatham ME5 8TD

Headline's policy is to use papers that are natural, renewable and recyclable
products and made from wood grown in sustainable forests.
The logging and manufacturing processes are expected to
conform to the environmental regulations of the country of origin.

HEADLINE PUBLISHING GROUP
An Hachette Livre UK Company
338 Euston Road
London NW1 3BH

www.headline.co.uk
www.hachettelivre.co.uk

For my cousin, Allan Case. Who lived life to the full.

9 September 1952–9 December 2006

ACKNOWLEDGEMENTS

Lovely Kev and I spent several wonderful days back in Liverpool doing research for this book. It was great to visit places again that I hadn't been to in years – the Cavern Club, Penny Lane and we even took a ferry across the Mersey in the pouring rain. The city is looking very spruce. If you haven't been to Liverpool, it's well worth it and the people are second to none. I highly recommend it.

Thanks to top mate, Paula DeGiorgio, for giving me the guided tour of her Liverpool, including a very enlightening morning at Great Homer Street market – or Greatie. Never have so many clothes cost me so little. The Duck Bus was fun too.

For authenticity, there are a couple of chapters set at the Tate Liverpool – a fab gallery – but all of the events and characters in this novel are completely fictitious.

Spencer's home, Alderstone, was inspired by a trip to Althorp Hall in Northamptonshire, seat of the Spencer family and childhood home of Diana, Princess of Wales. Another great place to visit for the day – the gallery of Diana's clothes is simply gorgeous.

Chapter One

Sally Freeman, Single Mum and Superwoman to the rescue once again.

'Let me take those for you, love,' I say to Mrs Kapur, who is struggling up the first flight of stairs, a heavy bag of shopping from the local Save-It supermarket in each hand.

'Lift's out again, Sally,' she mutters at me. 'Little buggers. It's the third time this week they've stuck up those buttons with chewy. I'll give them a bloody clip round the ear if I catch them.'

It would probably be the last thing that she did. Mrs Kapur's a tiny woman — all wrinkles and sinew — no match for the hulking great youths who hang around the flats looking for trouble and, invariably, finding it. I'm about a foot taller than her and I'm a little shorty myself.

Living on the tenth floor isn't easy at any age — I'm out of puff when I get up there. When you're well past pensionable age, as my lovely neighbour is, it must be a nightmare. The old lady stops and leans against the wall while she catches her breath. It's about 80 degrees out there. The sun's cracking the flags — those that haven't already been cracked for years because the Council never gets round to fixing them. Despite the heat, Mrs Kapur's still wearing a thick coat and a headscarf over her sari.

Super Sal takes the bags from her. 'Stocking up?' I ask.

'I'm out of everything,' she says with a shake of her head. 'No bog roll. No cat food.'

Technically, we are not supposed to have cats in our tower block but no one minds Mrs Kapur's big ginger moggy, Gandhi — apart from the Council, of course. That cat's the only company she has these days. He was originally called something else, something more cat-like — Tiddles or Puss-puss — but all the residents rechristened him and it kind of stuck. Now even Mrs Kapur calls him Gandhi. 'Got my pension today, though.' She gives me a gappy smile.

'I hope you've treated yourself to a nice big cream cake.'

'I have that,' she chuckles. 'Got Gandhi a bit of fresh fish too, as well as his tins. Probably why my bags are so heavy.'

'I've told you before,' I remind her. 'I'll do your shopping for you. All you have to do is give me a knock and tell me what you want. I'm up there every day.'

'I don't like to bother you, doll.'

'I've got naff all else to do, Mrs K. It's no trouble.'

'You're a sound girl, Sally Freeman. What would I do without you?'

Get one of your lazy, good-for-nothing sons to look after you, I want to say, but I don't. She adores them all – lazy bastards that they are – and wouldn't have a word said against them. They deign to pop in for five minutes once in a blue moon and then, strangely, she never seems to be able to find her pension money when they've gone. And I thought Indian families were supposed to be close?

Hoisting up the Save-It bags, I say, 'Ready for the assault on the north face?'

She laughs at that.

Unlike other Superheroes, I don't have my own cape or Lycra outfit emblazoned with an eye-catching flash of lightning. No. All I've got is a Matalan T-shirt, charity shop jeans – very last season – and cheap shoes off one of the stalls on Kirberly market. No silky padded knickers and star-spangled corset for this Wonder Woman.

'Come on, Mrs K. You can make me a quick cup of tea when we get to the top.' Most Superheroes get to save the world; all I do is stop frail old biddies from having heart-attacks because some bored-senseless little shite thought it was fun to vandalise the lifts.

I put my hand under Mrs Kapur's elbow and give her a bit of encouragement up the stairs. 'Ever thought of applying to the Council for a bungalow, Mrs K? Or what about sheltered housing?' Even if she lived on the second or third floor it would have to be better than this.

She takes the steps painfully slowly, lifting one tiny foot to the next stair then a mammoth effort until the other joins it. My son, Charlie, walked like this when he was two years old. Now he's ten and he runs up here like a wildebeest with a hungry lion at its bum.

Mrs Kapur stops and takes a few laboured breaths. 'I've lived here all my life, doll. I can't move now. This is all I know. Where would I go?' She shakes her head again and her scarf falls over her eyes. I put down one of the bags and push it back for her. 'I'll be going out of here in a wooden box.'

Sooner than she'd like if she has to keep using these stairs. The Council has given up bothering to come and fix the lift, no matter how many times I ring and complain. It works for about three days – sometimes not even that long – then someone kicks in the door or pulls off the control panel. Once there was a big pile of poo in there and, frankly, I couldn't swear that it was from a dog. In my role as Superwoman, I had to clean it up, of course. I'm on first-name terms with everyone in the local Housing Department – not that it does me any good. You'd think they'd be nicer to one of their regulars. Frankly, their customer service isn't what it should be.

While we catch our breath, I'll tell you a bit more about where I live. It's what's commonly called a 'sink estate' on the outskirts of Liverpool. Our tower block – one of three on the estate – is bordered by a rag-tag of run-down Council houses and prefabs which probably should be condemned by now. Row upon row of grey, box-like houses that were built as a temporary measure during the Second World War with nothing more substantial than Lego bricks, they still manage to defy the elements and stay standing to this day. William Shankly House – named for the legendary manager of Liverpool Football Club – was built in the late 1960s and should have been knocked down in the early 1970s. Why some bright spark thought this would be a fitting tribute to the great man, I'll never know. Bill Shankly would never have put up with this crap. He'd be spinning in his grave now, bless him, if he could see this. It's a concrete monument to all that was bad about British architecture at that time. Whoever decided that high-rise city living was desirable? Some over-paid architect living in a low-rise cottage surrounded by rolling countryside and nothing but the sound of skylarks, no doubt.

The outside of the building is unpainted pebbledash stained with dark streaks of damp that meander down its pock-marked sides. Inside isn't any better. The stairwells are dark and dingy; the lights are always on the blink, and after dark they're a mugger's paradise. As there aren't any public lavatories around here and the youths of today clearly have very weak bladders, the entrance hall is frequently used as a toilet. I wedge the front door open every day, but no amount of fresh air can get rid of the all-pervading putrid smell. When it's hot, like today, it makes you want to heave.

3

While Mrs K and I tackle the steps to the next floor, I'll tell you a bit about me too – other than the fact that I'm an unpaid Superwoman. I'm twenty-seven years old, but feel as if I've lived three lifetimes already. I've got lots of 'smile' lines for my age – even though, sometimes, there's not been a lot to smile about. I'm fit as a flea from climbing ten flights of stairs a dozen times a day. Think of all the money I save on expensive gym membership! You have to look on the positive side, don't you? My friend, Debs, highlights my hair every few weeks for nothing, which I like to think makes me look younger. I've got one of those trendy, short bobs – also courtesy of Debs – which is borne mainly out of a need to have low-maintenance hair because, despite being unemployed, I never seem to have time to do it. Most of my life is devoted to my ten-year-old son, Charlie, who's the best thing that's ever happened to me. I might be crap at most things in life, but I'm a bloody good mum. Despite what the *Daily Mail* might have you believe, not all single mums are slappers, sponging off the state and spending their benefit on Smirnoff Ice.

Having vented that, I have to take a deep breath and say, perhaps needlessly, that Charlie's dad isn't around. What a charmer he turned out to be. Left me when I was six months' pregnant for a Mrs Robinson-type woman from that hotbed of sin, St Helens. Thank goodness that we never married. I reckon that I had a lucky escape. He did suggest that he do the decent thing but, to be honest, he wouldn't have known the decent thing if it had bopped him on the nose. To prove my point, I can tell you that the onetime love of my life is now a permanent guest of Her Majesty – spending his days in Walton Prison for armed robbery. In my book, that means he's given up any rights to see me or Charlie ever again.

As it happens, I left the space for the father's name blank on Charlie's birth certificate. Very wisely, as it turns out. But it's something which the Child Support Agency are a bit put out about. They probably imagined that I'd had a different fella every night and didn't know which of the lucky souls was the dad. I wish. I'd been with Charlie's dad for three years – not exactly a flash in the pan. To call him my childhood sweetheart might be pushing it a bit, but we met at school when we were fourteen. He'd been my only proper boyfriend; the only person I'd ever slept with. I wasn't like my mates either, crossing their fingers as their favoured method of contraception. Charlie was the result of a dodgy condom – must have been. In my mind I was being really careful.

4

We never, ever did it without protection. And look what happened. I wonder, one day, will all single mums rally together to sue condom manufacturers? If I'd known about the morning-after pill – or if it had even existed then – my life could have turned out very different.

All my big career plans, such as they were, went out of the window once my squawking bundle of joy was born. I had to abandon my childcare course at the local Technical College which I'd only just started. But what little I did learn certainly came in handy. Now I feel older – much older – and wiser. And I wouldn't change a thing, as Charlie – now a ten-year-old grunting bundle of pre-teen angst – has brought me nothing but happiness. He's my sole reason for getting out of bed in the morning.

Now we're at the top landing and we both stop and puff for a bit. Even if you're fit and a Superhero, this is a long way up. My flat's opposite Mrs Kapur's on the top floor and just a bit further down the landing. I got the flat when I was seventeen. I'd just had Charlie and, believe me, I was *so* grateful at the time. I didn't know where else I was going to go. Mum had not long since died and I knew that I couldn't stay in the house with Dad. You don't want to bring up a baby around a raging drunk, do you? I could never have left Charlie alone with him. The man just wasn't safe. He'd always had a drink problem, but with Mum gone he went completely to pieces. One minute he'd be sober and all smiles, the next – when he'd had a few too many bevvies – he'd be crashing round the place, cursing fit to make Gordon Ramsay blush and trying to pick a fight with the telly. Anyway, he's gone too now. I know it sounds harsh, but good riddance, I say. He never was a father to me.

I look round at the peeling paint and listen to Mrs Kapur's breathless wheezing. This place felt like a sanctuary when I first moved in, my own little oasis, somewhere I could call home. I didn't even mind lugging the pram up ten flights of stairs. Funny how your opinion changes over the years.

Chapter Two

I unpacked Mrs Kapur's shopping for her too. Not that she had much, bless her. There's hardly anything in her cupboards. I felt guilty taking a cuppa from her *and* she wanted to share her cream cake. She's such a love. Turns out she'd only bought the cake because today was its sell-by date and she'd got it half-price. Is this what our poor pensioners are reduced to? Buying about-to-go-off cream cakes? Makes you proud to be British, eh?

Now I'm back in my flat, I go to see what's lurking in my own kitchen cupboards. It's not exactly a treasure trove of gourmet delights in here either, but Charlie and I never go hungry – that's one thing I'm very particular about. The rest of the kids round here seem to exist on nothing but pizza and turkey twizzlers. I'd rather not pay my leccy bill than go without food. I'm sure my power company don't feel quite the same. They'd rather see us starve. Bastards. I make sure that Charlie gets fresh veg every day; at the worst, when times are hard, frozen peas. He can only have cola once a day. And I buy the cheap crap from Save-It, so he actually doesn't like it that much. He just complains about it because that's what kids do. No doubt he thinks I'm a mingy old bat, but I tell him it's for his own good. One day when he's big and strong and has all his own teeth and isn't dying of obesity or heart disease, he'll thank me.

Glancing at my watch, I realise that I'd better get moving if I'm going to get to my computer course on time. Sorting out Mrs Kapur has taken much longer than I bargained for, so now food will have to wait. Unfortunately, my exemplary dietary habits only extend to when my son's here.

Probably couldn't eat, anyway. This is only the third week of my course and I'm still feeling very nervous about the whole thing. It's the first time that I've ever done anything for myself – just for me – and there's a certain amount of anxiety involved in that as I'm *so* determined not to fail. I was completely useless at school, mainly because I used to spend half my nights looking after Mum when she was ill, so all that I wanted to do during the day was put my head down on the desk and go to sleep. Often, I did. Then I ditched my college course when I got knocked up. So, this is the first time I've ventured back into any form of education since then and, frankly, I'm bricking it.

There's a knock at the door and I know who it is. I also know that I don't have time for this. Sighing inwardly, I go to open it. As I suspected, Johnny's standing there. His little dog Ringo's at his feet, as always.

'I've got five minutes and then I've got to go,' I tell him as I walk away from the door.

Johnny and Ringo follow me into the living room, where I start to check whether I've got my phone, my purse, my notebook, my pen.

'I came to see if you wanted me to pick Charlie up from school,' Johnny says to my back.

'You could have phoned me.'

Johnny shrugs apologetically. 'I was out and about.' He stands awkwardly, filling the small room.

Softening, I smile at him. I've nothing to be cross with Johnny about, for goodness sake. Plus it's very hard to stay mad when he's around. He grins back at me, running his hands through his shock of dark hair which always looks as if it's been styled by a Saturday girl. 'Thanks, Johnny. You're a mate.'

At that, his smile fades. Even Ringo looks at me with limpid eyes, tail tucked between his legs. I guess the worst thing that you can tell someone who's in love with you is that he's a mate. Even their dog gets naffed off.

Okay, so this is how it is. Not too long ago, Johnny and I were more than just mates. John Paul George Jones – even his dad, the world's biggest Beatles fan, balked at adding Ringo to his son's names – and I were together for about five years. On-off. Off-on. It was always me that called it off and always me that asked him to come back. Johnny might be irritatingly laid-back, but he's also a hard person to live without.

I finally split with him about six months ago, this time for good. Honestly. It was horrible and really hard, because – essentially – there's nothing really wrong with Johnny. (Apart from the dodgy name, of course.) He's handsome, funny and, to be honest, pretty fab in bed. He's great at remembering to take the bins out. He knows what to do with

7

the working end of a Black & Decker. He can use the washing machine. What more could I want in a fella, you might ask. It's just that he and I have different ideas about how we should live our lives. I'm trying to better myself. I don't want Charlie to spend all his life here. I want to get out of this dead-end place, make a nicer life for us. I'm not sure where yet, but I know that the universe doesn't begin and end in Liverpool. I'm going places. I have ambition.

Johnny, on the other hand, has none. He's a dreamer, drifting through his life, being buffeted along by the current, going where it takes him. Which doesn't seem to be any further than the end of his street. I can't do that. And I can't be with someone who thinks like that. It's dragging me down, keeping me under, pinning me to this place. He's happy here, happy with his lot. He loves the place. Johnny doesn't have a full-time job because he's the primary carer for his mum and that doesn't really bother him – and I think it should. He's young, fit, bright – he should want more. He doesn't think what else might be out there, just waiting around the corner, if only he'd try to stretch himself. I'm sure my former lover thinks that people like us shouldn't have ambition. That we should be content with our given place down in the gutter of the planet. But I can't do piss poor for the rest of my life. I've had enough of it. I want more. And that's what's driven us apart. Simple as that.

The Government have started up a 'Back to Work' programme round here – or, as I like to put it, a 'Get Off Bloody Benefits and Earn Your Own Way, You Miserable Scroungers' programme. Because it's free and held just down the road from me, I've signed on for 'Computing for Beginners' – proof that I've moved on and have begun to build the kind of life that I want for me and Charlie. Okay, so I'm never going to be the next Bill Gates, but it's a step in the right direction, yeah? I'm twenty-seven, for goodness sake – positively a raddled old bird to be thinking of taking on the world of work for the first time – and I'll admit that there's a panic welling inside me that if I don't do something now to break away, then I never will. I'll be stuck here forever like Mrs Kapur, grunting up the stairs with my meagre shopping and my cream cakes that are on the turn until the Grim Reaper comes for me.

To be honest, I'm not sure that computing is entirely my bag. I don't really see myself as nine to five office material, but it's a start. Everyone needs to know about computers, right? Even the telly seems to be a complicated beast these days with its digital and analogue and terrestrial and Freeview and all that stuff. You need a flipping degree to get it to record *Who Wants To Be A Millionaire?*. And at least I'm *doing* something.

'Shall I go and get Charlie then?'

'What?' I'd forgotten that Johnny was still waiting patiently for my answer.

'I remembered that you were at your course today and wondered if I should meet Charlie. I'm sure he'd like to see Ringo.'

'Oh,' I say, all thoughts of doom and gloom receding. 'That's nice. Thanks, Johnny.' Charlie's being bullied at the moment, probably because I can't afford the latest trainers for him. You know what kids are like. Little bastards. Every one of them except my own, of course.

'I miss him,' Johnny says quietly.

The hardest part about this break-up is that Johnny adores Charlie and, for better, for worse, Charlie adores Johnny. But am I supposed to stay with a man simply because my son loves him more than I do? I've spent many nights lying awake at three o'clock worrying about this. If I could get air miles for my guilt trip, I'd be in the Bahamas now.

When he was younger and Johnny and I broke up, it didn't really matter to Charlie. A day, a week or even a month . . . as a child you just don't register the passing of time; it could be ages before he'd cotton on to the fact that Johnny wasn't around. Now, of course, it's very different. Charlie, unfortunately, has his own opinions on the matter. Frequently, they seem to differ from mine.

'I know you miss him. He misses you too.' I sling my bag on my shoulder, indicating that it's time for me to leave as I try to ignore those nipping guilty feelings again. 'You know that you can come round to see him anytime anything you want. Why don't you stay for your tea tonight? We're only having pasta. I can throw a bit more in. Stretch the mince between the three of us.'

'I'd like that,' Johnny says, and I can't look at him because his voice sounds choked.

Johnny hasn't moved on. As I said, Johnny, I'm sure, is still in love with me. What can I do?

I give a little tsk at my watch. 'I've got to go,' I say. Avoid the issue, that's what.

Chapter Three

Crossing the road, I head off to my computer course. The organisation that's running it has taken over a council house that previously looked like it had been bombed out. To be fair, they've given it a lick of paint inside, mended the smashed windows and, what was a separate lounge and dining room have now been knocked together to form one big space. There are eight computers in there and the course has a full house. I had to wait six months to get a place.

It's been a long, hot summer. Now it's early September and the weather is still bestowing its blessings on us. Frankly, I love global warming. I'm guilt-free when it comes to my carbon footprint, since I don't have car, I've been on a plane twice in my life, I'm frugal with my power consumption because I can't afford not to be, and I use my Save-It Bag For Life every day because now they have the audacity to charge 5p if you want a new one. The only benefit I get out of all this is the nice sunshine. Bring it on!

All the grass at the front of the house has been burned to a nice brown crisp by the sun and is waiting patiently for the rain to return. I swing in through the open front door, humming to myself. This is the third week of my course, and it's fair to say that I'm not proving to be a natural. To be honest, I'm even struggling to remember how to turn the damn thing on. In my own defence, my only skirmishes with technology so far have been programming the DVD and making calls on my mobile phone. I haven't even used a typewriter, so this whole computing thing is just a bit scary.

I go in and head for the computer that I've bagged as mine. It's near the window, so if I get too bored I can stare out to see if there's anything happening on the estate. Which there never is. Not that I've had much time to do that in previous lessons. I know all the other people on the course, but I won't bother to introduce them because, frankly, they're not that interesting. They're mainly all dossers from this estate, long-term unemployed and social misfits. There's a couple of car thieves, each supposedly turning over a new leaf – which will be a severe blow to the second-hand car market round here. There's a disabled guy, Tom, who comes in his wheelchair and he's the best of us all. But then he spends the rest of his life playing computer games, so technically he should be. Davy in the corner is a career burglar. He can rob you anything you want to order. Not sure how much use a computer will be to him in his business ventures. He already knows that he can pick one up and run through the door with it or lob it out of the open window to his waiting accomplice – does he need to know any more? Is he going to do a spreadsheet to make sure he doesn't burgle the same place twice? Make a pie chart of the house most worth plundering?

I look round as I take my place. I'm the only single mum. Another drain on society, right? I'm the only woman on the course, in fact. No girlie chats to pass the time for me. This lot mean business and, un-usually for Scousers, hardly say a word. They get their heads down and crack on. But I shouldn't be scathing about the others, it's mean of me. You're hardly going to get lawyers in pinstripe suits on Government-funded courses on sink estates. These guys are only here trying their best. Like me. Maybe they, too, have realised that there might be a better way.

Our tutor is waiting for us. And – I can't entirely blame this on the wonderful weather – I go all hot. Think computers and you think, baldy bloke with greying, bushy beard wearing Jesus sandals with brown socks. Am I right? Spencer Knight, our tutor, is *well* far removed from that. He is one hot mother. Actually, no – *I'm* the hot mother! I can feel myself redden in unusual places as he comes over. What looks like measles springs out all over my chest.

'Hello, Sally,' he says.

'Hiya. Sorry I'm late.'

'You're not late.'

No, I'm not. I'm bang on time. It's just that I have no idea what else to say. My tongue, which seems to have expanded to twice its normal size, is now lolling uselessly in my mouth. There's a hint of a smile at Spencer's lips. I think he might be laughing at me.

'Have you managed to do any practice this week?'

I shrug. 'Haven't got a computer.'

'Sorry,' he says. 'I forgot. Would you like me to see if I can get hold of one for you?'

He could do worse than ask Davy. That's about all I could afford to pay, knock-off prices. 'It'd have to be cheap,' I say. 'But that'd be sound.'

'Sound?'

'Great,' I correct. 'That would be great.' Spencer's not from round here. He's from somewhere posh. He talks like the Queen. Everything comes out with massive long vowels. He doesn't say 'yeah', he says 'yaaah'. We all have to repeat most of our sentences so that he understands us. Everyone round here has a really thick Scouse accent; it comes with the turf and it can be hard to get your head round. But I try very hard to speak nicely and still he doesn't understand a word I'm saying!

Spencer Knight doesn't dress like us either. This estate is shell-suit city – shiny nylon rules. In a place where putting on the latest Liverpool or Everton football shirt is considered dressing up, Spencer's style stands out a bit. Today, he's wearing an ice-blue tailored shirt over black trousers with fine, blue pin-stripes in them. The shirt has enormous cuffs with huge cufflinks in them. His brown hair's all ruffled up. But it's a stylish mess – a fifty quid cut – not like Johnny's which is a plain and simple mess. He's got the most flawless skin I've ever seen on a man and I bet if I peeked in his bathroom cabinet, I'd find a whole range of expensive moisturising products. He's probably thirty, maybe even a couple of years older, but he looks like he's had a life of ease. His demeanour speaks of exotic holidays, business-class travel and fast cars. His eyes are clear blue, offset perfectly by the shirt, and when I look at them my mouth goes dry. No one's eyes have done that to me before. In short, Spencer looks like a catalogue model. But in a good way. I'm talking Versace rather than Littlewoods.

My jeans and T-shirt feel cheap and nasty in comparision and I've never really noticed that kind of stuff before. For the first time in my life, I wish I had stacks of designer labels in my wardrobe. Trouble is, if you wear labels round here then everyone assumes that they're fakes or knock-offs. No one would be stupid enough to pay the prices they want for the real McCoy.

The other students are all here now. One's a builder who wants to do his accounts on his computer – must have had a tug from the tax man and has seen the error of his ways. I haven't had a chance to talk to the other two yet, so we nod our hellos and then I switch on and try to pick up where we left off last week – creating a Word document. Despite my fears, I can actually remember what we did, even though there's been a heap of other useless crap through my brain since then.

When we're settled in, Spencer does a tour of the class, moving us onto the next part of the workbook. He gets to me and scoots a chair up next to mine, resting his arm across the back of it. My heart beats faster and it's not just because I think he's going to find fault with what I'm doing. My fingers hit all the wrong keys.

'Looks good,' he says over my shoulder. Despite it being like an oven in here, Spencer is as cool as a cucumber. The Council might have stretched to a new coat of paint and some computers for this place, but it didn't think about air-conditioning, and the windows are screwed shut.

I smile shyly at him. 'Thanks.' Then he sits and watches me while I type, arms folded, legs stretched out. His shoes are amazing. I know very little about shoes, but I'd bet a pound that they're handmade. I'd swear that his socks are silk too. I look at him and wonder what he's doing here, down among the low-lifes and the socially-deserted.

'You're staring at me,' he says, giving me a smile that offers a glimpse of his perfectly white, perfectly-spaced teeth.

'Sorry, sorry.' I switch back to my computer, embarrassed to have been caught out, and bash at the keys again.

He leans towards me. 'I rather like it,' he says.

'I was just admiring your shoes.'

Spencer laughs at that. 'My shoes?' He stares at his own feet, shaking his head. 'My shoes.'

'They're nice,' I say a little crisply. So I like his shoes — so what? It's no big deal. I'm not asking him to marry me.

'Thank you.' Spencer puts a hand on my chair and swivels me towards him. His face is very close to mine and he smells wonderful, of freshly-laundered clothes, soap and expensive aftershave. Even his scent is out of place here and I want to inhale him, fill my senses with him, drive the smell of damp and piss and poverty out of my brain. He glances over at the others, but they're all engrossed in their work. 'This is probably highly inappropriate behaviour,' he says, lowering his voice. 'But would you let me buy you dinner tomorrow night?'

'Dinner?'

'Or a drink. You're not busy, are you?'

Busy? *Moi?*

'Dinner's great.'

'I'll pick you up at eight.'

'I'll meet you somewhere.' There's no way I want him coming to the flats.

'I know where you live,' he says. 'It's on the register. I thought we'd drive out somewhere. I'll come for you.'

He knows where I live and yet he still wants to ask me out!

I nod. 'Okay.'

'Sound,' he says in his cut-glass tones as he stands up, a smile curling his lips. He's teasing me but, for some strange reason, I really don't mind.

Chapter Four

'Are you all right there, Mam?'

'Right as rain, son,' Mary Jones replied, trying to smile despite her pain.

'I'll get you some tea ready now,' Johnny said, heading to the kitchen through the crowd of furniture that was too big for the room. 'I'm going over to Sally's for mine.'

'That right?' His mother's voice brightened. She turned the volume down on the television, fading her best friend, Noel Edmonds, into the background. Finding out about her son's love-life was clearly more important than discovering whether the contestant went for a *Deal or No Deal*. 'Does that mean that yous two are back on?'

'No way,' he told her. 'I just want to spend some time with Charlie.'

'Breaks my heart,' Mary said, suddenly sounding teary. 'That boy's like a grandson to me. I love the bones of him. You should have married that girl while you had the chance, Johnny Boy.'

'I don't think I ever did have the chance, Mam.'

'You were such a lovely couple.'

'I thought so too. Sometimes it just doesn't work out as you want it to.' Wasn't that the story of his life?

'It wasn't because of me, was it?' Mary wanted to know. 'It wasn't because I'm a burden to you? You've said nothing about why you split up. Not many women would want to take on an invalid mother.' She hit at her leg with her walking stick.

'Don't do that, Mam,' he chided. But it was true, his mam was like a walking medical encyclopaedia.

Mary Jones had every 'itis' known to man. Arthritis, phlebitis, diverticulitis, gastritis, fibrositis and a few other ones he couldn't remember the name of. She'd suffered ill-health for as long as he could recall. At Charlie's age he'd been doing the ironing for the whole family because his mam couldn't stand for long enough to manage it.

He looked round the dingy, damp room. Perhaps it had been living here that had made things worse for her. All winter, condensation ran down the inside of the walls and the windows. His mam coughed non-stop from October through to April, phlegmy, wracking hacks that shook right through her body and set the teeth of the casual observer on edge. Worryingly, even the brilliant summer this year hadn't seemed to have offered her much respite. She was still comparatively young, especially in these days when sixty was the new forty – but you wouldn't think it, to look at Mary Jones. Instead of spending her twilight years on cruises or skateboarding or whatever it was that pensioners did today with their leisure time, Mary was confined to her armchair. Her daily intake of tablets were lined up on its worn arms. She was a one-woman drain on the NHS and Mary Jones could never say that she hadn't had her fair share of free medicine in her lifetime.

Her hair was thin due to the drugs; her skin grey through lack of sunshine. And it broke Johnny's heart to see her like this. His mother had been a looker in her day, with bright, clear eyes and high cheek-bones; now she was plump, soft with the folds of inactivity. A couple of years ago, when it became too hard for her to climb up to her bedroom every night, Johnny bought a single divan out of the local paper and they'd set it up in what used to be the dining room. They'd also got a grant from the Council to convert the understairs cupboard into a loo with a tiny washbasin. Now his mam's entire world was confined to the ground floor of her house, with only occasional trips to the doctor or the hospital to liven up the monotony. Could he really blame Sally for wanting to get away from this? Perhaps she looked at his mam and could see herself in years to come. Who in their right mind would want that?

'They'd have put me down years ago if I was a dog,' Mary said sadly. 'Isn't that right, Ringo?' At the mere mention of his name, Johnny's scruffy Jack Russell, who was lying at Mary's feet, wagged his tail enthusiastically. 'I feel so useless.'

Johnny went and put his arm round her shoulders. 'Don't think like that, Mam. You're not a burden, and you never will be. You're my mam and I love you to bits. It's nothing to do with you. It was all my fault.' There was a truth in that which was still painful to accept. 'Sally loves you.'

'I never see her now.'

'She's busy. She's started a new computer course. I'll make sure she comes to see you when she's got a minute.'

'Computers?' His mother shook her head in bewilderment. 'What would our Sally want with computers?'

She wants to break free, Mam. Fly away from here – from me, from you, from everyone. She wants to take Charlie away. 'I don't know, Mam,' he said instead.

In an attempt to divert the conversation, he then asked, 'What do you want for your tea?'

'The Meals on Wheels was nice today,' she said. 'Cottage pie. And it was hot. Makes a change. Just do me a little sandwich, son. I think the bread's fresh enough.'

'What about a nice bit of corned beef?'

She rubbed her hands together. 'Sounds lovely, Johnny. I'll have a drop of piccalilli on it too, there's a good lad.'

Johnny went into the poky kitchen as Noel Edmonds's voice filled the lounge once more. His interrogation was over for now. Gripping the chipped work surface, he closed his eyes tightly. Only the doubts in his own mind remained.

Chapter Five

'Hiya, Johnny.' Charlie sauntered out of the playground and over to the wall where Johnny was sitting waiting.

'All right, lad?'

The boy nodded as he knelt down and ruffled the fur on Ringo's neck. 'Good doggy. Good doggy.' The doggy – not usually that good – went into seventh heaven.

'Thought you might like to take Ringo for a walk. He's been stuck in the house for the best part of the day and he's going mad.'

'Sound.' Charlie took Ringo's lead.

Johnny's dad might have stopped short of naming him for all four of the Beatles, but there'd been nothing to stop Johnny giving every one of his subsequent dogs the moniker. This feisty little Jack Russell was the third incarnation of Ringo. The previous Ringo had been a Staffordshire Bull Terrier; the one prior to that, a chocolate Labrador with a dicky heart. 'Thought Mum might have sent you to get me because of the bullies.'

'Nah,' Johnny said, indulging in a white lie. 'How's it been today?'

Charlie shrugged and studied the ground. 'Not so bad.' Which meant it was shite, but it would be worse if he told. They'd be breaking up from school for the summer holidays soon, and at least he'd have some respite from it for a while.

Johnny threw his arm round the boy's slender shoulders. The child had only been five years old when he'd first started going out with Sally. In the intervening years he'd spent many days collecting Charlie from school and walking him home. It was something he enjoyed and it gave them time to talk – if not man-to-man, then man-to-boy. Next year Charlie would be going up to the big school – more than likely the sprawling comprehensive, a bus ride away. That would be the end of their walks, maybe their chats too. With him and Sally no longer together, it was getting harder to keep in touch with Charlie. They texted each other regularly – a couple of times a day – and he tried to see him a few evenings in the week, but he didn't like to make a nuisance of himself. Sally had her own life to live now. He couldn't help but feel that the boy was slipping away from him though. Much like his mother had.

Up to a few months ago, he'd be over at Sally's place nearly every night. You could count on one hand the number of nights he'd actually spent at his own place. They only held onto it because Sally would get her benefits cut if she was found to be co-habiting with someone. And he managed to sub-let a room on the quiet to a lorry driver called Jeff for three nights a week which helped with his running costs. Good job he had kept on his own flat, as it turned out. The lorry driver, a guy in his fifties from Glasgow, had turned out to be decent enough company when he was around too. Johnny's place was actually in a slightly nicer location than Sal's, on the other side of the estate, near to some scrappy fields that had somehow escaped the relentless march of development. His place was a maisonette, just two floors, and more modern. Those stairs at Shankly House would be the death of him yet. The maisonette wasn't very homely, though – a typical male crash pad, he supposed – but they could have fixed it up nicely together, if Sally had wanted to.

Now, he ought to give up his place and move in with his mam full-time. It was getting to the point where she needed more care and, in truth, he really didn't like the thought of her sleeping alone every night. He'd taken to staying over at his mam's place a couple of nights a week, anyway. Maybe it was time to make it a more permanent arrangement. He knew that his mam would like that, even though she'd never admit it.

Every night he'd been at Sally's he had taken to reading Charlie his bedtime story or just talking to him, soothing him for the night ahead. Every morning he'd been there to get him his breakfast, find his rucksack, remind him if it was the day for PE, so he wouldn't forget his good trainers. Now there was nothing but a big hollow where all that used to be. Charlie wasn't his own boy, not by blood, but that didn't matter to Johnny. Emotionally, it certainly felt like he was his son. You can't spend so long with a kid, watching them grow, wiping their nose and then just turn it off because things don't work out with their mam.

The two of them walked across the scrubby park, taking the long way home. Charlie let Ringo off his lead and the dog bounded away,

19

barking madly at the clouds, glad of some freedom. Did everyone round here – even the flipping dog – feel like that? Was it something they were putting in the water? Maybe he should go all poncey and start buying that bottled stuff, so that he didn't start feeling the same way too.

He turned his attention back to Charlie. 'So, what did you learn in school today?'

'Nuffin'.' His young companion scuffed his feet along the ground. It drove Sally mad when Charlie did that, what with the price of shoes nowadays. 'Everyone messes about so much, we don't learn nothing.'

'*Anything*,' Johnny corrected. 'You don't learn anything.'

'That's what I said.'

Johnny decided to let it go.

Now it was Charlie's turn for a question. 'Did you do any painting today?'

'Nah,' Johnny replied. 'Too busy.'

'Doin' what?'

'This and that,' Johnny said.

'Doesn't sound as if you were busy,' Charlie observed succinctly. 'You said you were going to go for it. When we last talked about it, that's what you said.'

'So I did.' Johnny was always full of good intentions when it came to his painting, but it was always the thing that seemed to get the left-overs of his time. 'Not sure you saw the one I started last week.'

'Can we go and have a look at your garage then – before we go home?'

'I'm staying for my tea tonight,' Johnny told him. 'At your place.'

The boy grinned at him. 'Gear.'

'Better not be late or your mum will skin us both.'

'She's completely hyper when she gets home from that computer course.'

'Yeah,' Johnny agreed. 'I've noticed that too. As long as we're back by half five, we can get the tea on for her.'

'It's nice having you around again, Johnny,' Charlie said and, because no one else was around to see, the boy slipped his small hand into his.

Chapter Six

Johnny opened the garage door which creaked in protest. He must get round to oiling those hinges. The dog whined at the noise. 'Shut up, Ringo.'

This was his secret place, his retreat. Charlie was the only other living soul who'd been here – apart from Ringo. Sally, unfortunately, had never had any interest in his paintings. Which was a shame. This was the only thing he'd ever been any good at, and it was probably the only thing he was ashamed of too. Say that you were an artist round here and someone would likely want to take a swing at you for no more reason than that.

Charlie flicked on the switch. 'Wow!' he cried as the fluorescent tube flooded the place with a harsh glare. Thankfully, Sally's son was a much more appreciative audience. 'Did you do this?'

Johnny wondered who else Charlie thought would be painting in his lock-up, but decided not to push his small friend's reasoning skills. 'Like I said,' he reminded him. 'I started it last week.'

'Wow,' the boy breathed again as he stood in front of it. Ringo sat down next to him and stared up at the canvas too, stumpy tail thumping against the paint-stained concrete floor. 'That's what you call a top painting, bro'.'

Johnny smiled. 'Thanks.' The canvas hung from the rafters of the garage. It was ten feet square. An angry-looking Superhero was beginning to punch his way out of the middle of the canvas, Superman-style. It was his own face, grimly determined, that looked out from the canvas. He wondered what the subject-matter said about his current state of mind. Come to think of it, maybe it wasn't just Sally who wanted to break out, after all.

'I'd like that in my bedroom.' It was probably bigger than Charlie's bedroom. The boy mimicked the pose, making Johnny smile.

'I'll do you a smaller version, if you want. If your mum will let you have it.'

21

'Aw! Thanks, Johnny.' Charlie ran his finger over the canvas. 'Is it dry?'

'No!' Too late. Charlie held up a finger smeared with bright red paint. 'Not yet, lad.'

The boy flushed. 'Sorry, Johnny.'

'No worries. I needed to touch that bit up again, anyway.' He didn't want to tell Charlie off for something so trivial; Sally was hard enough on him already. Johnny knew that she only did it because she wanted Charlie to stay on the straight and narrow, but sometimes she came down on her son like a ton of bricks for nothing.

'You could sell these,' Charlie said, looking around at the other canvases that were starting to stack up against the walls.

'Well . . .' Now it was Johnny's turn to scuff the floor with his foot. He followed the boy's gaze. This place was okay for the summer, but it was going to be hard to keep the finished paintings from warping, as it was likely to be damp in here. You could poke a finger through the door it was so flimsy. It was a miracle that he hadn't been robbed. Mind you, who would want to nick this lot? Didn't stop people from trying, nevertheless. His only heating was a poxy three-bar electric fire and he'd needed that when he'd done a couple of late-night sessions already. Not exactly cosy. In the winter, he could see himself having to paint in gloves. But artists were supposed to struggle, weren't they? Maybe he should take some of the smaller pictures to a car boot sale or get a stall at either Kirberly or Great Homer Street market, see if anyone was interested.

'If I was rich, I'd buy one,' his young friend piped up, still admiring the painting.

Johnny had started to rent the garage a few months ago, just after he and Sally had split. It helped to take his mind off things. It was a bit of a stretch affording the paint and the canvas, but what else did he have to spend his cash on? He'd never been one to pour it down his neck like his mates did. Drink wasn't his vice; the odd tipple was enough for him. Sally would never take any money from him – said it compromised her independence, whatever the hell that meant. He couldn't really paint at home as it made too much mess. Nice as the guy was, the lorry driver would probably complain or leave, and then Johnny wouldn't be able to afford the paint anyway. Another one of life's little quandaries.

'You should bring Mum down here,' Charlie said. 'I bet she'd like them.'

22

Johnny shook his head. 'I don't think so.' Sally thought he was a waster, that he didn't have any dreams. But this was his dream. He wanted to be a painter. A good one. But Sally didn't see being a painter as a real job. Given the fact that he was never likely to earn any money at it, she probably had a point. She'd rather he went out and got a proper nine to five job with a regular salary – in a factory or down on the docks or as a nightclub bouncer. Anything. But how could he do that when he had his mam to look after? Life was all about compromise, but Sally wasn't prepared to do that. She knew what she wanted and that was all that mattered to her.

Johnny looked again at the painting, trying to see it with impartial eyes. He had no idea if he was good or not. These could be nothing more than amateurish daubs. So, Charlie liked them, but being appreciated by a ten-year-old self-styled art critic wasn't going to make him his fortune.

Johnny surveyed the canvas. He'd been trying out different paints, different styles, attempting to find his groove. He shrugged at the painting. Maybe one day. 'Come on,' he said to Charlie. 'Let's get you back and get that tea on.'

Chapter Seven

When I get home from the computer course, the kitchen windows are steamed up and there's a great pan of pasta bubbling on the stove. Minced beef sizzles in the frying pan, filling the room with the appetising scents of home cooking.

Instead of being pleased, somehow it's irritating me that Johnny's here – even though I've invited him. That's women's logic for you. It's just that he looks so comfortable here in my flat. Even his flipping dog is at home here too, sprawled out on my clean kitchen floor. Johnny's alternately stirring the pot of pasta and the mince. Charlie, next to him, is wearing my pinny and is chopping onions. An everyday scene of domestic bliss. Except that it isn't.

'Be careful with that knife,' is the first thing I say, then instantly regret snapping.

My son turns his red-rimmed, teary eyes to me.

'You shouldn't cut through the root,' I say more softly. 'That's what makes you cry.' I go over, turn the onion around and show him the correct way to do it.

Charlie wipes his sleeve across his eyes and says, 'I like doing the garlic cloves in the thingy.' My son points at the garlic press. 'It's like squashing eyeballs.'

I stifle a sigh and turn to Johnny. 'You needn't have done this.'

'I don't mind,' he says chirpily. 'Got to look after the worker.'

I throw my bag down. 'Hardly that.'

Johnny pauses in his stirring to add Charlie's chopped onions and tears to the mince. 'Did you enjoy your course today?'

I can feel myself flush. After Spencer Knight asked me to have dinner with him – me, plain boring Sally Freeman – I didn't remember anything else he said the entire afternoon. At this rate I'm never destined to be a top computer operative. Bill Gates can rest safe in his bed. 'It's good,' I say and then, stretching the truth, I add, 'I'm learning a lot.'

'Great,' Johnny says. 'Really great.' But he doesn't sound as if he thinks it's too great. 'Make your mam a cup of tea, Charlie.'

'I'll do it,' I say, and pick up the kettle. They're making me feel redundant in my own kitchen. 'You can lay the table, son.'

'Already done.' Johnny gives me a warm smile and I laugh at that.

'You've been watching too much Nigella Lawson!'

The mention of the television cook clearly makes my son realise he could be doing something less constructive and he pipes up, 'Can I go and watch telly?'

'Five minutes,' I instruct. 'Tea won't be long. Go and wash your hands first.'

Charlie heads off to the bathroom.

'Take Ringo with you.' The dog's not exactly in the way, but it always feels as if he's under my feet.

'Come on, Ringo!' Charlie shouts and the dog's up and scampering after him. The stupid thing's an eternal puppy.

'He's a good kid,' Johnny says, when my son's out of earshot.

'Yeah.' And I'm determined to make sure that it stays that way. Charlie's best friend Kyle Crossman isn't exactly a shining example of good behaviour, but he's done nothing quite bad enough to make me split them up yet. He's not a good influence on my son though.

There are, however, too many kids like Kyle on this estate who are roaming wild like feral cats because no one's watching them, getting into mischief because they're bored out of their skulls. Doesn't help that the last time someone tried to set up a youth facility, some of those same youths burned it to the ground. Sometimes you just can't help people to help themselves.

'It was nice to be able to walk home with him. I could do it every day, if you want. Save you the trouble.'

I shake my head. 'You can't do that, Johnny.'

'What else do I have to do? I like spending time with him.' He busies himself pouring a tin of tomatoes on the meat. 'He's the closest thing I've got to a son, Sally. I still want to be there for him. I can't simply turn off my feelings for Charlie just because you and I aren't together any more.'

'I know. I know.' I don't want to tell Johnny that I also know that my son feels exactly the same way. The whole situation makes me feel like a complete cow. Sometimes I wonder if Johnny's more bothered about losing Charlie than he is about me. 'You can take him out any time that you like. Or come over. You know that.'

'But it's not the same, is it?' Johnny notes.

'It's different,' I agree. 'But it doesn't have to be difficult between us.'

'I've been thinking about it. I've no legal rights. It's not like I'm Charlie's dad. What about if you meet someone else? Where does that leave me?'

'Don't be ridiculous,' I say, feeling the guilty flush return to my face. 'Where am I going to meet anyone else?'

'It's bound to happen, Sally. You're a beautiful woman.' He abandons any pretence at stirring the Bolognese sauce and looks at me.

'You'll always be in my life, in Charlie's life.' I try to sound light-hearted. 'You're my best friend. What would I do without you?'

Johnny fixes me with his big brown eyes and says, 'I hope that I'll never find out.'

Chapter Eight

My living room stinks of peroxide. Debra is parting Dora the Explorer's hair and is slapping on the mauve-coloured bleach with what I'd consider reckless abandon. If she gets a blob on my carpet, I'll kill her – good friend or not.

'Sit still, Dora,' Debs instructs, yanking at her customer's hair.

'Sorry, love.' Dora tries to stop fidgeting.

We call Dora 'the Explorer' because she has a tendency to wander about the estate in nothing but her nightie and beddies. Most of the time she's fine and often dresses like a normal human being and behaves quite rationally, but occasionally she can get a bit confused when life becomes too much for her. If it's all going a bit pear-shaped on *Corrie*, even that can set her off. We had to stop her from watching *Desperate Housewives* as that was sending her completely over the edge. She kept thinking that Bill Shankly House would morph into Wisteria Lane and she'd end up locked in someone's cellar.

Dora lives three floors below me and, like Mrs Kapur, I sort of look out for her too. My neighbour with wanderlust should probably be in a home or on regular medication, but no one in authority's interested enough in her to pursue the issue. Everyone on the estate knows her and we just all do the best we can to make sure that she doesn't come to any harm on her expeditions. I frequently get phone calls to go and round her up from somewhere she shouldn't be.

Debs lives on the fifth floor, same block. We've been friends since school. Debra Newton is a trained hairdresser and does a roaring trade on the estate – all cash in hand, of course, which helps to supplement her benefits. As befitting a hairdresser, she's got fancy dark brown and blond striped hair. Debs spends a lot of her cash on fake tan and fake labels.

Once a week my flat is turned into a hairdressing salon. Super Sal's Salon to the Stars. A chair is plonked in the middle of my lounge floor and the carpet (such as it is) is protected with last night's *Liverpool Echo*. That hasn't stopped a ring of suspiciously bleached-out spots from appearing on it, even though I constantly nag Debs about being messy.

I've never managed to work out why Debs doesn't do the hairdressing in her own flat, but I've never tackled her about it either. Maybe she thinks her carpet is better than mine and won't risk damaging it. I don't really mind. I keep up a steady supply of coffee and, to be honest, I like the gossip. Plus my mate does my hair for free and, when money's tight, Debs sometimes slips me a tenner to help out or she might treat me to a spray tan if I'm feeling low. She's been a great mate to me over the years, more like a sister really.

The doorbell rings and, when I open it, Mrs Kapur is standing there. Debs is giving her a set today. 'Come on in, Mrs K. Kettle's on.'

'You're a doll, Sally Freeman.' She shuffles into the lounge and eases herself into the sofa, rearranging her sari and taking off her headscarf to reveal her thinning grey locks. 'All right, Dora?'

'Will be when I get my hair done, love. I don't want that Martin Kemp popping round while my roots are showing.' Dora nearly laughs herself to death at that. 'I love him in those DFS adverts. Lights up my night when I see him. He could bring me a settee any time he likes. And he wouldn't need no interest free credit!'

'You wouldn't catch a man getting over my doorstep again,' Debs says bitterly. 'Sofa or no bloody sofa.'

It's fair to say that Debs has been unlucky in love. She's done adulterous, murderous, fickle and feckless, randy and reckless, brainless, penniless and the downright criminally insane. I've no idea where she's actually managed to find such an appalling quality of bloke – but then there are a lot of weirdos out there. She thinks that I'm mad to have split with Johnny simply because he and I have different attitudes to life, and takes every possible opportunity to tell me. So much so, that I think Johnny might even have her on the payroll. Debs will think she'll have found her soulmate the day her man doesn't try to kill her, con her, or confess that his wife really doesn't understand him.

Hovering by the kitchen door, I realise that I haven't yet shared with her my news and think that this could be the time to come clean. 'I've got a date lined up myself,' I say in a rush. That brings a stunned hush to the room and my friends all look at me.

'Good for you, girl!' Dora exclaims.

Debs is arrested, mid–daub. She stares at me and hoists her fulsome bosom. 'You kept that quiet.'

'Only happened yesterday,' I tell her apologetically. 'My computer teacher has asked me out. He wants to take me for dinner tonight.'

'Ooo!' Dora says, clapping her hands in glee. '*Dinner!*'

'Is he nice?' Mrs Kapur asks. 'You deserve a nice man.'

I come over all shy. 'He seems lovely.'

'She's been on about him for weeks now,' my friend informs them loudly.

'I have not.' Well, not much.

Debs frowns at me. 'Have you said you'll go?'

I shrug. 'Yes.'

'I thought we were going out tonight? You said we'd go out for a couple of bevvies this week.'

'I don't remember saying that we'd go tonight.'

She dabs away furiously at Dora's hair. The poor woman will have dents in her scalp.

I dread asking this question, but I can't help myself. 'I was hoping that you'd babysit Charlie for me.'

'I can't,' Debs says, without looking at me. 'If we're not going out tonight, then I said I'd do my sister's hair.'

'Couldn't you do it another night?'

'I've promised,' Debs says, unmoved. 'Get Johnny to do it.'

'How can I ask Johnny?' I say, rolling my eyes. '"Hey, Johnny, I'm just going out with another guy, will you watch Charlie for me?"'

'So what?' Debs tugs her comb through Dora's hair. Dora ricochets in the chair.

My friend's in a funny mood, which I think is not only down to my impromptu date, but also the fact that she isn't similarly troubled with invites – and I'm glad that Dora's not getting a haircut otherwise she might end up with a Britney Spears shaved–off job. Despite declaring my insanity at my newly-established single status, I think she might have been secretly a teensy bit pleased that Johnny and I had split up as now she's got her old drinking mate back. The only thing that stops Debs from dragging me out clubbing every night is my lack of cash – and Charlie. Debs has never had a boyfriend for more than ten minutes for the last few years and can't see why anyone else would want to do otherwise. And whilst I might like clubbing every now and again, I certainly wouldn't want to be doing it every night. I've changed. I've got responsibilities. I've got soap operas to keep up with.

'The man's got to move on,' Debs says decisively. 'You've dumped Johnny. From a great height. Live with it.'

'He loves seeing Charlie.' Reluctantly, I think back to my conversation with Johnny last night. 'He'd sit with him like a shot, but I can't use him like that.'

'Suit yourself.' Debs shrugs her indifference. 'Looks like you'll have to cancel your dinner date.'

'You can't do that, doll,' Mrs Kapur chips in.

'I'll look after him,' Dora volunteers.

Debs laughs out loud at that one and I shoot her a look. Just because she's in a mood she shouldn't take it out on Dora.

'Don't worry yourself.' I pat Dora on the knee. Frankly though, Charlie's more capable of being left on his own than Dora is. I wouldn't rest for a minute if he was with her. What if she went on one of her walkabouts? What if she decided to divest herself of her nightie in our front room? Anything could happen and the Social Services are very funny about that kind of thing these days. 'I'll sort something out.'

Wonder how Spencer Knight would feel about having a ten-year-old chaperone on our first date? I haven't really discussed my domestic set-up with him. Actually, I haven't really discussed *anything* with him other than creating and saving computer files. 'I'll go and make the coffee.'

While I'm in the kitchen banging about with the cups and wondering what I'm going to do tonight, Mrs Kapur comes up behind me.

'I'll look after Charlie,' she says.

'I can't let you do that, Mrs K. You go to bed at nine o'clock. I might be later than that.' Much later, if I'm lucky.

'I can stay awake for once. It won't kill me. I can have a lay-in tomorrow to make up for it.'

'Would you do that?'

Mrs Kapur leans on my work surface, the effort of standing up unaided making her breathe heavily. 'You do enough for me, doll. It would be nice if I could help out for a change.'

'Then you're on,' I say. 'Charlie should go to bed at nine. He'll be no trouble.' I'll threaten him with three years' grounding before I go through the door – that usually works. 'You can watch telly until I come home. I promise I won't be too late.'

'You have fun. Don't mind me.' She inclines her head towards the living room. 'Don't mind Debs either. She's only jealous. I bet she puts my rollers in too tight just for spite.'

We have a giggle at that. To be honest though, I'm a bit pissed with Debs. I was hoping to borrow something to wear from her. Because she's got such a thriving black-market business going, she can afford much nicer clothes than me on a much more regular basis. It's more than once I've been dressed in her cast-offs. What the hell am I going to do now? I can't see Spencer taking me anywhere crummy and I wanted to look my best.

'I hope whoever this man is that he's as nice as that Johnny,' Mrs Kapur says, as she shuffles back towards the living room and the torture that awaits her. 'He's such a love. I always hoped that you two would stay together.'

I sigh out loud as the old lady leaves the room. Johnny *is* a lovely bloke. Everyone thinks so. Am I the only person who can see that he has his flaws?

Chapter Nine

Kyle Crossman kicked his heels against the wall. Charlie did the same. They were round the back of Bill Shankly House, hanging out in the skanky old garden there. No one ever came in here any more because it was such a dump, so it was a good place to hang out.

'Smoke?'

Charlie shrugged. Kyle handed him the cigarette even though Charlie had meant the shrug to say no. He coughed as he copied Kyle and tentatively inhaled. Kyle tutted at him, shaking his head in exasperation at Charlie's inability to look cool. Charlie wasn't really bothered about looking cool. He just knew that if his mum saw him now, she'd kill him stone dead with a look. Charlie turned away from the flats, just in case.

'My mum's going on a date tonight,' he confided as he tried to work out how to hold the cigarette properly.

'So what?'

'Why do old people go on dates?'

Now it was Kyle's turn to shrug.

'What have they got to talk about?' Charlie wanted to know. 'They don't do anything. My mum never goes anywhere.'

'Perhaps that's why she wants to go on a date.'

That's what Charlie liked about Kyle. He had an answer for everything. It would have taken Charlie weeks to work that out for himself.

No one really liked Kyle, but Charlie thought he was great. Now that he was friends with Kyle Crossman, the bullies kept away from him. Well, pretty much. They weren't as bad as they had been before, anyway.

The funny thing was that Kyle had been one of the worst in the class, always punching him when no one was looking, and now he was Charlie's best friend. It was odd, that. But that's how it was now. Wherever Kyle went, then Charlie went too. They were like Batman and Robin.

Best friends, doing everything together, but with one being a bit more in charge than the other. Charlie didn't mind Kyle being the boss though, because Kyle usually had good ideas.

Kyle had showed him the first magazine he'd seen with naked ladies in it. Kyle had shown him how to wee his own name against the wall – although Charlie took a bit longer than Kyle and sometimes he ran out before the end. Now he'd had his first cigarette.

At that moment, his friend nudged him in the ribs and took the ciggie back. 'Don't hog it,' Kyle said. 'We share everything now. We're like brothers but with different mums and dads.'

Charlie nodded his solemn agreement.

'I look out for you, and you look out for me.'

Charlie didn't think that Kyle needed anyone to look out for him, but he didn't say that.

'You've had loads of dads, haven't you?' Charlie asked.

'Yeah,' Kyle said. He spent a moment thinking about it. 'Three. Or it might have been four. What about you?'

'Just Johnny.'

'But he's not your real dad.'

'He's like one though. I never knew my real dad.'

'Me neither,' Kyle said. 'Mum said he was an arsehole.'

'My mum never talks about my dad, but he probably was too.' Whenever he tried to ask his mum about his dad she just shushed him up, so he hadn't bothered for ages. Not since Johnny had been around really. Having Johnny was just as good as having a dad, he was sure. How could it be better? Johnny was sound.

'I don't like this stepdad,' his friend mused. 'He's a knobhead. My others were better.'

Charlie thought he loved Johnny but he didn't like to say it or Kyle might think he was soft.

'Johnny's nice.' Charlie left it at that.

'*Nice*?'

Charlie thought he should have used a cooler word, but he couldn't think of one.

'Your mum's a bit fit too. For an old girl.'

'Thanks.'

He didn't understand why his mum didn't like Kyle, but she didn't and that was that. Nothing he could say would change her mind. And he didn't think that Johnny was that keen either, but Johnny *was* nice and he still taught Kyle how to play football even though Kyle was even more rubbish at it than Charlie was.

Kyle nudged him again and passed over the cigarette. 'Don't suck it in too deeply this time,' he instructed.

'Okay.' Charlie smiled at him through the smoke.

Whatever anyone else might think, Charlie thought it was great having a mate like Kyle.

Chapter Ten

It's six o'clock and I'm panicking. Charlie's had his tea and now he's sitting on my bed while I sort through my wardrobe. It's the tenth time I've done it today. 'Be good for Mrs Kapur,' I say over my shoulder. 'I want you to be grown up.'

'Yes, Mum.' Charlie picks aimlessly at the duvet. This room, like the rest of my flat, needs doing up. The duvet is about a hundred years old – seriously, it's a museum piece. It started off as a bright floral print, now it's been washed so much it's all pastel shades. The wallpaper is curling up at the bottom and hanging down at the top. Black speckles of mould do nothing to add to the pattern.

'Take yourself off to bed at nine o'clock and no later.'

'Yes, Mum.'

'I mean it, Charlie. She's not a well woman. I don't want you playing her up.'

'No, Mum.'

'And don't "yes, Mum, no Mum" me.'

'No, Mum.' I turn round to shout at him, but he's grinning his cheeky grin at me and I can't tell him off.

Charlie has more freckles on his nose than I've got specks of mould on my wallpaper. His hair's brown like mine was before Debs got at it with the bleach and, apart from his freckles, I like to think that he's inherited none of his father's characteristics. If he grows up to be nothing like him, I'd class that as a good thing.

I sit down next to my son and hug him. He's the one good thing that came out of the relationship. In some ways it's a shame that my ex never got to know his son. In other ways, I'll be happier if they never meet. Don't get me wrong, I'd love for Charlie to have a good dad, but no dad at all is better than a crap one. I should know. Johnny's more than made up for any shortcomings in the father-figure department and

I get a pang of guilt when I think of my date tonight. I know that Johnny would be upset if he knew.

'I won't be late.'

'You've said that seventeen times,' my son points out.

'Well, I'll say it eighteen times. I don't want to come home and find you still up. School tomorrow.'

'Why didn't you get Johnny to come round?' he moans. 'Why Mrs Kapur?'

I go back to the rickety wardrobe and flick furiously through my meagre selection of clothes. 'Johnny's probably busy.'

'He's never busy,' Charlie protests. 'He just spends his time at the garage painting.'

I wheel round. 'He's painting again?'

Charlie colours up and nods, looking as if he wishes he could slice out his own tongue. 'They're good.'

That makes me laugh. 'What do you know about painting?'

My son's face goes a furious shade of red. 'I know what I like.'

'I'm sorry. I'm sorry.' I shouldn't criticise his precious friend. 'I'm sure Johnny's paintings are really good.'

'Then what?'

I sit back down next to Charlie and try not to ruffle his hair, which he hates – except when Johnny does it. 'Johnny's full of dreams,' I try to explain. 'I am too. Dreams for us. Dreams that will get us a better life. The thing is though, when you have dreams you have to put a lot of hard work in to make them come true. Johnny doesn't do that.'

'He might do one day,' my son says defensively.

'I hope so.' And I do. I really hope that Johnny makes something of himself. 'Now help me to pick my outfit.'

I pull a black tunic top off the pillow – George at Asda, a £5.99 sale bargain. The fabric's sheer and there's a bit of lace round the neck-line, pretty even though it's a bit itchy. 'Like this?'

Charlie shrugs.

'What if I put it with my best jeans?'

'You always look nice, Mum.'

'Thank you.' I kiss him on the head. There's a knock at the door. 'Be a love and go and see who that is.'

Charlie hauls himself from the bed and stomps to the door while I strip off my T-shirt. Pulling the black tunic over my head, I check myself out in the mirror. Not too bad. Even if it wasn't, it would have to do.

My son puts his head round the bedroom door. 'It's Mrs Kapur.'

I rush into the hall. My neighbour's standing there in her dressing-gown, coughs wracking her frail frame. 'What's wrong?'

'I've come down with a terrible cold, doll,' she says apologetically. 'Just this afternoon. It must have been getting my hair wet. I thought I might be able to manage, but I'm going to have to take to my bed. I don't want to pass this on to you or Charlie.'

She looks terrible. 'Don't worry. Let's get you straight under those covers and wrapped up warm.'

Taking her arm, I lead her back down the corridor to her flat. Poor love can't even manage to open the door, so I take the key and let us in. I steer her straight to her bedroom and help her into the bed.

'Can I get you anything?'

'I've got cough mixture, love.'

'Want another spoon?'

Mrs K nods at me and I pour out some of the Veno's on her bedside table, then hold the spoon to her lips as she swallows it.

'Think you'll be all right?' God, I hate leaving her like this. I should kip down in her lounge tonight.

'I'm sound, doll,' she wheezes. 'It's just a cold.'

Came on pretty quickly if you ask me, but then that's the joy of living in a damp box; you've no resistance to anything. 'I'll come round in the morning and see if you're okay – bring some brekky.'

'Thanks, Sally.'

As I close the door behind me and make my way to my own flat, I wonder what I'm going to do now. I realise that I haven't even got a contact number for Spencer, so he's going to turn up anyway. I could invite him in, but do I really want him to see this place? The answer to that is no. I hate to say this, but I'm even ashamed that he knows where I live and is going to see the outside. How can I bring him in with the broken lift and the piss-filled entrance hall? It's times like these when I feel even more determined to get out of this place.

While I'm still stressing, Charlie pops his head out of the bedroom door to greet me.

I chew at my lip. 'Fancy coming on a date with your old mum?'

'No,' Charlie says emphatically. 'Phone Johnny. You should have done that in the first place. He'll come round.'

And my problem is? I know that he will and that's the trouble.

Chapter Eleven

'There's a Porsche Cockster parked outside,' Johnny says as he comes through the door just before eight, Ringo obediently at heel. 'With a bloke with a suit in it. It's a sound car. Won't last five minutes round here without the wheels being robbed. No idea who it is. Thought it must be CID.'

I don't even need to look out of the window to see who it is, but I do anyway. Ringo runs to the window next to me and puts his paws on the sill. He wags his tail. 'Get down, you silly dog.' Ringo doesn't get down.

I'm ten floors up, so I can't actually see him, but I know by instinct that the man in the very posh Porsche is Spencer Knight, my date for tonight. To help me though, in case there was any doubt in my mind, I can just about pick out the number-plate which looks like a person-alised one – SK something or another.

When I turn back from the window, Johnny is staring open-mouthed at me. 'You look fab.'

'Thanks.' That gives my confidence a boost, although it feels wrong to be getting emotional uplift from your ex-lover. I must admit that I've taken more time than I usually would with my make-up and hair. Normally, I would have let Debs straighten it for me, but I'm glad that I didn't today. She'd have probably turned my hair to toast.

'What time is Debs coming?'

I'm collecting my belongings, which gives me a great excuse not to look at Johnny. 'I'm not going out with Debs.' Even I can hear the hesitation in my voice. I didn't actually tell Johnny that I was going out on a date. I just told him I was going out. I didn't lie. It was he who assumed I'd be going out with Debs. On any other occasion, he'd have been right.

My saviour in the form of Charlie comes into the room. He and Johnny high-five each other.

'Hiya, champ! What's new?'

'I was going to have to go out with Mum and her new boyfriend if you hadn't come round.' Charlie wrinkles his nose.

Johnny looks over my son's head directly at me. 'That right?'

I nod because I can't do anything else. Caught in the act. Guilty as charged. Thanks, Charlie. Remind me to get out all of your baby photos when you bring home your first girlfriend.

'The guy in the Porsche?'

I swallow the lump in my throat. 'Yes.'

'He's got a Porsche?' Charlie runs to the window. Maybe now he's regretting that he didn't agree to come with me. Fickle child. Though, with just the two seats, quite where we would have put him, goodness only knows.

'Do you mind?' I ask quietly of my ex.

Johnny lets his arms hang by his sides. 'I don't know what to think.'

I lower my voice. 'I don't have to go if you don't want me to.'

Johnny matches my tone. 'How can I say that?' Then he sighs at me. 'Sorry.'

'I guess it's none of my business any more.'

'I really appreciate this, Johnny. I know it's a lot to ask.' Even though I know it's bad form, I can't help glancing at my watch. 'I have to be going,' I say. There's no way I want Spencer coming up here. 'Charlie, come and give your mum a kiss.' My son reluctantly obliges. 'I won't be late.'

'Good,' Johnny says.

And, as I don't know what I can say to make this right, I hurry up and leave.

Chapter Twelve

I fly down the stairs – all ten flights of them – and, as I get to the ground floor, Spencer is hanging up his mobile phone and getting out of the door.

'Sorry, I was delayed,' he says, all smiles. 'An urgent call.'

'Everything okay?' My breath is ragged and my heart is thumping. Only one of them I can blame on the stairs.

'Fine,' he says. Spencer stands back to admire me and all I want to do is jump in the car and get the hell out of here. 'You look absolutely wonderful.'

As Johnny said, he's wearing a suit – black, beautifully-tailored and a crisp white shirt. My jeans – even though they're my best ones – maybe weren't the best choice. 'Hope I'm not underdressed.'

'You're perfect.' He holds open the door of the Porsche and, gladly, I hop in, fighting the urge to look up to see if either Charlie, or more importantly, Johnny, are watching me. Spencer gets in beside me.

'Thought we'd drive out into the country a bit. Explore.' My date slides the car into gear. 'I haven't had a chance to get out and about yet much. You're not in a rush to get back?'

'No, no,' I hear myself say. What a liar. Johnny'll have a fit if I'm late. I might turn into a pumpkin or a mouse or whatever it was that Cinderella was threatened with. Didn't realise what that girl had to go through until now. Poor cow.

'I've booked us a table at a little place near Formby. It comes highly recommended.'

'Sound. Great,' I correct myself.

He gives me that million-kilowatt smile again and a little laugh, and we set off.

I try to relax in the plush car, but I'm too tense. Despite the air-conditioning that's chilling it to the perfect temperature, my palms are sweating. There's some classical music playing on the CD and I can honestly say that I've never known a real person before who actually liked classical music.

'This okay?' he asks. It's probably not wise to ask if he's got any Oasis.

'It's very nice.' I hate to show my ignorance, but I can't help it. 'Who is it?'

Spencer laughs again and I wonder if my inadequacies are going to provide a constant source of amusement for him. 'Vivaldi,' he says.

'Nice.' Not frigging Oasis, but nice.

We drive out of Kirberly, taking the main road towards Formby. The car eats up the miles smoothly and soon we're leaving behind the council estates. The rows of terraced houses give way to smart semis, the narrow streets become wide dual carriageways, until soon we're winding our way through country roads. I've never learned to drive, never owned a car and, consequently, I've never been anywhere. Well, I've been to Ibiza – twice – with Debs, which was okay. Hot, with cheap booze and a packed beach that we didn't manage to hit before lunchtime. But I've never really been anywhere in this country. And I certainly don't know the countryside within a twenty-mile radius from my own flat. Looking out of the windows at the rolling fields, lush in their summer livery, I realise that I didn't know that the world so close to my home was quite so pretty.

'I didn't know it was so nice round here,' I say.

'It's certainly a little more picturesque than Kirberly,' Spencer agrees. 'Not that there's anything wrong with it,' he adds hastily.

'It's a dump.' I voice what he's probably thinking.

'It could do with some regeneration,' he concedes.

I snort. 'It could do with a bomb under it.'

'Have you never lived anywhere else?'

I shake my head. 'No. But I don't intend to stay there for ever. I have big plans.'

'Those are the very best kind.'

'What about you? What's a nice boy like you doing in Kirberly?'

'Helping out,' he says with a shrug. 'I thought it was about time that I shared some of my skills.'

'With those less fortunate?' I can't help but sound cynical. We see plenty of do-gooders through the estate and they usually last all of five minutes. What's to say that Spencer Knight is different from any of them?

'I see it as a fresh challenge,' he tells me earnestly. 'I've worked in the City down in London, done the flash job, earned the big money. I wanted to see if there was anything else out there.'

'So you came to the arse end of the earth to teach computing to a bunch of lame brains in Kirberly?'

'There's no need to sound quite so incredulous.' Spencer laughs. 'I've had a very privileged upbringing. My childhood was idyllic. I was brought up on a beautiful estate in Surrey. I feel that I should give something back to society. I realise that not everyone's as lucky.'

I certainly think that Lady Luck's ignored me so far. As Spencer steers the car skilfully through the narrow lanes, his handsome face set with determination as he concentrates on the job in hand, I settle back in my seat. Maybe all that is about to change.

Chapter Thirteen

Johnny poured Charlie some cola. 'One glass,' he said, 'or I'll be in trouble with your mam.' The boy went to protest. 'No arguing or she won't let me babysit you again.'

'I don't need babysitting,' Charlie insisted. 'I'm not a kid. She was going to leave me with Mrs Kapur until she got a cold.'

'There was no need for her to do that.' Johnny shook out two bowls of crisps for them. 'I'll always come round. I've told you that.'

'I know. I reminded Mum, but would she listen?' Charlie shrugged his world-weary, ten-year-old shoulders. 'You know what women are like. I think it was because of this new boyfriend.'

This was dangerous territory, Johnny thought. It wasn't really a place he wanted to go. Primarily because it had been such a shock to find out that Sally was seeing someone else – especially when she'd ridiculed the idea only the night before. Why couldn't she have been upfront and told him straight out if she'd met someone? But then again, would that have made it any easier? While there was no one else on the scene, he'd always harboured the hope that they might get back together. Looked like that was the end of that, then.

'Let's go and choose a film,' he said to Charlie.

He and Charlie went through to the living room. In a Save-it carrier bag by the sofa there was a pile of pirate DVDs Sally had borrowed from Debs, who seemed to be able to get an endless supply of the latest films. 'Nothing too scary,' Johnny said as Charlie rummaged through them.

The boy pulled one out. '*Casino Royale?*'

'I've seen it.'

'So have I,' Charlie said. 'Five times. It's gear. I like it when he rolls the Aston.' The boy made suitable tyre-screeching noises and pulled on an imaginary steering wheel.

Johnny slotted the DVD in the player and while they waited for it to load, Charlie stopped his tyre squeals and said, 'Why don't you and Mum become boyfriend and girlfriend again?'

'Your mum and I have too much history,' Johnny said, shaking his head.

Charlie screwed up his face. 'What does *that* mean?'

What exactly *did* it mean? Johnny asked himself. 'It means that we used to go out together and a lot of stuff happened and now we don't.'

'But she liked you once.'

'She loved me,' Johnny said frankly. 'I think.'

Charlie's eyes brightened. 'Then she could do it again.'

'I think your mum's a bit more choosy now.' Johnny thought how it felt, watching her drive away in that bloody ostentatious Cockster. He'd never wanted to slash anyone's tyres before, but somehow he knew now that there were occasions when nothing would be able to beat it.

'Kyle said that women don't know what they want.'

'Kyle is clearly a genius when it comes to women's psyche.'

'What's syki?'

Johnny laughed. 'It's something you get when you're older.'

Charlie pulled his best sulky face. 'Everyone says that when it's something difficult that kids aren't supposed to know.'

'Ask Kyle.'

Charlie folded his arms and pouted. 'I bet he'll know.'

Johnny bet he would too. Kyle Crossman was Charlie's new best friend, a ten year old who knew far too much about life. He wasn't the type of boy that Johnny would have chosen to be Charlie's closest confident. Johnny helped to run an after-school sports club and Kyle came along there with Charlie; Johnny knew that the other boy came mainly to keep away from a stepdad who was a bit too handy with his fists, rather than for his love of the sport. Kyle might be a nightmare, but Johnny couldn't help but feel sorry for the lad too.

'Which flavour crisps do you want?' Johnny held out the two bowls as a peace-offering, one that he hoped would derail this conversation. 'Smoky bacon or salt and vinegar?'

Charlie peered at the bowls. 'I don't know.'

'See?' Johnny teased. 'It's not just women who don't know what they want. Kids don't either.'

'I know that I want you to come back,' Charlie said softly. 'Even if you've not got a Porsche.'

Johnny put his arm round the boy's thin shoulders. 'I don't think it's going to happen, lad.'

The DVD had finally loaded. The Bond theme blared out and he turned the sound down, so that it wouldn't bother the neighbours through the paper-thin walls.

'You could try, Johnny,' Charlie pleaded. 'You could try your hardest and then Mum might love you again.'

'Yeah.' And James Bond might turn out to be gay.

Chapter Fourteen

D inner was fabulous. The restaurant sublime. My companion attentive. My outfit – not appropriate. I was the only person in the
place not wearing a Diane Von Furstenberg wrap dress. Truly. And I
was very conscious of it. Still, it didn't spoil the evening. Once I got
behind the table, I pulled the cloth over my jeans and didn't move for
the rest of the dinner. Good job I have a bladder formed of steel.

Now the sun has nestled below the treetops. The green hedges are
falling away behind us, being replaced by the silhouettes of chimney
pots and high-rise blocks. We're heading back to Liverpool and yet the
night is still – like me – relatively young.

'Do you want to come back to my place for a nightcap?' Spencer
asks. He looks across at me and a warm glow spreads through me that
isn't strictly down to the amount of fine wine and good food that I've
managed to put away.

'I can't be late,' I say. 'My son's babysitter will want to go home.'

Spencer stiffens in his seat. 'Your son?'

I'm not sure how we managed to get through the whole evening
to this point without talking about Charlie, but we haven't. We've
discussed pretty much everything else, I think – but the fruit of my
loins was a notable omission. Maybe we just got carried away. Maybe
I wanted Spencer to think that I was capable of leaving my motherly
duties behind for the evening. And I don't know where the time went.
We got on so well that the evening just flew by. I'm not normally into
poncey statements like this – I live in downtown Kirberly, not Beverly
Hills – but I think that we really connected. And, to be honest, I sort
of assumed that Spencer would know that I'd got a child – I don't
quite know how. Do I look like carefree, single totty? I don't think so.
I have the lines of harried motherhood etched into my face. How could
he not tell?

'You could come back to my place,' I say, 'but Charlie will be in bed by now.' *And my place is a dump, and I'd rather poke out my own eyes than let you see it.* Or maybe I should just poke out Spencer's eyes? Plus there's the little matter of my ex-boyfriend being my babysitter. That's probably a situation that's best avoided. Johnny's not usually up for a fight, but there's always a first time.

'Charlie.' Spencer chews over the name as if it's something bad in his mouth – like broccoli or Brussels sprouts.

'He's a great kid,' I tell him eagerly. 'You'll love him.'

Spencer frowns.

'Everyone does,' I say, more lamely this time.

'I have a little bolt-hole,' Spencer says. 'We can go there.'

Perhaps it is a bit too early to introduce Spencer to my son. We've had one date. A very nice one, but that does not a relationship make. I should take this slowly, slowly – even though Spencer's possibly the best bloke I've ever come across. He's funny, sophisticated, smart and – did I mention this? – he drives a Porsche. Not that something as shallow as that matters, but . . . of course it bloody matters! I've never been in a Porsche before and, frankly, my head has been turned. Never will the number 19A bus seem the same again.

We pass the turning for Kirberly and keep going down the dual carriageway. 'I thought you lived in the flat above the computer centre?' I ask.

'Sort of,' he says a bit evasively. 'That comes with the job. This is more for entertaining.'

So, I'm going to be entertained? We head into the city centre and down towards the docks. This is the area that's seen some of the most extensive regeneration in the efforts to spruce up the city for 2008 when Liverpool becomes the European Capital of Culture. When I was a kid, only a certain kind of person came down here after dark; now it's the ritziest place in town. All the old warehouses have been converted into swish apartments – proper apartments, not knacky old 'flats' like mine. They change hands for money that I can only dream of. There are trendy restaurants, fashionable bars and even a branch of the Tate Modern Art Gallery – Tate Liverpool – that I've never visited because my appreciation of art, modern or otherwise, registers at zero. I glance over at Spencer. Bet this man knows his art. I'd stake my life on it.

Chapter Fifteen

Spencer's apartment is reached by an open, wrought-iron lift – the sort they have in warehouses, I suppose. We travel the four floors in silence, only the jingle of Spencer's car keys in his hand punctuating it every now and again. I stare uncomfortably at the exposed brick walls as we travel slowly upwards. The lift seems to be for his own personal use as it goes straight from the parking garage under the building and comes out right in his lounge.

He slides back the gate and we step into the room.

'Wow,' I say, without really meaning to. The place is enormous. I bet if you got all of the flats on my floor of Bill Shankly House and knocked them all together, it wouldn't be as big as this. So this is what Spencer classes as 'a little bolt-hole'?

There's a vast expanse of dark wood flooring and not much furniture except for a couple of red leather sofas and a huge glass coffee-table. One wall is entirely glass and there's a balcony that looks out over the River Mersey.

'This is amazing,' I tell him.

'Thanks. White wine?' While I stand and gape out of the windows, my date goes over to his minimalist stainless-steel kitchen and opens the fridge which is the size of an airplane hangar, busying himself with pouring me a drink. How is he affording this place? Certainly not on the salary of a computer tutor – if he even gets paid at all for his work at the Centre. He could be there on a volunteer basis, for all I know. Maybe Spencer made his fortune in the City or maybe he's from 'old' money. Perhaps this isn't his place at all and he's borrowed it from a loaded mate for the night so that he could bring me up here and seduce me.

When he comes back, he says, 'It's not cold outside – shall we go up onto the roof?'

'The roof?'

'Prepare to be amazed,' he says with a twinkle in his eye.

I follow Spencer up a staircase with glass treads until we come to a steel door which leads out onto the roof terrace. He's right: I am amazed. The terrace has been tastefully landscaped with shingle and decking. Bay trees and black bamboos flourish in over-size stainless-steel pots. Two chrome sun-loungers grace the decking, and in the corner there's a hot tub. Steam rises gently from the surface and beneath the inviting water, lights subtly change hue from red to green, to blue.

'I didn't bring my cossie.'

'I beg your pardon?'

I nod at the hot tub. 'My cossie. Swimsuit. I didn't bring it.'

Spencer grins at me. 'That's not strictly necessary.'

I snort. Call me a prude, but I think it's a little early in the proceedings to get naked with Spencer – even though I can see that it might have therapeutic benefits.

He beckons me to the edge of the terrace which is bounded by a glass balcony. I join him and, as I do so, he slips his arm around my waist, making my pulse race.

'Look at that,' he breathes.

The moon is high and bright and sparkles like disco lights on the inky blackness of the Mersey. It's a clear night and the stars are out in force, adding their own special backdrop. On the far shore, the lights of Seacombe and New Brighton are spread out in front of us like a fairyland. Why didn't I know that my own city had such potential for enchantment? If I crane my neck, I can see the Pier Head and the Three Graces – the world-famous Royal Liver building with its Liver birds perched majestically on top, the Cunard building and the Port of Liverpool building. I'd like to say that I had a view like this from my tenth-floor flat, but I don't. My view consists of litter, burned-out cars and a big brick wall that's permanently covered in X-rated graffiti, and maybe that's coloured my opinion for too long. In Kirberly I feel that I'm in the middle of a shitty little island, cut off from all the renewal and revitalisation that's going on around me. I hadn't realised that my Liverpool, the place that I've lived in all of my life, had become so very wonderful while I wasn't watching.

For some reason, this revelation makes me feel tearful. 'I never knew that this city could be so beautiful,' I say, choked.

'Really? You were the one who was brought up here.'

'I know.' I shake my head. 'I love the place, but I've always seen it as a dump.'

'How can you say that?' Spencer squeezes my waist. 'It's fabulous. It has a colourful history.'

Maybe it's something about the familiarity of the place that has bred my contempt. Or maybe I've just never before taken the time to stop and think about it. But at this moment, I feel very proud to be a Liverpudlian. There's a warm feeling in my heart and the hot tears prick at my eyes again.

'The people are great,' he continues. 'Very feisty.'

That makes me laugh and I brush the tears away. 'Feisty?' It makes me sound like Johnny's dog.

Spencer moves closer to me and takes my hand. 'Some of them are very sexy.'

Now that's better. A welcome breeze lifts my hair and caresses my neck. Maybe it gives Spencer ideas because he takes my glass of wine, puts it down on a conveniently-placed café table and leans his body into mine. His fingers trace the contours of my throat, and his lips, hot and searching, find mine. It's shocking and exciting. The only person I've kissed for the last five years is Johnny, and Spencer's lips, his kiss, feel so different, thrilling, unfamiliar. And I want to know more, so much more. I can hear my own blood rushing in my ears and I feel weak with desire. Right now, I'd like to reconsider my decision about the hot tub, because there's nothing I'd like to do more than rip off my clothes and get naked with my host.

We part and I can feel that Spencer's heart is beating just as fast as mine. 'Stay,' he whispers breathlessly against my cheek.

'I can't. I have to get back.' My voice sounds unsteady. 'Charlie will be wondering where I am.' Not to mention Johnny.

'Another time then,' Spencer says sadly.

I nod eagerly. 'Another time.'

Chapter Sixteen

I haven't felt like this since I was fourteen, when I sneaked home late from a school disco, clothes dishevelled from letting John Ashton feel my top parts, pissed on cider with a socking great love-bite on my neck. It was a bad feeling then and it hasn't improved any, now that I'm twenty-seven. Even though I haven't got a hickey and Spencer hasn't been anywhere near my top parts, I still feel as guilty as hell. It's midnight and I'd never intended to be so late back. I have no idea where the hours went. What is it they say about time flying when you're enjoying yourself?

Spencer has pulled up outside my flat. He looks as if he's planning to get out of the car.

'Where are you going?'

That halts him in his tracks. He looks over his shoulder as he says, 'I'm seeing you back to your apartment.'

'No, no, no!' I say too emphatically. 'There's no need for that.'

'I'd feel happier.'

I damn well wouldn't! 'It's fine. *I'm* fine.' I give him a peck on the cheek. 'Thanks for a lovely evening.'

'I'm sorry it had to end so soon.' Spencer finds my lips again and sears them with a kiss. I pull away. I can't snog in a Porsche with my ex-boyfriend a hundred feet above us. It's not right.

Before I change my mind, I fumble for the door handle. 'I'll call you.'

'You don't have my number,' Spencer points out quite reasonably. 'And I did hope that I'd see you at the computer course tomorrow.'

Oh. The computer course. I'd forgotten all about that. 'See you tomorrow, then.' My voice sounds ridiculously chirpy.

All Spencer does is smile at me. 'See you tomorrow, Sally Freeman.'

I'm out of the door and across the grass before you can say, 'Take me on the bonnet of your Porsche. *Now.*'

★

51

I pause outside my front door, letting my breathing return to normal. Biting on my lips, I hope that I don't look like I've been thoroughly and expertly kissed. I can still taste Spencer on my mouth. When I've smoothed down my top and fluffed my hair, I let myself into the flat.

'Hi,' I say as cheerfully as I can manage when I go into the living room. 'Sorry. I never meant to be this late.'

Johnny has arranged himself casually on my couch. He looks like he's been reading tonight's *Liverpool Echo*, but he's given himself away by holding the newspaper upside down. Ringo's also being traitorous by looking out of the window, wagging his tail. Seems that man and dog both witnessed my arrival.

Johnny puts down the paper. 'Good time?'

'Yes. Thanks.'

He stands. 'I'll be off then.'

I shrug. 'I was going to have a cup of tea.'

'I can't hang around,' Johnny says. 'I want to look in on Mam.'

'Is she okay?'

'Missing you,' he tells me.

'I'll try to call in this week.' We both know that I've been avoiding Mary and her probing questions. She's devastated that Johnny and I have broken up and I can hardly bear her pain. It's been easier not to go round there, but I know that it only makes things worse.

'She'd like that.' Now my ex-lover doesn't know what to do and it makes me feel awful to see him like this. 'I'd better be off.'

'Was Charlie good?'

Johnny nods. 'He always is. He's a great kid.'

'Thanks,' I say. 'For standing in at short notice and all that.'

'No worries. Any time.' We both sound ridiculously stilted and over-bright. Johnny clicks his fingers. 'Come on, Ringo. Mustn't outstay our welcome.'

'Johnny . . .'

'I'm finding this very difficult, Sal. It's probably best if you don't say anything.'

'He's just a friend.'

Johnny snorts in a way that says he doubts it.

'Really.'

Johnny looks at the floor. 'I could change, Sally. I could change, if you give me another chance.'

'We've had this conversation before, Johnny.' Too many times.

'I'm painting again.'

'So Charlie said.'

'I think they're good,' he says, and it breaks my heart to see him so desperate. 'Maybe I could sell some this time. Make some money.'

'And maybe you won't.'

'Come down to the garage, have a look at them.'

'I don't think so. I know nothing about painting.'

'You're trying to improve yourself. Why do you think that I don't want to do the same?'

'I'm doing it through courses and studying – hard work. All you're doing is daubing about in your garage.'

'If you saw it, you might like my painting.'

'Perhaps I would, but you can't make a living doing something like that.'

'People do.'

'Not people like us,' I remind him.

'That's my dream, Sally.'

'Dreams don't come true. Not round here. Look at this place.' I cock my head to take in the flat, the estate, the whole dump of an area. Perhaps I'm feeling bitter because I want a flat like Spencer's. I want a magical view over the Mersey. I want more than I can ever possibly have. 'People like you and me have to graft for everything we get. There are no free rides for us.'

'This is where the Beatles came from. I bet the world's glad that they were dreamers. My painting could be like a proper job,' he says earnestly. 'I really think so this time.'

'A proper job would be if you bought a ladder and a van, possibly a roller and paintbrush, a few tins of magnolia and did some decorating. That's what painters do as proper jobs.'

'If I did that,' he says, 'would you take me back?'

My head hurts and I feel dizzy with emotion. One minute I'm elated, the next I'm in despair. Both times I'm fairly confused. 'I don't know, Johnny.'

His handsome face breaks into a hopeful smile. 'That's not an outright no, then.'

I think that it is, but – for some stupid reason – I can't bring myself to say it.

Chapter Seventeen

Johnny had spent the night on his mother's sofa, which had seemed like a good idea at the time. After leaving Sally's house, he hadn't been able to face going back to his own miserable maisonette and the delightful sounds of Jeff the lorry driver snoring. The next afternoon, trying to run round a football field with twenty-two hyperactive teenagers, he realised that his muscles weren't quite as young as they used to be and were objecting to his night curled up on the soft cushions.

'Kyle! Kyle! Pass the ball to Charlie. Pass it! Pass it!' Johnny ran up and down the pitch, yelling instructions and encouragement to the kids. He'd been coach to this after-school football team for over two years now. Most of these kids had no one waiting for them at home – or no one who'd be pleased to have them under their feet. Johnny had wanted to offer them an alternative to kicking round the streets getting into trouble through sheer boredom.

It had been a struggle to set up, get the kids committed, but finally they were shaping up quite well. Somehow, Johnny had managed to persuade a local business to sponsor them and provide some kits. He wasn't sure how cool it was to have KEN'S CUT PRICE KITCHENS plastered all over your back, but at least they looked like a team. It was unlikely any of these lads would end up playing for Liverpool FC, but from small acorns many an oak tree had flourished. This wasn't the school football team – Lord Sefton's had their own coach, their own stars, their own little prodigies who would end up trialling for the under-sixteens at Anfield or Everton. In Johnny's football team were the kids who no one wanted to play. They were the troublemakers, the rebels, the ones with special needs and, of course, the ones who were completely crap at football. Charlie, unfortunately, fell into the latter category. The boy had clearly inherited his mum's skill with ball control and comprehension of the off-side rule. Despite the hours they spent playing keepy-uppy together, Charlie – to the lad's eternal disappointment – was never going to make the A-team.

On the other side of the pitch, Kyle's stepdad, Paul, was standing there shouting encouragement to the youngest of his six inherited kids. Johnny wondered why the man couldn't be like this more often. Although he was unemployed, he very rarely turned up to see the training sessions, let alone the matches. He seemed to spend most of his time in his armchair at home thinking up more and more creative ways to reduce Kyle and his mother to pulverised wrecks. One day – maybe the next time he saw Kyle with the big black bruises that were the bastard's trademark – Johnny would go round there and give the guy a taste of his own medicine.

Johnny looked over at Charlie trying to get a touch of the ball. What would he do if Sally took up with some tattooed, meat-fisted bloke like Paul? If anyone laid a finger on a hair of Charlie's head, they'd have him to answer to. From what little he'd seen of the guy in the Porsche who'd brought her home last night, he didn't look like a child-beater. He looked like a rich tosser who'd be able to give Sally everything she could ever want. But, if he was truthful, it didn't make it any easier for him to think of Sally shacked up with someone like that either.

The ref blew the whistle, signalling half-time. Johnny was grateful for the break. He was absolutely knackered. All he wanted to do was lie down on the hard ground and sleep for the rest of the evening. Charlie, untroubled by forty-five minutes of running around, came bounding over to see him.

'Wotcher,' he said, and flopped down on the ground next to Johnny. 'You looked buggered.'

'Language,' Johnny said.

'Tired,' Charlie corrected. 'Was Mum late home?'

'Nah,' Johnny said. 'Not really.' He might not have liked the fact that Sally came home after midnight, but he wasn't about to run and tell tales to her ten-year-old son.

'She looked bug . . . *tired* this morning too,' the boy observed.

As well she might. Johnny wondered whether Sally had spent sleepless hours, as he had, thinking about what the future might hold.

'Johnny,' Charlie's voice broke into his thoughts. 'It's the salsa thing at the Community Centre on Friday night.'

'And?'

'Mum's gonna be there.' Charlie's eyes were bright with excitement. 'You should go too.'

'Who's going to look after you?'

Charlie wrinkled his nose. 'I've got to go with her. If you went, we'd all be there.'

'Is her new bloke going too?'

The lad shook his head and said empathetically, 'Nah!'

'Do you think I'm going to impress her with my Latin-American dance skills?'

Charlie gave him a guileless shrug. 'You might do.'

Johnny laughed.

'If you were there, she might want to go out with you again.'

'It isn't that simple, lad.'

Charlie pulled a face. 'If you're there, then I won't hate it so much,' he pleaded. 'Please come. For me.'

Johnny held up his hands. 'Okay, okay. I'll be there.'

Charlie grinned. 'Maybe you can have a dance with Mum too. Women like that kind of thing, Kyle said.'

Johnny ruffled his hair. 'Get back on the pitch. You've got a match to win.'

The boy turned and raced away. Johnny sighed. So, he was to impress Sally with his salsa skills and make her fall in love with him again. If only he had the blind enthusiasm of a ten year old again, he might just believe it was possible. As it was, he knew that he had about as much chance of doing that as Charlie did of playing in the Cup final.

Chapter Eighteen

We're on our weekly trip to Kirberly market and it's heaving today. This place has been going for as long as I remember. Before she fell ill, my mum used to bring me down here as a kid for our cheap fruit and veg. The same bloke that ran the bread stall then is still here today, flogging his loaves for fifty pence. Now, the fruit and veg are largely gone, and the stalls stretch out along the road before us as far as you can see, selling knock-off designer gear and the best of fakes. Want Chanel sunglasses? Yours for three quid. The latest Burberry handbag? A fiver. Whatever you want, you can usually pick it up here for under a tenner.

Debs and I ease our way between the rows of stalls, winding through the crowds. You have to dress up to come here as most of the women look like they're on their way to a nightclub with their short skirts, high heels and hooped earrings. Debs and I are no exception as we totter along on our heels. My friend tugs my hand as she spies her favourite clothes stall – a place that features more sequins and glitter than a drag queens' convention. I've no idea why I let Debs convince me to go shopping today because I'm absolutely skint. I should have been sensible and stayed at home.

'What about this?' Debs picks up a silver shift covered in sequins that shimmer in the sunlight. She holds it up against her.

'That Wayne Rooney's bird was down here last week, girls,' the stall-holder shouts over at us. 'She bought the same dress. It's sixty-five quid in Debenhams.'

I nod. 'Looks great.'

Debs does a few slinky moves that are reminiscent of a lapdancer. 'Think I'll knock them dead at the salsa night on Friday.'

'Ah,' I say, and I feel a look of fear flit across my face.

With a menacing frown, Debs casts her dress aside. 'You haven't forgotten?' she says. 'How *could* you have forgotten?'

She's right. How could I? The thing is, this salsa night has been planned for ages. The Council have threatened to pull our Community Centre down, so we all thought that we'd better start making use of it to try to prove that it's needed. The trouble is, that like everywhere else round here, it's a dump. The walls are covered in graffiti, the windows are covered with metal grilles. It's not exactly the place you'd plan to spend an evening out of choice. But we have what's commonly known as a chicken and egg situation – because the place is a dump, we don't use it and, because we don't use it, it's becoming even more of a dump. I'll swear that the roof is held up by fresh air alone.

'You have to come,' Debs says. Her arms are folded and she looks a moment away from stamping her foot.

I wince before I say, 'I'd agreed to go out with Spencer again.' Since our date earlier in the week, my brain has been completely scrambled, and when he asked me to have dinner with him again tomorrow night, it never occurred to me that there might be something else looming on my busy social calendar. I thought I'd just be missing *EastEnders*.

'You're not wriggling out of this,' my friend insists. 'You promised that you'd do an hour behind the bar.'

So I did. 'I'd completley forgotten. I was so amazed that he even asked me out again, I just said yes without thinking.'

My friend's frown deepens. 'You've not said much about your first date with him at all.'

I give a wistful little sigh. 'It was lovely. *He's* lovely.'

'Nicer than Johnny?'

'Different,' I reply. 'He's different from Johnny.'

'Where did you go?'

'He took me to this really posh restaurant and then back to his apartment. He has an amazing place down by the docks. It's got its own lift and a roof terrace.'

'I need to meet this bloke.'

'I think you'll like him.' My friend likes very few men, but I think that Spencer's charm, sophistication *and money* could win her over.

'You'll have to bring him along then,' my friend tells me.

'I can't do that!'

Her frown morphs into one of her best scowls. 'And why not?'

Why not? Think, think. 'It's probably not his sort of thing.'

'You're not ashamed of us?'

I try a tinkling laugh and fail. 'Don't be ridiculous.'

'Then bring him. He could meet Charlie too.'

Crumbs. Don't know if I'm ready for all this.

'Christ,' Debs says. 'There are worse places than Kirberly Community Centre.'

If there are, then I can't think of any.

'You're turning into a right snob, Sally Freeman.'

Shrugging, I say, 'I'm not. I'm just worried about this all moving too quickly. I don't want to introduce him to Charlie if he's not going to be around.' And the quickest way to make sure that he's not around is to take him for a wild night out at the Kirberly Community Centre.

Debs has on her I-won't-be-messed-with face.

'I'll see what he says,' I concede. I'm going to have to cancel our date, see him another night. There's no way on God's earth that I'm going to be taking him to Kirberly Community Centre for a salsa dancing night. Does she think I've lost my mind?

'See if he's got a mate he can bring.' Debs smiles to herself and picks up the spangly dress again. In the street, she wriggles it on over her jeans and T-shirt.

'It looks very nice,' I concede.

'Better get yourself one then.'

The dress is very sexy. And not too scratchy. I pick one up in black. It's incredibly short.

'Black's too boring. Get silver. Then we'll look like twins,' she tells me as she tugs off the dress again.

Debs and I will never look remotely alike. Or, if we do, I will kill myself.

I stroke the dress that's over my arm. It glitters alluringly. 'It's lovely.'

'And a bargain.'

The dresses are £14.99 each, but they might as well be £1499.00. Then I sigh. 'I've no money. *Absolutely* no money.' Not even £14.99.

My friend takes both of the dresses and flings them at the stallholder. 'And when did we ever let that stop us?'

Chapter Nineteen

Johnny stood at the weathered door in Walton Street, wringing his hands together. It was just a door with no hint of frontage to give away what the place might actually be. He knew in his heart that this was a really bad idea, but sometimes in life you were compelled to do things by a power that was beyond reason. This was one of those moments.

He rang the doorbell before he could think better of it. Ringo sat at his feet whimpering anxiously. Moments later, the door was whisked open. A man stood there in pink Lycra trousers with kick flares and a white silk blouse with ruffled sleeves. This must be Ronaldo. Johnny took a step backwards.

The man waved his arms. 'Don't do that, lover. Come in, come in.' His voice was high-pitched, heavily accented with what could have been Mexican or Brazilian, but there was more than a pinch of Scouse in there too. 'No need to be shy with me!'

Johnny wasn't shy, he was terrified. 'I'm Johnny Jones,' he offered. 'I phoned earlier and left a message.'

'Come in, come in, Johnny Jones.' There was more arm-waving.

Jerking a thumb at Ringo, Johnny asked, 'Is it okay to bring the dog in?' It was the first time in his life that he'd wished Ringo was a Rottweiler.

'The more the merrier.' And the man minced away from the door.

Johnny followed him into the building, Ringo trotting so close beside him that he kept tripping his master up. They all trooped up the badly-lit, narrow staircase with fraying carpet, and into a spacious room with a wooden floor that had to be the nerve centre of *Ronaldo's Latin-American Dance Centre*. The place was painted a hideous shade of lime green, except for one wall, and that was covered with floor-to-ceiling mirrors. Johnny hadn't bargained for that. He wanted to learn to salsa but he certainly didn't want to watch himself doing it.

60

In the harsh light of the studio, the dance instructor looked older than his leery outfit suggested. His Day-glo tan couldn't hide the lines on his face, and his black, bouffant hair looked unlikely to be his own. It was clear that, like his dance studio, Ronaldo had seen better days. The teacher fluffed his sleeves. 'What can I do for you, lad?'

'I want to be able to salsa.'

'A beautiful dance.' Ronaldo rolled his eyes in ecstasy. 'So sexy.' He sang a little tune and threw a few moves. 'We can book a course of private lessons for you, my friend, or you can join my dance classes. They are Monday, Wednesday and Thursday at seven o'clock.'

'One lesson,' Johnny said. 'That's all I can afford. I've got twenty-five quid on me.' He pulled the money out of his pocket and held it out. 'What can you do for that?'

Ronaldo pouted thoughtfully. 'I can take you through some of the basics.'

'I need to learn by tomorrow night. I need to be impressive.'

'Hmm.' Ronaldo put a finger to his pursed lips. 'That may be a little more difficult to achieve.'

'My future happiness might depend on it.'

'Then, Mr Johnny, we had better start right away if I am to turn you into a wonderful dancer overnight.'

'In an hour.'

Ronaldo shrugged. 'Nothing is impossible. You will be the belle of the ball.'

That was hard to imagine.

'I will be the woman,' Ronaldo said.

That was easier to imagine.

He came and gripped Johnny in a close embrace. Ringo growled. 'Go and sit down, boy,' Johnny said. 'I'm fine.' And he hoped that he would be.

The little dog sloped away to the corner of the room, tail between his legs. He circled a spot suspiciously before settling cautiously on the space. The dog fixed his eyes on Ronaldo. Johnny shifted uncomfortably. Ronaldo pulled him tighter. Ringo bared his teeth.

'You have very good hips,' Ronaldo said.

Johnny avoided eye-contact with him. 'Thank you.'

'I hope that you have a natural rhythm.'

'I wouldn't count on it.'

Ronaldo put his hand on Johnny's bottom and pressed their bodies together. 'This woman you want to impress? You love her very much, I think.'

'I guess I must do,' Johnny said.

'Chassis. Chassis. La, la, la. Swing those hips. Volta turn.' Johnny's arms were held high, his back was aching and his feet were killing him. His dance instructor was still twirling him round the floor and they sashayed to the perky beat.

'Mambo. Mambo. Cucaracha. Cucaracha. Oh yes, move those feet to the beat!'

It was coming up to three o'clock. School home-time. He'd been learning to salsa since mid-morning without a break and, frankly, he'd had more than enough of bloody cucaracha-ing. Ronaldo, however, was still in full flow. For an older man, he had boundless energy.

'One more time,' Ronaldo instructed.

Johnny glanced again at his watch. His feet hurt. 'I've got to go.' He broke away from his teacher. 'I'm picking up a friend's son from school. Can't be late.'

Ronaldo looked disappointed. 'You have done very well, Mr Johnny. You are a salsa star.'

Johnny somehow doubted it. But in five hours' worth of private lessons, he supposed that he *ought* to have learned something. He might not be feeling as if he could be the winning contestant on *Strictly Come Dancing*, but at least he wasn't likely to fall over on his arse tomorrow night. Or stand propping up the bar like he normally did. It might not be a big start, but surely even something like this would prove to Sally that he was capable of changing?

'Thank you,' Johnny said. 'I've taken up too much of your time. You've been very kind. I'm sorry that I can't pay you more.'

Ronaldo waved his comment away. 'How can I stand in the way of true passion? Now you must go and make her fall in love with you all over again.'

'It might take a bit more than some fancy footwork to do that.'

'You must come back and tell me all about it.'

'I will.' The two men shook hands warmly. As Johnny walked to the door, he gestured at the lurid lime-green walls. 'Do you like this colour?'

'Hate it,' Ronaldo admitted, with a dismissive wave, his accent slipping to pure Scouse. 'Looks like frog puke.'

'If you pay for the materials, I'll come and spruce it up for you.'

The elderly man's eyes brightened. 'You have a deal, Mr Johnny.'

Now he had to wait until tomorrow night and see whether his newfound dancing skills would make Sally go head over heels for him, or whether she'd simply laugh her head off.

Chapter Twenty

'You don't have to do this,' I say.
'It'll be fine,' Spencer assures me. 'Stop worrying. I'm sure I'll have a great time.'

I, on the other hand, am not sure at all. Because I couldn't think of any way out of it, I took the bull by the horns and decided to ask Spencer to come to the salsa evening with me at the Community Centre. Now I'm panicking and thinking that this wasn't a good idea at all.

'Do you like to dance?'

Spencer nods his head, and then says, 'No. Not really.'

We both laugh at that.

I really wanted to avoid doing this when we've only had one date, but at the end of the day, this is my life, and the sooner Spencer sees me for what I really am, the better. Then there'll be no pretence between us, with me trying to make out that I'm something that I'm not. I'm not going to put on any airs and graces for him. This is how I am. This is where I live. And Spencer Knight will have to like it or lump it. Besides, Debs will never speak to me again if I don't take him.

Spencer thought we were going to some upmarket restaurant and has dressed appropriately in a smart black shirt and trousers. In some ways, he's probably relieved that we're going to a salsa night as he did look slightly shocked by my silver sequinned slip dress. He'll probably be even more shocked when he sees my bezzie mate, Debs, wearing the same frock. My date hands over a beautiful bouquet of red roses.

'Thank you. They're lovely. No one ever gives me flowers.' I kiss him on the cheek and he smiles. 'I'll try to find a vase.' Don't think I even possess one. I'll have to go and borrow one from Mrs Kapur. Johnny was never much of a flower buyer – simply because he never had the money to spare for such fripperies.

Spencer's eyes sweep round my flat and he's probably trying to take in quite how skanky it is compared to his place. His face is an inscrutable mask. If he wants to wrinkle his nose then he's making a good job of hiding it. 'I've got a computer in the boot of the car for you too.'

Now I'm even more taken aback. 'A computer?'

'I promised I'd find you one. So you can improve your skills at home.' He flicks a thumb towards the door. 'Shall I go and get it?'

I nod and Spencer heads back to the front door and downstairs.

'Charlie!' I shout as soon as he's gone. My son appears from the bathroom. 'Aren't you ready yet?'

'Yeah,' he says. Actually, he looks kind of cool. He's wearing his best T-shirt and baggy jeans. His hair's freshly washed and gelled into submission.

'Good boy. I want you to go and borrow a vase for me from Mrs Kapur.'

'What for?'

I throw a glance at my roses. 'For these.'

Charlie scowls at them. 'Are they from *him*?'

'From Spencer,' I supply. 'Now scoot, he'll be back in a minute.'

'Why does *he* have to come?'

'Because he's new to the area and doesn't know anyone.' And I couldn't think of a reason not to invite him and not have Debs murder me. 'So be nice to him. And be on your best behaviour, otherwise you'll be grounded for a month.'

'Aw, Mum!'

I turn him round and slap him on the backside. 'Vase. Run.'

He ambles to the front door and down the corridor. I find the scissors and, in the kitchen, start to snip the ends from the roses because I think that's what you're supposed to do. Minutes later, Charlie comes back and plonks a glass vase on the side. 'Thanks, son.' I set about arranging them.

My child leans on the work surface and huffs pointedly.

'I thought you were looking forward to tonight?'

'I *was*,' he says sullenly.

Then I hear Spencer come back and go into the lounge to see him struggling with the computer monitor. Ten flights is a long way to carry something so heavy. He's puffing and panting.

'Put it on the table. Here, here.'

He lowers the monitor gingerly and then straightens up, massaging his back.

'Wow! Charlie,' I yell. 'Come and look at this!'

My son lopes into the living room, shoulders dropping, arms hanging at his sides like a baboon's, a look of extreme discomfiture on his face.

'Look what Spencer's brought for us.'

'Cool,' he says, although he doesn't sound like he thinks it's cool at all.

Spencer holds out his hand and bends towards Charlie. 'Hello, little man.' He sounds like he's about to recite a nursery rhyme.

Charlie looks at me to see if Spencer's joking. I look at Spencer to see if he's joking. He isn't.

I nudge Charlie and, reluctantly, he shakes Spencer's hand.

'What a big boy you are,' Spencer continues in his sing-song voice. 'And how old are you?'

Charlie, incredulous, looks at me again. I glare at him. 'Ten,' he replies.

'That's lovely.' Spencer straightens up and rubs his hands together as he glances at me. 'So who's going to babysit for Charlie tonight?'

'He's coming with us,' I explain. Charlie now looks even more like he wishes he wasn't. 'It's a family event.'

'Oh,' Spencer says. Looks like he hadn't imagined that as part of the plan.

'Charlie, go and get your jacket.'

'I don't need a jacket,' Charlie says. 'It's hot.'

'Go and get your jacket,' I repeat in my don't-mess-with-me voice.

Charlie stomps off to get a jacket that he doesn't want and doesn't actually need as it *is* hot.

I lower my voice. 'You're okay with Charlie coming along?'

'Yes, yes,' Spencer assures me.

'My son's my life.'

'I understand that.'

'Have you had much to do with children?'

'Nothing at all,' Spencer admits. 'Does it show?'

I laugh, not unkindly. 'Just a little.'

'I'll try harder,' he says.

'Just be yourself,' I tell him. 'I'm sure you'll both get along fine. He's a good kid.'

'He seems delightful.'

Charlie is a lot of things, but I'm pretty certain that 'delightful' isn't one of them.

'I'll pop down to the car and get the rest of the computer, shall I?'

'This is very kind of you, Spencer. There's no need to do this. I hope it's not too expensive.'

'My treat,' he says. Then, before I can offer a protest, he comes to me and slips his arms round my waist. I stiffen slightly and hope that Charlie doesn't come out of his room right now. He's not used to seeing his mum canoodling with a strange man, and I bet he won't like it. 'I want to help you out, Sally. Will you let me do that?'

'Yes,' I say, because it seems the quickest way to untangle myself and because I can't quite believe that someone like Spencer wants to look after me and care for me and buy me roses and computers.

'I'll go and get the rest of it.' He strides towards the door. 'Back in two ticks.'

I watch him go with his immaculate clothes and his handmade shoes and perfectly-manicured hands, and I wonder what they'll make of him down at Kirberly Community Centre.

Chapter Twenty-One

The scruffy hall of the Community Centre is packed with bodies and the lights are dimmed, so it doesn't look too bad at first glance. Perky music with a salsa beat is already blaring out. I take a deep breath and slip my hand into Spencer's as we walk in. Charlie immediately makes a break for it and bolts across the room to find Kyle. I hoped that he would hang around at least for a few minutes to get to know Spencer, but that's probably the last I'll see of him until home time.

Debs comes straight across to see me. Spencer's eyes widen slightly as he takes in her silver sequins and her vertiginous second-hand hooker heels as worn once by a Supermodel. I'm suddenly hoping that I don't look quite so tarty as that. 'Hiya, Sal,' she says, though her gaze never leaves Spencer's face.

'Hiya. This is Spencer.'

'Pleased to meet you,' he says, and holds out a hand for her to shake. 'Spencer Knight.'

'Debra "Dynamite" Newton.' Debs winks salaciously at me as she holds onto his hand for a moment too long and I want to curl up and die. A man from the other side of the estate comes towards us, swaggering cockily.

'You dancing?' he asks Debs.

My friend smiles sweetly at him. 'Women with arses like mine don't dance with men with faces like yours.'

'Piss off,' he says as he walks away, swagger gone.

It's no wonder that Debs struggles with long-term relationships.

'I'll get us a drink, shall I?' Spencer asks.

'I'll have a vodka and Coke, please,' I say.

'Same for me,' Debs pipes up, toasting the air with her half-empty glass. 'A double.'

I die a bit more inside. Spencer smiles at me sympathetically and then heads to the bar. I hope he doesn't get beaten up. Already, I'm

68

wondering why on earth I brought him here. This is a close-knit community and Spencer has 'outsider' stamped all over him.

'Way to go, girl,' Debs gushes. 'I'd like to see that knight out of his shining armour. He's gorgeous.'

I shake my head. 'He's like a fish out of water.'

'We'll get a few drinks down him, knock the corners off,' she says. Which I assume is meant to reassure me. It doesn't. My friend looks longingly after my date which, if I didn't know her so well, would annoy me. 'Thought he might bring a mate.'

'I asked. He hasn't got any friends.'

'Huh,' she snorts.

Yeah, let's knock that double-dating idea on the head right away.

Debs inclines her head towards the dance floor. 'Have you seen *that*?'

On the floor, an elderly couple from my flats – Tom and Winnie Hunt – are doing a beautiful waltz to the salsa beat. The fact that their steps aren't co-ordinated to the music isn't bothering them one jot. They sweep together happily in perfect rhythm with each other and that's all that seems to matter to them.

'Aw, bless,' I say.

'Not that, you idiot.' She flicks a thumb towards the stage. '*That!*'

There's only one other couple on the dance floor and the sight of them makes my mouth drop open.

'Who does Johnny think he is?' Debs wants to know. 'Patrick frigging Swayze?'

If you ask me, Johnny's doing a remarkable impersonation of Patrick frigging Swayze. In his arms is Bootle Bev – a brassy, bottle blonde with a big bosom – and he's twirling her round in a expert fashion, in time to the music and everything. I'm stunned. He looks fantastic. At this time in the evening, Johnny would normally be propping up the bar and he'd stay like that until closing time, eking out a couple of pints. Perhaps that was the problem – he never drank enough to be a uninhibited dancer. He'd have to be seriously drunk and at a wedding, or something, before he'd even consider gracing the dance floor.

'Blimey,' I say. 'Am I hallucinating?'

'He must have been having lessons.'

'Johnny?' That one cracks me up. 'No way.'

At that, the music stops and Johnny catches me watching him. I try to look as if I'm not. Bootle Bev totters off and my ex-boyfriend heads towards me.

69

'Can I have the pleasure of this dance?' he says to me.

'Where did you learn to do that?'

Johnny shrugs and looks embarrassed. 'Too many hours watching those dance shows on the telly. Some of it must have rubbed off. Are you going to risk a twirl with me?'

I glance towards the bar. 'I'm here with Spencer,' I say to him, even though it makes me want to shrivel up. Johnny's face falls. 'I'd better not.' My date is still queuing three-deep at the bar. He'll never get served unless he shoves in. It's no good being polite here, every bugger will get in before you.

'He'll be ages yet,' Johnny notes, clearly thinking exactly the same thing as me. 'I'll have you back in just a minute.'

The salsa beat picks up again. It's tempting. Tom and Winnie could do with some company out on the floor. My foot starts an involuntary tap. It wouldn't take long. Johnny flutters his eyelashes at me and I crack. 'Okay then. Just one dance.'

I give my handbag to Debs and join Johnny on the dance floor. He holds me close to him and, I hate to admit this, but my heart sets up a salsa beat too. 'I don't know how to do this.'

He presses me closer. 'Just follow me.' Johnny leads my body through a series of twists and turns. It's great fun and I start to laugh as the beat takes over and I relax against my old lover. For some silly reason, it feels good to be in Johnny's arms again.

'When did you become such a smoothie, Johnny Jones?'

'I've always been a smooth mover.'

'You have not!' I giggle against his shoulder. 'Why didn't we do this when we were together?'

'Because there was never a salsa night at the Community Centre.'

'I had no idea that you could dance like this. Debs thought you'd been having lessons.'

I see a flush come to his cheeks. 'No way!'

Hmm. I'm not so sure. Maybe the gentleman protesteth too much.

'I thought we could have some fun tonight,' he says near to my ear as he arches me into him. 'I didn't know you were coming with your new fella.'

'It was a last-minute decision,' I tell him truthfully. 'I'm not sure it was a good idea.'

'He looks a bit out of place.'

The music stops as Johnny twirls me away from him and I stand there awkwardly, breathing heavily. 'I'd better get back to him. He doesn't know anyone else.'

Johnny's eyes are bright when they look into mine. 'We were just getting warmed up.'

'Dance with Debs. She's gagging for it.'

'As usual,' Johnny remarks. He takes my arm and leads me back to where Spencer and Debs are standing together. While they're still out of earshot, he says, 'Maybe later?'

'I'd better not,' I answer, even though there's nothing I'd like more than to have another spin with the new, masterful, twinkle-toed Johnny Jones. 'That was a lot of fun.'

Spencer is standing holding my drink. He grins at me as Johnny and I approach. 'That was superb. Well danced.'

'Come on, Debs,' Johnny says. 'You're on next.' And the two of them head off together.

I wave my hand in front of my face as I swig my vodka, trying to cool down. 'I'm hot.'

'Looked like you enjoyed yourself.'

'It was great,' I enthuse. 'You don't mind, do you?'

'No, no,' he assures me. 'And the guy?'

'Oh, that's Johnny,' I say and feel my face fire up. 'My old boyfriend. I'm sorry, I should have introduced you. Everyone round here knows him.' Which probably makes Spencer feel even more like an outsider. 'You'll like him. He's like a dad to Charlie.' Then I realise that it's probably the wrong thing to say as well, so I blabber on, 'We're great mates now. That's all.'

'We all need friends,' Spencer says.

The music starts again and I see Johnny take Debs in his arms, just like he held me moments ago. My feet start to tap of their own volition once more. Salsa dancing is a lot of fun. Now the dance floor's filling up and I lose sight of Johnny and Debs and I get a sort of achy pang that I can't quite identify. If I didn't know better, I might put it down to jealousy. 'I love dancing,' I say to my date. 'But I don't get the chance to do it much these days.'

'Maybe I can do something about that,' Spencer says enigmatically.

Chapter Twenty-Two

Charlie and Kyle had sneaked out from the Community Centre, unnoticed. They huddled up next to the big dump bin round the back of the hall, trying to remain unnoticed.

'It's boring in there,' Kyle said, dragging deeply on his cigarette and then passing it over to Charlie. 'Why doesn't anyone tell old people that they can't dance?'

'Johnny was doing okay,' Charlie pointed out.

Kyle received that information with a derisive snort.

'I was hoping that it might make my mum fall in love with him again.'

More snorting. Charlie passed the cigarette back to his friend. He didn't think that he really liked smoking now that he'd tried it, but Kyle said it made them both look older. All Charlie thought it did was make him want to cough.

His friend nodded at the Community Centre. 'Was that her new bloke?'

'Yeah,' Charlie said. 'He's a right prat. Drives a Porsche.'

Kyle's eyes brightened. 'Wow. A Porsche?'

'Yeah, but he's a tosser.'

'My mum goes out with loads of tossers, but they don't drive Porsches.'

Charlie shrugged at that logic. 'I thought your mum was married to your stepdad.'

'Yeah,' Kyle said. 'But that doesn't mean that she can't see other men.'

This was news to Charlie. He didn't even like his mum seeing one new man, let alone more than one. And his mum wasn't even married. 'That'd be horrible.'

'It's the way things are now,' Kyle informed him. 'Being married now is like a part-time thing.'

'Oh.' Charlie scuffed his feet on the floor. It was actually a bit more boring being out here than in the Community Centre watching old people trying to dance. 'I didn't know that. Is that what your mum said?'

'Yeah.' Kyle nodded sagely. 'But you don't have to say anything about it at home. That's the rules.'

'Oh.' There was always a lot to take in with Kyle. 'Doesn't your stepdad mind?'

'Not really,' his friend mused. 'He gives her a clock round the mush if she does it too much and then she stops for a bit.'

To Charlie's mind it didn't seem like the right way to go about things.

Kyle nudged him in the ribs. The cigarette, now becoming damp at the end, was passed between them again. Kyle always made them spitty, but then he paid for them so Charlie couldn't really complain. He looked much older than Charlie, so he was allowed to buy them from the cigarette counter in Save-It. Plus his aunty worked there, so he sometimes got a packet for free.

'Do you like your stepdad at all?'

'No,' Kyle said.

'Not even a bit?'

'No. He's a right wanker.'

'Why did your mum marry him?'

His friend shrugged. 'Some women like wankers the best.'

That didn't make sense to Charlie. You would have thought that women would like someone who'd treat them nicely – like Johnny, for instance.

'Do you let him know that you don't like him?'

'Yeah,' Kyle said.

'What do you do?'

'I become the Child from Hell,' he said in a menacing voice.

The Child from Hell. 'But doesn't that just get you told off a lot?'

'It's worth it,' Kyle concedes.

'I don't like getting told off,' Charlie admitted. He hated upsetting his mum at all, but sometimes it was quite easy to do. In fact, he'd better get back inside soon. If she missed him, there'd be hell to pay.

'That's because you haven't got a real dad,' Kyle continued. 'Stepdads don't love you like real dads do. It's never the same.'

'It seemed like it was with Johnny. He was like my dad.' But then Charlie had to confess that he didn't have anything to compare it with. He just got a funny feeling about this Spencer bloke. He didn't think

73

it would be the same with him. 'Spencer, her new fella, speaks to me like I'm a kid.'

Kyle blew out a steady stream of smoke and then ground the butt of the cigarette into the ground with his heel. 'Harsh,' his friend concluded.

'I don't like her seeing him. What shall I do?'

'Child from Hell.' Kyle nodded to reinforce his point. 'It's the only way. It'll be you or him. Always is.'

'Me or him?' As he trailed back after his friend into the Community Centre, Charlie thought that he didn't like the sound of that at all.

Chapter Twenty-Three

They were in the garage that Johnny used as his workshop. Johnny was painting, putting the finishing touches to an abstract canvas he'd mentally entitled *Saturday and Feeling Fucking Awful*. Primarily because it was Saturday and he was feeling fucking awful.

He'd danced with every single woman in that place last night – impressing even himself with his moves – and not one of them felt as good in his arms as Sally Freeman did. The way they'd swayed together, the feel of her soft body against his . . . Johnny sighed. He would have made Ronaldo proud of him. He had cucaracha-ed like an old pro. And it was pointless. All of it bloody pointless. She'd still gone home with the posh bloke in the Porsche. And that had cut him to the quick.

Had he really been so stupid as to think that a bit of fancy foot-work on the dance floor was going to win Sally back? If he hoped to have any chance with her at all, he'd have to start thinking about what she really wanted out of life. What she wanted, clearly, was a well-turned-out bloke, with a good job and a flash motor. She wanted to be someone and she wanted to be with someone who was someone too. He knew that. In his heart, he knew that. But even if he managed to get a job again – no mean feat after being unemployed for so long – not many employers would tolerate the amount of time he had to take off to look after his old mam when she decided to take a turn for the worse. What would happen to her? Who'd care for her? What about the kids at the football club? Who'd look out for them if he couldn't be there after school?

Was it just a ridiculous dream to think that he'd ever be able to make any money from his painting? Shouldn't he simply knuckle down and do something solid, a sensible day job like everyone else?

He'd painted the canvas black all over and was now flicking splatters of grey and white paint at it. Ringo, asleep at his feet, was also splattered in monotone paint making him look part-Dalmatian, part-Jack Russell. The little dog would have to go in the bath later, which he'd love.

Charlie was mooching round, picking up and discarding all that he could lay his hands on. An occasional disgruntled huff emanated from his direction.

'Don't get paint on yourself, lad, or your mother will have my guts for garters,' Johnny warned. If Charlie went home splattered with black and white paint he'd never hear the last of it.

Eventually the boy settled, coming to perch on a pile of old towels that Johnny had to one side for cleaning up. He put his head in his hands. 'I didn't know she was going to bring *him*,' Charlie moaned.

Me neither, Johnny thought. 'He seems like a nice bloke.' That was the truth. More's the pity.

'Seems like a complete divvy,' Charlie corrected. 'He called me "little man".' The lad's nose turned up in a sneer.

Johnny smiled to himself. 'There are worse things to be called.'

'Tosser,' Charlie said.

'That's one of them,' Johnny agreed. He wagged his paintbrush at the boy. 'Mind your language.'

'Do you think Mum's in love with him?'

He did hope not. 'It's early days, Charlie,' Johnny said with more confidence than he felt. 'They've had a couple of dates. That's all.'

'She goes all *girly* when he's around.'

'Women can be like that,' Johnny said. 'It doesn't mean that they're in love.' Though sometimes it did, he had to concede.

'Kyle says women go all silly when they're in love. Mum's gone all silly. She poured me out a bowl of Ariel Automatic this morning instead of cornflakes.'

That was very silly, he had to admit.

'Your relationship adviser might not be right one hundred per cent of the time,' Johnny reminded him. 'Does Kyle have a lot of experience with women? Bearing in mind that he's ten years old.'

Charlie shrugged. 'He's been going steady with Britney Evans for three weeks now. He's kissed her and *everything*.'

Johnny had no desire to know what 'everything' might involve. Maybe it was time that he and Charlie sat down and had a proper man-to-man talk. Cover the birds, the bees, the sexually-transmitted diseases. The whole gamut. But then he remembered that Charlie wasn't really his responsibility any more. Perhaps Sally wouldn't take kindly to him talking to her boy about such intimate subjects. Perhaps she'd want Spencer to sit down and have cosy chats with her son now.

An awful feeling of being cut loose overwhelmed him once more and, aggressively, he hurled the paint at the canvas. Watching the paint travel through the air and make its mark on the canvas felt good, therapeutic. He stood back and admired his handiwork.

'That's looking gear, Johnny. Can I have a go?'

'No,' Johnny said. 'You'll get me killed.'

The boy puffed unhappily again. 'I don't want her marrying him, Johnny.'

You and me both, he thought.

Chapter Twenty-Four

So, it's Monday and my computer lesson has come round once again. I couldn't go back to Spencer's wonderful apartment on Friday, because I wasn't able to find anyone to look after Charlie. I spent all night long lying awake having visions of me and Spencer romping together, naked, in his rooftop hot tub. I was so knackered the next day that I narrowly avoided poisoning my only child by trying to give him washing powder for breakfast. Good job one of us was awake.

Now Spencer's standing behind me, looking over my shoulder – ostensibly to try to improve my computer literacy skills. He's burbling on in his cut-glass voice about Word documents, but frankly my mind is so filled by thoughts of his closeness that there's no room for anything else. As I try to open and close files and look like I give a fuck, his fingers stray to the back of my neck and linger there. I look round to check what Davy, Tom and the others are up to, but they're too engrossed in their screens and doing proper computer stuff to notice the fact that Spencer and I can hardly keep our hands off each other.

'I missed you this weekend,' he says close to my ear. 'I normally go home to Surrey, but I thought we might do something together next weekend. Something special. You're not busy, are you?'

I was planning to spend an exciting Saturday scraping mildew from my windowframes. That's hardly going to stop me from doing something special. 'No. No, I'm not busy,' I tell him.

He squeezes my shoulder and smiles at me. 'Leave it with me.'

I carry on plodding my way through my workbook trying to take in the basics of page set-up, but my head is all over the place. Wonder what 'something special' entails? I bet he's planning to take me up to his spa and seduce me. Another expensive dinner could be involved. I feel like giving myself a little hug. How did I manage to get such a fab boyfriend? And Spencer missed me! He said so himself. Even after our disastrous date at the salsa night, he's still coming back for more!

Actually, Friday wasn't entirely a damp squib. We had quite a nice time at the Community Centre although he did attract a lot of funny looks. He didn't want to dance either – I had a few twirls with Debs, but that's hardly the same. But then I can't blame Spencer for feeling a bit intimidated after seeing Johnny on the dance floor. What an eye-opener! No one could have competed with that. It makes me smile, thinking of it. Who'd have thought that my ex-boyfriend had it in him to throw out better moves than Ricky Martin?

'What are you grinning at?' Spencer's behind me again.

'Nothing,' I say. 'Just something silly.'

He pulls a chair up next to me, close, close in my personal space. 'We're all set,' he says. 'I've organised everything.'

'Great.' It's all I can do to stop myself from rubbing my hands together with glee.

'The tickets are booked, the visa's organised.'

'Tickets? Visas?'

'We leave from Heathrow on Friday night,' Spencer informs me. 'Our connecting flight leaves from John Lennon Airport at six o'clock.'

'Heathrow?' I squeak. 'John Lennon?'

Spencer frowns. 'You have got a passport?'

'*A passport?*'

'Have you?'

I nod. It's been used twice. Both times to go to Ibiza with Debs – but you know that.

'I thought we'd go to Cuba.' He says it like he's suggesting we go down the road to the local pub for a swiftie. Perhaps he sees the shock on my face as he continues quickly, 'I saw how much you liked salsa dancing. Cuba is *the* best place to go to do it.'

I have no doubt about that. 'Cuba?'

'It's glorious,' Spencer assures me. 'We'll have a great time. Take in some clubs, sample a few mojitos.' He shrugs. 'We'll be back on Monday morning.'

'I can't go to Cuba, Spencer. I haven't two pennies to rub together. It's way out of my league.'

Even if he'd said we'd have a weekend in Blackpool that would be stretching my finances.

'Don't worry about that,' he tells me. 'It's all taken care of.'

He's paying too? Wow. I daren't admit it, but I haven't a clue where Cuba is. How long is it going to take to get there? Is it do-able for a weekend? I thought it was miles away. Near America or somewhere. Geography isn't my strong point – principally because I haven't actually been anywhere. Never mind that! I don't care where it is. It could be in Timbuktu or Outer Mongolia for all I care. What will I need to wear? I'm going to Cuba and Spencer's forking out for it! I can hardly contain my excitement. I'm going to Cuba! For the weekend! I'm going to dance until dawn. Knock back mojitos like they're going out of fashion. Then something in my brain brings me up sharp.

'Charlie,' I say quietly. 'Is Charlie coming with us?'

That question looks like it pulls Spencer up sharp too.

'Charlie,' he murmurs, and I see a lump travel down his throat. 'Couldn't you get someone to look after him? It's only for a couple of days.'

So, my son isn't featured in the plans to trip the light fantastic on the other side of the globe. 'Oh,' I say. Charlie would love Cuba. I'm sure of it.

'Havana really isn't the sort of place that you take children.'

'Isn't it?' What would international jet-setter Kate Moss do in this situation? If a hunky bloke was wanting to whisk her away for a weekend of pleasure would she consider having her kid in tow?

'Perhaps your friend would take care of Charlie?'

'Debs?'

'It's all booked up now.' Spencer looks worried. 'You said you weren't busy.'

I said I wasn't busy, I didn't say that I didn't have commitments. My lip gets an anxious chew. When do you see *any* of these celebs with their offspring, for that matter? I suppose they all have a barrage of nannies who can step into the breach when a bit of hedonism calls. Most people have family that they can call on. But I have no one – except Johnny.

Because everyone else on the computer course is working away and no one's paying a blind bit of attention to us, Spencer reaches out and strokes my hair. 'We could have a really fabulous time.'

We could. I know that.

'Do you think Debs would do it?'

'I could ask her,' I say. But I think I know what the answer will be.

Chapter Twenty-Five

'No,' Debs says, dragging deeply on her cigarette.

'Think about it,' I beg.

My friend arranges her face into an expression of thought. Then she says, 'No.'

'You're such a cow.'

'Do you mind,' she says. 'Even us heartless bitches have feelings too.'

Debs's flat is nicer than mine. Marginally. Because she works cash in hand, she has a bit more money to spend on her home. My flat's cleaner and neater, but Debs's stuff is more trendy.

'Cuba,' she says for the tenth time. 'I don't even know where the fuck Cuba is.'

'Me neither,' I tell her. 'I had to look it up on Google.' One of the few things I *have* learned from my computer course. I can Google anything now. I just did it when Spencer wasn't looking. 'It's the largest of the Caribbean islands. Just off the coast of America.'

'And you're going all that frigging way for a weekend, girl?'

'Yes.' I'm sprawled out on her leather sofa, nursing a cup of tea. I put the mug against my forehead to ease my headache. I don't know whether it's excitement or stress.

'Has your fella never heard of the Lake District?'

'I'd love to go.' I make my eyes go all moony. 'If I can get someone to look after Charlie.'

'No. No. No.'

Putting down my tea, I make a pious steeple with my hands. 'It's for two days,' I plead. 'Two tiny, weeny, little days. That's all.'

'All day Saturday. All day Sunday. And Friday night and Monday morning. That's more than two days. That's nearly four days.'

'It'll fly by,' I promise. 'And Charlie will be good. I'll threaten him. You'll hardly know he's here.'

'I'll hardly know he's here, because he *won't be here*.'

81

'Debs,' I say in a censorious tone. I ask very little of my friend.

'What would I do with him? Charlie's a great kid, but how am I going to entertain a ten year old for days on end?'

'I'll break all of my rules,' I tell her. 'You can leave him in front of the Playstation for hours on end and just give him junk food.' You can tell that I'm desperate and I'm hoping that a weekend of bad habits won't harm my son too much. Charlie, the little sod, would love it.

'Did you ever notice that I lack a certain maternal streak?'

'You'd have made a great mum.'

'I don't think so. But if I was hankering to look after something cute with way too much energy, I wouldn't go for a kid. I'd get a puppy. Better to ruin my carpets than ruin my life.'

My powers of persuasion are failing me.

'Johnny'll do it,' my friend says. 'Don't sweat. You can still go trotting off with Little Lord Fauntleroy.'

I frown. 'Don't call Spencer that. He's lovely.'

'I must admit,' Debs says sulkily, 'hitting Cuba is a bit more imaginative than your average date round here. You're lucky if most blokes stump up to go to the chippy.'

Perhaps that's really her problem. It's not just that she doesn't want to look after Charlie for me, it's that she's a little bit jealous that I've got a fab new man who wants to treat me like a princess and whisk me away to exotic lands – at his expense. 'I can't ask Johnny,' I say. 'He'll think that I'm using him.'

'You are.'

'Well, I can't do it,' I say. 'It's not fair on him.'

She stubs out her cigarette. 'Don't you think all that dancing on Friday was for your benefit? Did you see the state of the man? Desperate.'

'He was not! He was good.'

Debs snorts.

'Johnny isn't like that, anyway. He knows that our relationship is over. We've both moved on. What we have now is a mature friendship.'

Debs snorts louder.

I try changing the subject. 'It looked like it was a big success on Friday though.' Johnny's *Strictly Come Dancing* routine aside.

My friend's eyes light up. 'I'm well chuffed. Can you believe how many people turned up? The place was rammed. We'd sold a load of tickets, but even more people turned up at the door. Even after paying the DJ we're up about a hundred quid.'

'That's fantastic.'

'Maybe I should go into event management,' she muses. 'What shall I do with the money?'

'I dunno.'

'Give it some thought,' Debs says.

'It would be nice to do something for the estate.'

'I've already done enough for the estate. I was thinking I might spend it on shoes and handbags.'

'You were not!' I throw a cushion at her. 'This whole thing was set up to save the Community Centre from closure.'

'The rickety old dump will probably fall down of its own accord before they get a chance to close it.'

'I was talking to Mrs Kapur a couple of weeks ago. She said it used to be lovely round here. There was a real sense of community.'

'There still is.'

'Yeah, but a lot of it's gone. Look at the state of the place. It could be twinned with Beirut. No one cares. Would you have got kids pissing in the lifts twenty years ago?'

'Probably.'

'I don't think so. Mrs K said that everyone used to look out for each other. Wouldn't it be nice for it to be like that again? Why let a tiny percentage of idiots ruin it for the rest of us.' I stretch out on the sofa. 'When I was on Spencer's roof terrace last week . . .' My friend fakes a theatrical yawn which I ignore '. . . I looked out across Liverpool and thought what a wonderful, magical place it was. I'd sort of forgotten that. And now that I've seen it, I don't want to be living in the arse end of the city.' I look over at Debs. 'We could change things.'

'With a hundred quid?'

'Everyone has to start somewhere.'

'It'll never happen,' Debs says with a shake of her head. 'Might as well spend the cash on shoes and handbags.'

'I'll think of something,' I assure her. Why should everyone else be benefiting from regeneration when we're not? 'You see if I don't.'

In the meantime — before Super Sal saves the world — there's the more pressing little problem of what to do with my dear son next weekend.

Chapter Twenty-Six

I haven't seen Johnny's mum for weeks and I'm feeling really guilty about it. So, I thought I'd pay her a visit and see if maybe I could bump into Johnny while I'm there and perhaps chat to him about the possibility of him maybe, *just maybe*, looking after Charlie for me next weekend.

I know that I said I wouldn't put upon him like that, but I can't think of anything else and, frankly, I have so little excitement in my mundane life that I really, really don't want to pass up this once-in-a-lifetime chance of going to Cuba. Who would? Plus it's all booked up. How could I cancel now? Spencer would lose all his money. If I grovel enough, then Johnny might have some sympathy with my dilemma.

When I ring the doorbell, I hear Ringo barking and I know that it's a fair assumption that Johnny's here too. When he opens the door a minute later, it's confirmed. He's standing there unshaved, hair all rumpled as usual, but still there's a tug at my heart. Old habits, it seems, do die hard. Maybe it's the way his eyes light up when he sees me or the way his easy smile broadens. How many times in a lifetime do you meet someone who you have that effect on? Even though we're just friends now, it's still heady stuff.

'An unexpected pleasure,' Johnny says as, standing aside, he lets me in.

'Thought I'd stop by and see your mum. It's been a while.'

'Something she moans about constantly.'

'I'm sorry,' I say, feeling even worse that I've neglected her. 'I've been busy.'

'I know,' Johnny replies. 'You don't have to explain to me. It's just that when Mum's entire world is these four walls, she tends to notice these things. Go on through.'

Ringo wags his tail enthusiastically and trots at my heels as I make my way down the hall, smiling his adoring doggy smile up at me. That mutt's a pain in the neck. I'll kill him if he leaves dog hairs all over my jeans like he normally does.

In the living room, Mary Jones is watching *Cash in the Attic* on the television. The sun's beating down outside, another glorious summer day, but the curtains are closed against it. Her face breaks into a beaming smile when she sees me. 'Sally, love. What are you doing here?'

'I've come for a cuppa,' I tell her as I sit down opposite her. She doesn't look well, greyer and more frail than when I last saw her. It makes me sad to see her like this. Wonder why Johnny didn't say anything? 'See how you're doing.'

At that Johnny says, 'I'll put the kettle on.'

'Good lad,' Mary throws over her shoulder. 'Get the best biscuits out too.'

'It's our Sally that's come to visit, Mam. Not the Queen,' he teases.

'She's a queen in my eyes,' Mary answers fondly. 'Always will be. Use the best china.'

'Give us a break, Mam,' he says as he heads out of the cramped room.

Mary beckons me to her. 'Come and give us a kiss, doll.'

I go over and kiss her, wrapping my arms round her. Despite her weight, she feels insubstantial as if there's nothing inside her shell to give her strength or substance.

'How's that boy of yours?' she asks, patting my hand. 'Still growing up to be a cracker? The girls will have to watch out for him. He'll break some hearts one day.'

'As long as it's not mine, Mary, I'll not mind.'

'He's a good lad,' she says. 'Salt of the earth. Just like mine.'

'One of the best,' I agree.

I see a tear come to her eye. 'Thought you might make an honest man of Johnny Boy for me.'

'Well . . .' It makes me feel terrible to think that I can't give this woman the only thing that she really wants in her life.

'I worry about him being on his own,' she continues. 'It's not right at his age. I won't go to my grave happy while he's not wed. He deserves to be happy.'

'I'll just go and see how he's getting on with the tea.' And, coward that I am, I make a bolt for the kitchen door.

Johnny's stirring the tea in the pot. He's one of the few people I know who still turns making a quick cuppa into an art form. No tea bags for Johnny. He still uses real leaves and the pot has to be thoroughly warmed. On it goes. I have to admit, though, Johnny's tea does taste great. Needless to say, I'm back on the old Save-It own brand tea bags now he's gone.

He looks up as I come into the kitchen. 'Getting the third degree?'

I nod.

He gives me a sympathetic smile. 'Now you'll be remembering why you stopped coming round.'

'It's probably because she's been storing it up,' I suggest. 'I'll definitely call in more often, then she might forget.'

'No,' Johnny says, rescuing me. 'I don't think she'll ever give up hope.' He pours out a cup of tea for me – one of Mary's best china cups, as she instructed – and hands it over. 'Like me.'

I distract myself by stirring the tea, avoiding Johnny's eyes. 'You know that I'm seeing someone else.'

'Do you love him?'

I shrug. 'I really *like* him.'

'*Like* I can live with,' Johnny says. 'Just about.'

I nurse my cup. 'I've got a favour to ask.'

'Ask away.'

'Do you think you could look after Charlie this weekend?'

'Sure. Let me know when.'

'*All* weekend,' I admit. 'I'm hoping to go away.'

'Away?' Johnny raises an eyebrow. 'With Spencer?'

Honesty, I think, is probably the best policy. 'With Spencer.'

Johnny lets out a long, steady breath. 'Sometimes you really take the piss, Sally.'

'I know, I know,' I say in my best apologetic voice. 'But it's all booked up and—'

'Charlie is surplus to requirements?'

I sigh the sigh of the defeated. 'Spencer's not used to children.'

My ex-boyfriend frowns. 'Bit of a shame when you've got one.'

'I couldn't leave Charlie with anyone else,' I say. Maybe I'm not being entirely honest by omitting the fact that all my begging to Debs was to no avail. That woman is as hard-hearted as they come. 'If you say no, then I'll have to cancel. But this is my big chance. I've never been anywhere, Johnny. I've been trapped in this place all of my life. It's like an adventure for me.'

'So,' Johnny says. 'No pressure then.'

'I'll owe you,' I tell him. 'Big time.'

'You will,' Johnny says. I'm relieved to see that he's still able to smile about this. 'I'll make sure you pay. I just can't think how right now.'

'Anything, anything,' I promise rashly.

'Oh, Sally,' he sighs.

'I know. You're the best mate in the world, Johnny,' I tell him.

'Tell me about it,' he mutters.

I put my arms around him and hug him tightly. He might be an unshaven wreck but he still smells wonderful and so familiar. I resist the urge to nuzzle into his neck.

'So,' Johnny says as I untwine myself. 'Where are you going with Hot Shot?'

'Cuba,' I tell him with an anxious shrug.

'Christ,' he says, rocking back in surprise. 'I thought you were going to say Wales or somewhere. Cuba? The man doesn't do things by half.'

I can't really say much to that.

'Why Cuba?'

'Spencer says the salsa dancing there is great.'

'You're going all that way to *dance*?'

'It looks like it.'

'Bloody hell,' Johnny says. 'There's a great salsa dancing school in Bootle. Couldn't you go there?'

'It's not quite the same, is it?' I laugh softly. Then, 'What exactly do you know about salsa dancing schools?'

Johnny flushes. 'I'm doing some work there. That's all.'

Could Debs have been right about Johnny taking dancing lessons? Who knows. 'I won't forget this.'

'Cuba,' he repeats in a dazed way. 'Supposing that you fall in love with him while you're there?'

'I don't know,' I say.

My friend looks thoroughly deflated.

'I'm so sorry, Johnny. Thanks for doing this. You don't know what it means to me.'

'I think I do,' he corrects. 'Otherwise, I'd be telling you to get lost.'

'I don't deserve you,' I say.

'No,' Johnny agrees. 'You don't.'

Chapter Twenty-Seven

Johnny and Charlie stood on the kerbside outside the flats and watched as Spencer loaded Sally's small weekend bag into the boot of his shiny sports car. Good job Sally hadn't taken a lot of shoes, Johnny thought. It might be a forty-grand motor, but the boot was completely useless.

The boy leaned awkwardly against him and Johnny slid his arm protectively round Charlie's shoulders. Cuba, Johnny thought. To salsa dance. Maybe he had thrown the gauntlet down just a little too hard in front of his rival. There was no way he could compete with that.

Sally was panicking. 'Now be good,' she said. 'Don't be any trouble for Johnny.'

'Aw, Mum,' the boy complained.

Charlie was never any trouble, Johnny thought. Sally should know that by now.

'He'll be sound,' Johnny said. 'Don't worry.' Though why he should be reassuring her when she was leaving behind her only child to jet off on a romantic weekend break with a strange bloke, Johnny couldn't quite understand. 'We'll manage won't we, our kid?'

Charlie nodded vigorously.

Sally came over and brushed the hair out of her son's eyes. 'I'll be back before you know it, son.' She gripped him in a bear hug.

Charlie shrank away from her embrace, making Johnny smile to himself. 'Don't fuss, Mum.'

'If there's any trouble, anything, you'll ring me right away, won't you?'

'There'll be no trouble,' Johnny said calmly.

'But if there is—'

'You'll be the first to know.'

'Thanks, Johnny.' Sally hugged him.

Spencer, he noticed, glanced at his watch. 'We need to leave, Sally.'

Her eyes were teary and she looked as if she was never going to see her son again, rather than just be away for a few days.

'They'll be fine,' Spencer said.

'We will,' Johnny agreed crisply.

Spencer held out his hand and shook Johnny's. 'Thank you so much for this. Sally and I really do appreciate your thoughtfulness.'

'No worries, mate.' The bloke was confident, assured, loaded. He looked as if he'd never lost so much as a night's sleep in his whole life. And he was stealing Sally away from him right under his nose. Good job Spencer Knight's manners were impeccable. If he wasn't such a nice fella, Johnny really would have liked to deck him. He could have easily said no to Sally, but what would that have achieved? What right had he to deny her this bit of happiness when he had so little to offer her himself?

Sally squeezed her son again, making him squirm in embarrassment.

'Sally . . .' Spencer held open the door for her.

Reluctantly, she let go of Charlie and fed herself into the car. 'Bye bye, sweetheart. Be good.'

'Bye, Mum.'

The car roared away. Charlie and Johnny waved after it. Sally hung out of the window and shouted at the top of her voice. 'Mummy loves you!'

Johnny and Charlie looked at each other.

'*Mummy loves you?*' Charlie said, shaking his head. 'She's lost the plot.'

'She's worried, that's all.'

'Then she shouldn't be going,' the boy pointed out. 'Who wants to go to Cuba anyway?'

'Your mum,' Johnny conceded.

'Why does she like him better than you?' the boy wanted to know. 'What has he got that you haven't, Johnny?'

'Good looks. Money. A sports car.' *And your mother.*

Charlie looked miserable. 'Kyle says that getting a rich bloke is all that girls think about.'

Johnny smiled to himself. One day he must take time to educate Kyle about sexual equality. 'That's not true,' he explained.

'Kyle's girlfriend, Britney Evans, wants to marry a footballer and live in a mansion in Cheshire.'

Ah. It was all suddenly clear. So that was why Kyle, who was normally reluctant to do anything that involved effort, had started to attend the football club so religiously.

'Kyle wants to be a train driver though,' Charlie added.

Sensible career move, Johnny thought. Seeing as there wasn't much call for footballers with two left feet.

'Train drivers don't get paid a lot, do they? Unless they work overtime. Do you think she'll dump him?' the boy asked.

'Not all women are after men for their money, but sometimes they like to be treated nicely.'

'Can't you treat them nicely round here?'

'Yes. But you have to be a bit more creative.'

'You could do that, Johnny. You can do anything.'

Yeah, he was a regular Superhero. 'I'm trying, son,' Johnny said. 'Believe me, I'm trying.'

Chapter Twenty-Eight

Sally Freeman, Single Mum and Superwoman has touched down in Havana. Oh, *yes*.

Our hotel is five star. *Five star*! My only other brush with five stars was when I had a McJob as a teenager and I won Employee of the Month. How to be a winner and a loser at the same time, eh?

And we flew Business Class. *Business Class*! All the way! Never in my wildest dreams did I think that I'd ever be in a position to travel in such style. Bet I drove Spencer nuts, because I had to try everything out at least once. I pushed all the buttons, tried all the recline angles on my seat, watched all the DVDs I could fit into our eleven-hour flight. Charlie would have loved that bit. I also ate my own weight in handmade truffles and recouped the cost of the airline ticket in personal champagne consumption. To be fair to my companion, he never complained once.

We arrived in Havana in the dead of night, so it was pitch black and I couldn't see a thing, and all we did was take a taxi to the hotel and fall into bed, exhausted. But now Spencer and I are having breakfast on the roof terrace, and the whole of Cuba's capital city is spread before me.

It's already hot and the heavy air is filled with the scent of spices, jasmine and bougainvillaca. We're overlooking one of the main garden squares in Havana, the tall, leafy trees – not a clue what they are – providing much-needed shade for the throng of people already bustling below. Beneath us, a slow stream of 1950s American cars cruise by – Cadillacs, Chevys, Buicks and Oldsmobiles, Spencer tells me – all of those glamorous vehicles that they use in the movies. Some are the size of my flat and it's clearly obligatory for the drivers to hang out of the window, smoke a fat cigar and steer with one hand. Even at this hour, loud Latin-American music pumps out of them all. Next to them, little open-sided, two-seater cabs called cocotaxis in a custard shade of yellow that make them look like children's toy cars jostle for space. Over-shadowing both are enormous, double-length buses painted pale pink that are so tightly packed with people that I wonder how they manage to breathe. The city is virtually gridlocked, but never before has a traffic jam looked or sounded quite so pretty.

Spencer's hand slides across the table and finds mine. He looks so relaxed whatever his surroundings, a man at ease with himself. I, on the other hand, am like a kid with ADHD. A sweet-toothed addict let loose in a candy store. I can't wait to get out there and at it. We're here for such a short time and I don't want to waste even a minute. 'We'll take a walking tour of the city when we've eaten,' he says. 'Does that sound okay?'

'Spencer, it sounds fabulous,' I say gratefully. 'I can't believe that I'm really here.'

He lifts my fingers to his lips and kisses them gently. 'You'll fall in love with the place.'

I look across at his handsome face, his crisp white linen shirt, his flawless complexion. He's with me. That hunk is here with me in a foreign land. I feel like a princess, an heiress, a pop star. Surely even Paris Hilton was never so spoiled. And I'm sure that I *will* fall in love – and not just with Cuba.

Chapter Twenty-Nine

As soon as we've finished breakfast, Spencer and I stroll down Habana Street, hand-in-hand, looking like any other couple in love. Which maybe we are. On closer inspection, the magnificent buildings exhibit a certain faded elegance. My own personal guide tells me a bit about the buildings. Remnants of Moorish and Spanish architecture are all suffering acutely from years of trade sanctions by the USA against Cuba. Most basic supplies that we take for granted in our local B&Q, Spencer informs me, are notoriously difficult to come by and ridiculously expensive. So, of course, the buildings have fallen into a perilous state of disrepair. Some of them make Bill Shankly House look in great nick.

Despite the difficulties, the crumbling façades are still vibrant in primary colours, sunshine yellow, pillar-box red and cornflower blue. A few of the buildings have murals painted on the side – people dancing, market scenes, more flowers. Even the bright colour of the cars complement the cityscape perfectly. It looks like the whole place has been painted with the colours from a kid's paintbox. If it was any brighter, I'd worry that my retinas might shatter or something.

The spirit of the people here is amazing too. Every single person we've seen so far is smiling, grins splitting their weathered, nut brown faces. I wonder why us Brits, when we have so much, have become such miserable, ill-mannered and grey bastards? A wizened old man runs along next to us and, in seconds, sketches me and Spencer on a rough piece of paper. Spencer hands over a few dollars and, in return for our patronage, we get our portrait. Then he's off to tag some more tourists.

'Good grief,' I say as I examine our portrait. 'It looks just like us! How did he do that so quickly?'

'The people here are very enterprising,' he tells me.

I'll say.

Before we reach the end of the street, we're offered sunflowers by a woman on a bicycle wearing layers and layers of crisp white Broderie

Anglaise and a yellow turban bedecked with flowers. Something sweet and sugary in a paper cone is thrust into our hands and Spencer duly passes over the required payment. A man in a multi-coloured shirt comes along with the biggest cigars I've ever seen and insists that I take a puff while Spencer is coerced into recording the event on his camera. I inhale the bittersweet smoke and it leaves my head reeling and my lungs burning.

There are flowers everywhere. Terracotta pots brimming with red geraniums stand guard at every doorway. Windowboxes drip with exotic blooms in every conceivable hue that I can't begin to name. Outside even the poorest-looking house there are cleaned-up tin cans filled with an explosion of sunflowers and begonias. Little dogs in packs run amok, barking happily. A carnival follows in our wake: musicians playing a salsa beat; dancers in gaudy costumes with frilled sleeves totter past us on tall stilts. We pause to let them pass and already I'm tapping my feet.

'This place is so alive that it hurts,' I say.

'Come on.' Spencer tugs me towards a street café. 'You need refreshment.'

Even though it's not yet lunchtime, he orders mojitos for us both – a potent blend of Cuban white rum, soda water, sugar and mint, served with lots of ice in a tall glass. Nectar. The Cubans, it seems, drink them like we drink tea – and from as early in the morning. I sip it through a striped straw, enjoying the sharp taste of the mint, cooling and refreshing on my dry throat. I could stay here all afternoon drinking these, kick back, go native.

'Better?' Spencer asks.

'Mmm. Delicious.' I sink back in my chair and look out over the street. Forgetting about the Factor 30 that's in the bottom of my handbag, I let the sun beat down on my face which, even though it will give me millions of wrinkles in years to come, feels oh so good. A small band of musicians comes to our side to serenade us. There's a guitar, someone playing maracas. They sway along to their own soothing rhythm, voices like honey.

'They're singing a song of love,' Spencer explains. 'About a beautiful woman who has two men in love with her.'

But I'm not really listening. I'm staring at this colourful, exciting city and thinking, If these folk can lift themselves from the gloom and do so much with some paint and flowers and a whole heap of passion, then why can't the people on my estate do exactly the same?

Chapter Thirty

'I got you some Coco-Pops,' Johnny said as he poured them out into a bowl.

Charlie, at the table, said, 'Mum doesn't let me have those.'

Johnny grinned. 'I know.'

Charlie grinned in return. 'Ringo. Ringo.' In response to his name the dog trotted to Charlie's heel where he was fed a handful of the sugary breakfast cereal for his trouble.

The boy had been a bit down since Sally left. Even watching *Borat* together last night on DVD – something else that probably wasn't allowed – had failed to lift Charlie's mood completely. Sally had texted them both a dozen times before she even left the airport to find out if all was well, and Johnny had been able to reassure her that it was. They'd heard nothing from her since. But then, exactly what would she do if he texted back to say that the flat had burned down or that Charlie was in hospital with a broken leg? It was all very well appearing concerned, but the reality was that she was on the other side of the world having fun and could do nothing about it. Still, he didn't really mind. If he blocked out the fact that Sally was with someone else, then at least it gave him the opportunity to spend some time with Charlie.

'Everything all right?' Johnny wanted to know.

Charlie shrugged that everything was, indeed, all right.

'Not missing your mum too much?'

'No,' the boy answered, but he nodded his head subconsciously. Johnny smiled to himself.

'She'll be back before you know it.'

The Scissor Sisters 'Don't Feel Like Dancing' blared out of the radio.

'They're playing our song, Charlie,' Johnny said and jumped out of his chair.

Charlie jumped up too and they enjoyed a frenzied bout of 1970s disco-dancing together while the song lasted. Ringo yapped along enthusiastically. It was something silly that they'd done together since the tune had been at the top of the pop charts. They both loved it. When the song and their dance ended Charlie sat down again, smiling, and tucked into his cereal.

'It used to drive Mum mad when we did that,' he said, mouth full.

'Yeah,' Johnny said, and he couldn't see the lovely Spencer strutting his funky stuff with Charlie in the kitchen just to make the boy laugh. Maybe Sally would view that as a good thing.

'Mum says that you act like a big kid,' Charlie informed him.

Perhaps not.

'But that's why I like you,' the boy added, grinning. 'You're not like a real adult. You're silly.'

Johnny sighed inwardly, relief washing over him. That moment of madness had cheered Charlie up a bit. If that branded him as silly, then so be it.

Today, it would have been better if they could have done something fun together, taken off to the fair at Southport maybe, but Johnny had promised Ronaldo that he'd do some painting at the dance studio in return for his lessons. Charlie, for a fee, had agreed to help him out.

'Sure you don't mind coming with me today? I'd got it fixed up before your mum decided to go away and I don't want to let the fella down.'

Charlie shook his head. 'I've never done painting before. You like it. I might like it too.'

'Finish up your breakfast then. We'd better get going,' Johnny said. 'We've got a lot to do.'

Chapter Thirty-One

Ronaldo greeted them at the door wearing a rather more conservative outfit than he'd worn last time Johnny saw him. The bouffant hair was still in evidence and the Perma-tan, but the Lycra and frills had been replaced by jeans and a pink polo shirt. It didn't make him look any less camp.

'Come in. Come in, lover. This Johnny Junior?'

Johnny hated questions like that. How could he encapsulate his relationship with Charlie in one glib sentence? He opted for, 'This is Charlie. My apprentice.'

Ronaldo shook Charlie's hand. 'Very pleased to meet you, Charlie the Apprentice.'

Johnny smiled as the boy bristled with pride. They followed Ronaldo up the stairs and into the studio, lugging paint and stepladders with them. The rest of the stuff was in Johnny's beaten-up old van which was parked on a double yellow line with his mam's disabled sticker in the window.

'What are you going to do for me, Mr Johnny? All lessons are cancelled for today.' Ronaldo made a sweeping gesture. 'I hand my precious studio over to your care.'

'I've got this.' Johnny held up one of the cans of paint. 'Soft Sunflower Symphony.'

Ronaldo looked puzzled.

'In other words, pale yellow. Sort of lemon.'

'*Limón?*'

'Just to freshen the place up. Then I thought I'd paint a mural over it.'

'I love a muriel!' Ronaldo clapped his hands in joy. 'What kind of muriel?'

'Dancers,' Johnny said with a shrug. Seemed appropriate. 'Something like that.'

'Dancers!' Ronaldo was in seventh heaven. 'A muriel of dancers!'

Charlie tugged at Johnny's T-shirt and leaned into him. 'What's a muriel?' he whispered.

'A picture,' Johnny said. 'A big one. All over the wall.'

Charlie's eyes widened in approval. 'Cool.'

'I'll get the rest of the stuff from the van. You can start with a roller and do the bottom of the wall. I'll follow round and do the top.'

'I could go up the ladder,' Charlie suggested.

'I'll do that,' Johnny said. 'You might fall off and brain yourself. And then I'd get brained by your mother for letting you go up a ladder when I'm supposed to be looking after you.'

'I'm not a kid,' Charlie said with a pout.

'That's exactly what you are,' Johnny pointed out. Then he ruffled the boy's hair. 'But you're my favourite kid.'

The boy hopped about from foot to foot. 'What do we do first?' he wanted to know.

'We do what all good British workmen do before anything else . . .'

Charlie waited expectantly.

'Ronaldo,' Johnny instructed. 'Get a brew on.'

'Did my superb salsa lessons get you the girl, Mr Johnny?' Ronaldo asked as he brought them their tenth cup of tea of the day.

Johnny stood back to admire the mural. He shook his head. Charlie wasn't listening, but Johnny lowered his voice anyway. 'The lady in question is currently in Cuba salsa dancing with another man.'

'That is not good.' Ronaldo shook his hairstyle. 'Cuba is the beautiful island. Sexy, sultry, so romantic. The perfect place for love.'

'Too much information, mate.' Johnny held up his paint-smeared hand before Ronaldo volunteered any more depressing facts. Even while he was painting, visions of Sally, lying scantily clad on a white sandy beach, surf lapping at her toes, had tormented him. And he didn't even know if there was a beach in Havana. He wondered why he'd never taken Sally away for the weekend while they'd been together. Because he'd never had any money. Because he'd always considered Charlie. Because he had his mum to think about. A thousand and one excuses and all of them valid, but lame. He should have treated Sally like the special person she was. He knew that he'd taken her for granted. But he'd been happy. He'd thought she was happy too.

'The bloke's a tosser,' Charlie threw over his shoulder. Maybe the boy had been ear-wigging after all.

'Language, Charlie,' Johnny said. Then to Ronaldo, 'A *rich* tosser.'

The dance instructor pursed his lips. 'That is very bad.'

'He's with my mum,' Charlie added. 'He might want to be my dad one day.' The boy wrinkled his nose. 'That'd be horrible.'

Johnny silently agreed that it would.

'Mr Charlie the Apprentice,' Ronaldo said. 'You have done a very good job.'

The boy climbed down from the top of the ladder – Johnny had lost that battle within ten minutes.

Turning to Johnny, Ronaldo said. 'The muriel is wonderful, lover.' He sighed contentedly. 'People will come to my studio just to see it.' The dancer waved his arms round the room. 'They will travel for miles and miles.'

Johnny studied his artwork. He was pleased with it. On the Soft Sunflower Symphony background, life-size couples in vibrant colours danced together, bodies entwined, heads close together. They all looked happy, in love.

'Perhaps if your lady doesn't love you for your dancing, she might love you for this.'

'I doubt it,' Johnny said.

He looked at his dancers again. He really hoped that Sally wasn't being embraced by Spencer in a similar fashion. In fact, to be brutally honest, he hoped that, for his sake, she was having a really shite time.

Chapter Thirty-Two

Late in the evening, Spencer and I head for the Cuban equivalent of the Community Centre which is a world away from the dreary and dilapidated one at Kirberly, I can tell you. Spencer explains that even the little villages out in the country have a dedicated centre for music which everyone goes to on a Saturday night to boogie on down.

This particular one is open to the stars and a deliciously warm breeze blows over the dance floor, taking some of the heat from the steamy night. On the stage, a dozen or more musicians waft lively music into the swaying crowd. It's an amazing place. When Spencer says that everyone comes here, he's right; there are as many teenagers here as there are pensioners and it costs less than a Cuban peso to come inside where we've both been welcomed warmly.

The dance floor has been constantly filled with a crush of people from the moment we got here, one dance flowing seamlessly to the next, the dancers weaving in and out of each other like a slowly meandering river.

'To be unable or unwilling to dance in Cuba is considered a terrible social faux pas,' Spencer whispers to me. 'We'd better join in.'

He leads me onto the floor, easing our way through the mass of bodies until we're right in the middle of the throng and he takes me in his arms, moving me skilfully to the lilting beat. He might not have all the moves and turns that Johnny has, but he can still groove.

Already I know half of the songs as you can't sit down for five minutes in this place without someone popping up behind you with a guitar and a pair of maracas. I've been serenaded half to death. Then the ubiquitous retail opportunity springs up too. Spencer is very generous and now must own the most extensive collection of salsa music CDs outside of the Caribbean. My date/benefactor/boyfriend – I'm still not entirely comfortable with what his title should be – swivels his slinky hips against mine, turning me with him.

I look up at him. 'Thought you couldn't dance?'

'I can hold my own,' Spencer says with a smile.

'Why didn't we see this hidden talent at the Kirberly Community Centre?'

'I just didn't want to get into a duelling situation with your ex-boyfriend,' he says.

Probably wise.

'Men can be very territorial. Particularly when confronted with their love rival.'

'Johnny's not your rival,' I explain. 'He's my mate. He looks out for me.'

Spencer looks unconvinced, but his smile doesn't falter. 'I'll just have to make sure that I don't give him a reason to steal you away from me.' He pulls me closer as if to reinforce it.

My conscience has been pricked at the mention of Johnny. I wonder how my two men are getting on, if they're both okay and whether they're missing me. This morning I managed to place a brief phone call from the hotel to Charlie; getting a line out of Cuba isn't all that easy and the quality was terrible. Mobile phones don't work at all. Despite my best efforts, his responses were non-committal and we were cut off after two minutes. I think my son's less than happy with me for leaving him behind, and who can blame him? It's probably the first time he's been excluded from anything in my life. If there was another occasion, then I can't remember it. He'll be fine with Johnny though. Charlie adores him – as do most other people. What's more, I'd trust Johnny with my son's life. So I should just relax, and make the most of my time as a footloose and fancy free Superwoman.

I turn my attention back to my partner. All the mojitos we've knocked back today have loosened my hips. The silver sequinned number has been given another outing and I'm feeling fabulously sexy. Our bodies move together in time and it feels so good. I throw back my head and laugh and laugh while I'm spun round and round. There has been far too little of this pure, unfettered fun in my shitty little life. Charlie's the only ray of sunshine that I've got. And, much as I love my son, maybe sometimes that's not enough. Shouldn't I be allowed a life too?

My head's reeling and not just from the strong alcohol and excessive spinning combo, but because of all the sights and sounds that have bombarded my brain today. Cuba has blown me away and I've fallen in love just as Spencer said I would.

The music stops and the band leave the stage for a break. We're both breathing heavily. 'Let's get another drink,' Spencer suggests as he takes my hand. 'I need to sit down and get my breath back.'

I touch his arm, stopping him in his tracks, and stand on tiptoe to kiss his beautiful lips. 'Thank you for this,' I whisper. 'Thank you so much.'

'It's been my pleasure.' Spencer's lips are hot on mine and I can't wait for the music to start again so that we can rub our bodies together!

This weekend has shown me a way of life that I never knew existed. Despite crushing poverty, the Cubans have somehow managed to make their country bright, vibrant and full of life. In the dark recesses of my mind, I'm still wondering how I can bottle all of this and bring it home with me.

Chapter Thirty-Three

It's raining now that I'm back in Britain. The elements are playing make-believe it's winter and have everyone huddled back into thick jackets and sturdy footwear. Because of the weather Kirberly market is quiet today and I'm able to buy some really cheap fruit and veg that the stallholders are trying to get rid of.

My friend isn't really interested in shopping today – unusual. So Debs and I call it a day and head off to the nearest greasy spoon café on the fringe of the market. Starbucks it isn't. We pull two of the white plastic chairs together at a table covered with a stained gingham cloth and then, while Debs picks at a bacon butty, I proceed to sink three coffees in quick succession in an effort to caffeine away that jet lag and, in the process, blow my week's budget. So much for the cheap veggies. Charlie and I are going to be down to plates of pasta *au naturel* by the time my benefits are due.

My son was already in school by the time I got back from Cuba, which was disappointing. I'd have sent him a text, but they're not allowed to have their phones on during lessons. Fair enough, I suppose. Kids find enough to distract themselves from lessons without having gadgets to assist them.

Spencer dropped me off at my flat and then headed off home to get ready for his afternoon shift teaching plebs – including me – the finer points of computing. I still don't know why he does this. Do I believe all that 'putting something back into society' schtick? I don't know. He does seem to be incredibly generous with his time and with his money without being flash. I guess I just can't believe it. My old mum taught me that if something seems too good to be true, the chances are that it probably is.

Checking my watch, I remind myself that I mustn't be late for my lesson this afternoon. Now that I'm teacher's pet, I don't want to mess up.

The greasy spoon is packed with wet people steaming gently and it would be nice just to shut my eyes for a few minutes, recover from my hectic weekend. The minute I close my eyes I can take myself right back to Cuba. The dancing, the sun, the colours . . . they're all still locked in my head.

'You look knackered,' Debs observes. 'Too much salsa, sun and sex.'

'Plenty of the first two,' I say. 'But none of the latter.'

'All that way,' she splutters, horrified, 'and no nookie?'

'We didn't have the time,' I explain. 'Most of Friday night was spent on the plane, Saturday we went dancing and didn't get back until five o'clock in the morning.' To be honest, the five-star hotel was a bit wasted on me. Egyptian cotton sheets and we were in them for a few hours, max. We nearly got down to bumping uglies on Sunday morning, but I'm not going to tell Debs that. It's just that I couldn't wait to get out into the streets of Havana again and have a look around, and I think Spencer sort of sensed that my mind wasn't exactly on the job. And you don't want your first time to be a quickie, right? Frankly, I've still got my eye on that hot tub.

You want to remember your first time together as special, and although Havana might have been the perfect setting, basically there was too much else that I wanted to do. Is that a bad thing? Maybe I shouldn't have been feeling like that, but you have to remember that the only other man I've slept with for years and years and years is Johnny. Actually, I've made love with a grand total of two men since I was fifteen. Don't even have to get my socks off to count that lot. My relationship with Charlie's dad put me off men for years. You wouldn't believe how long it took Johnny to break down all the barriers I'd erected round myself. So, despite what the media would have you believe, not all single mums are slappers – get it? Just because I made one mistake in the condom department it doesn't mean that it should haunt me for the rest of my life.

That's why it feels weird to be contemplating getting naked with someone else. Now that it comes down to it, I'm more than a bit reluctant. I'm not exactly drawing my pension, but I'm not getting any younger either. I'm not in bad shape, but I'm not going to be giving Kylie sleepless nights. Because I had Charlie so young I've got stretchmarks on my stretchmarks – my stomach's like Nelly the Elephant's arse. No six-pack there. Come to think of it, my *arse* is like Nelly the Elephant's arse too. It wouldn't be so bad if Spencer had a bit of softening around the waist or some physical defect to comfort me, but the man's honed and toned. There's evidence that plenty of hours have been spent in the gym.

'Christ.' Debs is wide-eyed, clearly still struggling to come to terms with the fact that I haven't been shagged senseless all weekend. 'Didn't have time? What were you doing?'

'Sightseeing.'

'Fuck me.' She looks put out. 'I'd rather have gone to Blackpool and come back bandy.'

'That's where you and I differ,' I note haughtily. 'I appreciated the culture.'

'Culture?' My friend's agog. 'You're not interested in culture.'

'I am.'

'Since when? We're surrounded by the bloody stuff here,' a wave of her arm takes in the greasy spoon and environs, 'and I've never heard you wax lyrical about it.'

'Here? What culture?'

'We've got more culture than you can shake a stick at. We're the home of the naffing Beatles, the Fab Four, the band that rocked the world. That'll do for starters. We're the European Capital of Culture, for frig's sake. Someone must think we've got something to shout about.'

'That's different.'

'Like hell. Just because it's on the naffing doorstep and you don't have to fly eleven hours to get there you're not bothered.'

'It wasn't just about the culture.' Debs does have a point and I sound chastened even to my own ears. She's right about our fair city, but it isn't the same when you walk past it every day. Cuba was so different. How do I explain that to her? 'I wanted to experience everything there was to experience.' I drift back to Spencer and me going home from the dance in the back of a big black Cadillac the size of my living room, belching smoke and smelling of cigars with salsa music still ringing in our ears. Sharing this with my bezzie though would be a waste of breath. I just don't think Debs would get it. 'There's no point going all that way if you're not even going to leave the hotel room.'

'And Little Lord Fauntleroy had a good time – even though he didn't get any action?'

'Of course he did.'

My friend clearly still thinks I'm mad and that Spencer's a closet gay. 'You should see the place, Debs.' I don't know why I should have to justify myself to her, but I'm going to try. 'The people haven't got two halfpennies to rub together and yet they're full of life. There's an energy there that's gone from our estate. If they can have shit lives and still look like they're living in a Disney movie, why can't we?'

My friend rolls her eyes. 'Don't tell me,' she says, as she finishes her Danish pastry. 'Now you're going to become a one-woman crusade to re-energise Kirberly.'

I sit up straighter. Something goes *thunk, thunk, whirr* in my jet-lagged brain. 'You know that's not a bad idea.'

'Fabulous,' she says. 'Now what have I gone and done? Put stupid ideas into your head. You and your bloody do-gooding. No doubt you'll try and drag me into it too.'

My thoughts are whirling so quickly that I'm having trouble catching them. Yet, I think that in there, somewhere, a plan is hatching. 'Have you spent that hundred quid that was left over from the social evening yet?' I ask.

'No,' she admits sulkily. 'But we could go and blow it now on hand-bags. We'll pick up some great bargains on the market in weather like this, our kid.'

I give her my biggest grin. 'Or maybe there's something else much more useful that we could do with it.'

Chapter Thirty-Four

I ruffle Charlie's hair and he ducks away from me. 'Did you miss your old mum?' I ask.

'No,' he says.

'Bet you did.'

'Did not.' And he busies himself with his vegetable korma. I've been getting the cold-shoulder treatment since he came home from school. He avoided me by playing on his Playstation and watching crap on telly, but I didn't have the heart to tell him to turn it off. Now we're sitting together at the kitchen table having our tea.

'Were you and Johnny okay?'

My son shrugs. 'Yeah.'

'Aren't you going to ask me if I had a nice time in Cuba?'

'Did you?' he asks, but he fails to look interested.

'Yes. It was lovely. I'd like to take you one day.'

My only child gives me a withering look. Maybe not. Charlie'd probably prefer Alicante or Benidorm – somewhere with a water park that you can get to in two hours.

He pushes his cauliflower round the plate and avoids my gaze. 'Are you going away with *him* again?'

'I don't know,' I say honestly. 'But I'd like to. Would you mind?'

'I'd rather you went somewhere with Johnny,' he answers. 'Then he'd take me too.' The truth of that statement hurts.

I pick up a paper bag off the chair. 'Spencer bought you this,' I say. 'As a souvenir.'

Charlie's eyes brighten. That's kids for you. Can be bought off every time. He opens the bag and holds up the T-shirt. It looks ten times too big for him. What was I thinking, letting Spencer loose alone in the T-shirt shop at the airport? Kiddo here will probably be about eighteen by the time he grows into it.

He stares blankly at the face on the T-shirt. 'Who's that?'

'Che Guevara.'

'Who's he?'

'He was a Cuban revolutionary.'

'What's a revolutionary?'

'I'm not really sure,' I admit. 'But he was one of the good guys.' Then I show my lack of knowledge about Cuban military history and add, 'I think.'

Charlie puts the T-shirt back in the bag.

'You must remember to thank Spencer.'

'Yeah.'

'So what did you and Johnny do?' I must remember to call Johnny and thank him too. Despite having a minor case of the strops, Charlie seems to have survived the weekend unscathed.

'We painted a dance studio,' my son mumbles.

That probably wasn't the answer I was expecting.

'And he took me to Burger King.'

'Whoa, whoa,' I say. 'Back up. More about the dance studio.'

'We painted a muriel. Johnny let me do some.'

'A mural of what?'

'Dancing people. I did a lady's skirt and some hair. Big hair.' My son indicates big hair in case I'm not familiar with what it is.

'At a dance studio?'

Charlie nods, forgetting he's in a mood and becoming animated. 'Ronaldo's. I think he's a bender.' He gives me a limp wrist.

'Language, Charlie.'

'But he's very nice. He had caramel wafers. Kyle said benders are very happy people.'

'Kyle knows a lot about everything, doesn't he?'

Charlie nods, still too young to grasp the finer shades of sarcasm. One day I must remind myself to strangle Kyle Crossman before he completely poisons my child's mind with his ten-year-old politically incorrect and possibility perverted view of life.

'You should see it, Mum,' my son continues proudly. 'It's very good.'

'Has he finished it?'

'No,' Charlie says. 'Not quite. He's going there tonight to do the last bit.'

And I don't know why I say this, but I do. 'So we could go along and see it?'

My son looks up, eyes as wide as his grin. 'Yeah!'

'Then let's do it.'

108

Chapter Thirty-Five

Johnny was putting the finishing touches to a pair of cherry-red shoes when he heard the doorbell ring and saw Ronaldo mince out to answer it. Another hour here and that should do it. The studio would be fully operational once more.

'Not long now, boy,' he said to his dog. Ringo's tail thumped happily against the floor. Life as a dog must be so much easier, Johnny thought. Sleep, try to get a shag – even a chair leg would do – someone feeds you. There were worse lives to lead.

The studio didn't look bad. Not bad at all. Maybe if Ron wanted to stump up for the paint then he might do the hallway too. Maybe the front door as well. It was always the way, paint one room and it made the others look like shite. Come to think of it, the kitchen could do with a quick lick too.

A moment later, he heard footsteps behind him. Ronaldo coughed delicately and Ringo started to whine with joy. 'You have visitors, Mr Johnny.'

He turned and was surprised to see Charlie and Sally standing there. The boy was smiling brightly, but his ex-girlfriend seemed uncomfortable.

'Hiya,' she said, and came across to kiss him fleetingly. Even after just a weekend away in the sun she was looking tanned and lovely. Looked as if she'd had a good time. Damn.

'Hiya, yourself.'

'I brought Mum to show her the muriel.'

'Mural,' Johnny and Sally corrected in unison and then exchanged a wry glance.

Sally stood back and gazed at the wall. Actually, it was more like a gape.

'Johnny,' she breathed. 'This is fantastic.'

He scratched at his head, embarrassed. 'Thanks.'

'He is an artist,' Ronaldo put in. 'A true artist.'

'I did this bit,' Charlie said, pointing to a flowing skirt. 'And this.' The big hair was singled out for attention.

'That's very big.' Sally kissed her son's head and he let her. So he hadn't stayed mad at his mum for long, Johnny thought. That was good. 'That's great, love,' she said. 'You're a clever boy.'

Charlie glowed at the approval. Ronaldo beckoned to Charlie. 'Come with me, Mr Apprentice. I have some of your favourite biscuits in the cupboard.'

Obediently, Charlie followed Ronaldo. Even Ringo trotted after them. Both Johnny and Sally were conscious that they'd deliberately been left alone. Sal studied her feet.

'Why do you think Ronaldo did that?' she asked.

'Maybe he thinks that you'd like to show me your gratitude for looking after your only son.'

She laughed and it was a wonderful sound. He didn't realise how much he missed it.

'How was Cuba?'

'Amazing.'

He wasn't sure that he wanted to know anything else. Thankfully, nothing else was offered. Sally paced the floor staring at his artwork, slowly taking it all in.

'I saw some stuff just like this over there. On the buildings. Very colourful.'

'Yeah?'

'This is really very good, Johnny,' she said softly. 'I had no idea.'

It had been a sore point between them. Sally had always thought that he was wasting time with his painting. As a consequence, when they were together, he'd hardly done any at all. It was only after their break-up that he'd started up again. Now he felt he was getting into his stride.

He shrugged. 'I like doing it.'

'Is Ronaldo paying you?'

Trust Sally to ask the awkward questions. 'I owe him,' Johnny said, shuffling his feet. He hoped that she didn't ask what for. 'I did this as a favour.'

'I know that I'm forever in your debt,' she said with a smile, 'but can I ask you to do one last favour for me too?'

'Ask away.' He just prayed that she wasn't going to ask him to look after Charlie again this weekend while she jetted off somewhere else exotic with Spencer. That would be more than he could bear.

His ex-lover linked her arm through his and said, 'Fancy painting a "muriel" in the Community Centre?'

Chapter Thirty-Six

'Who put this computer together?' I must have been jet-lagged yesterday, because it's the first time that I've noticed it.

'Me and Johnny,' Charlie says over his shoulder, dragging his attention away from *Shaun the Sheep* on the television.

'You weren't half busy at the weekend, the pair of you.'

My son shrugs and I lose him once more to the ever-perky Shaun.

I pull up a chair and sit down in front of the computer, which has been mounted on a side table near the window. It feels like I'm taking my place at a grand piano. My fingers limber up over the keys and I should be flicking out the tails on my dress coat. Lesson number four – Surfing the Internet. Hmm. Let's see what I can remember.

'Johnny says we need Broadband,' Charlie offers from the sofa.

'Does he.'

'We'd get a quicker connection then.'

'How much does that cost?'

'Dunno.'

'Don't suppose the DHSS would pay for it,' I mutter to no one in particular. Then, before I make my first and momentous foray into the world of cyberspace, I stare out of the window.

Out there, across the city, Spencer is there somewhere. I wonder what he's doing now? He wanted to see me tonight, but what can I do? I've left Charlie alone all weekend with Johnny, I can't start doing that every evening of the week too. I can sense that Charlie's not comfortable with the situation either, so I can hardly invite Spencer round to hang out with us. Anyway, why would he want to spend his spare time in this dingy hole when he's got his own flaming penthouse to rattle round in? But I desperately want to see him. I had such a great time, and now I'm physically aching because I'm missing him so much. No one has ever made me feel like that before. He's fantastic. Fabulous. As well as being ridiculously handsome and ridiculously wealthy, he

112

also happens to be great company. And I don't want to lose him. How many men come along like that in a lifetime? How many women would give their right arm to be in my place? How many nights will he sit in on his own waiting for a single mum to make herself available, when he could have his pick of eligible women? If I were him, I'd be cruising the fleshpots of Liverpool looking for biddable wenches to take back to seduce in my hot tub. Come to think of it, that's exactly what he might be doing. How would I know?

Before I can send myself into a spiral of depression, I switch on the computer. At least I've remembered how to do that.

'Johnny's set you up an internet account,' my son informs me. 'Click the icon.'

'How do you know all this?'

'We do it at school.'

'Why didn't I know that?'

'Because we've never had a computer at home for me to work on.'

'Oh.' See, here I am again, holding back my child's education because I'm too piss-poor to buy a computer and have had to depend on the charity of others. I bash the keys harder.

'Your email address is SallySuperwoman.'

I don't know why, but that makes tears come to my eyes. 'Who thought that up?'

'Me and Johnny,' my son says.

And I wonder how much was Charlie and how much came from Johnny. Some Superwoman, when I can't even get my own kid a computer.

Taking my time, I work through the steps as Spencer showed us and – miracle upon miracle – after a few peeps, beeps and farty noises I'm connected to the information superhighway. I'm surfing the net singlehandedly for the first time! Woo-hoo! I'm almost giddy with excitement.

'I'm doing it, Charlie,' I shout. 'I'm doing it!'

'Sound, Mum.' My son's eyes don't leave the telly. Clearly he doesn't regard my first solo foray into the whirling maelstrom of information around us in the same momentous light as I do.

I go to Google – seems as if Spencer has taught me well – and tap in what I'm looking for. Sure enough, a list of sites pops up instantly. They're spread out before me for my choosing, offering more facts and figures than I can ever possibly need. My fingers move over the keys as I click my selections. I feel a real sense of achievement and joy. It's as if this isn't just connecting me to a whole load of bollocks that's out there that I'm never likely to use, but as if I'm somehow rejoining the human race again. I'm connected, online and I'm coming your way.

The world better watch out for Sally Freeman, Single Mum and Superwoman!

Chapter Thirty-Seven

I've called a meeting. Mrs Kapur from along the corridor is here, as is Dora the Explorer. Dora's having a nightdress day and has got Scary Mary hair, so I'm not sure how much use she'll be to us. Debs is sitting on the windowsill having a smoke out of the window. I don't mind her polluting her own flat, but she's not turning mine into an ashtray. It's slightly alarming that she's perching on my sill ten floors up, but I try not to think of the health and safety aspects of that. I've got the kettle on and we're all waiting for Johnny to arrive.

As I make the brew the doorbell goes and the final participant is here plus dog. Ringo yaps hello and is told to shut up for his enthusiasm. Johnny looks tired; dark circles ring his eyes. He normally looks unkempt but, literally, he looks like he's just fallen out of bed.

'You okay?'

'Bad night,' he says with a stifled yawn. 'Mam's not so good.'

'Want me to call in on her later?'

'She'd like that.'

'I'll take Charlie with me, but we won't stay long.' My son could wear out the Duracell Bunny. 'Is there anything she needs?'

'A new house that's not damp, an NHS that functions properly and twenty-four-hour care.'

'I meant milk and stuff.'

'No. Thanks for the offer. All that's sorted. Just go along and sit with her for a bit.'

I give him a hug as he looks like he needs one. 'She'll be all right, you know. She's got you to look after her.'

'I wonder how long she can keep soldiering on like this,' he confides. 'She never complains, but this can't be much of a life for her. I just wish there was something I could do.'

'You know if there's ever anything that I can do, you only have to ask.'

'Thanks for that.' Goodness only knows, I owe him enough.

'Have a KitKat.' I thrust one into his hand to try to lighten the moment. 'That'll cheer you up.'

Johnny gives me a weary smile.

I've got ulterior motives, so I've bought in nice biscuits to sweeten up my friends and neighbours.

'What's all this about?' Johnny asks, flicking a thumb towards my cohorts as he breaks open his KitKat.

'All in good time. Help me take these mugs through.'

We distribute the tea and I sit on the remaining chair while Johnny lounges on the floor between the two older ladies.

'Ah, Johnny lad,' Mrs Kapur says. 'You make yourself comfortable. A rose between two thorns.'

'I'm not a thorn,' Dora pipes up. 'I'm a little ray of sunshine.'

'Course you are, doll.' Mrs Kapur pats her knee.

Ringo snuggles in next to Johnny, curling up at his side.

It's about time we got started otherwise we'll be here all day. I clear my throat. 'I brought you all here,' I say, 'because I wanted to tell you my news.'

A look of alarm spreads over Johnny's face.

'It's nothing to worry about!' I laugh. 'As you all know, I went to Cuba for the weekend.'

'Aw, not again,' Debs says, blowing out a stream of smoke. 'Spare us the details.'

'I didn't know you went to Cuba,' Dora says, frowning. 'Where's Cuba? Near Scotland?'

'Maybe you are thinking of Cumbria,' Mrs Kapur suggests.

'It's a long way away, Dora,' I supply.

Then, before I can continue, she adds, 'What did you go there for?'

'Sun, sea and *no* shagging,' Debs chips in.

Johnny sits up straighter at that. Even Ringo lifts an ear.

Debs cocks her eyebrow at me in a challenging way.

I ignore my supposed best friend and carry on, 'It's an amazing place. The country's completely potless. Most of the people haven't got a bean to their name, but the place is full of colour and music and flowers.'

Only Mrs Kapur looks impressed by this revelation. 'Sounds lovely, doll.'

'It made me start thinking that maybe we could do something similar to liven the estate up.'

'What kind of music?' Dora asks nervously. 'I don't like all that loud stuff. You can't tell what they're singing these days, but you know it's not nice.'

'I didn't really mean the music, Dora. More the flowers and the colour.'

'I wouldn't mind some Frank Sinatra,' she continues. 'I like that kind of music. "Strangers in the Night" — I like that one.'

'I like that one too, doll,' Mrs Kapur says.

'What about "Fly Me to the Moon"?'

I wish I'd never mentioned the frigging music. It looks like Dora's planning to run through the entire Frank Sinatra back catalogue.

My bonkers neighbour starts singing her own rendition of 'My Way'. She *will* definitely face her 'final curtain' if she doesn't shut up.

'Ssh, ssh.' Mrs Kapur pats Dora's knee again, quietening her down. 'If we have music I'm sure Sally will let you be the one to choose it, Dora.'

Thankfully, Dora looks placated. Mrs Kapur winks at me and I smile at her with relief. 'I've been on to the Council this morning.'

'I hope you told them that the lift's still out,' Mrs Kapur says. 'I don't think my old knees will take much more of those stairs.'

'I did, actually,' I reassure her. 'But they still couldn't give me a date when they're coming to fix it.'

'Bloody typical,' the old lady mutters.

'However,' I press on, 'that wasn't my main purpose for calling them.'

'Get on with it,' Debs says, throwing her cigarette butt out of the window and coming to join us.

'I spoke to a really nice fella called Richard Selley,' I tell them. 'He's running a project called Urban Paradise. I found out all about it on the internet.' I pause while they register that small achievement. 'It's a Government initiative. They're providing funding in this area to regenerate sink estates, wasteland, that kind of stuff.'

'That's nice,' Mrs Kapur says. 'We could do with a bit of that.'

'I thought the same thing,' I tell her.

'Oh no,' Debs says, putting a hand to her head. 'I can feel a lot of work coming on.'

'They'll give us ten thousand pounds.'

'Ten thousand!' Dora exclaims. 'That's a lot of money.'

Think of all the nighties you could buy with that, Dora. 'I know.' I still can hardly believe it myself. 'We've to spend it on plants, trees, maybe some street furniture.'

Dora again: 'Street furniture?'

'Benches,' Debs supplies.

'Some of it can go on paint supplies.' I glance at Johnny and he nods.

'And the catch?' he says.

'We can't spend any of it on labour. All the work has to be done by volunteers from the estate.'

'The idea being?'

'If people have invested their own time and energy in doing up the estate, then they're less likely to sit back and see it succumb to vandals again. "Ownership" as the man at the Council put it.'

'I used to be handy with a paintbrush,' Mrs Kapur says. 'I can help.' Bless her, she looks too feeble to even lift one. 'Perhaps we can get those little buggers who've broken our lift to take part.'

'We could certainly give it a go. Even kids like that might see the point. Why wouldn't people want to live in a nicer environment?' Probably a thousand reasons, but I'm not going to let that notion rain on my parade. 'I thought we could all talk to people who we know, have a meeting in the Community Centre on Saturday morning and then decide what we'd like to do. We've got to submit our plans to Urban Paradise for approval before we get our hands on the cash. And there's a bit of paperwork to do, but they seemed pretty keen. Apparently this estate is marked down as a Priority Neighbourhood in the Council's Renewal Action Plan. It's something that's going on all across Liverpool.'

Mr Selley told me that the Council are selling off the worst of the tower blocks to private developers who come in and completely renovate them – put in new windows, new wiring, kitchens, bathrooms, the whole shebang. I'd certainly like some of that for Bill Shankly House.

'Sally, you're a wonder,' Mrs Kapur says. 'Isn't she clever? What a marvel.'

Single Mum, Superwoman, I think you'll find, Mrs Kapur!

The old lady claps her hands together. 'I can't wait to get started,' she says. 'We can make this place spic and span again. Like it was in the old days.'

'Johnny.' I look to my old boyfriend. 'Are you with us?' I don't think I could do it without his help.

'Yeah,' he says. 'Count me in.'

'Thanks,' I say gratefully. I know that I can rely on Johnny to watch my back.

I turn to my bezzie. 'What about you, Debs?'

'If we're going to be given ten grand by the Council,' she muses, 'does that mean I can spend the hundred quid I've got on shoes?'

Chapter Thirty-Eight

'I thought you were avoiding me,' Spencer says.

'I'm sorry,' I tell him. 'I've been mad busy all week and it's really difficult for me to get a sitter for Charlie.' This time, Mrs Kapur has been pressed into service, much to Charlie's disgust. I daren't ask Johnny again. Really, I daren't. You can push the bonds of friendship just too far. Besides, he's got his mum to worry about at the moment.

Spencer and I have seen each other at the computer course, but we don't have much time to talk there – at least, not openly. We do exchange a lot of longing looks though. Now it's Thursday night and we're in a tapas bar in Liverpool, a place that used to be an old Catholic church. The gothic architecture makes a grand setting and huge church candles provide the mood lighting. Religious murals cover the walls – God, the saints, that kind of thing. Totally amazing. We're sitting at the main altar that's now a bar eating chorizo sausage, spicy prawns and little bits of filo pastry filled with goat's cheese while drinking champagne. The place is busy and buzzy. I've been meaning to come here for ages with Debs, but have never been able to afford it.

My date brushes my hair away from my face. He's the most hand-some man in the entire place. Every woman that walks past Spencer clocks him. And he's mine. Hands off, bitches!

'I've missed you,' he says, as he gently caresses my thigh.

'I've missed you too. And I've got such a lot to tell you,' I gush. 'Cuba was sound and it gave me loads of ideas. I've been running around like a loony this week trying to get it all together.'

He can tell that I'm bubbling over with excitement and smiles at me as he says, 'Tell me more.'

'I've got a grant fixed up for the estate from an organisation called Urban Paradise. They're giving us ten grand to regenerate Kirberly. Ten grand! We're going to plant flowers and trees. Give everything that doesn't move a coat of paint.'

'Sally,' he says. 'That's a wonderful idea.'

'I know,' I say. 'And it was mine. I thought it up all by myself. But I want to thank you because you took me to Cuba and that's what started me off.'

'Glad to be of service.'

'We'll need loads of volunteers though. We've got our first meeting in the Community Centre on Saturday morning. I'm hoping that tons of people will come.'

'Oh,' Spencer says.

That stops me burbling. 'Oh, what?'

'It's just that I was hoping you'd be able to come away with me again this weekend.'

'I can't,' I say. 'Even if I wasn't committed to this meeting, then I couldn't leave Charlie behind again. The meeting's at eleven o'clock. It will only last an hour or so, I'd guess.' Then I decide to throw caution to the wind. 'Maybe we could go somewhere and take Charlie with us?'

'My friends are having a house party in the Cotswolds.'

Now it's my turn to go, 'Oh.'

Spencer purses his lips. 'It's not really a child-friendly type of get-together. I promised I'd be there.'

I shrug. 'Never mind. Another time.' I haven't been to the Cotswolds and I'd love to go. Bugger.

'I thought you could meet all the gang.'

Frankly, I'm not sure that I'm ready to meet Spencer's gang, so there is a silver lining.

'Maybe I could cancel and come to your meeting to support you,' he says next.

'No, no. Don't do that,' I insist. 'You can't let your friends down. And if this thing goes ahead, there'll be plenty more meetings.'

'If you're sure?'

'Of course I'm sure. You go. Have a great time.'

Spencer drains his glass, then checks the bottle. 'Looks like the last of the champagne.'

I tip my glass upside down. It's fair to say that I'm a bit tipsy. Maybe a bit drunk on joy. 'Mine's empty too.'

Spencer squeezes my hand and looks deep into my eyes. 'Let's go back to my place.'

Time's getting on and I should be thinking about going home. It's way past poor Mrs Kapur's bedtime, never mind Charlie's. The old girl's probably fast asleep on the sofa by now. 'I can't stay long,' I say.

We leave the Porsche in the centre of Liverpool – crazy! – and hail a cab back to the Albert Dock as Spencer's had too much to drink to drive and I can't drive at all, drunk or not.

Back at his place, he makes us both strong coffee then we take it up to the roof terrace. On the way, Spencer grabs a chenille throw from the couch and carries it up the stairs.

The night's cool; menacing clouds scud across the sky. Maybe it will rain tomorrow. 'Is it too chilly out here?' he enquires.

'No,' I say. 'I love this space.' Already I'm wondering if ten grand will get us a sky-high roof terrace on Bill Shankly House. Maybe not. Dora'd only fall off the top anyway.

Spencer lies down on one of the strategically-placed sunloungers and pulls me towards him. 'Come here.'

I lie down next to him and he arranges the throw over us. My eyes are rolling and I need to try very hard not to get too comfortable and fall asleep. On the deck next to us, there's a book which I pick up.

'*The World's Greatest Love Poems*,' I muse. 'Love poems? Is this your normal reading material?' This from a woman whose only reading involves browsing *Heat* or *Closer* magazines on the shelves in Save-It.

'Yes. Would you like me to read one to you?'

'No one's ever read poetry to me before.'

'Then I'll be delighted to be your first.'

I hand the book to Spencer.

'Maybe a little Elizabeth Barrett Browning, I think.' And he flicks through the well-thumbed pages until he finds a poem for me. 'Are you sitting comfortably?' he teases, and I snuggle in closer.

'"How do I love thee?"' he begins, his voice softening. '"Let me count the ways".' And he goes on:

> 'I love thee to the depth and breadth and height
> My soul can reach, when feeling out of sight
> For the ends of Being and ideal Grace.
> I love thee to the level of every day's
> Most quiet need, by sun and candlelight.
> I love thee freely, as men strive for Right;
> I love thee purely, as they turn from Praise.
> I love thee with the passion put to use,

In my old griefs, and with my childhood's faith.
I love thee with a love I seemed to lose
With my lost saints. I love thee with the breath,
Smiles, tears, of all my life; and, if God choose,
I shall but love thee better after death.'

'That's beautiful,' I say. Tears aren't far from my eyes.

'And so are you.' Spencer kisses me longingly. His hands, beneath the blanket, rove over me and I let out a shuddering sigh. 'Sally,' he whispers against my lips as he kisses me.

I sink into the sensation and then a little alarm bell sounds in my head and I know that I can't go any further. 'This is so nice. Wonderful. But I have to go.' I ease myself up and look at my watch. 'I'll get killed if I'm any later.'

'Just stay a little longer,' he murmurs against my neck.

'I can't. Mrs Kapur will be asleep on my sofa. She'll probably have a permanent crick in her neck and it will be all my fault.'

Spencer laughs. 'She'll be fine. You worry too much.'

I think maybe he doesn't worry enough, but I don't say that. I'm spoiling the mood enough by wanting to hightail it out of here in the middle of an outpouring of passion. The bloke's just read naffing poetry to me! 'I'm sorry,' I say. 'I can't. I have other people to think of.'

My hot man looks at me and then lets out an exasperated sigh. 'Okay.' He holds up his hands. 'I know when I'm beaten. I'll phone a cab and take you home.'

'I'm sorry,' I repeat. 'Really sorry.'

'Sally.' Spencer frowns at me. 'You do want this relationship to continue?'

'Yes, yes. Of course I do.'

'I had to ask,' he says.

'Spencer, you have taken my miserable black and white life and have filled it with colour.' I take his hands in mine and kiss them, then hold them against my cheek. 'Please be patient with me. This isn't easy. I have other people in my life who have to come first.'

'Forgive me.' He kisses me again. 'I fully understand.'

But I wonder if he really does.

Chapter Thirty-Nine

The cab pulls up outside Bill Shankly House. Now that plans are afoot to spruce up this area, it suddenly looks worse than ever. I bet the driver thinks I'm a prostitute or something. Otherwise, why would I be with a guy like Spencer. He gives me a look like he thinks I am.

Spencer is getting out of the cab behind me, paying the driver. 'You don't have to come up with me,' I say. 'I'll be fine.'

'I want to make sure everything's okay.'

'There's no need.'

'Perhaps we could have a coffee here,' he suggests. 'The last one went rather cold.'

I laugh and relent. 'Coffee it is.'

The cab drives off and I push open the door to the flats. Inside, the smell of piss is overpowering. In the corner of the hallway, three hulking great youths are lurking. Christ knows what's in the food we eat these days, but why are all teenagers giants?

At this moment, I don't want to 'hug a hoodie' as David Cameron suggests. Frankly, I'd like to deck one. Bet he's never had a hoodie pissing in his Notting Hill hallway.

The heckles on the back of my neck rise and I say coldly, 'Have you been peeing in my hall?'

'Fuck off, bitch,' the spottiest of all tells me.

'Don't speak to the lady like that,' Spencer says, pulling himself up to his full height.

'Fuck off, toff,' another says to him.

This is in danger of turning nasty and I don't want to ruin the mood of the evening further.

'Leave it,' I say to Spencer. 'They're not worth it.'

'I can handle this, Sally.'

'*I can handle this, Sally.*' One of them mimics his cut-glass tones.

'Grow up,' I throw over my shoulder as I tug Spencer up the stairs behind me.

'What ruffians,' he says, and I start to laugh. *Ruffians*? Yeah, they're ruffians all right.

'*Ruffians*?' I'm becoming hysterical. Wouldn't they take the piss if they could hear him now?

Spencer looks offended. 'Well, they are.'

'Fucking little bastards,' I say. 'That's what they are.'

'Big bastards,' he corrects. 'Fucking *big* bastards.'

Then he laughs and we climb the rest of the ten floors clutching our sides.

In the living room, Mrs Kapur is curled up on the sofa snoring. For a little lady she has a very big snore. I take her hand and gently shake her. 'Mrs Kapur,' I say softly.

My neighbour starts herself awake and blinks up at me. 'What time is it, doll?'

'Late,' I say. It's nearly midnight. 'I'm sorry, I should have been home earlier.'

'It's my fault,' Spencer says apologetically.

'Don't worry about me,' Mrs Kapur says, as she eases herself up. 'Can't stop the course of true love.'

We both flush at that. 'I'll just see her down the hall, Spencer. You put the kettle on. All the cups and stuff are in the cupboard above it.' Then I turn to Mrs Kapur. 'I'll pop in and see Charlie while you get your things together. Has he been good?'

'Sound as a pound,' she says, as she gathers a half-empty packet of sweets, a trashy novel and her knitting. Clearly, she'd come prepared for a long night, which makes me feel even more guilty.

In Charlie's cramped bedroom, I see the hump of my baby snuggled under his duvet. I go over, pull up the cover even though it doesn't need it, and smooth down his hair. Then I kiss his head which smells of hair gel and it doesn't seem long ago at all when it still smelled of baby powder. 'Night, night, Charlie.'

He snuffles in his sleep.

I start to tiptoe out and then, in the corner of his room, I see his brightly-coloured Super-Soaker propped up against the wall. Hmm. Picking up the machine-gun-styled water pistol, I take it out and prop it up in the hall. 'Ready, Mrs K?'

'Coming, doll.' She wanders out to me, still looking slightly dazed.

I open the door and usher her out, collecting the Super-Soaker on the way.

'Where are you going with that, Sally love?'

'I've a little errand to do,' I reply. 'Can I fill it up in your sink?'

She nods sleepily, too tired to question why. I take her arm as we make our way to her front door. Mrs Kapur hands over her key and I let us in.

'You go and get yourself ready for bed,' I tell her. 'I'll fill this, then I'll come in and see you right.'

My lovely neighbour shuffles off to the bathroom, while I nip into the kitchen and fill up the Super-Soaker, pumping it up to full pressure.

Then I go into Mrs Kapur's bedroom and she's there swamped by her white cotton nightie, climbing into bed. She snuggles down like a child.

'Thanks,' I say. 'Thanks for looking after Charlie.'

'He's a good lad,' she tells me. 'One of the best. Makes a nice cup of tea too. Besides, you do enough for me.'

'Go on with you,' I say. 'I do nothing.'

'You're a good girl, Sally Freeman,' she says, and I kiss her on the forehead.

'See you tomorrow.' I leave her to her sleep, and as I close her front door behind me, I can already hear her snoring.

Chapter Forty

L ike some kind of ace Superhero, I take the ten flights in my stride, stealthily. When I get to the landing of the last flight, I can still hear the 'ruffians' giggling to themselves. I round the last corner.

One of them is pissing up the wall. The other two are writing on it with cans of spray paint. I point the Super-Soaker at their backs. 'Don't piss on my patch,' I tell them, and without warning launch a Super-Soaker attack.

They emit loud screams as they're soaked with cold water.

'We'll get you for this,' one shouts over his shoulder at me.

'I don't think so,' I say. 'This is war. Unless you're at the Community Centre on Saturday morning, I'm going to the police. I've had enough of you and your behaviour. We all have. And it's not going to happen any more. Get it?'

Surprisingly, they look rather cowed.

'Get it?' I give them another blast for good measure.

'All right, all right,' one says. 'Keep your knickers on, girl.'

'I fully intend to,' I retort.

They all scowl like the teenagers they are.

My water pistol is resting on my hip, still aimed at them. 'Community Centre,' I repeat. 'Eleven o'clock, Saturday. I know who you are and I know where you live. If you're not there I'm coming after you. And next time it won't be with a Super-Soaker. Got it?'

'Got it,' they mutter.

'Now git,' I say in the style of a frontier-town Marshall.

Thankfully, they scurry out of the flats without argument.

I blow on the end of the Super-Soaker. If I had a holster, I'd probably holster it. Perhaps they'll start to realise that I mean business. No one – I mean *no one* – messes with Sally Freeman.

Then a voice comes out of the darkness. 'What exactly do you think you're doing?'

127

I jump, spinning round, Super-Soaker at the ready. 'Johnny?'

'Put that thing away,' he says. 'It might go off in your hand.'

'What are you doing here?'

'I was walking home from the garage. I've been thinking about the mural that you want me to do for the Community Centre. I heard a commotion and thought I'd stick my head in.' Johnny smiles. 'Should have realised that you'd be in the middle of it.'

I laugh. 'Just trying to clear the bad guys off my turf.'

'Be careful,' Johnny says. 'They might be nothing but big kids, but you never know when these big kids might be carrying knives these days. A Super-Soaker wouldn't be much use against that.'

'They'd have to get near to me first,' I say with false bravado. Never thought that they might be holding. It's always the same kids and they're barely older than Charlie. I just think of them as over-grown naughty boys, not real criminals.

'All quiet on the Western front then?'

'For now,' I say.

Johnny leans on the doorframe. 'You could invite me in for a nightcap.'

I feel the guilty gulp travel down my throat. 'You're more than welcome to come up,' I say. 'But Spencer's here. In the flat.'

'Oh.' Johnny's face falls. 'Why are you down here fighting your own battles then?'

'I slipped away,' I admit. 'Spencer doesn't know I'm here.'

He laughs sadly. 'When will you ever realise that you don't have to take on the rest of the world all by yourself?'

I don't know what to say to that. My Super-Soaker is leaking onto the floor and my mouth seems to have gone dry. I shrug at my ex-lover. 'I'd better go.'

'Yeah,' Johnny says. 'Me too.'

'I'll call you tomorrow. About the meeting.'

'Yeah.' He gives me a cursory wave and I watch him walk out of the door, but still I stand there looking after him.

Now what? I have a hot man waiting for me upstairs who can show me a different side to life, help me to get out of the gutter. So why do I feel so awful when this is exactly what I wanted?

Chapter Forty-One

'You've been a long while,' Spencer says as I go into the living room.

'Couldn't settle Mrs Kapur,' I say. 'Ooo, coffee. Lovely.' I turn down the lights so that you can't see the damp patches on the walls and join him on the sofa. He's found my knock-off Nora Jones CD and the soothing songs float through the flat. Picking up the remote, I turn it down a notch. 'Can't have it on too loud.'

'Charlie,' he says.

'He sleeps like the dead usually, but he's got school in the morning and I don't want to risk waking him.'

Spencer slips his arm round me and I nestle into the crook of his shoulder. He sighs happily. 'This is rather nice,' he says. 'It seems as if the most difficult thing to do is find time alone with you.'

'I guess you've never dated a single mum before?'

'No,' he admits. 'This is a new experience for me.'

'I'm probably very different from the type of woman that you usually go out with.'

'Yes.' He smiles a little squiffily at me. 'Most of the women I've had relationships with aren't nearly as fiercely independent as you are.'

It's maybe not a good idea to share with him that he's the second man to mention that in a very short space of time tonight. What am I supposed to be? A clinging drip? Would they like that better?

'I meant I bet you've never been out with someone living in a tower block, existing on benefits.'

'No,' he says. 'But then you know that I'm not after you for your money.'

'Me neither,' I say. 'I mean I'm not after *your* money.'

'That's the other thing that I like about you.'

'I like the fact that you've got a flash car and can whisk me off to

Cuba at the drop of a hat, but what would be the point of that if you were an arsehole?'

Spencer laughs.

'I like you for you,' I tell him. 'I like you a lot.'

He turns to me and his lips find mine. 'Do you like me enough to let me stay here tonight?'

I ease away from him. 'This is a big decision for me,' I admit. 'The only person who's ever stayed overnight here is Johnny and we went steady for nearly a year before I let him do that.' I pluck absently at the cushion. 'I've never wanted Charlie to be the sort of boy who has loads of "uncles".' God only knows there are enough of them on this estate, running wild because their mother wants them out of the way for a few hours to entertain her latest man. I've never been like that and never intend to be. I don't want my boy brought up to think that his mother's a slapper. 'This has to be serious. If I let you stay, then you have to be around for a while. I can't let you wake up here, use our bathroom, share our breakfast-table, if you're then not going to call me. I can't do that to my son.' This is hard for me to say. 'If I'm just another conquest, if I'm a bit of fun for you, then don't do this. Tell me where I stand. We can keep this light and commitment-free, I'm okay with that. But if that's the case, then no, you can't stay here.'

'Sally,' he says. 'This may be going too quick. For me, for you. For both of us. But I want you to be absolutely sure of my feelings.' He takes my hand and toys with my fingers. 'I think I'm falling in love with you and I want to be in your life. In Charlie's life.'

Guess that makes it pretty clear. I smile at my guest and then stretch out and fake a yawn.

'Tired?' he says.

Gazing at the handsome man before me I say, 'I think we should get an early night, don't you?' Taking Spencer's hand, I lead him through to my cramped bedroom.

Going to the window, I look out over the estate, before I close the curtains. Spencer comes and stands next to me. I place my hands on his chest and feel his heart pounding beneath my fingers. 'I love you,' he says, voice husky.

Do I love Spencer? Maybe I do, but the words won't come.

Instead, in silence, I slowly unbutton his shirt – his crisp, designer label, upmarket shirt – and slip it from his shoulders. I lift my arms while he tugs my T-shirt over my head. Unclipping my bra, I let it fall to the floor. He cups my breasts in his strong hands and I forget that I'm fiercely independent or that I'm on a one-woman crusade to save the world – and I let him love me.

Chapter Forty-Two

He knew it was wrong. He should have kept on walking. Gone home. As soon as he knew that Sally was all right, he should have left her to it. But he hadn't.

Instead, he'd sat on the kerb outside Sally's flat and tortured himself by imagining what might be going on inside. Ringo lay on the pavement next to him whining plaintively. For his pains, Johnny had been rewarded with a peepshow of his ex-girlfriend – and current love – and the Boy Wonder slowly undressing each other. It was too much to bear while sober. When Sally turned out the light, he knew it was time to leave, otherwise he might just go mad. So, he hauled himself to his feet and continued his journey one miserable plodding step at a time. He clicked his fingers at his dog. 'Come on, boy.' Ringo trotted along at his heel.

Johnny hoped that Sally knew what she was doing. It was clear that her new man was going to spend the night there, and he knew that was a big deal for her. It had taken ages for her to allow him to stay over, and the thought that she'd let this fella stay there so soon after meeting him depressed Johnny immensely. It was early days in her new relationship and while he appreciated that Sally was a grown woman and could make her own decisions, he was worried for Charlie. The boy hadn't got over their split-up and already she was introducing him to someone else. It was too soon. Way too soon, if you asked him. Sally should have left it longer, maybe a year. Two would be better. Better still, she should never find anyone she got along with as well as him. Was that too much to ask? Johnny knew that Charlie wasn't happy with the situation, but what could he do? He'd just have to be there for the boy and reassure him that this man wouldn't replace Johnny in his life and that his mum wasn't going to go off into the wide, blue yonder with Spencer Knight.

When he reached his mam's house, he knew that he couldn't stay there tonight. There was no way he was going to get any sleep.

As he opened the front door, his mam shouted from the dining room where her bed now was, 'Is that you, Johnny Boy?'

He stuck his head round her door and saw her curled up in the bed. 'Can't sleep?'

'Legs are giving me gip,' she said. 'I might put the light on and read.'

'Shall I make you a cuppa?'

'Aye,' she said. 'Make me one of your special brews that'll send me to sleep. Where've you been to so late?'

'Painting,' he said. 'Sally's got an idea to do up the Community Centre and brighten up the estate. She's ask me to do a mural. Apparently, she's managed to get some money out of the Government.'

'Good for her. She'll go places, that girl,' his mam said proudly. 'Always got something on the go. She's one of the best.'

'Yeah,' he agreed miserably. 'We've got a meeting about it on Saturday.'

'I'll like to go to that,' Mary said. 'Give her my support.'

'Yeah? We'll get the wheelchair out then.'

'You're a good lad, Johnny. I'm glad that you're helping her.'

Johnny clicked on the bedside lamp. 'Here's your book.' There was a half-naked man on the cover with a flowing mane, entwined round some buxom, tousle-haired brunette in a gypsy blouse. It was one of those ridiculous romances, the ones where the girl always gets her guy and he's always rich and arrogant, but with an understanding streak and an urge to do social good and be kind to small animals. Johnny hated blokes like that, but it broke his heart to think that his mam had never had anyone to treat her special in her life. It made him think of Sally and her new man. Who could blame her for wanting a piece of that? He should just get over her, move on, maybe ask Debs out – she'd give him more than enough trouble to keep his mind off Sally.

'I'm just at a good bit,' his mam said, as he plumped her pillows and helped her to get comfortable.

'Does the girl get her guy?'

'Ooo, they always do,' she said. 'That's why I like them.'

'I'll go and get that kettle on.'

When he brought the tea back, he sat on the armchair in the room and flicked through the paper, not seeing any of the words, until she dozed off to sleep. What his mam didn't know was that his own mug was filled with neat vodka and he was slugging it back to try to achieve oblivion.

Soon his mam had dozed off, book fallen into her lap. Maybe someone else's fantasy love-life wasn't that riveting, after all. Instead of achieving his own oblivion, the vodka had just helped to make him wired. He was buzzing and restless. Ringo had curled up on the foot of his mam's bed. 'Come on,' Johnny said. 'You're supposed to be a man's best friend.'

The dog cocked his ear, then opened one bleary eye.

'I don't want to do this alone.' Ringo was off the bed and by his side in an instant. Johnny tiptoed out of the room, took the rest of the bottle and headed out into the night once more.

Chapter Forty-Three

To punish himself further, Johnny took the route back past Sally's flat. He stopped to look up at the bedroom window, but all was still in darkness. Ringo gave a cursory bark, for which he got a tipsy, 'Sssh . . .'

He'd drunk more than enough by the time he reached his garage and he knew that he was weaving. Fumbling with the key, he swayed back and forth until he managed to fit it into the padlock, then 'Sssh'd,' the garage door as it creaked open noisily. He shivered. Even in his bevvied state, he could still feel that it was cold in here. Earlier, he'd roughed out some ideas for a mural for the Community Centre, but he didn't have the focus to concentrate on that now. Instead, he wanted to paint something that would capture his mood.

Staggering into his working area, Johnny tried to set up a canvas, but he stumbled and fell, knocking the canvas to the floor. No worries. It would work just as well there, he thought with a shrug. Plus he was probably incapable of hanging it like he usually did. The heavy ropes that he normally used hung down from the rafters of the garage and he grabbed them, letting himself swing forward over the fallen canvas on tiptoe. It felt quite nice. He hadn't been on a swing since he was a kid. The motion of the ropes carried him backwards and forwards gently. He lifted his feet from the ground and started to let himself twirl round. It was good to be drunk and dizzy, it stopped him thinking about Sally. Well, almost.

Then, amidst the vodka haze, he had a moment of clarity. He jumped down from his home-made swing. Ringo, sensing his change of mood, barked in excitement. Somewhere he had some empty squeezy bottles put to one side, just in case he might ever need them; too much time spent watching *Blue Peter* as a kid, maybe. Clearly this was the time to press them into service.

With a bit of effort and staggering about, he managed to mix three different colours of paint – red, blue and green – and poured them into the bottles. Then he laid out two more canvases on the floor next to the first one. On the battered old CD player he'd purloined for the garage, he slotted in his favourite Beatles disc and turned the volume to loud.

Taking the bottles of paint, he eased himself up onto the ropes above the canvases until he was sitting on the sturdiest one. Giggling to himself and with a bit of shifting of his weight, he got the swing going. He whooshed backwards and forwards through the air, dangling above the canvases. The Beatles blasted out 'I Saw Her Standing There' and Johnny sang along drunkenly. Ringo's barking reached a frenzy and he ran madly round the canvases while Johnny swung like a pissed trapeze artist above him.

He leaned back, letting his head dangle down and the paint drizzle from the squeezy bottles onto the canvas. This felt great, liberating. 'Twist and Shout' brought forth great flourishes to the paintings. Swinging backwards and forwards, twirling as he went, Johnny covered the canvases – and the dog. Perhaps he could paint Sally right out of his head like this.

'She Loves You,' the Beatles sang out. But, in his heart, Johnny knew that she didn't any more.

Chapter Forty-Four

I had a fantastic night with Spencer – believe me, Bill Shankly House was shaken to its very foundations. Spencer is a great lover. I lie here watching him while he's asleep. Even naked and dishevelled from the night's activities, he still looks too posh to be in this flat. He opens his eyes and I pull up the duvet to my neck.

'Good morning,' he says, and strokes my face gently.

I'd forgotten that I hate new relationships. Moments like these make me cringe. What am I supposed to say now? 'Thanks for a great night?' Frankly, I would have liked Spencer to be up and out of here briskly as I can already hear Charlie moving around. Why can't my boy be like other people's sons and want to lie in until noon and have to be pulled kicking and screaming out of their beds? My kid's always up with the lark.

Spencer moves in close to me and starts to kiss me, stroking my back. Oh, that feels good. So very good. I push him away. 'I can't,' I say. 'Charlie's up and about. He might come in. He doesn't know that you're here.'

'Right,' Spencer says with a frown. 'Forgot about that.'

Already, I'm getting out of bed, turning my back on my guest so that he doesn't get an eyeful of me in the cold light of day. I'm not quite ready for that revelation. 'I'll bring you a cuppa and warn Charlie that you're here. Then you can have a shower.' I wonder will the hot water run to three people. My boiler is, at best, temperamental. 'Tea or coffee?'

'Have you any Earl Grey?'

I laugh. 'I've got builders' tea, Spencer, that's all. There's no Columbian fine roast coffee either. Everything in my cupboards is the cheapest I can find in Save-It.'

'Builders' tea is fine,' he says, looking slightly chastened.

'It'll put hairs on your chest,' I tell him.

'Hasn't done it for you,' he notes. Then he catches my hand and pulls me to him for a quick kiss. 'Thank you for last night. I'm honoured that you let me stay here. I know how much it means to you.'

'Thanks,' I say. 'I enjoyed it too. I just hope that you don't eat much for breakfast. All I've got is toast and cereal. If you normally eat smoked salmon or kedgeree then you're out of luck on that too.'

All he does is grin at me. 'Toast would be lovely.'

I'm taking a cup of good, strong Save-It own brand tea into the bedroom to Spencer when Charlie comes out of the bathroom, all smiles. Then he sees the two cups in my hand and draws himself up straighter. The smile disappears. He knows that second cup isn't for him.

'All right, love?'

Charlie nods brusquely.

I lower my voice. 'Spencer stayed over last night,' I tell him. There's a guilty quiver there. 'Hope you've left some hot water.'

My light quip goes down like a lead balloon and my son's expression turns in a flash to a dark scowl. 'Breakfast in five?' I ask.

'I'm not hungry,' Charlie says, lip pouting.

He's always hungry. There's no 'full' level on that kid's stomach. 'I'm sorry to spring this on you, Charlie.' I'd like to give him a hug, but my hands are still gripping the tea. 'It wasn't planned. I should have talked to you about it first.'

He doesn't look placated. And then Spencer comes out of the bedroom. My overnight guest is wearing nothing but his undies and a sleepy grin. I'm not sure who's more horrified, me or Charlie.

'Hello, little . . . friend,' Spencer says. The nursery-rhyme voice is back in evidence.

'Hiya,' Charlie mumbles reluctantly, studying the wallpaper.

Spencer gives up with my son and turns to me. 'May I use the bathroom?' he asks.

Charlie takes the distraction as an opportunity to shoot into his bedroom.

'Yes,' I say. 'Go for it.'

I hit the bedroom and in double-quick time, I throw on my jeans and a T-shirt. Washing can wait until later, until there are no strange men taking up my bathroom space. Through to the kitchen and I start flinging bread into the toaster and putting the boxes of cereal on the table.

Charlie wanders in, dressed now in his school uniform. He plonks himself down at the table.

'What do you want on your sandwiches today?'

One shoulder gets lifted and dropped.

'Peanut butter?'

The other shoulder gets the same treatment and I take it as an enthusiastic yes for peanut butter.

While I'm dashing off a couple of rounds of butties, the toast pops and I slap some butter and marmalade on it for Charlie. 'You can have a boiled egg tomorrow,' I say, 'when I've got more time. I'm running a bit behind this morning.'

I get a glare. I do the world's best boiled eggs and Charlie is just playing hard to get.

Then Spencer joins us. He's freshly washed and beautiful. Even in last night's recycled clothes, he still looks wonderful. He's buttoning his shirt cuffs as he comes into the kitchen. My heart lurches. I still can't believe that I spent the night with this man, but the flip that my stomach does confirms that I did indeed.

My unexpected house guest takes a chair next to my son and Charlie studiously avoids looking at him. More bread gets slapped in the toaster. I top up Spencer's mug with hot water and give it to him.

'Thanks.'

Then I squash Charlie's butties and two pieces of fruit – a banana and an apple – into the battered ice-cream carton he takes in every day. I'd buy him one of these flashy lunchboxes, but he'd only get it nicked. As a treat – and as a consolation for having woken up to find he's got a wanton mother – I've also put in a chocolate-topped flapjack. Not homemade, but then you can't have everything.

There's an uneasy silence at the breakfast-table. Charlie's clearly uncomfortable and so am I.

My new man clears his throat loudly and my son and I both jump. 'And what's on the agenda at school today?' Spencer says in jocular, sing-song tones.

'Nuffin',' Charlie mutters, sliding towards the table, concentrating on his toast as if he's planning to perform heart surgery on it.

Spencer looks to me for help.

'Charlie,' I say crisply. 'Play the game. Tell Spencer what you're doing at school today.'

'Maths, English, Games,' my son tumbles out in a rush. The last piece

139

of toast is stuffed into his mouth. 'I've gotta go. Late.' And he shoots towards the front door like a hare out of a trap.

I chase after him, sandwich box in hand and catch up with him as he's about to leave. 'Don't forget this.'

He stops and takes his butties from me. 'I love you,' I say, smoothing down the hair that, in his strop, he's forgotten to gel. 'We'll talk about this when you get home.'

'Don't want to.'

'I still love you more than anyone,' I say. 'Nothing will change that. Even if Spencer comes into our lives.'

Charlie looks up and his eyes are filled with tears. 'I want you to love Johnny again.'

'It's not that simple.'

My son sags in front of my eyes.

'I don't want you to worry about this.' I kiss the top of his head. 'Tell me you won't worry.'

'I won't worry,' he mumbles in a worried way.

Giving him a playful slap on the behind, I say, 'Go on, otherwise you'll be late for school.'

Back in the kitchen, I slump down next to Spencer with a big sigh. I take a slurp of his tea and nick a bit of the toast he's buttered for himself in my absence.

'That went well,' I say, relying on the British propensity for irony.

'I don't think he likes me,' Spencer says.

'Give him time. He doesn't know you and he's still very fond of Johnny. This isn't easy for him.'

'I'm not used to children,' Spencer admits. 'I don't know what to say to him.'

'Just be normal,' I tell him. 'You don't need to speak to him like he's three. He's a good kid. Relax. Be cool.'

Spencer tugs at his cuffs. 'I'd rather face a roomful of investment bankers than one ten-year-old kid.'

'That much is obvious,' I laugh.

'I'd better go,' he says, with a glance at his watch — a watch that would pay my rent for a year (if the DHSS didn't, of course). 'I'm due at the Computer Centre shortly and I want to shoot home and change.'

'I'll call you a cab.'

Spencer catches my wrist as I stand. 'I want to do this again soon,' he says, pulling me to him. My legs oblige by turning to water. 'Sure you won't reconsider coming away at the weekend? It will be a lot of fun.'

'I can't,' I say weakly. 'How can I?'

'I'd like you there,' he says. 'With me.'

And just when I have begun to think that he's understood my situation, how tied I am, I realise that he hasn't at all.

Chapter Forty-Five

I'm amazed – and more than a little pleased – to see how many people have turned up for the meeting at the Community Centre. Half of the estate is crammed in here. I had Charlie put some leaflets through the doors during the week; he did it with minimal grumbling which I'm taking as a sign that he's forgiven me for my indiscretion earlier this week.

The leafleting has clearly worked. I just hope that all these folks are as keen when it comes to putting their workclothes on and getting down to business. Even the hoodies with the weak bladders and the bad attitudes are here. They're in the back row and aren't looking very happy, but they're here. So I'd class that as a result.

Johnny's standing next to me by the stage. He seems very subdued.

'You okay?' I ask.

He shrugs non-committally.

'Thanks for bringing your mum.' Mary Jones is sitting at the end of the front row in her wheelchair. She's got her arms folded across her ample bosom and a big smile on her face. Mrs Kapur and Dora are sitting next to her. I can't remember when I last saw Mary out and about, so I'm pleased that she's made the effort.

'She wanted to be here,' Johnny says. 'For you.'

'I'm glad. We need all the support we can get.'

'No Spencer?' He tries to make the question sound casual, but fails. So, he's still smarting that Spencer was at my flat the other night. I just hope he doesn't find out that Spencer stayed over, as I made Johnny wait for ages before he was allowed anywhere near my bed. In hind-sight, I think it was the right choice – even though we did both have bad backs from snatched sex sessions in the rear of his Transit van.

I wonder where Spencer is now. It would have been nice to have him here today. He went off to his house-party in the Cotswolds and I feel a little flame of envy burn inside me – a feeling that I've rarely had before. I want to be at a house-party in the Cotswolds too – even though I've no idea what it might involve. But I bet there'll be plenty of champagne and nice things. There'll probably be posh birds too, with long legs and flowing locks.

I sigh out loud when I don't mean to.

'Penny for them,' Johnny says.

'They're worth at least ten quid.'

'In that case, you'll have to keep them to yourself, I'm skint.'

Impulsively, I take Johnny's hand. 'Thanks for being here. I don't know what I'd do without you.'

'Well, you'd be stuck for someone to paint the walls.'

'You know that it's so much more than that.'

Johnny avoids my gaze and looks out over the crowd in the hall. 'We'd better get started,' he says with a nod. 'The natives are getting restless.'

'There's probably footy on this afternoon,' I say, 'and they'll be wanting to make sure that they're back in time.'

'Liverpool versus Chelsea,' Johnny supplies, sneaking a glance at his own watch.

'Let's go for it, then,' I say, and pull him onto the stage behind me.

We take up our positions and Johnny claps his hands. Everyone starts to quieten down. He's rigged up the PA system and I stand up to the microphone with a sheaf of notes. 'I don't know about you,' I begin, 'but I'm fed up of this estate looking like the bad side of Beirut.'

There's a wave of muttered approval.

'I thought it was about time that we did something about it.'

Again much nodding.

'I want to live in a nice area. I want to see flowers and trees instead of burned-out cars and litter.'

Mary Jones is nodding so hard I think her head might fall off.

'I don't want vandals breaking our lifts and peeing in our hallways.' I direct my look to the hoodies and they shuffle in their seats. 'I want us all to be proud of our neighbourhood. Every single one of us.' *And, on a personal level, I want to bring home posh boyfriends and not cringe every time I do.* 'I want this to be a nice place to live.'

Everyone claps enthusiastically.

'It will mean a lot of hard work,' I say. 'For us all. I want to clear away all the rubbish, grass over the derelict ground, put flowers in neglected corners. Anything that can be painted will get a freshen up. Does that sound like a good start?'

There are rumblings of consent, so I push on.

'We can get some money from the Government to use for plants, trees and equipment, but we have to do all the grafting ourselves. All of it. The whole shebang. If anyone thinks that they don't want to be involved, then now's the time to tell us.'

Neighbour turns to neighbour, deep in conversation.

'And when we're done,' I say, 'we all have to work to keep it that way. We have to police our own neighbourhood so that it doesn't fall into the hands of the vandals and the criminals. It won't be easy, but I think, together, that we can do it.'

For my impassioned speech, I get a round of applause. When I've milked it for all it's worth, I hold up my hand. 'Johnny's put some sketches on the walls round the hall. It'll give you some idea of what we'd like to do if everyone agrees. The work will start with sprucing this place up.' I sweep my hand to encompass the grotty hall.

No one looks as if they'd disagree with that. 'Shall we take a vote? Hands up if you want to get involved with this project.'

Across the room hands shoot in the air. Looks like there are very few objectors. The hoodies at the back remain still and I look over at them. Then one of the boys slowly raises his hand, the others look at him aghast and then, after a moment that goes on for an eternity, they too join in.

'Unanimous,' I say. God, there are tears of joy in my eyes. What have we started? I grab Johnny's hand and smile across at him. He's grinning too. Together we punch the air. 'Let project "All You Need Is Love" begin!'

Chapter Forty-Six

We were inundated with questions, offers of expertise and general good wishes. Several of the older men on the estate either run or used to run allotments and were quick to offer their horticultural services. That's a big relief, because I don't know one end of a plant from the other. I'm the sort who'd be ripping up rare orchids and nurturing common or garden weeds. We had a few people who professed to be dab hands with paintbrushes, so that'll be useful too. The rest of it is in the lap of the gods. How we're going to gainfully employ the hoodies, goodness only knows. But everyone can pick up rubbish and put it in a black sack, right?

Now Johnny and I are both sitting in rickety plastic chairs with our feet up taking a breather – shame that our budget probably won't run to replacing these uncomfortable old buggers. I feel high on a rush of adrenaline and I don't think I've ever experienced anything like this before. Mary's neighbour has wheeled her home for Johnny, and now Charlie and his all-knowing mate, Kyle, are stacking the rest of the chairs away for us.

'The girl did good,' Johnny says.

I blow an unsteady stream of air out of my lungs. Only now are my nerves kicking in. Only now am I realising exactly what a huge undertaking this might be. There will be a lot of people depending on me and, frankly, I don't know if I'm that dependable. 'Do you really think we can do this?'

'It's too late to back out now,' he tells me.

'I'm not thinking of backing out,' I assure him. 'It's just that I've never organised anything on this kind of scale before. Come to think of it, I don't think I've ever organised *anything* before.' I struggle to make sure that I've got enough food in the fridge for Charlie's packed lunch every day. That's the limit of my organisational skills. Can I really pull off a stunt like this? Li'l ol' me?

'If you're going to start,' Johnny says, 'may as well start big.'

'Do you think people really will rally round?'

'They seem keen enough. This sort of thing tends to bring out the old British fighting spirit.'

'I wonder will that exist in the next generation?'

'Depends if we hand it down to them.'

'I have a wonderful vision for this place.' My voice sounds wistful. 'Do you think we can stop the rot and turn it round?'

'I think it's worth trying.'

Suddenly all this thinking, planning and strategising is too much for me and I feel emotionally drained. 'I'm gasping for a cuppa.' My throat feels like it's lined with sandpaper.

'Me too.'

'Why don't you come back to the flat?' I suggest. 'We could spend the afternoon going through some ideas. Maybe you could sketch out a few things, draw up our masterplan.'

Johnny looks evasive. 'No can do,' he says. 'I've got stuff I need to see to.'

'Ah, the footy.'

'That and other things.'

'You're not backing out on me now?'

Johnny laughs. 'Prior engagement,' he says. 'I could come over tomorrow though. Haven't seen Charlie for a couple of days. If the weather stays nice we could go to Sefton Park together, kick a ball about.'

'He'd like that.'

'I'd better get off,' Johnny says. 'See you tomorrow.' I watch as my friend strides off purposefully. Wonder what he's up to?

'Are you nearly finished, boys?'

'Yeah,' Charlie and Kyle shout back.

I stand, stretch my back and look around the hall, taking in the peeling paint, the rising damp, the mouldy curtains. Can I do this? Can I really mobilise these people who have been so apathetic about the decline of their neighbourhood for years into a lean, mean, keen workforce? I'll have my work cut out, that's for sure. But then I remember that I'm not an ordinary human being. I'm Sally Freeman, Single Mum and Superwoman. And I can do anything I want.

Chapter Forty-Seven

Johnny opened up the garage, then stood back and looked along the row. These lock-ups could all do with a coat of paint too. They were all scruffy and his was the only door that wasn't completely buckled. Sally was right: how could people let their own estate become such a pigsty? He was only just starting to see things through her eyes and it wasn't a pretty sight.

He'd never before been discontented with his lot in life and he didn't like the way that it made him feel. Sally had often accused him of seeing the world through rose-tinted glasses and it seemed that for the first time, he'd taken them off. Johnny shook his head sadly. Sally, it seemed, was determined to shake everything up, reshape it, re-energise it. He wasn't finding it a comfortable process.

Now that he'd thought about making his own changes, his stomach was in a constant swirl. The core of contentment and stability that he'd always felt had gone, almost overnight. He felt scared, unsettled and excited at the same time. Johnny rubbed his hands over his face and breathed out a heavy sigh. *Sally Freeman, you crazy lady, where is all this going to lead?*

Inside, still on the floor, were the canvases he'd painted the other night. He stood back and scrutinised them. They weren't half-bad. Maybe some of his better work. He should get roaring drunk and paint to Beatles music more often. If nothing else, it was very therapeutic. Even the thought of Sally shacking up with this new man hadn't left him feeling quite so downhearted. Ringo had padded across the corner of two of them and, to be honest, the blurry doggy footprints only added to their charm. Johnny laughed as he lifted and stacked them against the wall.

Today's task was more important. Liverpool was famous the world over for having two great football teams – Liverpool and the Liverpool reserves. He'd been a lifelong fan like his father before him. He put the radio on so that he could tune into the Liverpool game, but he knew that his mind was only half on it.

Outside, the van he'd bought dirt cheap was waiting. When he'd cleared a space in the middle of the floor, he drove it inside. It was a small Ford van, ancient, and every panel looked like it had been customised with a hammer. He'd got it off a bloke who knew a bloke. The engine rattled a bit and there was more smoke than you'd ideally want puffing out of the exhaust, but it ran reasonably well. Seemed like a good buy at the time. Now he had it inside his workshop, he wasn't quite so sure. This was going to take some serious paint job to make it look good. Still, the sooner he got started, the sooner he'd be finished.

He'd borrowed a compressor and an airbrush from a mate who worked in a place that did these flash designs on motorbikes – Harley Davidsons and the like. He'd got to work quick as the fella wanted his stuff back for Monday morning before his boss realised that his precious equipment was missing. For a six-pack of Stella, his mate had also supplied the necessary paint. With a promise to redecorate his living room to return the favour, the guy was also going to make sure that his design was lacquered and finished in the right way – after hours, of course.

Johnny picked up the brush. It was years since he'd done this kind of thing and then it was only a fleeting interest. He hoped that he hadn't lost his touch and what little technique he'd acquired. Flicking open the art books he'd borrowed from the library, Johnny rubbed his chin as he browsed through them until he found what he wanted. Putting the book in a plastic bag so that it didn't get dirty or splashed with paint, he smoothed it down and laid it out on the nearby work bench. Then he cranked up the radio, listened in dismay as Liverpool went down to Chelsea, one-nil, and got on with his work.

Chapter Forty-Eight

At eleven o'clock on Sunday morning, the doorbell rings. I'm still in my dressing-gown and have a hedge where my hair used to be. I had a late night with Debs and a bottle of cheap wine or two. We put the world to rights, but it took a long time and plenty of drink. Plodding to the door, I wince as it creaks open.

'I've got something to show you,' Johnny says without preamble. There's an excited glint in my ex-lover's eyes.

'What?'

He tugs at my hand.

'What? What?' I pull back. 'I can't come out like this.'

'You look fabulous,' he says, giving me a cursory glance. I'm sure he actually winces at my hair, but nevertheless he yanks me out of the door. Then he stops. 'Get Charlie too.'

'Charlie,' I shout over my shoulder. 'Johnny's here. He's gone mad.'

My son sticks his head out of his bedroom door and his trademark grin is in place. 'Hiya, Johnny.' If only his face lit up like that when he saw Spencer.

'Come on, lad,' Johnny urges. 'Let's get this old mum of yours moving. I've something I want you both to see.'

So Johnny pulls and Charlie pushes my bottom and they get me out of the flat and to the stairs.

'I haven't even got any slippers on,' I mutter. 'I'll catch my death of cold. I'll get splinters in my feet. Look at the state of my hair.'

I look behind me and Johnny and Charlie are making comedy 'yack, yack' movements with their hands.

'Very funny,' I say. 'This better be worth it.'

We make it down the ten flights of stairs, me stomping and with them giggling like a pair of loonies at my back.

★

I'm pleased to say that at eleven o'clock on a Sunday morning there are precious few people lurking outside Shankly House.

'What do you think?' Johnny says.

And, to be honest, it takes me a minute to get my breath. Not because I'm knackered at having come down ten flights – that's a piece of cake these days – but because of the sight before me.

'Ohmigod,' I say. '*Ohmigod*!'

'Is that ohmigod good? Or ohmigod bad?' Johnny, watching anxiously, wants to know.

Charlie has raced ahead of me and is now also standing agog, bereft of speech. And it takes a lot to stop Charlie talking.

There's a van parked at the end of the path and it's amazing. It's got the most incredible mural all over it. 'Is that what I think it is?'

'The Sistine Chapel,' Johnny supplies. 'Well, part of it.'

Quite a large part.

'That's God's creation of Adam.' He points to a bunch of angels fronted by a big guy with a flowing white beard who's touching fingers with a reclining, blond-haired Adonis with an incredible six-pack. Adam, I presume. Then Johnny shuffles a bit self-consciously. 'The other side's got the creation of the sun and moon on it.'

I'm still struggling to take this in. 'When did you do this?'

'Yesterday,' he says. 'And during the night. I've not long finished, in fact. Actually, there are still some bits to do.'

'I'm stunned,' I say, as I start to circle the van to view it from every angle. Not an inch of its surface has escaped Johnny's airbrush. It's all covered in the most astonishing, brightly-coloured paintwork.

'This is the best bit,' Johnny says. 'This is what I want you to see.'

He takes my hand and guides me to the front door of the van. I follow him like a sleepwalker; any minute now I'm going to wake up and this will all be a dream.

'Look.'

My eyes follow his outstretched finger.

On the door, painted in large and beautifully curly script, are the words *Johnny Jones – Painter* and, underneath, in much smaller script it says *and decorator*.

'You're going to be a painter and decorator?'

Johnny nods. 'My first job is to paint the living room of the fella who loaned me all the stuff to do this, but I thought I'd give it a go.'

For some reason, tears come to my eyes. 'This is fantastic news. You can start a portfolio. With the mural you've done at Ronaldo's dance studio and the Community Centre, when that's done—'

'I wasn't thinking of doing this kind of stuff,' Johnny says with a frown. 'Who round here would want that kind of thing?'

'Durr,' I say. 'Ronaldo's studio, the Community Centre.'

'Yeah, but who wants to *pay* for that kind of thing? No one round here has the money.'

'No one in Shankly House, perhaps.' Although I'm sure Mrs Kapur would definitely have *God's Creation of Adam* on her kitchen ceiling if she had the spare cash. 'But businesses, bars, hotels would go mad for it. They love this sort of stuff. The other night I went to a swanky bar with—' then I realise what I'm about to say and falter slightly 'a mate.'

My friend's expression darkens.

'It used to be a Catholic church. Now it's got this kind of mural all over the walls,' I bluster on. 'We'll have to go there so you can see it.'

Johnny shakes his head. 'This van is just my gimmick. I have no illusions that I'm going to be able to make a living out of my art. I'll be slapping on the Dulux Brilliant White and a coat or two of magnolia and hoping to pay the bills.'

'Johnny,' I say, an exasperated tone creeping into my voice, 'this is a real talent. I never really appreciated it before, but you could definitely make a go of this.'

He looks at me uncertainly. Have I spent so long pouring cold water on Johnny's aspirations to be an artist that he now can't see just how good he is? 'At least try,' I add. 'For me. For yourself. That's all I've ever wanted.'

'Whatever I do it isn't good enough for you,' Johnny replies tightly. His ready smile disappears; the excitement in his eyes dulls. 'I'm not working because I want to look after my mam – and that's not right for you. You reckon I should be doing something more. Then when I decide that you've got a point, I *have* been coasting all these years, and set myself up with a little business, that's not good enough either.'

'It isn't that it's not good enough, it's just that I can see your true potential.'

'Oh, suddenly you're an art expert too,' Johnny snaps and I'm taken aback as he's never spoken to me like that before. 'I can't just do this for a bit of cash, I've got to be the next Picasso. Well, let me tell you, Sally, some of us are happy with who we are. We don't need big cars and trips to fancy bars to define ourselves. We don't constantly need to prove that we're better than everyone else. Some of us like ourselves just as we are!'

Then he stomps off, gets in his fabulously-decorated van and screeches off.

I turn round, open-mouthed, and Charlie is standing next to me kicking at the kerb.

'What was *that* all about?' I ask.

'Why can't you just like Johnny?' Charlie says and there's a crack in his voice. 'His van's great. Why couldn't you just tell him that? Why do you always have to upset him?'

Then my son stomps off too, leaving me standing in my dressing-gown on the pavement wondering exactly what it was I said.

Chapter Forty-Nine

I'm at the computer in my living room. Ostensibly, I'm downloading garden-design plans from the internet to give me some idea of how we can brighten up the neglected areas on our estate with our influx of cash from the Government. My computer tutor is here and, also ostensibly, he's supposed to be helping me. There are some great things on the internet but, at the moment, they're failing to hold my interest. Currently, Spencer's behind me stroking my back and kissing my neck while I try to remember what I'm meant to do with Acrobat Reader. I'm a bit of a lost cause.

'We could do this later,' Spencer murmurs in my ear as his hands slide over my shoulders and down to my breast.

'We could,' I breathe.

Frankly, I've no idea why we're on the computer when we have the place to ourselves for a few hours – except that I want to get the proposal in for the estate renovation really quickly, so that we can get our hands on the cash as soon as possible. Having drummed up some enthusiasm among the residents, I don't want it to wane due to unnecessary delays. One of which would be me snogging my boyfriend senseless instead of doing this.

I haven't seen my new love since his weekend away – socially, at least – and I feel we have a lot of catching up to do. The funny thing is that I don't really want to ask him what he did at the weekend. A certain amount of ignorance is bliss. I wouldn't want him telling me about all the attractive, single women who were there too.

Then I hear Charlie's key in the door. I'd given him a late pass to stay round at Kyle's until nine o'clock. But now it's barely eight and he's back. 'Hiya, Mum,' he shouts out as he comes in. Then, when he's in the living room and sees Spencer, he pulls up short and huffs, 'Not you again.'

'Charlie,' I snap. 'Don't be so rude. Spencer's here to help me with the plans for the estate.'

153

'Sorry,' Charlie mutters as if he's not sorry at all.

'I thought you were staying round at Kyle's until nine?'

'I came home early.'

'That's a first.'

'I'll go to my room.' Charlie turns on his heels.

'Don't do that,' I say. 'Come and help us. You can tell us what you'd like to see on the estate.'

'I don't care,' my son tells me.

'Then I hope that not everyone feels like you.'

With that he walks out and slams his bedroom door behind him. Hmm. Handled that well, Super Sal.

'Sorry, sorry,' I say to Spencer. 'He's not normally like that.' But then, I have to admit, when Spencer's around, he is.

'Not to worry.' He gives me a squeeze. But I can tell that the mood's been broken. 'Can't you come back to my place tonight? Perhaps Mrs Kapur would stay here. I've got a hot tub and champagne that are both at exactly the right temperature.'

My heart is urging me to say yes.

Then the doorbell rings again. 'Bloody hell,' I moan. 'It's busier than the M6 in here. Can't we get a minute's peace?'

Johnny's at the door. 'Hate to be the harbinger of doom, but there's a Porsche with its tyres slashed outside. I thought it must be Spencer's.'

'Oh, no,' I hear my boyfriend groan from behind me.

'Sorry, mate,' Johnny offers.

'I'll go down and look,' Spencer says, picking up his car keys.

'Did you see who did it?' I want to know.

Johnny shakes his head. 'I was on my way back from the garage. There was no one around by then.'

'This flaming place,' I say bitterly. 'I hate it. Why do we have to live in such a shit-hole?' Then, leaving Johnny standing in my wake, I follow Spencer down the stairs to look at the damage.

Chapter Fifty

Charlie was covered in grass stains and dirt. He walked along next to Johnny, football tucked under his arm. They were heading back to the changing rooms and a much-needed shower. Ringo was trotting obediently at their heels.

'Well played,' Johnny said. 'We'll get you a contract at Anfield yet.'

It was a lie. Charlie was a terrible footballer, but the kid looked like he needed something to lift his spirits. They'd been stomped on by the opposition today – a Catholic school from the other side of the estate who'd played dirty even though the match was supposed to be a friendly.

'What's the matter? Cat got your tongue?' Six-nil had to hurt in any league. There'd be as many bruised ten-year-old egos tonight as there were bruised shins.

'I was crap,' Charlie muttered.

'There'll be other matches. Then we'll paste them.'

The boy stared off into the distance. 'It's not that.'

'Gonna tell me what it is then?'

Charlie kicked at the turf. 'I'm glad that Spencer had his tyres slashed.'

'You don't mean that,' Johnny chided.

'I do.' Charlie sighed.

'Any idea who did it?'

Charlie shook his head. 'No.'

'Your mum would kill you if she thought you knew who did it.'

'I don't,' he insisted. 'Mum doesn't care about anything any more but *him*.'

'That's not true, Charlie.'

The boy turned an anguished face towards him. 'You're losing her, Johnny. He's always round at our flat now. He's stayed the night and *everything*.' The boy's eyes were round with horror. His nose wrinkled at the very thought of it. 'He stayed for breakfast. He sat where *you* sit.' He let out a heavy huff. 'I think Mum loves him.'

Johnny put his arm around the boy. 'She might do,' he conceded. 'But there's nothing much I can do about that, lad.'

'There is. I've talked to Kyle about it. He says you need to do something drastic.'

More drastic than learning salsa dancing? More drastic than getting off his arse and setting up his own painting and decorating business? 'Like what?'

Charlie's shoulders sagged. 'He's thinking about it.'

Johnny smiled to himself. 'When he comes up with a cunning plan, you let me know.'

Johnny had done his first decorating job today. Not paid. Returning a favour for the loan of the compressor and airbrush stuff. But it was a start. Something to build up his confidence, get him back in the game. He'd been so long out of the workforce that it was daunting to be thinking about rejoining it again. Plus he'd have to let the DHSS know so they could arrange to stop his benefits. The stupid thing was, he'd probably be worse off working. It was how people like him got stuck in a rut and how people like Spencer got richer and richer.

He might outwardly shrug off what Charlie said about Sally's new man, but inwardly it hurt to think that she was slowly but inexorably moving away from him.

'Now you look sad,' Charlie said.

'Well, you know,' Johnny replied. 'You never like your own team to lose.'

'If I get showered quickly,' the boy suggested, 'you could take me to the pub for a Coke. We could sit outside in the garden. I don't need to tell Mum.'

Johnny rubbed at Charlie's dirty hair and laughed. 'If you're quick.'

Charlie started to run ahead of him. 'Don't you worry,' Charlie said over his shoulder. 'I'm staying over at Kyle's tonight.'

'At Kyle's?'

Charlie nodded. Johnny thought that Sally must have lost her mind. But then, perhaps she had other plans for the evening.

'We'll talk about it then. He'll come up with something. He always does. We'll get Mum back for you.'

Great, Johnny thought. It was always reassuring to know that your future happiness was in the hands of a ten-year-old and his dysfunctional mate.

Chapter Fifty-One

I'm having a meeting with the man from the Council. Mr Richard Selley is very cute and he's smiling over his desk at me and Debs. I've dragged my friend along with me for moral support. Currently, she's making eyes at Mr Selley.

'You've done a great job with the plans, Ms Freeman,' he says, ignoring Debs's attempts at flirting. 'I'll organise for you to have access to the funds as soon as possible. You'll be able to begin work in a couple of weeks.'

'A couple of weeks?'

'Yes,' he confirms. 'We're keen to push the Renewal Action Plan forward as quickly as we can and, as you know, Kirberly has been designated as a Priority Neighbourhood. We're delighted that you've approached us first. That makes my life a lot easier.'

'Wow.' I sink back in my chair and try to take this in. Now I'm as panicked as I am thrilled. Two weeks to mobilise everyone on the estate. With Johnny's help, I'm sure it can be done. And with Debs's, of course. I put all the plans up in the Community Centre and there's been nothing but praise for them – thank goodness. What would I have done if everyone had been set on having their own ideas? As it is, the residents seem happy enough to let someone else take control. I have to say that the designs we downloaded from the internet are pretty impressive. Mr Selley has suggested a few tweaks, but he's more than happy with them too. Let's just hope they look as good on the ground.

'I'll come down and help you to implement the scheme,' he continues.

'You will?'

'It's a lot to take on,' he says, as if I didn't know. 'We can give you some assistance, help you to keep on track.'

'That's great.'

'Anything else you need to know?'

Yes: how can I make my ten-year-old son like my fabulous boyfriend?

But I realise that Mr Selley is solely concerned with my garden dilemmas not my personal ones, so I don't say that. Instead, I shake my head and say, 'I don't think so.'

'I'll be in touch, then,' he says and as I stand up, he leans over to shake hands with me. I realise my hand's trembling. I've done it. I've got the money to regenerate the estate. Have you any idea how this makes me feel? I'm walking on sunshine, to quote Katrina and the Waves.

Debs barges me out of the way and grabs his hand too, letting her fingers linger a little too long. The poor bloke looks terrified.

'Thanks,' I say, dragging my bezzie towards the door. 'We won't let you down.'

Outside, on the steps of the Council offices, I do a little happy dance. 'I can't believe it,' I shout out. 'This is the only thing I've ever achieved.' Apart from being mother to my wonderful, if moody, child, of course. 'Come on,' I say to my friend. 'I'll treat you to a coffee.'

'We don't need coffee, we need strong drink,' Debs insists. 'And you're paying. You can claim it as expenses.'

So we head to the nearest bar, which looks like it's just opened up for the day. Debs orders us both double vodkas and Coke and – true to her word – I pay. Then we find a seat and take up residence.

'All we've done is talk about bloody gardening for the last few weeks,' my friend complains. 'Though I'm glad I came today.'

'Thanks,' I say.

'Not for you,' she informs me. 'For the scenery. I could definitely have given that Council bloke one.'

'I'm sure he'd have been delighted.'

'Many men would,' she says wistfully. 'Actually, I'm thinking of asking Johnny out.'

I'm so horrified that I nearly spit out my drink. 'Why would you ask Johnny out?'

She swigs at her vodka and shrugs. 'Because it's about time that I did nice instead of nasty.'

'But Johnny?'

'Why not? He's a sound bloke.'

'I can't say that I'd be very happy about it.'

'It's not really up to you any more, is it?' my friend points out rather tartly. 'You're heading off into the sunset with Little Lord Fauntleroy.'

'Don't call him that.'

'What does it matter to you what – or *who* – Johnny does?'

But it does matter. Perverse as it may sound, I don't want him to go out with Debs. She might be my best mate, but she's an awful girlfriend. She can't stay faithful. Her hygiene habits are very suspect. If I was a bloke I wouldn't want to go out with her. And I wouldn't want Johnny going out with her either. Not that he would. He likes his women, well, *different* to Debs.

'So, how is life with Little Lord Fauntleroy?'

'Don't call him that,' we both say in unison, then laugh together.

'He's wonderful,' I say in answer to her question. 'He's a hopeless romantic.'

'I wouldn't want a *hopeless* romantic, I'd want a decent one.'

'You know what I mean. He can dance, he likes to read poetry, he knows his way round computers.'

'Great in bed?'

I nod.

'I think I might be in love with him too,' Debs quips.

'Now you can see why I'm smitten.'

My friend shakes her head. 'He sounds too good to be true. You know what the women's rule of thumb is – if it has tyres or testicles you're going to have trouble with it. Spencer, as wonderful as he sounds, will be no exception.'

'You're wrong,' I say. 'This time I really think that I've found the perfect man.'

'He's not one of us,' she tells me. 'He's rich. He's posh. Why's he hanging round our estate? Why's he shagging a single mum with a kid in tow when he could have his pick of women? No offence.'

'None taken,' I say, offended.

'Something doesn't add up,' my so-called friend says. 'More vodka?'

And, before I can answer, she sweeps up our glasses and goes back to the bar leaving me alone with my nagging doubts.

Chapter Fifty-Two

Dinner is perfect. Spencer's apartment is lit only by candlelight which dances in his eyes. There's some kind of mellow mood music drifting over us. I wonder if I could slip into this lifestyle on a permanent basis, wave goodbye to Bill Shankly House for good.

Don't get me wrong, I'd never be without Charlie now – he's my life – but I can't help thinking how different my lot could have been if I hadn't got pregnant so young. Could I now be living in a place like this, drinking champagne as if it was Diet Coke, enjoying fine dining every night rather than eking out my benefit and scoffing beans on toast by the end of the week? What would it be like to have a life without responsibility, without money worries, with only yourself to please? What would my life be like if it was just me and Spencer?

My boyfriend – still not sure that I'm comfortable calling him that yet – pads about the apartment, tidying away the debris of our dinner. He's wearing a loose white linen shirt, baggy grey combats and he's barefoot. The thing that amazes me most about this man is how at ease he is with himself; the only times he shows any signs of discomfort is with my son. When I'm with Spencer I feel gauche, naive and not worthy of him. Yet it's nothing that he does to make me feel like that. This is all down to my own insecurity.

Spencer comes back to the table with the champagne bottle. 'More fizz?'

I nod and Spencer tops up my glass.

'Happy?' he asks.

'Very. That was wonderful,' I say with a contented sigh as my tummy strains against my skirt. The man's an excellent cook too. The wild mushroom risotto was perfect. I'll swear that the tiramisu we had afterwards was shop-bought, but Spencer reckons that it wasn't. Says it was all his own work. Old family recipe. Not sure I believe that bit, but it's something else I can brag to Debs about. 'Is there nothing that you can't do?'

160

He reaches out for my hand. 'I can't persuade you to come away with me for the weekend again,' is his rejoinder which he softens with a kiss on my lips. 'All the crowd will be coming to my place soon.'

'Here?'

'No, to my family home in the country. I'd like you to meet them.'

A family home in the country? How appealing does that sound? And I thought that I remembered Spencer saying that he'd been brought up on a nice estate. Perhaps his parents have retired there or something.

'I have to ease into this. Slowly, slowly. I've let Charlie stay over at Kyle's tonight,' I remind him. Which, frankly, goes entirely against my principles. I'm sure Johnny would be furious if he knew that I was even considering letting him stay there. 'A snatched evening on a school night. That's a big deal. I'm not wildly happy about it. Kyle might be Charlie's best friend, but that kid's normally up to no good.' I glance at my watch. 'They should be in bed now, but I bet they're holed up in Kyle's room with a stash of porn or some X-rated Playstation game that involves extreme violence. No one keeps a proper check on that boy. I don't really want my son mixing with him. But, for you, I'm letting go. This is emotionally very expensive for me.'

'Thank you,' Spencer says. 'I appreciate the sacrifice. It's so hard to get you all to myself and your son makes it very clear that he'd rather not have me around.'

'Maybe all three of us could do something together this weekend,' I suggest. 'I'm sure if you got to know Charlie better then you wouldn't find him so daunting. He's quite grown up for his age. If he knew you better then he'd love you too.'

'Just like he does Johnny?'

I sigh. 'Johnny's been in his life for a long time. He's as near to a father as my boy's ever known. You're never going to replace him, but you could get along with Charlie just as well.'

'You're a very persuasive woman,' Spencer says, and he leads me from the table over to the fire. It's one of those modern ones, set into the wall. The flames flicker, licking at the shadows.

There's a huge sheepskin rug spread out in front of it and Spencer eases me down into the soft wool. He takes my champagne glass and puts it on the coffee-table along with his while I kick off my shoes. We lie on the rug, basking in the heat of the fire, even though the night isn't cold. His lips find mine and he kisses me deeply. I arch towards him in response. I can safely say that there have been very few

161

times in my life when I've been happier than this. Spencer's fingers find the buttons on my blouse and slowly undo them. My head spins and it's not because I've drunk too much champagne. All thoughts of what Charlie might be up to, Johnny's lurking presence, the problems on the estate, all fly away in the face of this tender assault.

'Sally Freeman,' Spencer says, 'I think that I'm falling in love with you.'

I know this is too soon, too quick. It's unwise to be swept away like this. But I feel as if I'm being carried along by a turbulent sea and I can no longer tread water. I can no longer tell where Spencer's body ends and mine starts. We're swirling together in the tide.

'I think I might love you too,' I answer.

Chapter Fifty-Three

T his was probably a very bad idea. But Kyle Crossman, Kirberly's self-appointed agony uncle, had decreed that drastic measures were required. How could Johnny argue with that? He'd tried wooing Sally back with sexy moves on the dance floor and had failed. She'd been equally unimpressed by his new career choice. Maybe this would do the trick.

Thankfully, not all of the streetlights in this area had been vandalised, so he could just about see what he was doing. Kyle, as yet, hadn't come up with a marvellous plan, so Johnny had decided to take matters into his own hands.

He made a few more sweeping strokes with his paintbrush. Then, standing back, he admired his work. As this could also be classed as making a start on sprucing up the estate, it might please Sally on both counts. He couldn't wait to get started on the project to regenerate the area. It was long overdue and he was so proud of Sally for having the energy and the vision to drive this whole thing forward. He'd always admired her determination and fighting spirit – this time she'd really come through for all of them.

'What do you think, Ringo lad?'

The little dog barked his appreciation.

'Do you think Sally will like it?'

Ringo wagged his tail.

'What do you know?' Johnny said. 'You're man's best friend, but you're useless when it comes to relationships. When did you last have a girlfriend, eh?'

The wagging didn't stop.

The night was cold. If he had any sense, he'd be tucked up in his bed right now. But he had no sense at all when it came to Sally. Despite them being parted and her having another man – someone he hadn't a hope in hell of competing with – he was still totally besotted with her. If only he'd shown her that more often when they were together, perhaps he wouldn't be in this mess now.

He turned and checked Sally's flat behind him. It was three in the morning and still she wasn't home. A knot of jealousy tangled his guts. She must really like this guy if she'd risk leaving Charlie with Kyle Crossman overnight. Goodness only knows what the boy might have learned by morning. And yet, here he was, a grown man clutching at straws and taking Kyle's advice himself. What exactly did that say about his state of mind?

He turned back to his handiwork. A few more strokes and he'd finished. Johnny checked it out again. It said all that needed to be said. He thought it looked great and hoped that Sally would feel the same. Satisfied, he tidied away his brushes and the paint, putting them into the cardboard box he'd brought along for the purpose. He'd clean off the brushes properly later on.

Then he crossed over the road to Bill Shankly House and settled down on the broad, concrete doorstep of the flats. He'd wait for Sally, make sure he was here when she discovered exactly what he'd been up to in the early hours of the morning.

Now that he wasn't active, the chill of the night started to set in — and also the doubts. Had he done the right thing? Johnny turned up his collar and huddled into the corner of the doorway. Ringo, completing three circles, snuggled down next to him with a contented sigh. Only time would tell.

Chapter Fifty-Four

I leave Spencer in bed and get a taxi home. My lover was all keen to get up with me and see me home, but I insisted he stay where he was. He looked so warm and comfortable that I couldn't make him go out into the cold light of dawn. Waking up in his arms was just wonderful and it took all of my willpower to drag myself out of bed.

It's not yet six o'clock, but I want to make sure that I'm home long before Charlie. I told him that he had to come and get ready for school here rather than going straight from Kyle's. To be honest, I just want to make sure that he's still in one piece – that he hasn't come home with a piercing or a tattoo. Being slightly less melodramatic, I also want to make sure that he has a decent breakfast and his packed lunch for the day. Kyle, poor kid, seems to live on nothing but crisps.

The taxi pulls up outside Bill Shankly House and, still yawning, I pay the driver. I watch him drive off and then make my way up to the flats. As I get to the doorway, I start as I see a figure huddled there, fast asleep. I start again as I realise that it's Johnny and he's cuddling a pint of milk. Ringo's sparko at his feet.

Going over to him, I give his shoulder a gentle shake. 'Johnny.'

The dog cocks his ear and Johnny rouses, blinking his eyes as he does so.

'What on earth are you doing out here?' I ask.

My friend is still trying to wake up and mumbles groggily, 'Waiting for you.'

'How long have you been here?'

'All night,' he admits, stretching.

'That could be classed as stalking, Johnny. Come on in before the neighbours start gossiping. I'll make you some breakfast.'

Climbing the stairs, Johnny follows, bringing the milk with him. Ringo trots behind. I flick a thumb at the milk bottle. 'Is that mine?'

165

'Yeah,' Johnny says. 'Your milkman comes at five o'clock. He's a nice fella.'

I humph at that. Johnny's everyone's bezzie within two minutes of meeting them.

'You owed him a month's money. I paid him for you.'

'Oh,' I say, having the grace to blush. 'Thanks. I'd been meaning to catch him.' Actually, I'd been hiding from him for weeks. 'I've got the money in a jar in the kitchen. I'll sort it when we get upstairs.'

'There's no need,' he counters sleepily. 'You know that.'

We say nothing else while we climb the stairs – me not knowing whether to be hopping mad or just sad.

I let us all into the flat – me, Johnny and the faithful hound. Chucking my bag on the sofa, I turn to Johnny and say, 'What were you thinking of? Now you know that I spent the night with Spencer, does that make you feel better?'

'No.'

We go through to the kitchen.

'In my defence,' Johnny says, 'it wasn't my entire reason.'

'Care to enlighten me?'

'Yeah.' He takes my hand and tugs me to the kitchen window. 'That's what I've been doing.'

'Ohmigod.' My hands fly to my mouth. Outside the flats is an enormous wall that's normally covered in obscene graffiti. It's such an eyesore. It was one of the first things on my plan to obliterate. Looks like that's been done. And in fairly good style.

Now it's decorated with hearts and flowers and there's a curling banner painted across the middle which boldly declares, *Sally Freeman, I love you.* Hot, stinging tears prick at my eyes and I start to cry. 'I don't know what to say.'

'Say that you like it.' Johnny's face is anxious and frowning.

'I love it,' I tell him truthfully. 'It's beautiful.' No one has ever done anything like this for me before. I don't think there could be a more public declaration of Johnny's love. It thrills me and it hurts me in equal measures.

'And the sentiments?'

'Not entirely a surprise.'

'Does it change things between us?'

I shake my head. 'No.' Looking over at my ex-lover, my heart aches for him. There is so much good in Johnny, I can hardly bear to cause

166

him this pain. 'I've just got out of someone else's bed, Johnny. Doesn't that tell you something?'

I see something inside Johnny shrivel up and die. Ringo whimpers. My friend chews at his fingernail. 'Do you love him?'

'I think so.'

'Then there's not much else for me to say.'

'Let me put the kettle on,' I blurt out. 'In times of crisis you can't beat a cup of tea.'

'A hug would work too.'

I only hesitate slightly before I go and put my arms round Johnny and we hold each other tightly. 'You are my best friend,' I whisper fiercely in his ear. 'I always want you to be in our lives. My son adores you.'

'What does Charlie think about Spencer now?'

'He's coming round to the idea. Slowly.'

'I'd still like to see more of him,' Johnny says, holding me away from him. 'I know that I've got no legal rights, not being his real dad and all that, but maybe we could come to an informal arrangement?'

'You can see him whenever you like.'

'It's more awkward with Spencer around,' he points out. 'Perhaps I could take Charlie for the weekend sometimes?'

'Of course you can. He'd love that.'

'And it would give you more time to spend with your new man.'

'Why would you want to do anything to help facilitate my relationship with Spencer?'

'Because I do love you, Sally Freeman. More than you'll ever know. If you're sure that this is what you want, then I love you enough to let you go.'

The tears are hot behind my eyes again.

'He can offer you so much more than I'll ever be able to. A blind man on a galloping horse could see that. Even *I* can see it.'

'It's not about his money,' I say. 'I'm not a gold digger.'

'I want Charlie to have a better life too,' Johnny continues. 'You've taught me that much. If this Spencer can give the lad a better start then I can't stand in the way of that.'

I hug Johnny again. His body's warm and familiar against mine. And, in some ways, I miss that so much. The sex with Spencer is new and exciting, sizzling. But after five years with Johnny, our love-making had become comfortable, loving and caring. I don't think that you can beat that.

'You're a wonderful man and the best friend that I'll ever have,' I tell him.

He eases himself from my arms. 'Either that or I'm a complete idiot,' he says flatly.

Chapter Fifty-Five

We're meeting Spencer at the Albert Dock outside the Tate Liverpool. He's organised a day out for the three of us. A bonding exercise with Charlie. I'm nervous and I know that I shouldn't be. I want so much for my son and my lover to like each other.

Charlie's very reluctant about this. There's some football practice this afternoon that he really didn't want to miss, but I think this is more important, particularly when Charlie isn't exactly showing any signs of having Beckham's skill on the pitch.

Spencer's already waiting when we arrive at the dock and my heart lurches when I see him standing there in his designer sunglasses and the smartest casual clothes I've ever seen. The sun's shining today, but there's still a cool breeze off the Mersey which is scudding the big white clouds across the sky. So much money has been lavished on this area and it's worth it because it looks fabulous. I feel guilty that I don't do more things like this with Charlie when it's on our own doorstep. Perhaps Debs is right. We don't appreciate our rich culture when it's right there under our noses all the time.

There's a museum dedicated to the Beatles, a Magical Mystery Tour in an old coach round the haunts of the Fab Four, and the Yellow Duckmarine Bus – one of those old amphibious crafts that bobs visitors around the waterfront and the docks. Charlie would love all of those and I wonder what Spencer has in store for us.

'Hi,' I say shyly, as I kiss him on the cheek. I was naked and getting low down and dirty with this man just a couple of days ago, but now I feel strangely embarrassed in his presence.

'Hey,' he says softly and gives me a squeeze. Then he bends down and shakes Charlie's hand. The volume increases. 'Hello, Charles.'

No one calls my son Charles. Not even when they're cross with him. He wasn't even christened Charles. Actually, he wasn't even christened. 'It's Charlie,' I say, putting my arm round my lad's shoulders. 'Just Charlie.'

Already, my son has stiffened.

'We're both looking forward to our day out together, aren't we, Charlie?' Now I'm speaking in sing-song tones. Must be catching. 'What did you have in mind?'

'Thought we'd go to the Tate,' Spencer suggests as he gestures at the big blue and orange building behind us. 'There's an exhibition of Chinese contemporary art that I think will be very interesting.'

Chinese contemporary art? Very interesting? My heart sinks. I was hoping to sit on a coach and sing Beatles songs. Charlie looks like he feels the same.

'Do you know much about modern art, Charlie?' Spencer asks – still a decibel too high.

My son looks nonplussed. 'No.'

'Sounds great,' I say too brightly. My own voice has gone to pot too. 'We've never been here before. What do you think, Charlie?'

My son shrugs. 'Whatever.'

Spencer rubs his hands together, clearly pleased. He beams wildly as he says, 'The Tate it is then.'

We go into the gallery and I have to admit that it's the first time I've ever been in here. I also have to admit that it's the first time I've been in *any* art gallery, modern or otherwise. I've been bringing up a kid single-handedly, okay? So, my appreciation of modern art has been a bit neglected – get over it. I have.

Inside the Tate, the foyer is bright and airy as is, I guess, befitting of a modern gallery. A few paintings in bold colours grace the walls. If the entrance is anything to go by, it looks nice. This could work out much better than I imagined. Charlie, however, doesn't look quite so impressed. He's currently trying to curl in on himself in an attempt to look invisible.

Spencer makes a donation in the clear glass box for the purpose and then ushers us up the stairs to the first floor and to one of the galleries. Opening the glass doors, we go inside. The room is painted bright white and grey steel pillars support the vaulted ceiling in exposed brick with soft lighting.

I don't really know what to do in here and neither does my son, so we both hang on to Spencer's coat tails exuding nervousness. It's as quiet as the grave and there seem to be more security guards than there are customers. Our feet clonk too loudly on the polished wood floor as we walk. What do I do? Should I go up to the artwork and linger, trying to look intelligent, or should we just shuffle past with admiring glances making informed-sounding murmurs? The first wall seems to consist of a series of painting of dismembered bodies. Not sure what to make of that.

My son's eyes are out on stalks and I'm not at all surprised. The last time Charlie saw this amount of slaughter was probably on one of Kyle's Playstation games. I thought we'd be looking at the sort of stuff that's painted on Johnny's van. But no, this art is out to shock. What I want to do is rush my boy straight out of here, but then that would make me look like a pleb.

'Why is this art, Mum?' Charlie whispers to me.

'I don't know,' I whisper back. We both get a fit of the giggles. Spencer smiles indulgently at us. Perhaps he wouldn't if he knew what we were laughing at.

The three of us make our way along the rows of exhibits, paintings, sculptures, some things that defy description.

'Wow,' Spencer says, enraptured. 'Fabulous.'

Charlie and I exchange a glance. 'Care to shed some light on it for us?' I venture. 'We're not really used to this kind of thing.'

'Sure, sure,' Spencer says, stroking his chin in a thoughtful manner as he admires another painting of a cut-up corpse. 'A lot of the art stems from the new generation of Chinese artists,' he intones. 'I'm full of admiration for them. Unlike the generation before them, they're really moving toward a self-confidence and maturity that comes from a greater understanding of their place in the contemporary global village.'

'Really?' Charlie and I look at each other. My son's face is as blank as my own. Clearly neither of us have a clue what Spencer is talking about.

'I like the way that they're able to contemplate their own positions within a society that's going through an immense period of rapid and profound cultural upheaval. Don't you?'

'Absolutely,' I say.

Charlie chokes on a giggle. I give my son a surreptitious kick.

'The paintings are full of vivacity, imagination and energy.' Spencer is unaware that he's lost his audience. They're dead bodies, for heaven's sake. Lots of them. I can't imagine why he thought that this would be a fun way to spend a morning with a ten-year-old boy. Does he really know so little about kids?

For an hour – a long, long hour – we trail round after him while he tries, and fails, to educate us in the appreciation of modern Chinese art. As well as the corpses, there's a pile of rubble that's supposed to say something meaningful about the Great Wall of China, and a blow-up sex doll dressed in a Maoist uniform which I don't get at all. I'm just grateful that, at this point, my son has given up asking questions.

After a while, there's a tug on my sleeve. 'I'm hungry,' Charlie whispers.

'Me too,' I confess.

'Can we go now?'

I ruffle his hair. 'Had enough of Chinese art?'

He nods vigorously, then adds, 'Johnny's paintings are miles better than this.'

I sigh at yet another severed and bleeding limb. 'I can't help but agree with you,' I say.

Chapter Fifty-Six

We go into the Tate Liverpool Café to have our lunch. It's a stylish venue next door to the gallery and is currently decorated with an art installation that involves brightly-coloured plastic streamers draping from the ceiling and an indecipherable message in big, black letters all along one wall. Don't understand that either – but the colours are pretty and at least there's no blood. The menu is lovely, but it's all goat's cheese and polenta, and we struggle to find something that Charlie likes to eat – and believe me, my son isn't a picky eater.

Eventually, we settle on a chickpea burger with sweet potato chips for him. We've just finished eating when Charlie's mobile phone beeps. 'It's a text from Johnny,' he says when he checks it.

'Go outside to text him back,' I tell him. Other diners are already staring at us. 'I don't want you doing it in here.'

He slips down from the table and goes outside. And before you say anything about what's a kid of ten doing with a mobile phone when I'm on benefits – I'm like any other parent: I want to know where he is every minute of the day. Especially where we live. So if some of my measly income support has to fund my son's Pay As You Go, then so be it. Through the huge windows I watch him texting, frowning in concentration, tongue out to aid him. It makes me smile to myself and a rush of love for him floods through me.

Spencer's fingers find mine. 'That didn't go well, did it?'

'No,' I say with a smile. 'A bit too highbrow for a ten year old.' A bit too highbrow for me too.

'I thought he'd like it.'

'Oh, Spencer,' I say. 'You really don't understand children, do you?'

'I loved art galleries as a boy,' he protests.

'Did you?'

'My father always used to take me up to London when I was home from school in the holidays. It was our special time together.

I could lose myself for hours in the Tate, the National, the Royal Academy.'

'Well, maybe Charlie just hasn't had enough exposure to them.'

'What do you want to do this afternoon? I'm so hopeless at this, maybe you'd better choose.'

'I think Charlie's had enough for today.' Personally, I think he's been marvellous. There were times when *I* felt like lying down on the floor and kicking my heels. Chinese art might be great, if you like that kind of thing, but you can have too much of it. Ten minutes was my limit. 'You go off and do your own thing. There's a football practice that I'm sure Charlie would like to go to instead.' It would run off some of his pent-up energy.

'I hoped that we'd spend the whole day together. I could come to the football practice too.'

'Do you know anything about football?'

'I'm more of a rugger and polo man,' he admits.

I laugh. 'Why doesn't that surprise me? Look, Johnny has said that he'd like to have Charlie at the weekends sometimes. If you want to organise that party at your house, then perhaps I can fix it to be there.'

Spencer's smile melts my heart. He might be rubbish with kids, but he's certainly got it off pat with the female of the species. 'Are you sure?'

'Yes,' I say. 'I'm sure.'

'I'll miss you today,' he tells me earnestly. 'I enjoyed our night together. I'd like to be able to do it more often.'

'I'd like to do that too, Spencer. But this is like eating an elephant. Let's take it one small bite at a time.'

Chapter Fifty-Seven

'So?' I say to Charlie. 'What do you want to do now?'

Spencer said goodbye to us, looking a bit downcast, but also the slightest bit relieved. He feigned pressing engagements for Charlie's sake and left both me and my son sitting on the side of the Albert Dock in the warm sunshine.

I buy Charlie an ice cream from a nearby cart because he's still hungry. The chickpea burger didn't really do it for him. Then we dangle our legs over the wall, letting them hang high above the water. There's a floating sculpture in the slate-grey water. It looks like an over-sized chandelier, and a million rainbow-coloured sparkles glitter on its surface. It's absolutely stunning. Maybe this appreciation of art isn't entirely wasted on me.

'What do you think of that?' I ask, pointing at it.

'Sound,' Charlie says, but he's too busy making his own sculpture with his ice cream using his tongue to take any real notice.

'We can get back in time for your football practice if you want to.'

'Johnny texted me to say that it had been cancelled. Not enough people could go.'

'Oh,' I say. 'That's a shame. Want to do something together? Just the two of us for a change?'

Charlie shrugs, but it's an 'okay' shrug not a 'get lost' shrug. I thought it was only when you became a teenager that you carried on all your conversations with your shoulders. He's supposed to be three years away from that yet.

I stroke my son's hair. 'I'm sorry that it wasn't much fun for you with Spencer this morning.'

More shrugging.

'He's really a nice guy. I wish that you could like him.'

Charlie pulls a face. 'He doesn't like me.'

'He does,' I assure him. 'He loves you. It's just that he doesn't get kids. Give him time.'

We sit and watch the sculpture turn gently in the breeze. The glass droplets tinkle musically.

'Did you really think that Johnny's paintings are better than those in there?' My son flicks a thumb back towards the Tate Gallery.

'Yeah,' I say. 'I did.'

'What about the one that's outside the flats?' Charlie keeps staring straight ahead.

Ah, so my son – who never notices anything – has noticed Johnny's declaration of love. Would be hard to miss it, seeing as it's ten feet high and the same wide.

'Johnny did that, didn't he?'

'He did,' I confirm. 'And I like it very much.'

'I do too,' Charlie says.

Then, to change the subject, I make a suggestion. 'What about we go on the Magical Mystery Tour this afternoon? See where the Beatles came from?' Like all good Liverpudlian kids, he's been brought up on a diet of the Fab Four.

'Okay.'

So I blow a considerable part of our weekly allowance on two tickets for the tour. We're just in time to see the rickety 1970s coach painted in psychedelic colours coming round the corner, *Magical Mystery Tour* painted on the side in yellow and blue.

We jump on board, bagging the front seats even though we were probably the last to pay up. Tourists from all over the world troop on behind us – Beatles fans from Japan, Australia, Germany and goodness knows where else.

Singing along to Beatles songs at the top of our voices, we set off, heading out of the city, taking in the sights of Strawberry Fields and Penny Lane, all the local places made famous by the records.

We make stops to visit the homes of George, John, Paul and Ringo. All small, unassuming homes. Ringo's former house, a two-up, two-down terraced place is in the Dingle – another area designated as a Priority Neighbourhood, prime for redevelopment. In the Dingle's case this seems to involve knocking most of it down and starting again rather than planting a few flowers and giving it a lick of paint.

We get off the coach and follow our guide to the house. Charlie and I stand outside and look at the faded net curtains, the tiny front door, the grime-blackened brickwork.

'They were people just like us,' my son says in wonder. 'They all lived in little houses – and look what they did.'

'They took on the world. And they won.' I hug my boy to me, fiercely. 'So will we. We'll do great things. We're not going to spend the rest of our lives in Bill Shankly House, Charlie,' I say to him. 'I promise you that.'

Chapter Fifty-Eight

'It's not going well,' Charlie said.

They were both sitting in Kyle's bedroom. The window was open and Kyle dragged deeply on the cigarette; he passed it to Charlie who did the same. Simultaneously, they then wafted the smoke out of the window with frantic waves.

'I had to go to an art gallery with them on Saturday.'

Kyle pulled a suitably appalled face.

'What can I do?'

'Child from Hell,' Kyle reminded him.

'I can't,' Charlie told his friend. 'Mum'd kill me. And she really likes him.' The thought made him take another worried drag on the cigarette. 'We have to find a way to make her like Johnny more.' He passed the cancer stick to his friend. 'He painted a great picture on the wall outside our flats telling her that he loved her.'

Kyle stuck his finger in his mouth and feigned vomiting.

'I know,' Charlie agreed. 'It's a bit soppy, but grown-ups can't help it. Even that didn't work. I thought it might.'

'Johnny does paintings?'

'Yeah. He's got a lock-up over the other side of the estate. He's really good.'

'Can we go and look at them?'

The boy shook his head. 'I haven't got a key.'

'Since when did that matter?'

Kyle leaned out of the window and stubbed out the cigarette on the brickwork. Then he wrapped it in a piece of toilet paper that he'd purloined earlier for the purpose. The mummified butt then went into his pocket so that any incriminating evidence could be disposed of well away from the house.

'Come on. Let's go and look in the shed.' Both boys jumped down off the bed and Charlie trooped after his friend, down the stairs, through the kitchen and down the worn scrap of grass that constituted the Crossman family's back garden.

In the long-neglected shed, Kyle rooted through a motley assortment of rusted tools. 'These all belonged to my real dad,' he told Charlie as he passed one then the other to his friend for him to examine. 'My current dad's a useless fucker when it comes to DIY. That's what my mum says, anyway.'

Charlie brushed away cobwebs as he tried to peer over his friend's shoulder into the treasure trove. 'What are you looking for?'

'These,' Kyle said and produced, with a theatrical flourish, a large pair of bolt cutters.

'What are we going to do with those?'

'Get into Johnny's garage.' His friend handed them over. 'Put them up your T-shirt.'

'Why?'

'Because we don't want to be seen with them, knobhead.'

Charlie put the bolt cutters up his T-shirt. They were dirty and the metal was cold against his skin and he knew why Kyle didn't want to put them up his own T-shirt.

'Bring a screwdriver too,' Kyle said and, pre-empting Charlie's next question, added, 'In case we need one.'

A screwdriver joined the bolt cutters and the pair made their way out of the shed and back down the garden, carefully avoiding being seen from the kitchen window as Kyle's mum was in there having a cup of tea with one of her mates before they went to Bingo.

'What are we going to do when we get to Johnny's garage?'

Kyle looked at him as if he was mad. 'Break in.'

'Why?'

'We've nothing else to do, have we?'

Charlie couldn't really argue with that.

Chapter Fifty-Nine

The postman comes and I hear a few bits fall onto the mat. The deliveries are getting later and later everyday. Not that it bothers me. All I ever get is bills and I'm certainly in no hurry for those.

I go out to the hall and retrieve the post. Today there's a letter from the Council and I tear it open. Inside, there's a cheque for ten thousand pounds and it takes me a minute to absorb the fact. Ten grand. I blink at the amount of noughts. I've never seen a cheque for ten grand before. I've had to set up a separate bank account for the fund, and Johnny and I are joint signatories. I guess it's an attempt to stop you defrauding the Council, but frankly I'd consider running away with Johnny for this amount of money.

A thrill runs through me. I've done it. I've got the money. I have to tell Johnny. Shrugging on my jacket, I grab the cheque and race out of the house. Minutes later, I'm knocking on the door of his mam's house, excitement bubbling inside me, but I can tell from the amount of time it takes for the door to be opened that Johnny's not at home.

Puffing and panting, leaning heavily on her walking stick, Mary Jones hobbles to the door. 'Hiya, our Sally,' she says, as she tries to catch her breath.

'Sorry to drag you to the door, Mary,' I apologise.

'Don't worry, love. That's my exercise for the day sorted.'

The sad thing is that it's probably true. 'I take it Johnny's not here?'

'Got his first job,' she says proudly. 'He's over at that Les Flynn's, painting his living room.'

'I've got some good news.'

'The only good news I want to hear is that you and our Johnny Boy are back together.'

'It's about the money for the regeneration project.'

'Then that's nearly as good,' she concedes. 'Go round there and tell him. You know where Les lives.'

'Yeah. Want me to make you a cuppa while I'm here?'

'Nah, doll. Just had one. Thanks all the same.'

So I take off again, wings on my feet, while I think of Mary painfully shuffling her way back to her chair for the rest of the afternoon.

When I get to Les's road, I see Johnny's van parked in the street and he's just coming out of the door heading towards it. His hair's standing on end and he's got magnolia highlights. 'Johnny!' I shout, and break into a run to cover the last few metres.

That stops him in his tracks. 'What?' He looks worried.

'The money came through,' I yell joyfully, as I throw myself into his arms.

He lets out a triumphant whoop too. Then he spins me round and round while I shriek with glee. When he puts me down, we hug each other tightly and then break away self-consciously.

'That's great,' Johnny says. 'Just great.' He shakes his head in bewilderment. 'You did it.'

'I know, I know.' I sit on the pavement before my legs give way beneath me. 'I can hardly believe it.'

Johnny sits down next to me. 'Now the hard work starts.'

'It'll be okay,' I say. 'You'll see, we'll get them all going.'

My ex laughs at that. '*You* will!'

'I couldn't do this without you, Johnny. I'd be terrified.'

'I'm very good at hand-holding.' He takes my hand and I let him. 'Friends?'

I nod. 'Friends.'

'I'm just finishing up here.' He flicks a glance back at the flats behind him. 'Then I'll come round and paint that bit of nonsense off the wall opposite your place.'

'It's not nonsense,' I tell him. 'It's very flattering. I love it.'

'Makes me look stupid,' he points out.

'No,' I say. 'Not stupid. Just very caring. Besides, it's a great mural. Seems a shame . . .' But I can't be selfish. If I don't want Johnny then I can't force him to leave it there for all the world to gawp at. Not sure that Spencer would be too enamoured either.

'Maybe I'll just come and paint the name out,' he proffers. 'Then people will know that there's a vacancy in the love-life of Johnny Jones.'

'I'll leave it to you, Johnny. You decide.' Then I notice the time. 'I'd better get back,' I say. 'Charlie's due home soon. There's been some sort of teacher training day at school so it's shut. He's playing round at Kyle's.'

My good friend frowns at me. 'He's spending a lot of time with Kyle. I know it's none of my business, but that lad's not a great role model.'

I shrug. 'He doesn't seem too bad, despite his reputation. Perhaps he's just another misunderstood kid with too little love meted out to him. They have been spending more time together and it doesn't seem to have had a detrimental effect on Charlie's behaviour. I'm keeping my eye on it though.' The minute it does, I'll be clamping down on the time he spends round there, that's for sure.

'Good,' Johnny says. 'I knew you would be.'

I give him a wave. 'Catch you later.'

'Sally,' Johnny shouts after me. 'What did Spencer say about the money?'

'Haven't told him yet,' I confess at the top of my voice. 'I came straight round here.'

And, for some reason, that makes Johnny smile.

Chapter Sixty

'Keep a lookout,' Kyle hissed.

'What for?'

'Anything.'

Charlie put his hands in his pockets and whistled nonchalantly as he paced up and down behind Kyle. The bolt cutters bit effortlessly through the flimsy padlock on Johnny's garage and, seconds later, the boys were lifting the creaking garage door.

Finding the lights, Charlie flicked them on, flooding the lock-up with a harsh glare. They shut the door carefully behind them.

'It's a bit of a dump in here,' his friend noted.

'I think it needs to be like that if you're a painter,' Charlie assured him with more enthusiasm than certainty.

It might be a dump, but there was something nice about the garage. He liked coming here. He liked the way it smelled, all sort of funny and musty. He liked all the stuff that was lying around – the paints, the brushes, the tools. It was better when Johnny was here too though. He wasn't sure why they'd had to break in. Johnny wouldn't have minded Kyle coming here with him, Charlie was sure of that. Johnny enjoyed having kids around. Not like that Spencer.

'Hmm,' Kyle snorted, casting his eyes around the place. 'So these are Johnny's paintings?'

'Yeah,' Charlie said. There was a big one hanging from the rafters. It was a woman's face and it looked a bit like his mum, but it was just made up of lines so Charlie couldn't be sure.

'Hmm,' his friend said again, while he massaged his chin just like Spencer had done at the art gallery. Charlie decided to do the same to see if it made the paintings look better. It didn't.

Another 'Hmm,' from Kyle.

Charlie didn't know why, but it suddenly seemed terribly important that Kyle should like them. 'These are some of his best,' Charlie told his friend. He went to where the canvases were stacked up against the wall. 'What do you think?'

Kyle flicked through them. 'Hmm.'

'Say something else except "hmm"!'

'You reckon these are better than the ones in the art gallery?'

'Yeah,' Charlie said earnestly. 'Much better.'

'Does he ever sell any of them?'

'Nah.' Charlie shook his head. 'I keep telling him he should, but he never gets round to it.'

'Perhaps we could give him a little bit of help.'

'How?'

'Let's take them down there. To the gallery,' Kyle said. 'See what they think.'

'Why?'

'They might pay us for them.'

'But how would that help Johnny to get my mum back?'

That one seemed to stump Kyle. He chewed at his lip for a minute before he came up with, 'Say if we sold one of his paintings to the gallery, we might get fifty quid for it. More.'

Fifty quid. Charlie felt his eyes widen. Could they really get fifty pounds for one of Johnny's paintings? It seemed like a lot of money.

'We could keep twenty-five and we could give Johnny twenty-five. He could take your mum out for a nice meal with that. Or buy her some shoes.'

Gosh, that sounded like a great idea. Kyle was brilliant. He was the best friend you could have.

'We'd have to ask Johnny if we could take the paintings,' Charlie said, scratching at his head.

'Not necessarily,' Kyle said mysteriously. 'It might be better if we just took a couple. Check out the lie of the land.'

'The lie of the land?'

Kyle gave an exasperated sigh. 'See if they're interested.'

'Oh, right,' Charlie said. 'Wouldn't that be stealing?'

'No.' Kyle shook his head vigorously. 'Johnny's your friend. He's like your dad. You can't steal off your own dad.'

'But he's not really my dad.'

'He's near enough that it doesn't matter,' Kyle pointed out. 'You said so yourself. And it would be a nice surprise for him.'

184

That was true. Yet although he didn't know why, Charlie still didn't think it was a good idea just to take the paintings.

'We'd only be borrowing them,' Kyle continued. 'If they're not interested, we could have them back before Johnny noticed.'

That didn't sound too bad.

'Would it still be open now?' Kyle said.

'I don't know.'

'Let's just take a couple each. We can get the bus down there.'

'I've got to be home soon.'

'Phone your mum and tell her that something important came up.'

'Like what?'

Kyle rolled his eyes. 'Make something up, knobhead.'

'Okay.'

'Have you got any money for the bus?'

'I've got a bit,' Charlie said, fiddling with the change in his pocket. 'But I don't know how much the bus is.' Or which one they should get, for that matter. 'I don't know if I'm allowed to go into the city on my own.'

'She'll never know,' Kyle reassured him. 'We'll be there and back in a flash.'

'Okay then,' Charlie agreed. 'Which ones shall we take?'

'These three,' Kyle said. 'They look like they match. And this one.' He picked up the Superman painting that Charlie particularly liked. 'Good choice,' Charlie said.

'The Superman looks like Johnny,' his friend noted.

'I think it is supposed to be him.'

'Hmm,' Kyle said again. Then he stacked the paintings together, a couple for each of them. Kyle manhandled his pile until he'd got a firm grip on them.

His friend was dwarfed by the canvases.

'They're a bit big,' Kyle said. 'Hasn't he got anything smaller?'

'I don't think so.' Charlie heaved his paintings up and wrapped his arms round them as best he could. They weighed a ton too. 'I think they have to be big to be proper art.'

'Oh.'

The boys made their way to the garage door.

'If we sell these,' Charlie wanted to know, 'and we get fifty quid . . .'

'Huh.' His friend grunted underneath his load.

'. . . what will we do with our twenty-five quid?'

'Sometimes,' Kyle said, 'you're a right spaz, Charlie Freeman.' But he didn't tell him any more than that.

Chapter Sixty-One

I'm just passing the Computer Centre – not that it has such a grand title, but I don't know what else to call it – when Spencer's coming out. My heart does a little flip and I hurry towards him.

'Hello,' he says, in surprise. 'I'm just finishing for the day.'

It's not my turn to be trained in the delights of word processing, so I hadn't been due to see Spencer today. 'Hiya.' As I'm in the street, he has to make do with a peck on the cheek.

'I did think about calling round for a cup of tea,' he tells me.

'Kettle's always on in my place,' I say. 'Charlie's on his way home.' I think I see his smile falter a little at that, but I can't be sure. 'Fancy a quick one?'

He raises an eyebrow. 'I take it we're still discussing tea?'

'Come on,' I say, linking his arm through mine. 'You can tell me about your day and I'll tell you my good news.'

Spencer casts a worried look at his newly-shod Porsche. 'Do you think the car will be safe here?'

'No,' I say. 'If I were you I'd trade it in for a knackered old Ford Escort then you wouldn't care so much.'

I tug him and with one anxious look behind him we head off to Bill Shankly House.

Making the tea, I say, 'We got the money through for the regeneration project today.' If I wasn't holding the kettle, I'd clap my hands in glee again.

'That's great,' Spencer says, but he doesn't sound wildly enthusiastic.

'What?' I hand him his tea. 'Why the glum face?'

'It's going to be even harder to see you, once this is up and running. We'll never get away.'

'It won't be for long,' I tell him. 'A few weeks, maybe a bit longer.'

He looks suitably horrified at the thought.

'And there's nothing to stop you picking up a shovel and joining in. A couple who dig together stay together.'

Spencer's frown relaxes into a smile. 'Is that so?'

'It's an old Liverpool saying.'

'I'm sure.' His big baby blues lock onto mine. 'Come to my place this weekend,' he urges. 'Before this all starts in earnest. Everyone's going to be there. You'll really enjoy it and my parents are dying to meet you.'

'Your parents will be there?' He wants me to meet his parents! This is the first time he's mentioned that. Should I read anything significant into this?

Spencer shrugs. 'It's their house.'

'Oh,' I say. 'And where will we stay? Is there room enough for all of us?'

'Oh, yes.' Spencer waves a hand dismissively. 'There's plenty of room.'

'I don't know if I can,' I admit truthfully. No point stringing Spencer along.

'I thought you said that Johnny would like to see more of Charlie.'

'He would, but I can't just spring this on him at short notice. He might have plans.' Unlikely, but you never know. I can't take it for granted that Johnny will drop everything to accommodate my every whim. Even though he normally does. Plus I'd quite like to spend the weekend with my kid myself, as it happens.

Spencer pulls me down onto his lap and kisses me. Then he lets out a long sigh. 'I love you, Sally Freeman. Do you know that?' He toys with my fingers. 'I want to be in your life permanently, not just relegated to the periphery.'

'I'd like that too, Spencer,' I assure him. 'I promise you, I'm working on it.'

'I suppose tonight's out of the question?'

'You're right,' I tell him. 'Big girls' night tonight.'

'Oh really?'

'Mmm. We've got some woman coming to try and flog us cheap jewellery. It's just an excuse for a bottle of plonk. Debs is coming round. Plus Mrs Kapur and Dora the Explorer.' If Dora's remembered. 'Not that we're going to be able to buy much as we're all broke.'

'Let me give you some cash.' Spencer reaches for his wallet. 'I'd like to treat you.'

'No, no, no,' I say. 'You can't do that.' I push away the sheaf of ten-pound notes that he's handing me. 'I can't take money from you. It would feel really funny.'

'Let me,' Spencer implores. 'I want you to have a nice evening.'

Then I get a brainwave. 'Let me treat Mrs Kapur and Dora. They have nothing. I'd love to be able to buy them something.'

He smiles at me lovingly. 'I think you're one of the kindest people I've ever met.'

'I'm not,' I say. 'They do a lot for me. It would be nice to spoil them, even though it's your money.'

'Take it.' Spencer folds the money into my palm, which still feels a bit odd. It's clear that he could buy and sell me under the table a million times over, but that's not why I want him.

'Thank you.' I give my lover a kiss. 'You're also very kind.'

'I'd better go,' Spencer says. 'There's a microwave dinner and some very interesting television waiting for me.'

'Now you're making me feel terrible!'

'Good,' Spencer says. 'That means that you're in my debt and you'll have to come away with me at the weekend to repay me.'

'I will think about it,' I promise. 'I can't do any more than that.'

'I'll leave you to it.'

I give Spencer another kiss. 'Yeah. Better find something for our tea too.' Then I glance at the clock and wonder why Charlie isn't home by now.

Chapter Sixty-Two

Kyle had phoned his big brother who'd told them which bus to get and where to catch it from. Charlie was getting worried; it was growing nearer and nearer to the time he should be home and still the bus hadn't turned up. He was just on the point of telling Kyle that he couldn't do this, when the bus arrived. They struggled on with their load.

'Can't bring those on my bus.' The driver held up his hand.

Charlie felt his face fall.

'It's an urgent delivery for the Tate Liverpool,' Kyle piped up in an important-sounding voice.

'Yeah? And I'm Sir Paul McCartney,' the driver said, but he took their money and let them on anyway.

It felt like an adventure riding on the bus into the centre of the city. Even Kyle shut up talking for once and just looked out of the window.

Now they were down at the Albert Dock, standing outside the Tate Liverpool just as Charlie had done with his mum and Spencer last weekend, and Charlie was feeling just as nervous.

'What shall we say to them?' he wanted to know.

Kyle chewed his lip, deep in thought. 'We should ask to speak to the boss,' he decided.

'Okay,' Charlie said. Then his mobile phone rang. His eyes widened in panic. 'It's my mum. What shall I tell her?'

'Tell her that you've been unavoidably detained,' Kyle advised.

'What does that mean?'

'I don't know,' Kyle admitted. 'But it's what people say.'

Charlie answered the phone. 'Hiya, Mum,' he said, trying not to sound guilty. 'I'm still at Kyle's. His mum's not come home from the Bingo yet, so I'm waiting with him. He doesn't want to be on his own. Yeah. Won't be long.' He glanced nervously at Kyle. 'Love you too, Mum.'

Kyle wrinkled his nose in distaste.

Charlie hung up.

'Inspired,' Kyle said. 'Apart from the last bit.'

'I have to say that, otherwise she gets funny.'

'Come on, then.' Kyle set off, pushing his way into the entrance, wrestling the paintings through the revolving doors.

'Mum says I have to be home in half an hour.'

'We'd better get a move on, then.'

There was a lady with a uniform and blond hair behind a desk and they decided to start with her. The place seemed a lot bigger to Charlie, now that he wasn't here with his mum. Kyle marched up to the desk and Charlie trailed in his wake.

'We'd like to see the man in charge, please,' Kyle said, and Charlie was relieved that his friend had been polite, because sometimes he wasn't.

'I'm afraid that our Chief Executive, Mr Stokes, isn't available this afternoon.'

Oh. That was a blow. Now what?

'Can anyone else help you?' the lady asked. She was being very nice.

Kyle pushed Charlie forward. 'We've brought these paintings for him to see,' the boy explained when he found his voice. 'I came here with my mum and her new boyfriend, Spencer. We went to see the modern Chinese art.' He was sure that was right. 'It was horrible.'

The lady seemed to smile at that. Perhaps she thought it was horrible too.

'These are much better,' Charlie explained as he pointed at the canvases. 'My friend Johnny does them. In his garage. Well, he's more like my dad really.'

'And you wanted to show them to the Chief Executive.'

'Yeah.'

'We wouldn't normally do this,' she said kindly. 'There are proper procedures.'

'I wanted it to be a surprise,' Charlie told her. 'Johnny always says he's going to do something with his paintings, but he never gets round to it.'

She gave one of those sighs that grown-ups often do. 'You could leave them with me,' she said. 'Just this once, mind. I'll make sure he looks at them.'

Charlie and Kyle exchanged a worried glance. If he couldn't look at them now, then how were they going to put them straight back in the garage? What if Johnny noticed that they were missing?

'When do you think he could do it?'

'I'm afraid that I couldn't really say. As I told you boys, this isn't really our proper procedure.'

Kyle shrugged. 'Okay then.'

'Leave me a phone number.' She pushed a piece of paper and a pen towards them. Charlie took the pen and in his best writing, he put down his mobile phone number.

'And your friend's details,' the lady added.

So Charlie, very carefully, wrote out Johnny's name and address and his age. He thought he'd better put Johnny's phone number too in case he was at school when the man phoned and his mobile had to be turned off. He also wrote that he had a dog called Ringo.

'Thank you,' Charlie said, as he handed back the paper.

The lady came from behind the desk and took the paintings, but Charlie was disappointed when she didn't even look at them.

'You'll be hearing from us,' she said.

'Can you tell us where to get the bus back to Kirberly, please, miss?' Kyle said.

'Just across the street.' She pointed across the cobbled courtyard outside. 'The numbers are on the shelter.'

And then, because there was nothing more they could do now, they left the art gallery.

Chapter Sixty-Three

'I need a smoke after that,' Kyle said, and he pulled the packet from his back pocket and lit one up for them to share.

'We'd better get going,' Charlie warned. 'Or I'll be killed.'

They both had a quick puff and then the two boys rushed off towards the bus stop. When they had it in their sights, they could see the bus already at the stop and they put on a spurt. As they did, they ran headlong into Spencer, who was coming round the corner, making him drop his car keys on the ground. Oh no! Charlie had completely forgotten that his mum's new boyfriend lived round here in one of these posh flats. This wasn't part of the plan.

'Hey, hey,' Spencer said, in his usual nursery-rhyme voice. 'What are you doing down here?' He was holding Charlie by both arms.

Charlie looked guiltily at the gallery behind him. 'Nothing.' Spencer followed his gaze, but remained silent. Then his eyes dropped to the cigarette.

'That I can't condone, Charlie.'

He dropped Kyle's cigarette to the ground, much to his mate's horror, and stubbed it out with his heel.

'Does your mother know that you're in the city on your own?'

'Yeah,' Kyle said loudly. 'What's it to you?'

'This is my mum's new boyfriend,' Charlie whispered. 'Shut up.'

Kyle's jaws clamped together firmly.

Spencer fixed Charlie with a stern stare that seemed to bore into his mind. It was the very same look his mum always gave him when she knew he was telling lies.

'Not really,' Charlie admitted with a huff. 'We were just getting the bus back. She said I'd got to be back in half an hour. I'm late. Are you going to tell her?'

His mum's new boyfriend let go of him and crossed his arms. 'What if I put you both in a taxi – and pay for it? That would get you home a lot quicker than the bus.'

Charlie's eyes widened. A *taxi* instead of the *bus*? Why would Spencer be nice to him? Grown-ups were usually the first to tell tales in situations like this. Not that he'd been in many situations like this, but there were definitely more of them now that he was best friends with Kyle.

'I'd take you in my car,' Spencer threw in, 'but there's no room for the two of you.'

If his own eyes had widened, Kyle's were out on stalks as he cast his gaze over Spencer's gleaming Porsche. To be honest, Charlie was a bit disappointed himself that they couldn't go in the flashy sports car. A taxi was good, but a Porsche, well . . .

'What do you think?' Spencer said. 'Do you want me to call a taxi?' Kyle nodded emphatically.

'And you don't want me to tell your mum that you were down here? Or tell her that I caught you smoking?'

Now it was Charlie's turn to shake his head emphatically. He'd never be allowed to go out again in his entire life if his mum found out he was smoking – even though they were Kyle's cigarettes.

'Then I'd like you to do something for me.' Charlie noted that the sing-song voice had gone, even though Spencer's smile was still in place. 'I'd like you to tell your mum that you'd really love to spend this weekend with Johnny.'

'With Johnny?'

'I want to take your mum to my house in the country and I know that she's worried about leaving you behind. It would make her feel much better, if you said that's what you wanted.'

Charlie *would* like to spend the weekend with Johnny. There wasn't a problem there, as far as he could see. And Johnny would want to see him. He always did. They did cool stuff together. Sometimes stuff that his mum didn't let him do. However, something didn't feel quite right about this, although Charlie didn't know what it was.

'It'll cost you,' Kyle said bravely. 'A taxi home. No splitting on us. And twenty quid each.'

Charlie was appalled.

Spencer laughed. Charlie hadn't expected him to find it funny. 'Your friend drives a hard bargain, Charlie.'

Without further comment, his mum's new boyfriend got out his wallet and peeled off a twenty-pound note for each of them. Charlie felt funny putting it in his pocket.

'Now I'll get you that taxi.' Spencer flicked open his mobile phone.

Minutes later, a cab pulled up by the kerb next to them. Spencer gave the driver some money and told him the address of Bill Shankly House. 'Get him to stop round the corner,' Spencer advised. 'Then you won't have to explain to your mum why you're in a taxi.'

That seemed like a good idea.

'Remember, Charlie,' Spencer said, as he closed the door, 'we've got a bargain. I hope you'll keep your end of it.'

The taxi set off and Kyle turned round to stare out of the window, waving to Spencer as they headed back towards Kirberly.

'What was he doing round here?'

'He lives here,' Charlie said glumly. 'In one of these posh flats.'

'He seems like a nice fella.' Kyle craned his neck to get a last glimpse.

Charlie still wasn't sure.

'If your mum stops going out with him,' Kyle said, 'can I have him for my mum?'

Chapter Sixty-Four

The collection of costume jewellery is spread out on a velvet cloth on my table. There are some very pretty things and I'm trying hard not to lust after them.

Dora the Explorer has on a necklace of sea shells, worn fetchingly over her Marks & Sparks floral nightie, and is dancing round my living room, singing 'Fly Me to the Moon'.

'That looks sound, doll,' Mrs Kapur tells her. My other neighbour is sporting a big, bling crucifix that's covered in red diamanté and is more Madonna than elderly Indian lady, and she's admiring herself in the hand mirror the jewellery lady, Kathy, has given to her.

'So you're off to Outerbumblefuck for the weekend with Little Lord Fauntleroy,' Debs says from her windowledge perch as she drags deeply on her cigarette and blows the smoke out into the sky.

'Looks like it,' I say. 'I don't know what came over Charlie. He announced out of the blue that he'd like to see Johnny this weekend. I was stunned. I was so worried about leaving him behind, but it's worked out really well for me. I can go away with Spencer – meet the parents . . .' We both grimace at that. 'It's good timing too, just before the project gets under way.'

'Yeah, no more free weekends for you, Kirberly's answer to Alan Titchmarsh.'

'I like a bit of Alan,' Dora chimes in. 'You know where you are with him. No smut. Lovely man. Lovely man.'

'Are you going to have that one, Dora?' I ask.

'Can't, love,' she says sadly. 'All my money's gone this week. Had to buy some new beddies. My others had worn right through.'

Perhaps if Dora didn't run round the estate in her slippers, they might last a bit longer. Still, it's not exactly as if she's blown her benefit on living the high life.

'I've got a little surprise for you. Spencer's given me some money

196

to treat you and Mrs Kapur. Pick whichever one you want.'

'Isn't that nice, Mrs Kapur?' Dora says, clapping her hands together. 'Our Sally's young man is buying us a necklace.'

'He doesn't have to do that, Sal,' Mrs Kapur says.

'I know, but he said that he'd like to.'

'Perhaps I'll have this one,' Mrs Kapur says, stroking her bling.

'It's frigging awful,' Debs says, carelessly flicking her cigarette out of the window and sliding down from the ledge. There'll be no more of that once this project starts. All litter will be properly disposed of. You're going to be able to eat your dinner off the pavements on this estate, come the revolution. 'Let me pick you something a bit more tasteful, love.'

Mrs Kapur eases herself from the sofa and shuffles to the table, smiling broadly. 'Perhaps we ought to try them all on again just to make sure which one we like the best.'

Dora clearly likes the idea and pounces on the jewellery again.

'That all right, Kathy?' I check with the jewellery lady.

Kathy, sitting contentedly in the corner with a big glass of wine, smiles on. 'No worries, girl.'

I sidle up to Debs as she's sorting purposefully through the chains, dangly earrings and bracelets. 'Do you think I'm doing the right thing?'

'About what?'

'Spencer wants me to meet his parents. Isn't it a bit soon for that sort of thing?'

'If you ask me, even the wedding day's a bit too early to meet the in-laws. It's best left until about five years after you're married. Preferably longer.'

'We're staying in their house.'

'In Outerbumblefuck?'

'Yeah.'

'Where exactly is that?'

'I'm not sure. Surrey somewhere.'

'You say that he's taking all his mates along too?'

'Yeah.'

'Can't be a little two-up, two-down then.'

'I guess not.'

'Isn't that a bit weird? What's a bloke like Spencer still doing living with his folks?'

'I don't know,' I say. 'But it looks as if I'm about to find out.'

Chapter Sixty-Five

'We'll take the football up to the school field, lad,' Johnny said. Ringo barked enthusiastically when he heard the word 'football'. 'I've just got to drop into the garage first.'

'You could go to the garage tomorrow,' Charlie suggested. 'Or maybe Sunday.'

'Best get it out of the way. I need to order some paint but I can't remember what colours I'm short of. It won't take long.'

'But it's still nice and sunny, Johnny,' Charlie whined. 'We could be playing football instead. It'll be dark soon.'

'Five minutes,' Johnny said. It wasn't like the boy to complain. Perhaps he was just edging nearer towards those teenage years when it was compulsory to complain about everything. 'That's all I'll be. I promise. I haven't been there for a few days and I need to get this done.'

He put his arm round Charlie's shoulder and shepherded him towards the door of Sally's flat. Ringo followed at heel. 'Normally you like to go up to my workshop.'

Charlie shrugged uncomfortably, and Johnny wondered if the lad was feeling a bit out of sorts because his mum had gone away with her new fella again. Though, if he believed Sally's account, it was Charlie who'd suggested that they spend the weekend together.

His ex would be on her way now to Spencer Knight's home in the country. It was best if he tried not to think about that. Every day that passed seemed to take Sally further away from him, and it was something that he was going to have to live with. He'd just try to enjoy the time that he had with Charlie before Spencer muscled in on that as well.

They walked up to the garages, ball tucked under Charlie's arm, Johnny burbling away to cover the lad's reticence. His little friend's steps got slower and slower as they got nearer to the workshop, and Ringo hung back with him.

'Come on, our Charlie,' Johnny said. 'Otherwise this is going to take a lot longer than five minutes.' And he tried to hurry the boy and dog along — without success.

As they approached the garage, Johnny could tell that something wasn't right. The up and over door wasn't fully closed. Not a good sign. 'Someone's been in the garage.' He put a spurt on, rushing towards it. The little dog chased after him, barking.

When he turned back, he saw that Charlie was rooted to the spot, his face white.

'Stay there,' Johnny instructed. He didn't want them both to go blundering in if any of the intruders were still inside.

When he got to the door, Johnny stood stock still outside. He put a hand out and Ringo was silenced too. Inside there was no noise. It seemed like whoever had broken in had already gone. Probably just as well, as Johnny would have liked to flatten them, the bastards.

Swinging open the door, Johnny gawped at the scene of devastation that greeted him. He felt like he'd been thumped in the chest. Paint had been thrown all round the garage, his canvases scattered all over the place. Some had been kicked in. He let out a deep, shuddering breath. Ringo whined in sympathy.

Then he heard a sobbing noise and turned to see Charlie standing behind him, crying.

Johnny put an arm round his shoulder and pulled the boy towards him. 'Don't worry, our kid,' he said. 'Probably looks a lot worse than it is.' He wasn't sure that was strictly true.

Charlie leaned against him and sobbed noisily. Ringo put his paws up on the boy's legs and licked at them.

'Little bastards,' Johnny muttered. 'I'd like to get my hands on the scum who did this.'

'Your paintings are ruined.'

'Not all of them.' Johnny wandered aimlessly into the garage. The splattered paint had now dried. This had probably been done a day or two earlier. He picked up and moved a couple of the broken canvases. 'Looks like some are missing though.'

Why couldn't people leave well enough alone these days? Why was it that everything that was good or clean or beautiful had to be sullied? Still Charlie sniffed loudly, tears rolling down his face. To be honest, Johnny felt like joining in. It was all very well, people like Sally wanting to champion good causes, clean up the area, but when things like this happened it made you wonder why anyone bothered. Why shouldn't all the decent people just move out and leave the trash behind to wallow in their own muck?

'I should call the police,' Johnny said. He felt Charlie start at that. 'But what would be the point? This is one of a dozen things like this that happen every single day. Where would they start? Besides, they're not interested in helping the likes of us.'

'I'll help you to tidy up,' Charlie said. 'It won't take long if we try really hard. We could get it done before Mum comes back.'

'Yeah,' Johnny said. 'Let's get some of these canvases stacked up again. See what the damage is.'

As he moved into the garage, Ringo started playing with something on the floor that had caught his eye. 'Leave it,' Johnny said, and the little dog stood aside. There was a piece of toilet paper with a cigarette butt wrapped carefully inside it. 'Hmm,' Johnny said. Where had that come from? 'Seems the vandals have left a little clue behind. Maybe I should call the police after all.'

At that, Charlie burst out crying again.

Chapter Sixty-Six

We've been driving for hours now. Down the M6, then the M1 and, finally, the M25. The Porsche has eaten up the miles and now we're winding down country lanes as dusk is closing in. My eyes are getting heavy and I'll be glad of my bed tonight. Wonder if Spencer and I will be sharing a room or whether his parents are the old-fashioned kind and I'll be sleeping chastely down the hall.

Spencer pats my knee. 'Nearly there.'

Minutes later we swing through a pair of majestic gates and head up a drive that's lined on either side with trees, possibly poplars. They're tall and straight, anyway. The lights from Spencer's car pick out a rash of bunnies hopping across the surrounding parkland, white tails bobbing as they scatter in alarm. In the distance, a mellow stone building looms ahead of us. It looks like a posh hotel. Welcoming lights blaze from every window.

'Are we stopping here for dinner?'

Spencer turns and grins at me. 'This is it,' he says. 'Alderstone House. My home.'

When I say Alderstone House, think as far away as possible from Bill Shankly House and you'll just about have it. I do a gasp and a gulp at the same time and nearly choke myself. I splutter out loud, 'No way!'

'Do you like it?'

My guess is that this place is Georgian, something like that. My lack of knowledge involving trees is second only to my ignorance concerning the architecture of stately homes.

'You're not a lord or something, are you?'

'Heavens no!' Spencer laughs. 'My family are commoners.'

Mine too. But some of us are way more common than others.

I still can't believe this is true. 'You're having me on.'

'No,' Spencer says. 'This is it. We're here.' And with that he pulls up outside the main part of the building, showering gravel in our wake.

Alderstone House has two enormous wings and, in the time I've got, I can't even begin to count all of the windows. The place is vast. It should be a hotel. I can't believe that normal people live here.

A man in a formal dark jacket comes out of the enormous front door and I wonder whether this is Spencer's dad.

'Good evening, Mr Spencer,' he says as he opens the car door. 'I hope you had a pleasant journey.'

'Wonderful,' Spencer says. 'This is Miss Sally.'

'Good evening,' the man says deferentially.

I feel as if I should curtsey for him.

'This is Brookes.' Clearly not Spencer's dad then.

'Hello, Brookes.'

'Cook has prepared a light supper for you in the dining room, sir.'

'Thank you. We'll just take a minute to freshen up before eating.'

It's fair, at this point, to say that I feel somewhat underdressed in my jeans and my Asda price military jacket.

'I've taken the liberty of putting Miss Sally in the Princess of Wales bedroom.'

'That's fine, Brookes.'

'I'll bring your bags straight up, sir.' And with that we sweep into the house, leaving this poor old bloke to carry our bags. Though, to be fair, we're not exactly packing excess baggage, Spencer's car having a boot the size of a ham sandwich.

If the outside of the house is breathtaking, inside the hall nearly makes my lungs collapse. It's bigger than my entire flat, much bigger. The floor is covered with black and white marble tiles. Huge paintings depicting horses cover the walls and, as you well know, I'm no art expert, but these look like the real deal. In the centre of the hall hangs an enormous golden lantern.

'That's beautiful,' I whisper. This is not a room you could talk out loud in.

'Ormolu,' Spencer says, as if that would mean something to me. 'Eighteenth century.'

'Has this been your home for a long time?'

'Five hundred years or so,' he says dismissively, as if he's told me they picked it up in 1975 for a song.

'Come on,' he says, taking my hand. 'Let's find your room.' Spencer leads me out of the hall and up the oak staircase ahead of us. Portraits of his ancestors line the walls and I have to say that they're all a handsome bunch. No wonder Spencer likes art galleries so much — his own home looks just like one. At the top of the stairs, there's a gold brocade chaise longue and above it hangs a painting of a formidable couple. The woman's slim with long blond hair and she's wearing a red evening gown and a single string of pearls. The man's in a black suit and looks like an older, harder version of Spencer.

'Mother and Father,' he confirms. They look like a force to be reckoned with.

I haven't got any pictures of my ancestors. They were probably all too poor to afford cameras, let alone commissioned portraits. Spencer guides me along the corridor, past a dozen different doors.

'This is a very peaceful corner of the house,' he tells me as he opens the door. 'You have lovely views of the gardens.'

A four-poster bed dominates the enormous room. The canopy and the headboard are covered in a lavish cream, green and terracotta fabric decorated with gold. The bedspread's made of cream and gold plush velvet which is just begging me to bury myself in it. A crystal chandelier hangs from the ceiling. More portraits adorn the walls and there's a gilt mirror above the marble fireplace.

'This is gorgeous,' I breathe in a hushed voice. I'm going to have to get used to talking at a normal level in this place, but it's all so overwhelming.

'Come and look at the view.' Spencer takes my hand and we walk to the window. Formal gardens border the house, then, for as far as the eye can see, there are rolling fields.

'You own all this?'

Spencer nods.

'Why didn't you tell me?'

'Could I have described this?' he says. 'I wanted you to see it for yourself.'

I look up at his handsome face that's glowing with pride. He clearly adores this place and I can easily understand why. 'What are you doing with me, Spencer Knight?'

'I love you,' he says, and holds me in his arms.

This is all too much to take in. It's as if I've been transported into a new world, a world that I didn't know existed, and in which I feel like I don't belong. 'Why is this called the Princess of Wales room?'

'Because Diana stayed here once,' he tells me. 'When she was a girl.'

'*The* Diana?'

'Yes,' he says. 'My parents have dined out on it since. But do you know what the best thing is about this room?'

I shake my head. He takes my hand again and tugs me gently over to a big oak door. He flings it open. 'It adjoins my room.'

'Oh?' That makes me smile. 'And what's your room called?'

'The Spencer Seduction Suite,' he teases.

And, for the first time, I think I might be able to relax and enjoy myself here.

Chapter Sixty-Seven

The dining room is just as vast as the other rooms – no cosy nook here. It's decorated in rich shades of burgundy and dark blue. Another rash of portraits cover the walls and I'm beginning to think that the Knights were a vain lot.

A mahogany table dominates the room. Around it are sixteen intricately carved chairs. Spencer and I sit opposite each other at one end. Our voices echo in the void.

'Hungry?' Spencer asks.

'Starving,' I say, though my stomach is a mass of anxiety.

Supper is a simple affair – a platter of cheese, some crusty bread and a tureen of home-made soup. Except that the platter and the tureen both appear to be silver, as is the cutlery. The crockery is white, edged with gold and is made of a china so fine that I can almost see through it.

'What was it like growing up here?'

'Wonderful,' Spencer says, as he cuts into the cheese. 'Although I spent a lot of time away at school.'

'I wouldn't ever want to leave somewhere like this.' Though it does feel a bit like living in a museum.

'I'll take you on a tour after supper, if you'd like. Help you to get your bearings. This place is a bit of a rabbit warren.'

'I'd love it.' The soup's hot and nourishing and I can feel my tension dropping away as it warms me through. 'Are your parents around tonight?'

'Brookes has probably told them we've arrived,' he says, 'but I expect we'll see them in the morning.'

How strange that they don't want to see their son as soon as they know he's here. Perhaps they're giving him time to get me acclimatised.

'When are your friends coming?'

'They'll be here after breakfast,' he tells me. 'Small turnout during the day, I'm afraid. There'll be just the eight of us. But they're all dying to meet you. Another crowd will be arriving in the evening, then things will liven up.'

Not sure if I'm feeling quite the same level of enthusiasm about meeting them. I've got this vision of them all being snooty Hooray Henry types who'll hate me on sight.

'You'll love them,' Spencer assures me, and I hope that he's right.

After our meal we wander through room after sumptuous room, each one seemingly more grand than the last. I want to know how Spencer's family made their money to be able to afford all of this, but it seems rude to ask. I'll have to Google him when I get back to my computer. Who knew that the internet would come in so handy?

We take in the picture gallery and our footsteps clonk on the oak flooring just like they did in the Tate. Charlie could skateboard the length of here. Then there's the south drawing room, which Dora would love as it has more sofas than DFS. After that comes a library and a room with a full-size billiard table.

Another dining room and I lose count at thirty chairs. Then there's a comfortable lounge which has more normal proportions compared to the rest of their house. This only has six sofas in it, along with myriad other furniture. I stifle a yawn.

'I think it's time for us to retire,' Spencer says.

'I've walked further round your house than I have in years,' I tell him.

He laughs at that – but, to be honest, it wasn't a joke.

'There's plenty of time. We can have a look at the rest of it tomorrow.'

The rest of it? I can tell that Spencer's not joking either.

In the Spencer Seduction Suite, I curl into his arms under a canopy of golden silk. This is a bed fit for a princess and – for all I know – there might have been one or two in here already. What a privileged existence Spencer has – and I'd really no idea. I'd pictured him living in a big, posh detached house in a prissy cul-de-sac, but nothing on this scale had even remotely crossed my mind.

The featherlight duvet floats above us as I sink into the contours of the bed and it cocoons me, creating a lovely sanctuary that feels safe from the world. Spencer's naked next to me and I think I might have died and gone to heaven.

'Oh,' I say. 'This is absolute bliss.'

'Can you imagine yourself living here?'

'No,' I say, 'my imagination's not that vivid.' He moves above me and kisses me deeply. My senses swim. 'What are you doing in my life, Spencer Knight?'

'I'm hoping to make it better,' he murmurs against my neck. Then he proceeds to show me how.

Chapter Sixty-Eight

We take breakfast in the same dining room as we used last night. Sunshine is flooding through the windows making the austere room feel warm and welcoming.

Mr and Mrs Knight are already seated at the table when we arrive.

'Mother,' Spencer says heartily, and goes over to kiss her on both cheeks.

'Hello, dear. Are you well?'

'Fine,' Spencer says. He takes my hand and urges me forward. 'This is Sally,' he announces.

His mother smiles at me, but I can't tell if it's genuine or forced. It's kind of wavering between the two. 'Spencer's told us so much about you,' she murmurs.

I do hope not.

By this time, Mr Knight has lowered his copy of *The Times* and is glowering at me over the top of it.

'Father,' Spencer says. 'This is Sally.'

I hold out my hand. Mr Knight sort of harrumphs at me. And I let my hand fall back to my side.

'You have a lovely home,' I tell him, at which he harrumphs some more. It's very hard not to start talking like Julie Andrews in their presence. Never have I been more aware of quite how Scouse I sound.

'Thank you,' Mrs Knight says, as her husband seems to have lost his tongue.

The room may feel warm and welcoming, but my hosts are most definitely not. I may not have good breeding and have been dragged up in a council house, but I'd like to think that guests to my humble home wouldn't be treated as rudely.

There's a buffet set out on one of magnificent sideboards and Spencer ushers me in its direction. 'Come on,' he says. 'Help yourself.'

I put a few things on my plate, some bread, some jam — can't say that I feel brave enough to tackle a boiled egg while I'm under such scrutiny. Spencer and I take our seats. There's very little in the way of conversation. How different from my own breakfast-table, with Charlie chattering on and Radio Merseyside burbling along in the background. When Johnny was with us, he'd chat away too and then there was always his dog under your feet. You could hear a pin drop in here and suddenly I get a pang of longing for my son and my own small, scruffy life.

Mrs Knight makes me jump when she speaks. 'Spencer tells me you have a son.'

'Yeah. Yes. Charlie. He's ten. He's a lovely boy. Isn't he, Spencer?'

'Lovely,' Spencer agrees.

'And Charlie's father?'

In Walton Prison for armed robbery, actually. 'We have no contact with him now.'

'Pity,' Mrs Knight observes.

'Not really. Charlie and I do all right for ourselves.'

More harrumphing from behind the newspaper.

'Family is so important,' Mrs Knight observes.

'Depends what your family are like,' I counter, and Spencer's mother stares at me levelly. I hold her gaze, as no one can outstare Sally Freeman, Single Mum and Superwoman.

Then, as my blood sets up a slow boil, Brookes comes to the door of the dining room. 'Miss Arabella Fostrup and Mr Toby Jessop have arrived.'

'Splendid,' Spencer says, putting down his napkin. 'Just four more, but they should be here shortly. I thought we'd all go riding this morning. It's a beautiful day for it.'

That pulls me up short. 'Riding?'

Spencer turns to me, looking vaguely aghast. 'You do ride?'

I lower my voice slightly. 'Spencer, you've seen where I live. I don't think I actually saw a horse until I was fifteen.' And then it was probably a police horse at the Liverpool football ground. 'Of course I don't ride.'

'You don't ride!' Mrs Knight exclaims in incredulous tones.

'Sorry, Sally,' Spencer apologises. 'I never even thought . . . I just assumed . . .' Clearly he has never dated a woman with inadequacies in her equestrian skills. 'We can do something else.'

'No, no,' I say. 'It doesn't matter. You can all go riding and I'll have a walk in the gardens or read while you're gone.'

'I had sort of promised the others . . .' Spencer says.

'That's fine. There are plenty of ways that I can entertain myself for a few hours.'

'We'll all get together for a picnic for lunch.'

That sounds more like it.

'I'll make it up to you,' Spencer says. 'I promise.'

And I ignore the chilly looks from his parents and think that sounds even better.

Chapter Sixty-Nine

At the back of the house and across the beautiful gardens are the stables. Set within a massive building in warm honey-coloured stone, they're almost as grand as the house. Lush green ivy meanders up the walls. The surrounding lawns are mown into regimental stripes, and the sky's a rich shade of Tuscan blue. I wouldn't mind being a horse if it meant that I could move in here.

Spencer is striding out across the gravel path in his hacking jacket and jodhpurs. I'm tottering alongside in Dolcis heels and outfit by Matalan. Some more of Spencer's friends have arrived and now the other couples are waiting in the stable courtyard, all suitably attired.

There's much hugging, kissing and backslapping. Except for me, of course.

'Sally, you must meet everyone.' Spencer urges me forward when, quite honestly, I'd rather melt into the background, vanish into thin air, go up in a puff of smoke.

'Arabella and Toby.' I get a rather cool handshake from both of them. Arabella casts a disdainful eye over my clothes. So I do the same to her. Unfortunately, she's immaculately turned out, whereas I'm not. Spencer and I made love again this morning, so the time I had for hair and make-up was deliciously eaten into. I smile at the thought. I may not be able to ride a horse, but at least my gorgeous boyfriend has a chin.

I wonder, are the rest of Spencer's friends going to be such hard work?

'This is Phoebe and Max.' Phoebe nods curtly at me. She has a perfect figure, perfect hair and a perfect face. And she knows it. Max is a little more effusive and shakes my hand so vigorously that I'm worried it might drop off.

The last of the couples is Tania and James. Tania kisses me warmly on both cheeks, which takes me aback. James is equally welcoming.

211

Just when I thought that this was going to be a very long weekend, there might just be some relief in sight.

'The horses are ready,' Spencer says, and a groom starts to lead them out in the courtyard. Tania hangs back as the others make their way towards their mounts.

'Don't mind that lot,' she says, as she links her arm through mine. 'Arabella and Phoebe are both Spencer's cast-offs and they're wildly jealous that he's finally found someone he wants to settle down with.'

He has? This is news to me.

'Spencer's told me so much about you. I'm sure you'll win them over. Arabella's just green with envy, wondering what you've got that she hasn't.'

Can't quite see it myself, I have to say.

The others are ready and waiting. With a friendly squeeze of my arm Tania leaves my side – although I want to beg her not to – and gets onto her own horse.

Spencer comes over and slips his arm round me. 'I'll be back as soon as I can,' he whispers. 'I feel awful leaving you behind.'

'Don't worry about me,' I say. 'Really. I'm going to have a wander in the grounds. Take as long as you need. Enjoy yourself.'

He kisses me again and bounds up onto his horse.

Arabella looks down at me. 'Not joining us, Sally?'

'I can't ride.'

She sniggers at that.

I might not be able to ride, but I have better manners than you, lady. 'But you all have a lovely time. I'll see you later.'

With that they all trot out of the stable courtyard, Spencer waving over his shoulder.

My spirit sinks as I stand alone and watch them disappear from view. Now what? I feel the hours stretching ahead of me and I should be grateful for this time to myself – an unexpected oasis of peace in this beautiful setting with no one to impress, no one to defend myself to. As soon as I get back to Kirberly I'll be straight into the regeneration project and my life won't be my own for weeks. I feel exhausted just thinking about it. There's such a lot to do and I'm so glad that Johnny will be alongside me, watching my back. I resist the urge to text my friend.

Taking the path behind the stables, I stroll further away from the house. The path is lined with mature trees, cool in the morning sun.

It's still hard to believe that I'm here in this place, Spencer's home. How strange it is that our lives have crossed, our worlds collided. At the end of the path, there's a large, oval-shaped lake. Ducks quack happily and I stop for the first time in my life and listen to birdsong.

There's a summerhouse at the end of the lake made of white stone with ornately carved pillars. Inside, there's a big stone bench and I ease myself down onto it, resting my head back. I haven't brought a book or a magazine, although I did rifle through a stash that was in the drawing room; it mainly consisted of *Horse and Hounds*, *The Illustrated Garden* and *Harpers and Queen* – none of which held much appeal. My eyes are growing heavy and I let them close, enjoying the sun on my face. I let my mind run over the plans I have for the estate back home. It might not involve a grand summerhouse and an oval lake, but I think that it will look so much better when we're done. There's a scruffy area of enclosed grass behind Bill Shankly House that I can see transformed as a secret garden where Mrs Kapur can sit and Dora the Explorer can roam free.

In the middle of my reverie, I hear footsteps on the gravel. Opening my eyes, I see Spencer's father approaching. He's wearing a blue open-necked shirt with a red spotted cravat and brown trousers. I feel as if he should be an Earl or a Duke or something and I'm sure that he does too.

Without saying anything, he sits down next to me and stares out over the lake.

'It's a lovely morning,' I venture, when it's clear that he's not planning to open the conversation.

'My ancestors built this lake,' he says. 'In 1868. The grounds were designed by Capability Brown.'

Even I've heard of him.

'Our line goes back a long way.'

Doesn't everyone's?

'It's very important to me that it's preserved.'

'I'm sure.' Not quite certain where this is leading. But I'm sure it involves me and I'm equally certain that it's not good.

'I wanted Spencer to go and have a taste of real life before he takes over the running of the estate,' Mr Knight tells me. 'Learn the skills that he'll need when dealing with our household.' He turns and looks at me for the first time. 'I realise that we have a very privileged life and that there are those who aren't quite as fortunate as ourselves. I wanted Spencer to fully understand that before I handed over the reins to him.'

Ah, so that's why Spencer's working in Kirberly. Because Daddy wanted him to get in among the under-privileged folk. It's all coming clear now. Perhaps it wasn't entirely for the altruistic reasons he'd have me believe.

'He was starting to run wild. Too much booze, too many women. I wanted him to see that he needed to settle down. With this estate comes heavy responsibility. My son needed to see what life was like on the other side of the fence.'

So you thought you'd teach him a lesson by sending him off to do a menial job to prove himself whilst dangling the running of the estate like a carrot. *Be a good boy and Daddy will let you have your reward.*

'The thing is, my dear . . .' Mr Knight turns to study the lake again '. . . I hadn't expected him to form an attachment.'

The phrase 'to one of you lowly scumbags' is left unsaid, but I can do subtext. So that's what this is all about. I'm to be warned off his precious son.

'Spencer is our only child,' he continues. 'The sole heir to our fortune. We have to protect that. You do understand?'

'Of course.'

'It's important that he marries someone suitable.'

Looks as if Spencer's father also thinks that he's got his cap set at me. I'm the only one, it seems, who's unaware of this.

'I'm sure that Spencer's perfectly capable of choosing a wife who'll make him very happy,' I say firmly.

'But this isn't about happiness, my dear.' He says 'my dear' again as if it's an insult. 'It's about duty. It's about choosing someone who will be the right person to run Alderstone with him.'

'You make the process of finding a wife sound like a job interview.'

Mr Knight smiles indulgently. 'Sometimes when one foolishly believes one is in love, all reason goes out of the window.'

'Spencer *is* an adult. He'll make the right choice for himself.'

His father tsks-tsks. 'I'm rather less sure of that. There are a lot of women who have their sights set on Spencer's fortune.'

'Well, I'm not one of them,' I tell him crisply. And his son's certainly not after me for my money. But I don't think that I need to point that out.

Mr Knight stands and pats my hand patronisingly. 'You're a very pleasant young lady to look at, but beyond that I can't see what hold you have over my son. You're not one of our kind.' He slowly, deliberately, takes in my cheap jeans, my cheap blouse. 'We'll tolerate you at Alderstone for as long as this relationship continues, but I wanted you to be absolutely clear that you'll never, ever be welcome here on a permanent basis. Not as long as I live.'

My mouth drops open. Mr Knight walks away from me. And, at that point, my mobile phone comes to life and the sound of Gnarls Barkley singing 'Crazy' slices through the atmosphere.

Chapter Seventy

On the other end of the phone, Charlie's crying. 'What's wrong?' I ask anxiously. 'Just calm down and tell me.' But the sobs only get louder.

'Come home, Mum,' he sniffs.

There's a chill round my heart. 'What's wrong? Are you hurt?'

My son takes a shuddering breath. 'Johnny's garage has been done over.'

'Done over?'

'Someone got in and smashed up his paintings. There's stuff everywhere.'

'Oh no.'

'Come home, Mum,' Charlie implores again. His tears make my inside tie up in knots.

'Is Johnny okay?'

'Yeah.'

'Is he there with you?'

'He's in the other room. He doesn't know that I'm phoning you.'

'Put him on.'

A moment later Johnny's voice comes down the line and I feel a surge of relief.

'Hi, Sal,' he says.

'What's happened?'

'The garage has been broken into, but it's not too bad.'

'Little bastards.' The sooner we manage to get a grip on this estate, the better. 'Charlie said that your paintings have all been smashed up.'

'Some of them, yeah.' Johnny lowers his voice. 'I'm not sure why Charlie's taking this so badly though. He's very upset. He's not stopped crying since we found the place in a mess last night.'

'You think there's something else?'

There's a pause and Johnny says softly, 'I think maybe he's just missing his mum.'

The words pierce my heart. 'I'll come straight back.'

'You don't need to do that, Sally. I can manage. He'll probably be all right now that he's spoken to you.'

'How can I enjoy the rest of the weekend knowing that Charlie's so upset? I'll come back. I have to.' My friend doesn't argue with me. I wish we had beam-me-up-Scotty machines and I could ping myself home in an instant. Surrey feels like a million miles away. 'Thanks for looking after him, Johnny. I should never have left him again so soon. Look, I'm really sorry to hear about your garage. We'll talk more when I get back. Can you put Charlie on again, please?'

I hear my son sniffing on the other end of the phone. 'I'll be home before you know it,' I tell him. 'Don't cry. Be my big boy. We'll sort this out. Try not to worry about it.' That sets him off again. 'I'm going to hang up now, but I'll be back as soon as I can. Okay?'

There's a mumbled 'Okay,' in response.

'Love you,' I say.

'Love you too, Mum.'

'See you soon.' Then I hang up. Hadn't quite thought through the logistics of my hasty departure, but I decide the first thing to do is go back to the house and pack up my stuff. As soon as Spencer returns he can take me to the nearest railway station and I'll be off.

Staying in my room keeps me out of the way of Mr Knight too. Won't he be delighted to hear that I'm high-tailing it out of here? After this, I want nothing more to do with Spencer's family, who clearly think that they're so much better than I am. I wouldn't run their precious house for them if they paid me. Just because they've got a stately home and horses and whatnot, they think that they can speak to me like I'm some kind of serf. Well, I can't wait to get back to Charlie and Bill Shankly House and people who love me. How on earth did two such crashing snobs manage to raise such a well-balanced son? While I'm pacing, I hear the sound of horses' hooves approaching the house.

Grabbing my overnight bag, I rush out of the bedroom, clatter down the stairs and dash out to the stables.

Spencer and his pals are all laughing breathlessly when they ride into the stables. I'm standing there clutching my bag. My lover slips down from his horse, handing the reins to a waiting groom.

His face is flushed from exertion, his hair tousled. He has an air of the Mr Darcy about him and my heart – worried as it is – flips when I see him.

217

'What's wrong?' he says, as he eyes my bag.

'It's Charlie,' I tell him. 'I have to go home. I have to go home now.'

'Is he hurt?'

'No.'

'Ill then?'

'No, no. He's upset. He's missing me. And there's been an incident. A break-in at Johnny's garage.'

Spencer leads me away from the group. 'But why do you have to go?'

'They need me.'

'I need you too,' Spencer says, stroking my arm.

'I can't be here,' I say. 'Not now.' Probably not ever. 'If you can take me to the nearest train station?'

'Sally,' he says with a sigh, 'I'll take you wherever you want to go – you know that. But I'd ask you to reconsider. The rest of my friends are coming this evening. I have a lovely picnic and dinner organised. You'll love it. We can leave straight after breakfast tomorrow and we'll be back by lunchtime. Won't Charlie be all right until then?'

'I can't stay,' I say. Now that I've made my mind up, I just want out of here. 'It's no good trying to persuade me.'

Spencer's shoulders sag. 'I'll drive you back.'

'You can't do that,' I tell him. 'You've got a houseful of guests to entertain. I can't drag you away.'

'I want to be with you, Ms Freeman. Don't you understand that?'

'I'll get a train. Really. I'll be fine.' There's a slight bit of bravado going on here, because I don't actually have the money to pay for a train fare. If Spencer agrees to drop me off, then he's going to have to give me a loan too.

'Let me at least get one of the staff to take you home,' he says with a resigned look. 'If you go by train you'll have to change in London. It'll take you hours. I'll sort you out with a driver. That'll be much quicker.'

'Thank you.' I'm on the verge of tears.

'I still wish you'd change your mind,' Spencer says. 'This isn't because I left you alone this morning? I would hate to have upset you.'

If he carries on being kind then I will cry. 'No, no,' I reassure him. 'I should never have left Charlie alone. This is too soon for him.'

He wraps his arms around me. 'This is my fault for being selfish.'

'No,' I say. 'I'm being a wimp, but I have to get back to my son.'

'I wish you'd let me come with you.'

'Please stay and entertain your friends. That would make me feel better.'

He kisses me. 'Then I'll see you tomorrow. I'll be back in the evening, but I'll come round to see you. Is that okay?'

'That's fine.'

'Sally,' Spencer says softly. 'You have loved Alderstone, haven't you?'

'It's been wonderful,' I lie. All I want to do is get out of here now. As fast as I can.

Chapter Seventy-One

Charlie was talking to Kyle. He was still feeling all girly and cry-babyish, but he was trying not to let his eyes leak all over the place in front of his friend.

They were sitting on a wall at the edge of the estate. A view of the whole of Liverpool was in front of them. If Charlie tried really hard and screwed up his eyes a bit, he was sure that he could see the Albert Dock and where they'd taken Johnny's paintings to the Tate Liverpool Gallery.

He passed the now obligatory cigarette back to his friend. 'We could be in big trouble.'

'Nah,' Kyle said, but Charlie thought that he didn't sound very sure.

'What if the police find out that it was us?'

'We didn't smash up the paintings,' Kyle pointed out. 'We just borrowed a couple. For Johnny's own good.'

'But it was our fault that the baddies got into Johnny's garage,' Charlie reminded Kyle. 'We could be blamed.' He felt like crying again. 'I only wanted to help Johnny.'

'I knew it was a bad idea,' his friend said.

Charlie tried to think. Hadn't it all been Kyle's idea in the first place? He felt so mixed up that now he wasn't sure at all. 'We could go to prison.'

Kyle shook his head. 'You don't go to prison for that kind of stuff,' he said confidently. 'You have to do really bad stuff before they lock you up now. Murder and . . . and . . . that kind of thing.'

That was a relief. Charlie didn't want to go to prison. They probably wouldn't let you have Coco Pops for breakfast there. Still, it was a worry. 'What will happen to us if they do find out?'

His friend's eyes brightened with excitement. 'We'll probably get an ASBO.'

That sounded dreadful. 'What's an ASBO?'

Kyle thought for a minute. 'It's an Anti-Social Boys Organisation.'

'And we'd have to join it?'

'It'd be great,' Kyle assured him. 'It makes you look big. Everyone's got one these days.'

'I don't think my mum would like it.' In fact, he was pretty sure that she'd kill him. 'What would your mum say?'

'She wouldn't mind as long as it didn't mean I had to stay in the house more.'

'Huh.' Charlie took his turn with the ciggie. Kyle's mum seemed different from his own mum. She didn't seem to mind what Kyle did. He could stay out really late and not get told off. He could eat what he wanted whenever he wanted. Sometimes he had ice cream for breakfast and she didn't say a thing! That must be great. 'My mum's on her way home. She's gone somewhere posh with that fella for the weekend.'

'That was so he wouldn't tell on us,' Kyle reminded him.

'Oh yeah.' Charlie had forgotten all about that.

'Did that bloke from the gallery ever ring you about the paintings?'

'Nah,' Charlie said. 'Perhaps he doesn't want to buy them after all.'

'You think he'd phone,' Kyle tutted. 'You can't rely on grown-ups these days.'

Charlie hoped that Spencer was reliable and remembered not to tell tales about them to his mum. The boy had missed her this weekend. His mum might tell him off a lot, but he liked it better when she was there.

The cigarette was finished and he stubbed it out on the wall. Sometimes he didn't think that he really liked smoking at all. It made his mouth taste funny. He jumped down. 'I'd better be getting back,' he said. 'Johnny'll be worried about me.'

'Everyone worries about you,' Kyle said, and there was something in his voice that Charlie didn't understand.

Kyle was right though. His mum would be worried too. He didn't cry very often and Charlie knew that she didn't like it when he did. He'd be glad when she was home again. The only bad thing about his mum coming back was that she'd know. She'd just *know*. She was a lot like Kyle really. Somehow, some way, she knew *everything*.

Chapter Seventy-Two

The journey home seems to take forever. I'm sure Surrey wasn't this far when we were going. One of Spencer's staff, Eddie, drives me all the way back without stopping. We don't speak much as we speed along the motorways and I sit in the back of the huge, posh car feeling self-conscious.

Eventually, hours later, he pulls up outside Bill Shankly House, his face inscrutable.

'Thanks,' I say. 'Thanks so much.' I don't know what to do now. Do I tip him, invite him in? The poor man's going to have to turn round and drive straight back – all that way. 'Do you want a coffee or something?'

Eddie casts a glance over the flats. 'No thanks,' he says. 'Better be going.' Bet he can't wait to get out of here in his shiny motor. Well, let me tell you, if he comes back here in a few months' time he won't recognise the place.

'Thanks again.' I drag my bag behind me as I get out of the car and then trudge the ten flights up to my home. Now, of course, I'm thinking that I shouldn't have been in quite so much of a rush to leave Alderstone House and Spencer behind.

But when I stick my key in the lock, I hear Charlie shout out, 'It's Mum!' and the next minute he barrels into me, nearly knocking me flying. It's like having my very own Andrex puppy in human form.

He grips me in a bear hug as if he's never going to let me go.

'Did you miss me?' I ask.

I feel my son's head nod against my chest. I kiss his hair, enjoying the smell of it despite the pound of gel that's in it. When I look up, Johnny's standing in the hall looking bashful. Even though we've split up I still get a rush when I see him. That's got to be odd, right?

'Good journey back?' he says.

'Okay,' I answer. 'One of Spencer's staff drove me.'

222

I see him flinch slightly at that. 'Spencer has *staff*?'

Turning Charlie round, I push him gently towards the kitchen. 'Go and make your old mum a cup of tea.' He clicks his fingers at Ringo, who trots after him, and then my son goes and does as he's told without argument. Definitely something wrong with him.

Johnny and I go through to the living room. 'Remember that old telly series *Brideshead Revisited*?'

'Yeah. Just about.'

'That's Spencer's life,' I tell him.

'Wow.'

'Wow indeed,' I agree. 'His house is a stately home and his mates are all Hooray Henrys.'

'Seriously?'

'Yeah.'

'So what's he doing round here?'

'Seems like Daddy wants him to experience the real world before taking over the running of the family estate.'

'Kirberly's certainly the real world,' Johnny muses. 'I'm sorry that you had to come back to it.'

'I'm not,' I reassure him. 'Not really.' How can I begin to explain to Johnny how like a fish out of water I felt in Spencer's world? How can I tell him that I couldn't wait to get back to Charlie, to him, to Mrs Kapur, even the mad, sad Dora the Explorer – people who love me. How can I tell him how much Spencer's father dissed me and thought I was some sink-estate gold digger?

While I'm contemplating all of this, Johnny says, 'Charlie's been inconsolable. I don't know why.' He gives his head a bemused shake. 'It's not like him.'

'Particularly when it was his idea to spend the weekend with you.' I sigh and flop down on the sofa. 'Maybe your assessment was right. Maybe he's just missing me more than he thought he would. I'm not going to go away on any more so-called "glamorous" weekends.' It doesn't matter how wonderful or exotic your surroundings are, if the people with you aren't very nice. 'I don't want to do anything that's going to mess up my kid.'

Johnny sits down next to me. I get the urge to curl up into his arms, but resist it. I'm feeling weak and vulnerable. It would be a Bad Thing.

'Sorry to hear about the garage.'

My friend sighs wearily. 'I might give up the painting as a bad job.

I'm just wasting time with it when I could be doing something more constructive.'

Heaven knows that I've told Johnny this often enough, but now I've changed my mind. He's good and he deserves to follow his dream – as we all do. 'Don't do that,' I urge. 'Stick at it.'

He looks unconvinced.

'For me,' I say.

He laughs. 'You know that I'd still do anything for you, you silly woman.' With that, he gives me a peck on the cheek. 'I'd better be going.'

'We should get all the stuff through to start the project by next weekend.' My own estate might not be quite like Spencer's, but my weekend away has made me even more determined to do something to stop the rot.

'I've put leaflets through everyone's door to ask them to be at the Community Centre for nine o'clock,' I go on.

'Optimistic.'

'That's me,' I say. 'You know, Johnny, I don't think I could do this without you.'

My ex stands, ready to leave. 'We'll make a formidable team.'

'We will.'

'I'm looking forward to it,' he says.

I kiss Johnny on the cheek. 'So am I.'

Chapter Seventy-Three

On Saturday morning just before nine o'clock a huge lorry arrives from the nearby DIY superstore. It's laden down with goodies, all paid for by our Government grant.

There's a good crowd of people here to greet its arrival. A cheer goes up when the lorry parks outside the Community Centre, leaving the driver looking very bemused. I record the moment for posterity on my mobile phone camera. Okay, so I might not bear comparison to ace photographer Annie Leibovitz, but I'd like to put a scrapbook together after we're all done. A sort of before and after. Proof that if I never, ever again achieve anything else in my life, that at least I once made a difference to something.

It's a beautiful morning. The sun's out already, the air's cool and crisp, which means that it's not yet too hot for grafting. Johnny's painted a banner on some plywood which he's attached above the door of the Community Centre. ALL YOU NEED IS LOVE is what it says. Actually, it seems we need a lot more than that, judging by the amount of stuff that's being delivered.

My friends are out in force. Even Debs, looking ever so slightly hungover, has made it here on time. Mrs Kapur in her usual sari in delicate fabric has found some pink flowery Wellingtons from somewhere that swamp her tiny frame and a big floppy hat with a daisy on it. She's clutching a paintbrush and looks ready for action. Dora the Explorer's in her second-best nightie and is well away singing 'I Could Have Danced All Night' and twirling herself round and round. Ringo's accompanying her by barking in circles, trying to chase his own tail. Dora sings louder. Clearly the excitement has got to her. All she looks ready for is the nut house, bless her.

'Dora,' I say. 'Mind the lorry.' And I herd her back onto the pavement where she continues to waltz with herself. Don't want to start the morning with one of the residents squashed. 'Charlie! Keep your eye on Dora for me.'

Charlie nods back to me. His friend Kyle is in tow, as always, and they're both looking a bit too keen to be helpful – which, in turn, is making me a bit suspicious. Would love to know what those two have been up to. Charlie's been clinging to my legs all week since I came back from Spencer's place.

Speaking of which – my lover is here too. Things have been a little cool between us this week, it has to be said. I still can't get over how mean his father was to me and I know that's not Spencer's fault, but . . . Well, it hurt, nevertheless. Just as it was intended to.

Spencer slips his arm round my waist. He's been a bit distant all week too and I wonder whether he's having second thoughts about ditching Arabella or Phoebe or Tania – all women who are eminently more suitable as the future Mrs Spencer Knight and mistress of Alderstone House than I would ever be. The knowledge of that fact doesn't make me feel any happier.

'Nervous?' Spencer asks.

'Yeah.' Perhaps not surprisingly, I am. There's a buzz of excited tension in the air and, somehow, I feel that I'm responsible for it. There is, I know, a lot of expectation resting on my slender shoulders. Am I woman enough for the job?

As if reading my thoughts, Spencer says, 'You'll be fabulous.'

The old guys from the allotments – Ted, Brian and Jim – have turned up too. More surprising, the three hoodies are here, although they're lurking on the fringes looking furtive and uncomfortable. We did communicate long enough for them to give me their names – Jason, Daniel and Mark – and I'm hoping that my faith in them isn't misplaced. I'll get them kitted out with some spades or paintbrushes and set them to work right away before they've a chance to think better of it and scarper. Or, even worse, scarper *with* the spades or paintbrushes.

If the hoodies turning up was a complete surprise, I'm even more stunned to see that Kyle's mum, Janice, and his stepdad, Paul, have bowled up too. I'm not one to gossip, but I'd be amazed if they're normally out of bed at this time on a Saturday morning. You wouldn't have 'gardening' down on a list of interests for either of them. Janice looks slightly out of place in her white crops and stilettos, but she's got a new pair of gardening gloves in her hand, so she's clearly intending to work. I just hope that doing something together as a family for their own estate helps them to become closer. Then I look at Kyle's stepdad, who looks as if he wishes he was in the bookies instead, and I think maybe that's hoping for just a bit too much.

While I survey our motley crew of helpers, Johnny's busy signing the paperwork. Once that's done, then we all start to unload our goods from the back of the truck. I'd hoped that his mum would come out today, but Johnny said that Mary's not feeling too good. Maybe we can persuade her to join us later. There must be a little job that she can do to make her feel a part of this.

On the lorry, there are tools too numerous to mention, a case of filler, a dozen different shades of paint, a colourful splash of plants, bags of compost and a box full of bits and bobs like sandpaper, white spirit and disposable gloves. I ordered all this over the internet and that in itself feels like no mean feat. I've also drawn up an Excel spreadsheet for both managing the project and keeping a grip on the budget. All this from a woman who hadn't even seen a computer a few weeks ago.

I give Spencer a squeeze. Without this man I wouldn't have had the courage or the vision or the wherewithal to even begin to tackle this.

'What was that for?' he wants to know.

'For being you.'

We each take a load of equipment and, as we're putting it all into the Community Centre – which is doubling as our project headquarters for the duration – a van pulls up. Out of it steps one of the most beautiful women I've ever seen.

As I stand and gape at her and my mind tries to work out what she's doing here, she strides over towards me. She's tall, with a skein of thick dark hair that's pulled back into a plait, and she turns everyone's head with her commanding presence.

'Do you know where Sally Freeman is?' she asks no one in particular.

I step forward. 'I'm Sally Freeman.'

She beams at me and holds out her hand. I take it and she has the handshake of an all-in wrestler. 'I'm Dana Barnes,' she tells me as she pumps my hand, even though the information makes me none the wiser. 'I'm from the Council. And I'm here to help you.'

Chapter Seventy-Four

Johnny lugged another heavy bag of compost towards the Community Centre. It was about the tenth he'd moved already and there was a pleasant ache starting in his shoulder muscles.

It had been great to see that so many people had turned up to help them this morning. He'd been worried that after the initial enthusiasm, the actual commitment might have proved too taxing for most people, but he was pleased to see that he'd been wrong.

He was wrong about other things too. Those he was less pleased about. He risked a glance over his shoulder to where Sally was standing. She was with her boyfriend, and Johnny, he had to admit, had been surprised to see Spencer here. For some reason, he thought it would just be him and Sally heading up the project – but it looked like that wasn't to be. No matter how much he promised himself that he wouldn't get hung up over Sally, that he'd move on, somehow he couldn't quite make himself do it. However hard he tried to ignore his feelings, he couldn't quite keep at bay how much it hurt to see her with another fella.

His life felt in such turmoil. Where the hell was he going with himself? Once upon a time, he had been quite happy with who he was, content around here, content in his relationship. Now the whole thing seemed to be up in the air and he couldn't get a grip on his emotions. Take the break-in at the garage. It wasn't that bad – he could rationalise that. Some of his good paintings had been destroyed, but most had escaped scot-free. It had taken him and the lad the best part of Saturday to clear the mess, but that wasn't so bad. So why did he feel so upset about it? Why was he currently trying hard not to break down and cry about it like Charlie had? Was it just symptomatic of how he was feeling generally? His dreams, literally, had been kicked around and he didn't know quite where to turn next. Should he just trash the rest of his paintings, close up the garage and be done with it?

'Can you give me a lift with this?' It was the woman from the Council and she was struggling to lift a bag of compost on her own.

'I'll do it,' Johnny said. 'You don't want to put your back out on the first day.'

'You neither,' she said, but nevertheless she put the bag down.

'I'm Johnny Jones,' he told her.

She shook his hand. 'Pleased to meet you. Dana Barnes.'

Ringo came trotting up, not wanting to be left out of the introductions.

'Is this your dog?'

Johnny thought about denying him. 'Yeah,' he said. 'Ringo.'

At the mention of his name, Ringo rolled over and presented his stomach for tickling. Old tart.

'I adore dogs,' Dana said, obligingly giving Ringo a good scratch.

'So now you've got a friend for life,' Johnny said.

She looked under her eyelashes at him flirtatiously. 'You or Ringo?' she asked.

'Both, I hope.' Johnny laughed. 'Are you going to be with us throughout the project?'

'Yes,' Dana said. 'This is a big undertaking. We want to make sure that it's all kept on course for you.'

'It'll be good to have an extra pair of hands.'

'Well, you seem to have done all right by yourselves so far,' Dana said. 'You've got a pretty good turnout here. That's not always been the case.'

'That's mainly down to Sally.' Johnny flicked a thumb in his ex-girlfriend's direction. 'She's the powerhouse round here.'

Dana looked over towards Sally. 'Seems like a great lady.'

He followed her gaze. 'Yeah,' he agreed. 'She is.'

'Are you her partner?'

'Used to be. But not any more.' Johnny hoisted up another bag and Dana took one end of it. As she did, their eyes met and she smiled at him. Something in Johnny's heart warmed up and he smiled back. They walked down the path together, the bag of compost between them, Ringo sticking close to Dana's heels. 'Done many of these before?'

'Yes,' Dana said. 'Loads. But I have a really good feeling about this one.'

Strangely, Johnny felt the same way too.

Chapter Seventy-Five

I look over towards the Community Centre and can see Johnny and Dana unloading the last of the stuff on the lorry together. Hmm. What happened to my nice man from the Council, Richard Selley? I thought he was the one who'd be coming along to oversee this project. What's this woman doing here, striding about looking all Lara Croft?

She looks like she's got Johnny organised already. Hope she doesn't think that she's going to start bossing me around or there could well be trouble. First and foremost, this is my project. The whole thing was thought up and instigated by me, Sally Freeman, Single Mum and Superwoman, and I just hope she remembers that.

Johnny laughs out loud at something she says and I realise that I haven't heard my friend guffaw like that in a long time. A frown settles on my forehead and I don't know why.

Ted, Brian and Jim from the allotments are armed with their own tools and have set about digging out the small area of wasteground bordering the Community Centre. Even after a half-hour they're accumulating a small pile of house bricks, bottles and general bric-à-brac. They're going to remove the remnants of some sorry-looking, weed-ridden turf and replace it with a mass of shrubs. We've got lots of glossy green, low-maintenance plants to go round there which should keep them busy for a while.

The hoodies are looking restless. 'What do you fancy, lads?' I ask. 'Digging or painting?'

Jason, Daniel and Mark look from one to the other and eventually mumble as a collective, 'Digging.'

'Good.' I hand them spades. They handle them as if they're grenades. Perhaps they're going to need some digging lessons from Ted, Brian and Jim. 'See that area behind Bill Shankly House?' I point to the area that's enclosed by a graffitied brick wall. 'We're going to try to make a garden out of that.'

Three sets of eyebrows shoot up in surprise and maybe horror or even fear.

'Yeah,' I say. 'It's a bit of a tall order and it will all be down to your hard work.'

They're looking like they wish they'd opted for painting now – or preferably had decided to stay in bed. But piss in Sally Freeman's hallway and there's a price to pay. If I get any trouble from them, I'll simply remind them of that.

'Here's a copy of the plan.' I hand them a piece of paper. Johnny and I downloaded the design from the internet and then jiggled it about a bit to fit the space and, more importantly, the budget.

They take it and, bless, try to work out which way up it is.

'This is the back of the flats,' I point out. 'Where the bins are. We're going to build a fence to screen them, covered with clematis.'

They look blankly at that.

'Flowers,' I simplify. 'We're going to cover it with flowers.' My finger traces a line on the paper. 'That's a winding gravel path. Either side is going to be lavender.' I see the blankness descend once more. 'More flowers. It smells nice. At the back there's going to be a sheltered bench . . .' won't risk confusing them with the word arbour '. . . and some more flowerbeds. Okay?'

They nod in unison, but they all look very confused and more than a little alarmed. I might sound more knowledgeable than my new young friends but this is only stuff that I learned on the internet last week, so I'm barely one step ahead of them.

'Go with Mrs Kapur.' My neighbour is already standing there, kitted out with her wellies, floppy hat and paintbrush. Despite her being the size of a seven-year-old child, the hoodies look terrified of her. 'She'll organise you and I'll be over in a minute to work with you.'

'Come on, lads,' Mrs Kapur says. 'We've not got time to hang about.' She marches off, lifting her sari above her wellies. There's a spring in her step that I haven't seen in years and it makes me smile to see it. Inside that frail frame, there's a steel core. The hoodies, heads down, hoods up, jam their spades under their arms and trail after her obediently.

I decide to go and see what Johnny and Ms Gardener of the Year are up to. They're chatting over a bag of compost when I approach. I fold my arms and, for some reason, I feel my shoulders squaring up. Ringo wags his tail, but I'm not in the mood for that now. 'Everything okay?'

'Yeah,' Johnny says. 'This is the last of the compost. Once that's all inside, I'm going to get cracking on painting the Community Centre. I'll do the outside first, I think, while there's so much stuff indoors.'

'And I'm going to help the guys here with their digging and planting,' Dana Barnes says. 'If that's what you want me to do.'

'Sound,' I say. 'Looks like you can manage without me.'

'Yeah,' Johnny says. 'We've got it under control.'

'Good. Lovely. I'll go and sort out the garden area behind the flats with Mrs K and the lads.'

'Good idea.' Johnny nods.

'Well, then,' I say. 'I'll be off.'

Johnny stands with his hands on his hips. 'Is there a problem?'

'No, no. I'm just letting you know where I'll be if you need me.'

He looks to Dana. 'We should be okay, shouldn't we?'

'Yes,' Dana agrees. Way too readily in my opinion. 'But we know where you are if we get stuck.'

'Yeah,' I say. 'That's all I wanted to tell you. So that you know I'm not far away. I'll just be over there.' They stand and look at me. 'Well. Can't hang around here chatting. Stuff to be done. Lots of it. Lots and lots of it.'

They both nod in agreement. Seems I'm not needed here then. So, with that, I stomp off in search of Mrs Kapur and the hoodies.

Chapter Seventy-Six

'Y ou're very cute when you're angry,' Spencer says.

'I'm not angry,' I snap in a tone that could possibly be interpreted as ever so slightly angry. I tug furiously at the weeds that surround me, snatching them from the ground, ripping them from the earth. That will teach the little bastards to grow where they're not wanted.

'Your face is looking a little bit thunderous,' he tells me as he patiently weeds next to me. 'Are you cross with me?'

'I'm not cross with anyone,' I insist. More yanking. This is clearly the place where all bindweed goes to flourish. 'I'm just busy. There's a lot to do.'

'And I'm here to help you,' he says softly as he touches my arm. 'We all are. You're not alone in this.'

At which point I want to burst into tears. I *am* alone. I've never felt more alone in my life. Johnny's supposed to be helping me, and instead he's helping Dana Barnes, even though she's from the Council and should know what she's doing without any help from Johnny. Isn't she supposed to be helping *us*? Well, she's not helping me!

'Last weekend was a disaster,' Spencer says miserably. 'I so wanted you to love Alderstone.'

'I did,' I say. 'It was wonderful.' But my voice is flat and unconvincing even to my ears.

'Was it really just because of Charlie that you rushed away?'

I sigh and stop exterminating the weeds. 'Yes,' I say. 'And no.'

That makes him smile. 'Care to throw any light on that?'

'I'm not like you, Spencer,' I try. 'I'm not one of your people.' Even here, helping to turn this neglected square of wasteland into a garden, he looks out of place. I told him to wear old clothes. This is what he looks like. He's wearing jeans, but they're barely-worn designer label denims. He has on a casual shirt, rolled up at the sleeves, but it's linen and as white as a snowflake. He's beautiful, flawless and he just doesn't

233

look right here. Even Kyle's mum in her white crops and stilettos looks less out of place than Spencer.

And that's what I felt like at Alderstone. I stuck out like a sore thumb in what I thought was my trendy gear which just looked cheap and tarty in that splendid setting. I fit in *here*, among the dirt and the weeds, the dog ends and the discarded condoms. This is my world. Spencer's designer jeans and linen shirt are meant for Alderstone. They're meant for acres of lawn, for stables, for oval lakes built in eighteen-whatever-the-fuck it was.

'What's that supposed to mean?' Spencer straightens up. He takes my shoulders and turns me towards him.

Over in the corner, I catch sight of the hoodies who are all concentrating on their digging – hoodies now discarded. Underneath their thin veneer of surliness, Jason, Daniel and Mark are turning out to be really lovely lads. Who'd have thought. Mrs Kapur is alongside them painting the wall with little bird-like strokes to cover the obscene graffiti.

I lower my voice so that they can't overhear us. 'You know exactly what I mean.'

Spencer narrows his eyes. 'What's this about? Everyone loved you.'

'I don't think so.' I shrug his hands off my shoulders.

My boyfriend frowns and somewhere cogs click together. 'Did my father say something to you? Is that what this is about?'

Either my love is very perceptive or this has happened before. And I guess this is as good a time as any to come clean. This relationship isn't going anywhere. It can't. 'Your old man warned me off,' I say. 'Told me I was nothing more than a sink-estate gold digger. Or words to that effect.'

'He said what?' Spencer is incredulous.

I blunder on. 'He told me that he'd never condone a relationship between us and that you were only here because he'd insisted that you get out and do a real job before taking over the estate, in order to teach you some kind of lesson.'

My boyfriend's face turns thunderous. 'Part of that is certainly true,' he tells me. 'I'd been living the high-life, enjoying myself too much as a bachelor in my father's opinion. All he wanted me to do was choose a wife and settle down.'

Someone more suitable than me to grace the halls of Alderstone, no doubt.

'Coming here was supposed to be some sort of punishment for me. A veiled threat that I was to see the error of my ways and settle down. "Show him a taste of real life, that should bring him back into line" – that sort of thing.'

That much I already know.

'The trouble is, Sally, that he hadn't banked on me loving it. Loving you.'

And I hadn't banked on that either.

'Don't let this come between us, Sally. You mean more to me than you can ever know. What my father said is indefensible and I whole-heartedly apologise for his behaviour. There's no excuse for it.' His eyes are bright. 'But we can prove him wrong. Prove that this isn't just a flash in the pan.'

'How are we going to do that?' I don't say that I'm in no hurry to make a return visit to Spencer's ancestral home.

Sweeping his arm round the tatty garden-in-waiting, my boyfriend says, 'We could bring him here. Let him see what you've done. How hard you've worked to make this happen.'

'Oh no,' I say. 'No way.' I might run this area down myself, but I certainly don't want anyone else doing it. Mr Whateverhisnameis Knight can keep his distance. There's no way I'm having him turn his nose up at Kirberly.

'Sally,' Mrs Kapur shouts across at me. 'Can you come and open the top on this white spirit for me, doll?'

'I'll be right there!'

'Let's not talk about it now,' Spencer suggests. 'We need some time and space to discuss this properly.'

'There's really nothing to talk about, Spencer.'

'I think there is,' he tells me. 'There's a whole lot more that I want to say to you.'

Well, it will have to wait, because now I've got stuff – important stuff – to do.

Chapter Seventy-Seven

The dusk is gathering and it's the end of a very busy day. The orange globe of the sun is hanging over Liverpool, threaded through a few stoic clouds, bathing everything in a golden glow. Virtually everyone else has gone now. Mrs Kapur and her hoodies have packed up after making fabulous progress on the garden. I've been amazed at how much work they've put in. I think they have been too. Every time the lads showed signs of flagging, Mrs Kapur prodded them along. Who'd have thought that my tiny little neighbour was great foreman material!

I stifle a yawn. The first day has been a great success and all I want to do now is have a hot bath and curl up in front of the telly with a takeaway. I'm so knackered that I can't even contemplate cooking tonight. Even sitting upright might be a bit of a challenge.

Charlie comes over and leans against me. I hug him to me. 'You've worked really hard today,' I say. 'Both you and Kyle. Thank you for that. If Kyle wants to, he can stay at ours for a Chinese.'

'Okay,' Charlie says.

'Have you enjoyed it?'

'Yeah.' He shrugs.

'Gonna do it again tomorrow?'

'Yeah.' He shrugs again.

'Come on then, let's make our way back. I've got to drop these bits off at the Community Centre then we're done for the night.' I need to put my trowel and rake away, hang up my gardening gloves.

Spencer's gone home to get a shower and change, then he's coming back later to join us for our tea. No sixteen-seater dining-table in my place; he'll get a tray on his lap tonight and like it.

The lights are still on in the Community Centre when I put my stuff away which I take it means that Johnny hasn't quite finished yet. I've hardly seen him all day and, this may sound funny, but I've really missed him. I thought that we'd be working shoulder-to-shoulder on this and, well, we haven't.

I head back towards Bill Shankly House with my arm slung round Charlie's shoulder. My son must be feeling mellow – or too knackered to object – as he doesn't shrug my arm away.

As we approach the flats I see Johnny, dog at feet and paintbrush in hand even though the light is failing.

'Still at it?' I quip as we both come alongside him. Then I realise what he's doing. 'Oh.'

'Said I'd do this ages ago,' he says, and makes another sweeping stroke with his brush. 'Thought it was about time.'

'Yeah,' I say. 'Yeah. I guess it is.' But I feel something like pain deep inside me.

With a final flourish, Johnny stands back from his work. 'Better?'

I feel a lump stick in my throat. 'Yeah.'

The beautiful banner that he painted for me with hearts and flowers and the legend *Sally Freeman, I love you* slap bang in the middle has been updated. My name and Johnny's bold declaration of his feelings for me have now been painted out. All that's left is the heart and the flowers and a blank space where I used to be.

'Thought I might paint "Kirberly" in the banner instead,' Johnny tells me.

'That would look nice.' Not quite as nice as my name but, well . . .

'I'll do it tomorrow, then.'

I try to choke down my emotions. I've gone. I've been painted over. I've been airbrushed out of Johnny's life. Swallowing the lump in my throat, I manage to croak out, 'Had a good day?'

Johnny is all smiles. 'The best.'

'Great. Sound.' I kick at the ground, lost for words.

'Have a relaxing evening,' Johnny says. 'More of the same tomorrow.'

'Yeah.' I turn to go. 'Johnny, we're only having a takeaway but you're welcome to join us if you like.'

'Well . . .' he says.

'Spencer's coming back too.' Thought I'd better throw that in, just in case Johnny gets the wrong idea.

At that moment, a familiar figure appears out of the gathering gloom. She's got a smut of dirt on her cheek, but she still looks fabulous.

'Hi.' Dana bends to ruffle Ringo's fur affectionately. The little dog nearly licks her to death and suddenly I want Ringo doing that to me

237

too. He's probably given up because I always push him away. And the thought of that makes me want to cry. 'You've done a great job today,' she says. 'You should be really proud of yourself.'

I have the grace to smile. 'Thanks.'

Then when she's finished charming his dog, she slips her arm through Johnny's. 'We've all worked really hard.' She kisses Johnny warmly on the cheek and he grins happily.

My friend clears his throat. 'Dana and I have already got plans for tonight.'

She laughs softly at that and gazes up at my very best friend and my ex-lover. My insides churn unpleasantly as if I've eaten something that doesn't quite agree with me.

'But thanks for the offer, Sal,' Johnny adds. 'Maybe another time.'

'Yeah, sure. Another time.' Turning my attention to Charlie, I say, 'Come on, young man. Let's get you home.'

We walk away from Johnny and Dana, arm-in-arm, and suddenly the evening feels cold.

'She's lovely, isn't she?' Charlie whispers as we get out of earshot. There's a distinct note of awe in his voice. 'Sound.'

'She seems okay.' The words seem to stick in my throat.

'She said I was very good at digging.'

'You are. You've done really well.

'And she said that I was very handsome too.'

Flattery works every time with the male of the species – whatever the age. 'Did she now?' I tease.

My son's ears turn pink and there's a twinkle in his eye and a contented grin on his face. Just the same as Johnny's.

Chapter Seventy-Eight

We all sit with trays on our laps, eating while we watch *Any Dream Will Do* – one of these television talent competitions destined to give some lucky soul a chance to fulfil their dreams and star in a West End production of *Joseph and His Amazing Technicolour Dreamcoat*. I love this kind of show. It makes me all teary when I see ordinary people – such as myself – realising their most long-held ambitions.

I've scrubbed all the dirt off me and I'm now dressed in my most comfortable – scruffy – tracky bottoms and sweatshirt. I've washed my hair, but couldn't hold my arms up for long enough to dry it, so I've pulled it back in a scrunchy. Spencer, as always, looks as if he's just stepped off a catwalk. It seems funny that last weekend we were eating together at his parents' grand mahogany table, using the finest china and silver cutlery, and now he's reduced to eating the traditional fayre of the Hong Kong Garden takeaway from plates bought on Kirberly market with free disposable wooden chopsticks.

Charlie and Kyle have chosen the menu so we're feasting on sweet and sour pork balls, spare ribs in special sauce, sticky white rice and prawn crackers. I'm so tired that I'm currently struggling to stay upright and I'm eating on autopilot, so I've no idea whether the food is good or not. It doesn't stop the boys from clearing their plates though.

'Can we go into my bedroom and play on the Playstation?' my son wants to know.

'You can,' I say. 'You've both been very good today.'

Charlie and Kyle exchange a shifty glance.

'Take your plates through to the kitchen before you go.'

Without a quibble, they meekly do as they're told. There's definitely something going on there. And I will find out what. Just give me time.

The boys disappear into Charlie's bedroom and the door's closed behind them, leaving Spencer and me in blissful peace.

Spencer finishes his Chinese and I give up with mine, the effort of eating proving too much to handle. I thought I was quite fit after bounding up and down ten flights of stairs at least twice a day, but I've got aches and pains in muscles that I never even knew that I had.

'Here,' Spencer says. 'Let me take that.' He picks up our trays and carries them into the kitchen. A minute later he reappears carrying two wine glasses and a bottle of fizz.

'What's that for?'

'For you,' he says. 'You've worked so hard to get this off the ground and I'm very proud of you.'

I allow myself a tired smile. 'Thank you.'

Spencer pops the cork with an expert flick of his wrist, splashes the fizz into the glasses and hands me one.

'To you, Sally Freeman.' He clinks his glass against mine. 'A very special lady.'

'Aw,' I say. 'That's nice.' I feel a solitary tear slide down my cheek.

'Why the tears?'

'I'm tired and emotional,' I tell him with a sniff. 'And happy. You don't know what this means to me.'

'I think I do.'

'No. No one does. This feels like my first step out of this place. I've achieved something that I never thought that I could do, not in a million years.' I then let the tears flow freely, enjoying the sensation of relief that floods through me. 'Just think what else I might be able to do.'

'Anything is possible,' Spencer agrees.

We clink our glasses together again and both sip our champagne. Then Spencer toys with my fingers. 'I wanted to do this properly,' he says. 'Whisk you away to Paris, get down on one knee, the whole thing . . .'

Suddenly, my heart has stopped beating. I take a hefty swig of my champagne to see if that will restart it.

My boyfriend's eyes search mine. On the telly, I can hear people cheering, manic applause, clearly someone has found their dream, but I can't tear my eyes away from Spencer's.

'But this seems like the perfect moment,' he continued. 'Sally Freeman, would you do me the very great honour of being my wife?'

I feel as if I want to splutter on my champagne, but I can't: nothing will come. No comedy cough, no clever words, no cohesive thoughts. Nothing.

Spencer smiles. 'Is it so much of a shock?'

A shock? Is it a shock? Of course it's a bloody shock! 'Yeah,' I finally manage. 'It's a shock all right.'

Spencer's friend Tania hinted at it, so did his own father, but I never thought that there was any substance behind the notion. Why on earth would Spencer want to marry *me*?

'Do you think that you might be able to say yes?' Spencer prompts eagerly.

'No! No, no, no!' I try not to look too aghast. 'How can I possibly say yes?'

Now it's Spencer's turn to look aghast. 'I want you to marry me and come to Alderstone House, leave all this behind.' He sweeps a hand round my poky living room. 'Is that so terrible an idea?'

'Of course not,' I tell him. Then I sigh. 'Oh, Spencer. You and I are from different worlds. It would never work out. Your family don't want me within a hundred miles of you.'

A frown crosses Spencer's beautiful brow. Have I really just turned down my Cinderella moment?

'I told you what your father thinks. He wants you to settle down with someone more suitable to your status.'

'What my father thinks isn't important,' he tells me. 'This is about you and me. That's all.'

'Surely you'd want their blessing?'

'They'll come around in time,' he says dismissively. 'When they've had time to get to know you.'

'Supposing they disinherit you or something?'

'I'm their only son, their only heir. My parents want to step away from the management of Alderstone. They've realised that if we want to keep it in the family, then we have to start running it as a business – host weddings, shooting weekends, corporate parties, that kind of thing. That doesn't interest my father. He doesn't want to be around to see the public tramping through his family home.'

He doesn't want to see *me* tramping round it either, from what he's said.

'As soon as I take over, he and my mother are going to retire to one of the smaller cottages on the estate.'

Probably a seven-bedroomed 'cottage', if you ask me.

'They can't wait. As soon as they see what you're capable of, they'll love you too.'

Tolerate, would be a good start.

'I don't know, Spencer.' I chew at my fingernails. 'You'd be better off with one of those haughty deb types like Arabella or Phoebe. They know your world. They know your kind of people.'

'But you're a breath of fresh air to me, Sally,' he insists. 'The reason I love you is precisely because you're *not* like Arabella or Phoebe.'

The possibilities whir round in my head. Would I be mad to turn down this opportunity? Charlie and I could get out of here to a better life in one fell swoop. No slaving away at a computer trying to claw our way out of the gutter; it's being handed to me on a plate – a silver plate. So what if my in-laws can't stand the sight of me? I'd be marrying Spencer, not his flipping mum and dad. Who ever likes their in-laws anyway?

I put my head in my hands. 'I can't think straight,' I say. 'I'm so tired and there's such a lot on my mind.'

'Perhaps I should have whisked you off to Paris,' Spencer says ruefully.

'Give me time to think about this, Spencer. It's a really big deal for me. There's a lot to weigh up.'

'Take all the time you need,' he tells me. 'Just make sure you come back with the right answer.'

Though what that should be is anyone's guess.

Chapter Seventy-Nine

Today, Johnny was going to carry on painting the outside of the Community Centre. Dora the Explorer and some of the other older women from the estate had been rubbing down the windowframes and the faded old double doors at the front.

His plan was to brighten up the place with one of his murals which seemed to be fast becoming his trademark. The mural he'd painted in Ronaldo's studio certainly hadn't done the dancer's business any harm. Ronaldo reported that he'd had record numbers attending his classes since the makeover which had revitalised the studio and had, effectively, saved it from closing.

They'd stayed in touch since Johnny's dance lessons and now Ronaldo was eager to help out with their project. He'd turned up this morning and was busily working alongside Dora, rubbing down, filling in and flirting outrageously all the time, which she was lapping up.

He shouldn't smile too much though at young love, Johnny thought; after all, he'd done his own bit of flirting last night – something that hadn't happened in a *long* time. He'd gone home and showered and then he'd popped over to see how his mam was doing. If the weather held this afternoon, he might wheel her over here to look at the progress. Sally had suggested that Mary might be able to help by putting some bedding plants in the hanging baskets which were to grace either side of the door at the Community Centre. Johnny thought that his mam would like that and it was typical of Sally that she didn't want Mary Jones to be left out.

After he'd made sure that his mam was okay, he'd left Ringo behind and gone to collect Dana in his van. Okay, it might not be a sporty little number like Spencer's, but it was a two-seater nevertheless and it had a certain kind of charm. Dana had been impressed by his paint-work anyway.

They'd gone to one of those trendy restaurants down by the Albert

Dock. And they'd had a great night, even though the meal and a few drinks had cost him way more than his week's benefit. Good job that he'd started doing some painting on the side. Dana was good company and they'd laughed a lot at nothing in particular – something else that had been missing in his life recently.

Dana rented her own little place in Everton Valley – an area that had already seen some benefits of regeneration – and he'd gone back there for a nightcap at the end of the evening. He hadn't stayed over, but Dana had made it clear that he was welcome to do so if he'd wanted. Johnny sighed to himself. This was moving way too quickly for his liking – he was more of a slow-smoulder man – but there was no denying that there was an extra lightness in his heart this morning which wasn't entirely down to the fact that the project was going so well.

'Hiya, doll,' Dora called out, and he turned to see Sally striding towards him.

'Hiya,' he said when she bowled up in front of him.

She nodded towards the hall. 'You're getting on well here.'

'I want to give the old place a base coat today – we've got loads of white paint. Then I can start on the mural in the week when I've got some spare time.'

'Have you decided what you might do?'

'Thought it would be nice if we had scenes of all the work that's been going on. A sort of arty-farty record.'

'That's a great idea, Johnny.'

He smiled. 'Glad you approve.'

'When did you suddenly become so clever?' Sally asked.

He shrugged. 'A lot of things seem to be falling into place for me.'

'I'm pleased.'

'Are you okay?' Sally looked tired today, a bit of her old sparkle missing.

'I've a lot on my plate, Johnny,' she admitted. 'With this and everything.'

Johnny didn't like to ask what the 'everything' might be. He hoped that Spencer wasn't cooling their relationship – or maybe he did.

With that, the Council van pulled up next to them and Dana got out. She smiled as she came towards them both, swinging her keys in her hand. Ringo scampered over to meet her like a longlost friend, a puppyish spring in his step and Johnny thought that he saw Sally scowl slightly.

'How did your date go last night?' she asked him in whispered tones.

'Good,' he said truthfully. 'Very good.'

'I'd better be off, then,' Sally said. 'See if Mrs Kapur's okay. Charlie said she was out there with her paintbrush at the crack of dawn, bless.'

She waved at Dana as she hurried away.

Dana came over and kissed Johnny casually on the cheek. He didn't know if they'd be self-conscious with each other this morning, but everything seemed cool. 'Sally's rushing off?' she asked.

'Mrs Kapur's on her own in the new garden bit,' Johnny explained. 'She was worried about her.'

'She is okay about me being around?'

'Of course,' Johnny said. 'Many hands make light work.'

'I meant being around you.'

'Oh, right,' Johnny said.

'Looked like she was trying to avoid me.'

'No, not Sal. She's fine.' Why did women always try to over-complicate matters? 'Sally and I are old news. We're just mates now. But I guess that she'll always be in my life.' He thought it was only fair to let Dana know that from the outset. 'I love her kid to bits. I told you that last night. He's . . . well, I know that he's not, but Charlie feels like he's my own boy.'

'He seems like a good lad.'

'One of the best.' Johnny picked up his brush. 'I'd better get on if we're to get this place painted today.'

'I enjoyed our evening together,' Dana said softly. Her hand rested on his arm. 'Want to do it again?'

'That'd be great.'

'Lasagne at my place later?'

'Sound.' Then his mobile phone rang and he answered it. 'Johnny Jones.'

'This is Matthew Stokes, Chief Executive of the Tate Liverpool, Mr Jones,' said the voice on the other end of the line.

'Yeah?' Johnny felt himself frown. The Tate were ringing *him*?

'We have some of your paintings here.'

'My paintings?' Johnny laughed. How could that be? 'You sure?'

'Yes,' Matthew Stokes said. 'And they're really rather good.'

Chapter Eighty

I've got complete brainache. All night I've been lying awake turning over Spencer's proposal in my mind. Every time I blink, my eyelids sandpaper my eyeballs. I wanted to be firing on all cylinders today, but I feel like I'm walking through treacle.

What am I going to do? This feels like a dream come true, but – as is usual in my life – it's not without its complications. The biggest one being, do I love Spencer enough to marry him? Put aside the fact that he's going to inherit this enormous estate and I'd swan off down there to become Lady of the Manor – do I actually love him enough to promise 'till death us do part'?

For some reason, I wanted to talk it through with Johnny. He's always been my sounding board and it's a hard habit to break. I wanted to catch him this morning, but I hadn't reckoned on Delicious Dana being there too. Why did my heart squeeze so painfully when I saw the loving way she looked at Johnny? Why did I want to scream, 'He's mine!' when he is so clearly no longer mine? I have no right to begrudge him happiness, but I do. Particularly when it comes in the shape of someone more beautiful, more curvy and more together than I am. It only serves to make me realise quite how magnanimous Johnny has been about my relationship with Spencer. Speaking of which . . . I also need to talk this through with Charlie. It's a fantastic opportunity for both of us, but I want him to be completely happy with it and maybe it's too soon for him. He'd be changing school soon anyway, so that wouldn't be too much of a wrench, but it means leaving behind his friends and, more importantly, Johnny. Not sure how he'll handle that. I couldn't have talked rationally to him this morning, because I can't even get my own thoughts straight yet.

There's no doubt that I still want out of here – who in their right mind wouldn't? But Surrey seems such a long way away. It took us hours to get there. *Bloody* hours. It'd be like moving to the moon or

New Zealand. I can't drive, so there'd be no popping back for coffee with Debs or our girly trips down to Kirberly market. I want out of here, but I didn't imagine going so far – either physically or emotionally. I thought maybe I'd move to somewhere like Ormskirk or the Wirrall. Somewhere nice, but still within striking distance. If I went to Surrey, I'd be leaving behind everything that I know – even the good bits.

When I get to the garden, Mrs Kapur is – as my boy said – hard at it already. Paintbrush in tiny hand, she's still working away, covering up the graffiti on the wall. Even more surprising, given the early hour, is that the hoodies are here too. Jason, Daniel and Mark are all digging away happily, chatting and laughing to each other. How quickly they've been transformed from disenfranchised hooligans with attitude into helpful, enthusiastic kids. Is this all it takes to bring people back into the fold?

'Hiya, Sally,' they say in unison as I approach.

'Morning, lads. Good to see you. You're making great progress there.'

They blush in unison too and all turn back to their spades.

I glance round the wasteland area. It's coming on in leaps and bounds. Spencer and I managed to clear nearly all of the weeds yesterday. In among them we found a few discarded tyres, a telly, two microwaves and even a couple of mouldy old teddy bears probably from the time when this place was last used as a garden.

Mrs Kapur's going great guns with her painting and the lads have dug over three borders and have just one left to do. After that we're going to lay a winding path down the middle and some new turf. This is going to be a quiet garden where the older residents of the area will be able to get away from the noise of the kids. I envisage it as their own little sanctuary, with roses round the arbour and lots of scented plants to cheer them up. I hope that Johnny's mum will love it and we can get her out here and in the fresh air a bit more often.

I look around me. Everything's shaping up nicely. We won't know this place when it's finished.

Then I see Debs tottering through the gate towards me. She's wearing her silver high-heeled shoes and is dragging deeply on a cigarette.

'Hiya.'

'Gardening on a Sunday morning is obscene,' she grumbles. 'Sunday mornings were made for lying in.'

'Hard night?'

'Very harsh,' she says. 'Very harsh.' My friend sniffs and flicks a thumb towards the Community Centre. 'Saw your man out with the woman from the Council at one of the bars. He was looking very into her. Did you know?'

'Yeah,' I say. 'Apparently they're an item.'

'That was bloody quick work on someone's part.'

Somehow I don't think that it would have been Johnny's.

'How do you feel about it?'

'Fine,' I say. 'I'm glad that he's happy.'

'Huh.' It's accompanied by a snorty noise of disbelief. 'Where's your man today?'

'On his way. He'll be here soon.' This would be a good opportunity to run Spencer's proposal past my friend, but I can't bring myself to voice it. I have a lot more thinking to do about it yet.

'I might be crap at gardening,' Debs says, 'but I've brought bacon butties for everyone. Shall I dish them out?'

I kiss my friend warmly on the cheek.

'What's that for?'

'You're a lifesaver, Debs.'

'Yeah,' she says. 'Don't forget it. You'd miss me if I wasn't around.'

And that's something else that I need to think carefully about too.

Chapter Eighty-One

'We're dead meat,' Charlie informed Kyle. 'Seriously.'

His friend took a drag on their communal cigarette. They were leaning on their spades round the back of the Community Centre out of sight of the others, taking a momentary respite from the strenuous activity of digging. Charlie had been enjoying himself, but Kyle wasn't so sure about gardening. Kyle was getting bored. But then Kyle was always getting bored.

'Your mum might not find out.'

'She will,' Charlie said. 'She *definitely* will.'

'Johnny might not go to his appointment at the gallery.'

'Why wouldn't he?' Charlie scratched his head. 'Isn't that what we want him to do? Isn't that the point?'

Kyle conceded that one in silence. 'That bloke was supposed to ring *us*,' he grumbled. 'How did he get Johnny's number?'

'I might have put it down on the paper,' Charlie confessed. Which earned him a scowl from the much more wordly-wise Kyle Crossman. If only he could think things through like his friend did. 'I had to. What if the man had phoned while I was busy?'

'Doing what?'

'I don't know. Playing football? Digging?'

'He could have left a message.'

'Oh.' Charlie hadn't thought of that. It was too late now. He had overheard Johnny telling Dana that someone had phoned and that he was going down to see him at the gallery. Then Johnny would find out that Charlie and Kyle had taken the paintings there, then he'd realise that Charlie and Kyle must have also broken into his lock-up, and then he'd tell Charlie's mum, and then . . . Charlie and Kyle would be dead meat. And then they'd get one of those ASBOs that Kyle was so keen on.

It was making Charlie very worried. 'I should tell her first,' he said.

'No,' Kyle warned. 'Say nothing. Let them drag a confession out of you.'

Charlie didn't think that he wanted anyone to do that.

'But they've got my name. On a piece of paper.'

'We should have gone in disguise,' Kyle said, tutting at the flaw in their plan.

'What would we have gone as?'

'I don't know.' Kyle huffed. 'You should have given them a false name.'

'And a false phone number too.'

'Then they wouldn't have been able to call you, knobhead.'

'Oh.' They'd phoned Johnny anyway, not him – but Charlie didn't want to argue with his friend. 'Should I just tell Johnny it was us?'

'*You*,' Kyle corrected. 'No. Say nothing. That's always the best way.'

Kyle sucked in the cigarette smoke and blew it out. He was trying to blow rings like his big brother could, but he hadn't managed to do it yet. Kyle said it would make them both look cool if they could do that. He was going to learn first and then show Charlie. Really, Charlie longed to tell him that he didn't want to smoke at all any more, but he thought that Kyle would be annoyed at him.

'How are things going with the other bloke?'

'Spencer?'

Kyle nodded.

'Okay. I think Mum's going off him. She came back from his house early last weekend.' Charlie didn't tell his friend that he'd cried down the phone. 'And she didn't say that she'd had a nice time or anything. Not like she went on when she came back from Canada.'

'Thought you said it was Cuba?'

'Oh, yeah.' Charlie remembered now. 'There too.'

'Well,' Kyle said. 'That's one less problem you've got to deal with.'

Charlie brightened. He hadn't thought of it like that.

'There's just this little matter to fix.' Having given up trying to blow smoke rings, Kyle stubbed out the cigarette. 'When's Johnny going to meet the man?'

'He said he'd go tomorrow, but I don't know when. He looked very happy about it.'

'If they give him a lot of money you might not get killed.'

'*We* might not get killed,' Charlie corrected.

'This hasn't got anything to do with me,' Kyle said. 'It's your name

on the paper. Johnny's your friend. It was you who said that his paintings were better than the ones that they had in there.'

Kyle was right. It *was* all his fault. And, no matter what his friend
said, tomorrow he'd be a dead man.

Chapter Eighty-Two

We've all worked really hard again today. Now though, my aching back is calling out for a long, hot bath. I stand up and stretch, trying to stifle the groan that wants to accompany it. We've cleared all of the weeds and I've just laid out the route that the path's going to take with string and pegs and I've set out the area for the bench and its covering arbour in the back corner, furthest away from the flats. Hopefully it will catch the afternoon sun, giving Mrs Kapur, Dora and their friends a lovely, peaceful place to sit and while away the hours together.

Ted, Brian and Jim, the old blokes from the allotments are going to come over tomorrow and lay the slabs for me. Mrs Kapur is still painting away furiously, eager to get the very last bit of wall finished before the dusk consumes us.

I survey the tidy garden that's starting slowly to appear out of the wreckage while I enjoy some juice that Debs has brought round for us all from the Community Centre kitchen. My friend is right, she may not be much of a gardener, but there's no doubt that Debs has excellent timing with refreshments.

Jason, Daniel and Mark have all stopped for a drink too. The lads have worked really well together again today and have finished digging over all the new borders and clearing them of weeds. Where there'd been hardbaked soil and bindweed, there's now fresh, rich pristine topsoil just waiting to be planted.

They've all asked if they could come along tomorrow, straight from school, to start the job. It's wonderful to see not only the transformation in the ground that they've worked, but in the boys too. I feel so proud of them. I've got a maternal glow just looking over at them chatting away together. There's a certain satisfaction in hard, physical labour that I've just discovered, and it looks like the hoodies have too.

Spencer comes over and slips his arm round my waist. 'Happy?'

'Mmm.' I smile up at him. After our shock conversation last night,

I wondered if there'd be an awkwardness between us today, but there hasn't been. Spencer had come along this morning, bright and breezy, and simply got on with all of the tasks that I set him without complaint. To look at him though, you'd never know. He's still managed not to be as filthy dirty as the rest of us.

'You've had so many volunteers come along to help that you'll get this done in no time.'

'It's been brilliant, hasn't it? Much better than I ever could have hoped for.'

'And all down to you.'

'With a little help from my friends.'

'I love you, Sally Freeman,' Spencer says.

'I love you too.' And I really think that I do. I kiss Spencer's cheek and nestle into him. Could I make my life in this man's arms? Could I take on him, his snotty family and his big, fuck-off stately home? It's something I should decide soon. If Johnny's moving on and away from me, what is there really to keep me here?

'Any more thoughts after our talk last night?' my boyfriend asks.

'Loads,' I tell him. 'I need to sit down with Charlie and talk to him about it and what it would mean.'

Spencer squeezes me. 'That sounds as if you're coming round to the idea.'

'Maybe,' I say.

'That's progress enough for me.'

The sun's sinking lower in the sky and my eyes are starting to roll with tiredness thanks to my sleepless night and the fact that I've shifted ten tons of soil this afternoon. 'Shall we call it a day?'

Spencer nods.

'You go straight back to the flat,' I say. 'See if you can find something to go with pasta for dinner. There might be some tins of tuna in the cupboard. Take Mrs Kapur with you. Although I think you might have to wrest her paintbrush from her.'

'Shall I see if she wants to join us for dinner?'

Not sure that I'd call pasta and tinned tuna anything as grand as 'dinner', but that's Spencer for you. 'That's a really nice idea. She probably needs a bit of carb loading after all her hard work. I'll go over and see how Johnny and Dana are getting on and lock all this stuff up in the Community Centre.'

And if they're standing there looking all loved-up with each other, then I'll try really hard not to mind.

Chapter Eighty-Three

Johnny's finishing up too before he loses the light. The whole of the Community Centre has been transformed with white paint so bright that I need my sunglasses.

For some reason, I'm relieved to see that he's on his own – apart from Ringo fast asleep at his feet, of course. 'Wow,' I say as I approach. The dog cocks his ear, but carries on snoozing. 'That's amazing.'

'This bit of the base coat dried so quickly in the heat that I've been able to start the mural already,' he tells me.

On one of the big concrete panels, Johnny has started to paint some figures. There's a little enclosed garden and they're digging it over. 'Hey,' I say. 'That's me.' Unfortunately, I can tell that from the way my hair's scraped back and Johnny has perfectly captured my knacky old red T-shirt and jeans. I've got a painted smut of dirt on my cheek. 'You could have made me look a bit more glamorous.'

His eyes meet mine. 'You look fine just as you are.'

I flush and ask, 'No Dana?'

'She's gone off to get changed and put some tea on for us,' he says with a corresponding blush.

'Right.'

'She's nice, Sally,' he says softly to me.

'Yeah, yeah. She seems great.' Then neither of us know what to say. So I look at Johnny's mural some more while I mull over the fact that my son is also obsessed with the lovely Dana and even Ringo is.

The mural's looking fab. Mrs Kapur's there in her beautiful sari all daubed with paint. Johnny's even got the hoodies in a huddle – the boys will like that. They're not likely to graffiti over or piss on that, right?

Then my own boy saunters over to join us. Charlie leans against me, letting me put my arm round his shoulders and he yawns tiredly. Can I smell a faint whiff of cigarette smoke on him?

'No Kyle?'

'Gone to the chippy with his mum and dad,' my son supplies.

Kyle's parents have been here all day too digging alongside their boy, and they even looked like they were enjoying themselves, laughing together. Kyle might be a little toe-rag, but sometimes my heart goes out to him.

'That looks sound, Johnny,' Charlie says. 'Can I be in it too?'

'Course you can. I'll have to catch you doing some work first.'

'I've been busy,' my boy protests.

I stroke his hair. Definitely cigarettes. 'Enjoyed today?'

'Yeah.'

'You too, Johnny?'

'Yeah,' my friend says with a heartfelt sigh. He stands back and admires his own mural. 'I'd love to be doing this full-time.'

I shrug my shoulders. There's no way I'm going to give my friend careers advice. Last time I did that, I got my head bitten off for my pains.

Johnny puts down his paintbrush and turns to me. 'Sal,' he says, suddenly serious. 'I had a call from a fella at the Tate Liverpool today. One of the top bods.'

'The Tate? That deserves another wow.'

Charlie squirms against me.

'I know.' Johnny folds his arms.

'What did he want?'

My friend frowns. 'He told me that someone had handed in some of my paintings.'

'The ones that were stolen?'

'Looks like it.'

'Did he say who?'

'No idea. He seemed to think that it was one of my friends rather than someone who'd robbed me. I didn't tell him they'd been stolen. Strange thing is, they gave him my phone number.'

'Seems a bit stupid if it was the bloke who nicked them.'

Johnny looks as puzzled as me. 'Thought you might know something about it.'

I shake my head. 'Not me.' My boy fidgets next to me. 'Stand still, Charlie.'

'He wants to see me. Tomorrow.'

'Are you going to go?'

'Can't do any harm, can it?'

'It might give you a lead to help you find out who busted up your garage.'

'Yeah. What wouldn't I give to get my hands on those thieving little sods.'

I think my boy's developed ADHD. Giving him a sharp nudge, I say, 'Charlie, stop wriggling, will you?'

My son breaks free. 'Got to go,' he says, and shoots off like a scalded cat.

'Don't you disappear, Charlie Freeman,' I shout after him. 'Spencer's making our tea.'

'Kids,' Johnny says. 'Who'd have them?'

'I'm going to start restricting the amount of time he spends with that Kyle. Could you smell ciggy smoke on Charlie?'

Johnny shakes his head, but I'm sure that they're up to no good. I'm going to keep a close eye on this.

'I'd better be going,' Johnny says, and he starts to clear away his brushes.

'Good luck for tomorrow. Hope this guy's got some good news for you.'

'Thanks.'

'Want me to come with you for moral support?'

'I'd like that,' he says. He stares deeply at me and looks like he's going to take my hand but thinks better of it. Then he adds, 'But Dana's already offered to do that.'

Oh. I'd like to be there for Johnny. After all, I've known him much longer than Dana. Shouldn't it, by right, be me who goes? But then I rally. 'That's good. Very good.'

'I can't let her down.'

'No, no. Wouldn't dream of it. Just glad that you've got someone to be there with you. Oh, is that the time?' I make a fuss of leaving. Over my shoulder, I say to Johnny, 'Make sure that you let me know how you get on. Phone me as soon as you know anything.'

'I will,' my friend says. 'Promise.'

And I walk away thinking that I really want to be with Johnny at the Tate Liverpool Gallery to find out what's going on, and wondering why I feel quite so much as if my nose has just been pushed out of joint.

Chapter Eighty-Four

It was Monday – which always seemed quite a depressing way to spend nearly 15 per cent of the week. The sun was playing coy today, hiding behind the burgeoning rain clouds that had seemed so reluctant to appear over the last few weeks – giving rise to myriad newspaper headlines about it being the driest summer in more than a century. People round here were rapidly embracing global warming as a wonderful way of saving money on expensive foreign holidays. Would you ever need to go abroad if it was wall-to-wall sunshine in Britain? Frankly, no.

Johnny had never felt moved to go abroad or on holiday at all. He liked where he lived – didn't see the need to escape from it for two weeks of the year. He liked English food. He liked English people. He even liked the English weather – although, as he hurried towards the Tate Liverpool, he hoped the rain would stay away long enough not to dampen the smart suit he'd borrowed from his mate, Carl, for the occasion.

The bold blue and orange frontage of the gallery blazed out in the greyness of the day. Dana was already standing outside waiting for him and he felt his spirits lift. She was there for him as he knew she would be. Already he was so comfortable in her company that it scared him. He felt that he'd never get over Sally, but now – after such a short time – it was frightening and exhilarating at the same time to find himself considering her less and less. He was no longer so worried about what Sally would feel, what she'd think, or whether she would approve. Perhaps her constant discontentment had affected him more than he'd realised.

Ringo, much to the little dog's chagrin, had been left behind with Mary. Good job that the little dog didn't know that Johnny was meeting his new girlfriend, otherwise he would have been even more miffed. Clearly, it wasn't only humans who could experience love at first sight.

257

Dana smiled when she saw him and he dashed forward just as great splots of rain started to drop on the tourists thronging the dock area.

'Hiya,' she said, and kissed him warmly.

'Let's go inside before we get wet.' Johnny took her elbow and steered her through the doors into the foyer. He'd never actually been in here before. It had always seemed too intimidating. Maybe he should have a look round when they'd finished his meeting, see what real artists did. Johnny smoothed down his hair as he approached the receptionist. 'I've got an appointment with Matthew Stokes,' he said.

'Who shall I say's calling?'

'Johnny Jones.'

'Ah, yes, Mr Jones. He's so looking forward to meeting you.' The receptionist pressed a buzzer and then spoke into her phone. 'Mr Jones is here.' She hung up. 'His assistant will be down to collect you in just a moment.'

'Do I look okay?' he whispered to Dana as they waited.

'You look gorgeous,' she said, and kissed him again. Johnny wondered if she'd left lipstick on his cheek.

A minute later, a well-groomed young lady came out of the lift. 'Mr Jones?'

'Yeah.'

'Come this way, please.'

He and Dana followed her back into the lift which took them up to the top floor. Then she showed them into a spacious boardroom where Johnny could see his paintings leaning up against the vast expanse of white wall. There were four of them altogether – the ones that were missing from his lock-up. Three were the ones he'd painted the night he'd got drunk and sung along with the Beatles, and which he'd collect-ively mentally titled *She Loves You* in honour of his drinking song and the fact that he'd been in mourning for Sally. The fourth was the painting of himself in the Superman pose which Charlie liked so much but which hadn't got a title at all.

When Mr Stokes's assistant led them into the room, the two men waiting there stood up.

One of them held out his hand and grasped Johnny's warmly. 'Matthew Stokes,' he said. 'Delighted to meet you. This is my buyer, David Nelmes-Crocker.'

The latter shook Johnny's hand too.

'This is my friend, Dana,' Johnny said, introducing her.

'We're just thrilled with your paintings,' Matthew Stokes gushed. 'To discover such a special local talent – well, we're both overwhelmed.'

'Thanks,' Johnny said, wondering if they were sure that they meant him.

'Of course, we'd love to put on an exhibition of your work,' Matthew Stokes continued. 'I take it there's more where this came from?'

'Yeah,' Johnny said. 'I've been painting again for a few months now.'

Both men laughed at that and Johnny wasn't sure why.

'We'd also like to make a purchase to form part of our permanent exhibits.'

You could have knocked Johnny over with a feather. He wasn't sure he'd heard properly. 'Buy one of my paintings?'

'We particularly like this series.' Matthew Stokes pointed at the ones he'd done when he was blind drunk, the ones with Ringo's paw marks adding to the composition. Both men from the gallery admired the splattered canvases with wide smiles. 'Wonderful.'

'Just one thing,' Johnny said, when he could find his voice again. 'Can you tell me exactly how you came to get hold of them?'

'Yes,' Matthew Stokes said. 'Rather oddly, two little boys brought them in on spec. You didn't know that?'

'No.' Johnny couldn't quite get his head round this. Were these the kids who'd vandalised his lock-up and stolen his paintings? Why would they bring them here? 'I've no idea who they might be.'

'Well, it certainly was most unusual. I have a name here, I think.' Matthew Stokes rifled through the papers on the boardroom table. 'Ah, yes.' He picked up a piece of crumpled paper and peered at it. 'One of the boys was called Charlie Freeman.'

Chapter Eighty-Five

J ohnny's hands were shaking as he and Dana went back down to the
ground floor in the lift, leaving Mr Stokes and the paintings behind
them.

'You okay?' Dana asked.

He nodded, speechlessly.

'There's a café next door,' Dana continued. 'I think you could probably do with a cuppa.'

Johnny felt that he could probably do with a double brandy, but he
couldn't find any words to express that.

Instead, Dana took his hand and he meekly followed her through to
the café, sat at the table she chose and didn't object when she ordered
a pot of tea for two in place of the desired alcohol.

The Tate Gallery – the *world-famous* Tate Gallery – wanted to buy
one of his paintings. A *series* of his paintings. Paintings that had been
half-done by his dog! A figure of £50,000 had been mentioned and
his brain was having a great deal of trouble trying to imagine why
anyone would possibly give him that amount of money for his amateur
daubings.

£50,000! Even with his weekly benefit plus an extra bit of carer's
allowance for his mam – and the few bob he managed to earn on the
side from his growing decorating business – it would take him years to
earn that. The gallery top bods were talking about a full-blown exhibition of his work next year.

The tea arrived and Dana poured it. He tipped in a couple of spoons
of sugar even though he didn't normally take it. Wasn't that what you
were supposed to do for people who were in shock? After a few sips
of the hot, sweet brew his heart started to steady, his breathing was
returning to normal.

'That's put a bit of colour back in your cheeks,' Dana said with a
grin. She reached across the table and took his hand. It was still shaking.

'Thanks for coming with me.'

Dana laughed. 'I wouldn't have missed it for the world! Who'd have guessed that I'd be witnessing the birth of Liverpool's latest talent?'

'Not me.' Johnny's voice wasn't entirely steady either. He let out a wavering puff of breath. 'I can't believe it.'

'I'm so proud of you,' his companion said. 'I know that you're doing the murals at the Community Centre and all that, but you never mentioned that you'd done other paintings. They were brilliant.'

'It's just a hobby,' he said. 'I never knew whether they were any good or not. I took it up again when Sally and I split, just to fill the time.' The mention of her name made him think of Sal. He had to call her as soon as possible. Or maybe he'd go round there – tell her in person. That would be better. He'd like to see her face when he told her. She'd be thrilled that he'd finally done something with his life, that someone felt he had something worthwhile to offer.

It also made him wonder what Charlie's role had been in all this. When had he taken the paintings from the garage? Did he know more about the break-in than he was letting on? If that was the case, he'd forgive him anything now! Wait till the boy heard of the outcome. How on earth was he going to thank Charlie for instigating this fantastic opportunity for him?

Johnny felt a lump come to his throat and hot tears pricked at the back of his eyes. He wanted to see the boy right now, pick him up in his arms and hug him half to death. A ten year old had believed in him more than anyone. However this had been cooked up, it looked as if Charlie had managed to hand him his dreams on a plate.

Chapter Eighty-Six

I had my computer course this afternoon, so I couldn't go along to the garden. It made me realise that I'm probably not cut out for nine to five life in an office. To be honest, I really struggled to concentrate on what Spencer was trying to teach me. All I wanted to do was get back into the garden and get digging. I like the feeling of dirt under my fingernails, the smell of grass, the sun on my back.

It also made me realise that I've learned a lot about computers by now. Our course is very soon to come to an end. What will Spencer do when all the courses are finished? Will he stay on and find something else, or is this his time to go back to manage Alderstone? It's a conversation that we need to have. But not today. I've just changed into my scruff and I'm heading right out now to see how my lovely hoodies, Jason, Daniel and Mark, are getting on. I had a quick peep out of the landing window and, sure enough, shortly after school let out they were there digging, weeding, doing good. Bless 'em. I'm really going to miss working with those guys and already, I wish that this project could go on for ever.

As I'm having this lovely daydream, my doorbell rings. When I open it, Johnny's standing there. In a suit. With his hair combed. Ringo at his heel. Blimey, even the dog looks spruce.

'Good grief,' I say. 'To what do we owe this?' I cast an eye over his suit. 'Have you been in court?'

'Very funny,' Johnny says, as he follows me into the living room, Ringo trotting behind. 'As it happens, I've come to tell you my good news.'

'Good news?' My interest perks up at that. Then I realise that it might involve Dana and my mouth goes dry. 'What kind of good news?'

'The Tate Liverpool want to buy some of my paintings to exhibit.'

'No way!'

'Way,' Johnny says.

'Ohmigod.' I jump up, hug him and we dance round the lounge. Him in his borrowed suit and me in my grubby gardening gear, Ringo in a barking frenzy. 'I knew you could do this. I just knew.' I squeeze him tighter. 'Oh, Johnny.' Tears spring to my eyes. 'This couldn't happen to a nicer man.'

'That's not all,' he says breathlessly. 'They're going to pay me fifty thousand pounds!'

Now the tears flow and I dab them away with my grass-stained sleeve. Johnny is finally going to get the recognition that he so truly deserves. 'No way!'

'Way!' And we do a happy dance again.

'Fifty thousand pounds,' he repeats in a dazed way. 'Just think of what I can do for Mam with all that.'

This kind of thing doesn't happen to people like us. First I get an offer to become the Lady of the Manor and now Johnny's going to be a famous painter. Has someone sprinkled us with fairy dust? Or maybe when you release your dreams into the universe, sometimes they just come true. 'You need to tell me all the details. I want to know everything. Every single thing. How, why, when, what, where?'

I sit on the sofa, giddy with excitement, and Johnny flops down next to me. We're still holding hands and it feels so nice even though mine are callused and rough in his. His eyes meet mine and I can hear both of our hearts thumping in time. Then, slowly, he leans towards me and he kisses me. He kisses me long and hard and my insides turn to water. He kisses me like I haven't been kissed in a long time, and I'd forgotten how good this could feel. Spencer's a wonderful kisser, one of the best, but . . . Then Johnny breaks away from me and gives me a self-conscious hug.

My friend sits back against my cushions and lets out a wobbly sigh.

'You're not going to believe this,' Johnny says. He laughs in an incredulous way while I sit with bated breath, my lips still tingling from his kiss. 'Charlie took them down to the gallery.'

'Charlie?' All lovey-dovey thoughts fly out of the window. '*My* Charlie?'

'Looks like it.'

'You didn't know about this?'

'No,' Johnny says. 'Not a thing.'

'When, how?' Now I'm frowning. 'He wouldn't have taken them without your permission. Plus Charlie's not allowed into the city on his own. How would he have got them there?'

'I don't know,' Johnny admits. 'But that's what the guy at the gallery said.'

I shake my head. 'He must be mistaken.'

My friend shrugs. 'He seemed pretty certain and *I* definitely didn't take them down there. So who did?'

Then I hear a key in the lock and the front door swings open. A tuneless voice sings an unrecognisable song. Charlie's home.

'Well, here he is,' I say to Johnny. 'Let's find out.'

Chapter Eighty-Seven

Charlie looks like a rabbit caught in the headlights. And that's before I've had the chance to ask him any questions. Just the sight of Johnny and I sitting on the sofa together has alerted him to the fact that he's been rumbled. I can't believe my boy's behind this. Now it's just a matter of finding out exactly what he did and didn't do.

Johnny breaks the impasse by standing up and scooping Charlie into his arms. He hugs Charlie to him. 'Thank you,' he whispers into my boy's hair. 'Whatever you did, I can't thank you enough.'

When he puts Charlie down, my son is still looking terrified. Johnny slings his arm round him and looks at him closely. 'Did you take my paintings to the art gallery?'

A big gulp travels down Charlie's throat and he nods.

'They want to buy them, our kid,' Johnny tells him. 'The boss there loves them.'

Charlie glances anxiously at me and then finds his voice. 'He does?'

Johnny can't keep the grin off his face. 'He wants to pay me a lot of money for them.'

My boy's face also breaks into a grin. 'Oh, wow!'

I fold my arms. 'Want to tell me exactly how this came about?' I think that Charlie can tell that I'm not yet sharing their joy over this revelation.

My son shuffles from foot to foot, his eyes shifting between me and Johnny. 'We just borrowed the paintings,' he eventually says. 'That's all.'

'*We* being?'

'Me and Kyle,' Charlie coughs.

I might have known that boy would have been slap bang in the middle of this somewhere.

'I didn't think Johnny would mind,' Charlie continues.

'Or you didn't think that he'd find out?'

My son says nothing.

'How did you get into the garage?' I ask. 'Did you have a key?'

Now Charlie flushes to an uncomfortable shade of beetroot. You could fry eggs on his cheeks. 'We used some bolt cutters on the locks.'

The smile disappears from Johnny's face at that.

'Where did you get them from?'

'From Kyle's mum's shed.'

'And you broke into Johnny's garage?'

Charlie starts to cry. 'We only borrowed four paintings,' he sniffs. 'We didn't think about leaving the garage open afterwards. We were in a big rush. It wasn't us who did the other stuff. I don't know who did that. We didn't mean for it to happen. All we wanted to do was take Johnny's paintings to the art gallery. When we went there with Spencer I thought all the things that were supposed to be art were crap . . . rubbish,' he corrects quickly. 'I thought Johnny's stuff was much better. And I was right.' He turns to Johnny for support. 'I was right. It *is* good.'

'And what about all the damage to Johnny's workshop?'

'I helped him to clear it up,' my son says in his defence.

'He did,' Johnny agrees.

'I'm really, really sorry,' Charlie looks downcast.

'That's okay,' Johnny tells him. 'It's all come good in the end.'

'No, it hasn't,' I intervene. 'Charlie, you've broken just about every rule I can think of.' I count them off on my fingers. 'You've vandalised Johnny's garage. You've taken his belongings without asking. You went into Liverpool without my permission. And I know for a fact that you're smoking.' Thought I might as well throw that one in as I'm on a roll.

My son hangs his head.

'I haven't brought you up to be like this. I'm so disappointed in you. Get out of my sight.'

'Mum . . .'

I hold up my hand. 'Go to your room while I think of an appropriate punishment.' Which will, of course, involve confiscation of the treasured Playstation at the very least.

'Sorry, Mum,' my son says tearfully. 'Sorry, Johnny.' And then he trails off to his bedroom, the picture of misery.

Johnny turns pleading eyes to me. 'Sal,' he says quietly. 'That was harsh.'

'I don't think so.'

'Your son has just made all of my dreams come true in one fell swoop. Can't you forgive him for some misplaced boyish enthusiasm? I have.'

'He's not your child,' I say. And instantly regret it when I see the look of hurt on Johnny's face.

'I might not be his dad, but I know a good kid when I see one.'

'He's breaking into garages, stealing stuff and smoking. From where I sit, I see a kid who's going down the wrong track.'

'Give him a break,' Johnny begs. 'He knows some of his behaviour was silly. But there's no harm done.'

'Silly?'

'He's ten,' my friend points out. 'We've all made mistakes.'

'And my mistake is to bring him up here in this shitty place where people don't know right from wrong.'

'That's not true, Sally. You're over-reacting.'

'I've every right to,' I shout. 'I'm his mother!' Now I'm crying. I realise that I'm probably ruining Johnny's big moment but I can't help it. It feels as if all my fears are coming true. My ten-year-old son's a burglar, a smoker, creeping round getting into mischief behind my back. I've always worried about the bad influences on him from being brought up here, but I thought I'd done a good job. A *really* good job. I thought I'd taught him how to behave properly. Seems that I've had my blinkers on. 'I want him out of here,' I say to Johnny. 'I want him away from this estate. The sooner the better.'

Chapter Eighty-Eight

Johnny has found the remnants of a bottle of cheap wine in the fridge. Must have been one that Debs brought round. He pours me a glass and hands it over.

'I'm sorry,' I say, calmer now. 'I've spoiled it for you.'

Charlie has yet to reappear from his bedroom and he must be getting hungry by now. I feel emotionally drained.

Johnny sits down next to me on the sofa and swigs at his own wine. He holds my hand. 'Want to tell me what this is really all about?'

'I don't want my son to turn out to be a criminal.'

Johnny gives me a sideways glance. 'Sally.'

I sigh at him. 'I want Charlie to know a different life than this. I want him to have the childhood that I never did. I don't want him breaking into garages for entertainment.'

'Your son did this for me with every good intention.'

'Isn't that what the road to hell is paved with?'

'He's a good kid, Sal. You know that.'

'He's great,' I say. 'And I don't want anything to change that. I have to get him away from the bad influences around here.'

'You've seen how people have pulled together over this project. This is still a great place to live. Underneath a thin veneer of shabbiness, there still beats a very good heart.'

'Do you really believe that?'

'There's a few bad apples, Sal. That's all. Don't think that means that the whole barrel is rotten.'

I massage my temples, a headache coming on.

'Maybe now that I've got this money coming to me I can do something to help you out.'

'I don't want you to do that, Johnny. Goodness only knows that you deserve the money yourself.'

'Then what can I do to help?'

I swallow down some more of my wine. 'You can support me in the decision I've made.' Within the last ten minutes, if I'm honest.

'I always back you to the hilt, Sal. You know that.'

Taking a deep breath, I say, 'Spencer has asked me to marry him.' The colour drains from Johnny's face. 'I've decided to accept.'

'Congratulations,' my friend says quietly. 'Spencer's a very lucky man.'

'I haven't told him yet.'

'You told me first?'

'You know how much you mean to me, Johnny. I wouldn't have wanted you to find out from anyone else.'

Johnny sighs. 'I'd hoped to be in his position myself at one time. How did it all go so wrong?'

'It means leaving here,' I continue. 'Leaving everyone behind.' I daren't meet Johnny's eyes.

'Are you sure that it's what you want?'

'It will be better for Charlie.' Voicing this out loud makes a lump come to my throat. 'Spencer's wealthy. His family home is enormous, set in its own grounds. Charlie will have freedom there that he could never have here. He'll have opportunities that I could never dream of giving him.'

'And you love Spencer enough to cut yourself off from everything you've ever known?'

I nod, unable to speak. *Tell me that I'd be crazy to turn this down,* I urge Johnny silently. *Or beg me not to.* That's the other stupid thought that's running through my mind. *Beg me to stay here. With you.*

My friend lets out an unsteady breath. 'For some reason, I didn't see this coming.'

'Me neither,' I confess.

'You've always wanted out of here.'

'But I hadn't imagined it happening like this.'

'If you think it's the right thing, then you have to do it. You have to go.'

'I do, don't I?' My voice is wavering. 'We'll keep in touch though. You and me. We've been through too much together. And, of course, there's Charlie.'

'We won't.' Johnny shakes his head sadly. 'You'll start your new life and will get caught up in it all. Maybe once a year you'll remember to pick up the phone to me.'

'It won't be like that,' I swear. Johnny has been my lover, my friend,

269

my confidant, my child's surrogate dad. 'I couldn't bear not to have you in our lives. We can organise for you to come down for the weekend, that kind of thing.'

'Maybe.' But my friend doesn't look convinced. Then he stands up. He looks like a stranger to me with his smart suit and his tidy hair. 'I wish I could have loved you better,' Johnny says flatly.

'I never felt as if you didn't love me,' I tell him.

'I should have done things differently,' he insists. 'I know that now.'

'And I should have appreciated you for the lovely, kind man that you are.'

Johnny sighs. 'It's feels weird to be having this conversation now.'

I nod in agreement, because I can't find my voice.

'I think I should be going. Come on, Ringo.' The little dog pricks up his ears and rouses himself from his nap to rub against Johnny's ankles.

'Johnny.' I don't want him to go. I want to hold him back. I want him to stay here with me. With me and Charlie. I don't even want his bloody dog to go.

I follow Johnny to the door, a million conflicting thoughts going through my mind and I'm struggling not to break down and cry. But that would do neither of us any good. I've made my decision and I have to stay strong. I have to believe that this is the right thing. 'I'm sorry that it didn't work out between us. We could have been great together. In different circumstances. I know that it was me that blew it, but I did love you very much.'

Johnny laughs. 'My circumstances *are* different now. But it looks like it's too late for us.' He kisses me on the forehead, letting his warm lips linger a moment too long for a kiss between friends. 'Be happy, Sally.'

'And you.' The words *I love you* want to break free from my mouth, but I won't let them. I don't love Johnny any more, not like that. I love Spencer. I'm going to marry him.

Johnny leans on my door. 'There's one thing you can do for me, Sally. Forgive Charlie. Just think of the wonderful opportunity he's created for me. Don't be hard on him.' He turns to go. 'And tell him that I love him. I love him very much.'

Chapter Eighty-Nine

I make my son his favourite tea. Home-made meatballs in tomato
sauce with Uncle Ben's rice – not the cheap Save-It stuff which, no
matter what you do, always sticks together in one big lump.

'Thanks, Mum,' he says as he eats. His face is all blotchy from crying
and now, of course, I feel terrible for shouting at him. Johnny's right,
he is a good boy and I ought to appreciate that more.

'I'm sorry for being upset with you,' I say. 'But you can understand why.'

Charlie nods. 'I won't do anything like that again,' he promises.

'Well, Johnny's certainly pleased that you did.'

He manages a wan smile at that.

'It turned out well this time, Charlie. You might not have been so lucky.'

'Yes, Mum,' he says.

'The people who got in after you were there could have caused a
lot more damage. They could have ruined everything Johnny had worked
so hard for – burned the place down, for instance. The police could
have been involved. You might have been blamed. It was a very silly
and thoughtless thing to do.'

'Yes, Mum.'

I toy with my own meatballs as we face each other across our tiny
kitchen table. Looking round, I wonder how much longer I'm going
to call this place home. Skanky as it is, I'm already starting to feel senti-
mental about it, perverse creature that I am. I have had some good
times here with Debs, with Mrs Kapur and with Dora. And with Johnny.

I plaster a smile on my face. 'I've got some news to tell you. Some
good news, I hope.'

Charlie's all ears.

'Spencer has asked me to marry him,' I continue. 'And I want to say
yes.'

My son's reaction is much the same as Johnny's. A slight blanching.
A resigned acceptance.

'I know that it's taken you a long time to get to like Spencer, but he really is a lovely man and he can offer both of us a much better future than we can have around here. His home is lovely. Very big. You'd have a massive room.'

He looks aghast. 'Spencer won't live *here*?'

'No,' I say. 'We'll go to Surrey to live with him.'

Charlie promptly bursts into tears, so I go round to his side of the table, kneeling beside him to comfort him.

'Don't cry, son.'

'Is this because I was naughty?' he sobs as he clings to me. 'I promise I won't do it again. Never, ever. Don't make me go to Surrey.'

He makes it sound like a prison sentence rather than an opportunity to make a new life and better himself.

'You've never seen it, silly,' I chide. 'You might love it.'

'I won't,' he cries. 'I know I won't. Johnny won't be there.'

Stroking Charlie's hair, I try to reassure him, saying, 'Johnny can come to see us any time he likes.'

'But it won't be the same,' Charlie insists tearfully. 'It'll never be the same again.'

'Sometimes things have to change,' I tell him. 'And sometimes they're for the best.'

'I could stay here,' Charlie suggests, suddenly hopeful. 'You could go to Surrey with Spencer. I could stay here with Johnny and Ringo and Dana.'

That takes me aback. My own child would rather stay here with Johnny and a strange woman than accompany me to a new life.

'You know that can't happen,' I say. 'You and I belong together. We're a team.' I punch his arm playfully and Charlie stares ruefully at the spot. 'I know this is a shock, but just think about it. Maybe then it won't seem quite so bad.'

'I don't want to go to Surrey,' my son tells me. 'And I don't want you to marry Spencer.'

'Sometimes,' I say, 'you have to trust me to do the right thing for both of us.'

At that he gets up and runs into his bedroom, slamming the door, his favourite meatballs abandoned.

I sigh and rub my eyes. He'll come round – I'm sure he will. But the worry is, can I, Sally Freeman, Single Mum and Superwoman, trust *myself* that I'm doing the right thing?

Chapter Ninety

'Where are we going?' Spencer wants to know.

'You'll see. Come on,' I say. 'We need to hurry up.' I pull his arm and we dash along the waterfront, making our way from his apartment in the Albert Dock towards the Pier Head.

I pay over ten quid for two tickets and we charge off down the gangway just in time to catch the *Royal Daffodil* ferry before it's leaving.

'Ferry across the Mersey,' Spencer says approvingly. 'How romantic.'

This is an epic journey across the famous river made popular by the 1960s hit 'Ferry 'Cross the Mersey' by beat combo Gerry and the Pacemakers – in the days before 'pacemaker' referred to a medical appliance, of course, and was a good name for a pop group. If you ever find yourself in Liverpool, a ferry across the Mersey has to be done.

We eschew the upper saloon which is done out like a bad 1970s disco with swirly carpet and patterned banquettes, and instead, make our way up to the promenade deck to stand on the back of the boat, shivering in the cold. The hit song blasts out over the PA system and I daren't listen too closely to the lyrics, which are all about never, ever leaving Liverpool, because that would make me well sad. And right now I want to feel nothing but happiness.

With a hearty belch of diesel smoke, we cast off. The *Royal Daffodil* lurches off on her well-trodden path and her engines chug and churn their way through the grey-green, foamy waters of the Mersey as they've done for years and years.

Because of the threatened rain, there are few tourists on here today, most of them probably sensibly opting for the indoor attractions of the museums and maybe the Tate Liverpool. I try not to think of Johnny and the fact that his paintings will soon be hanging in there alongside some of the most famous artists in the world, and that tourists will marvel over his work too.

Today is cooler, a definite change in the temperature. There's a biting breeze on the river and I wonder how much is left of the hot Indian summer weather we've enjoyed for so long. Are we already on the slow, steady slide into autumn? I'm certainly glad that I put a jacket on. We lean on the railings at the back of the ferry and look out. Spencer's hair is being whipped about his face, but he's still smiling.

The seagulls wheel on the air, calling out to no one in particular. A mist has settled on the river and the clouds are massing, but the sun is still making a valiant effort to puncture them. Spray from the bow wave dampens our faces. I pull my jacket around me and huddle into Spencer's chest for warmth.

'This is a nice surprise,' he says, his words being snatched by the wind.

Charlie's at school and I've persuaded Spencer to bunk off from doing all his paperwork this afternoon to take him on this mystery tour.

I think of my son and get a pang of guilt. He's still not happy about my decision, and nothing I have yet been able to say has changed his mind. Still, I have to remember that I'm doing this for the best and be sure in the knowledge that – like making him clean his teeth after every meal and feeding him broccoli at every opportunity – one day Charlie will thank me for this.

Spencer and I watch the magnificent Three Graces – the Liver Building, the Cunard Building and the Port of Liverpool Building – grow smaller as we make our way across the river. The new skyscrapers inch towards the sky and the converted warehouses along the Albert Dock give the area an affluent, upcoming feel. This is the port that first put Liverpool on the map as an important trading centre for the world, and now it feels as if Liverpool has stamped its place back on the map with a vengeance – and I'm kind of sad that I won't be here to enjoy it.

The predicted rain starts to fall, puckering the surface of the river. Soon all the wooden benches hold pools of water, which ensures that we have the deck all to ourselves.

As we get into our stride out in the river, and the posh houses over on the Wirral start to come into view, I turn to face my boyfriend and say, 'Remember you asked me a very important question recently?'

Spencer shrugs. 'Of course. I hadn't forgotten.'

'Neither had I.' Looking into his eyes, I swallow the gulp that's lodged in my throat. 'The answer's yes.'

It takes Spencer a moment to digest that as he tries to blink it into his brain. 'Yes?'

I nod. 'Yes.'

Spencer laughs out loud, shouting into the wind, 'She said yes!'

Then I laugh too as he picks me up and spins me round. The rain pelts down on us.

'You do mean it?' he asks.

'Sure.'

'Yes!' He spins me again.

At this moment, I know that I've made the very best decision that I could. It's the right thing to be doing. Spencer and I can conquer any opposition to our marriage. We'll make it right with Charlie. We'll make it right with Spencer's parents and all his snooty friends. Johnny and Dana will come and visit us regularly and we'll all be the best of mates. I *will* have my happy-ever-after.

'I brought something specially,' I say as I delve into my voluminous handbag. With a bit of rooting, I then pull out two plastic beakers and a half bottle of champagne. It was on offer at Save-It and it's probably not even proper fizz, but beggars can't be choosers. This could, however, be the last bottle of cut-price champagne that I ever drink.

Spencer pops the cork, letting it sail out over the Mersey where it disappears, consumed by the waves. He splashes the fizz in the beakers and then holds his up for a toast. 'To us,' he says. 'Mr and Mrs Spencer Knight.'

'To Mr and Mrs Spencer Knight,' I echo, and our cups knock together, the rain mingling with my tears.

'I should have had a ring organised.'

'You didn't know that I was going to spring this on you,' I remind him. 'And you know that I'm not bothered about that kind of thing.'

'That's why I love you,' he says, and kisses me again.

We toast ourselves once more.

'I can't believe it,' Spencer tells me as he leans on the rails and looks back towards Liverpool. 'You've made me the happiest man alive.'

I wipe my face on my sleeve and snuggle into him again, faces close together. 'And I'm the happiest woman.'

'Have you discussed it with Charlie yet?'

'Yes,' I say. 'That's the only cloud on the horizon.' Well, not quite the only one but, I guess, the most important one. 'He's not very happy.'

'He'll come round,' Spencer assures me.

'That's what I'm hoping.'

'He'll love Alderstone. I did as a boy. I couldn't wait to get home from school for the holidays.' Spencer laughs. 'We'll get him into my old school – he'll love it there. Every generation of Spencer as far back as we can remember has been to Langley. It will be nice for Charlie to carry on the tradition.'

'Sounds great.'

My future husband smiles contentedly. 'It's only about an hour's drive from Alderstone, maybe a little more. He could even come home for occasional weekends until he settles. Though I never wanted to once I'd got used to it.'

The shock makes my lungs fill with cold air and rain, and I start to cough frantically. 'You want to send Charlie away?'

Spencer frowns. 'Not away,' he says. 'To school. I told you, every generation of Knight has been to Langley. Charlie should go there too. He *must* go there.'

'No way,' I say. 'We can find somewhere local. There must be decent schools around Alderstone. I want my boy at home with me. That's final.'

'I never knew that you felt so strongly,' Spencer says.

'Well, I do.' I realise that perhaps there are a lot of things that our conversations have only skirted around.

'Let's not talk about it now,' my boyfriend says. 'There's plenty of time to make arrangements. We can discuss it at a later date.'

But I still won't change my mind, even at a later date. Spencer must know that. Charlie's my life. How could anyone contemplate sending their ten-year-old kid away to school? It's cruel, if you ask me. Don't have them if you can't be arsed to bring them up yourselves, that's my opinion. Don't farm them out to some posh school just because it's a family tradition. My heart's banging in my chest, excitement all but forgotten. It brings it into sharp relief that there are so many differences between us – things that I don't yet even realise.

Spencer touches his beaker to mine again, but somehow the moment's gone. I smile anyway. That always hides a multitude of sins.

'It would be good character-building for Charlie,' Spencer muses, even though the subject is supposed to be closed. 'It wouldn't hurt for him to be more independent.'

Then it occurs to me that maybe Spencer views my one and only son as I see Johnny's little dog, Ringo. He's always around, getting under your feet and, while he may be cute enough in his own way, he can be really annoying too. He's there all the time, even when you don't want him to be, wagging his jolly little tail and depending on you for affection and approval. And I just can't see why Johnny adores him so much and it pains me to think that's exactly how Spencer views my own son, Charlie. Does he just see my child as a necessary nuisance? Quite nice in his place, but to be tolerated rather than cherished. Does he think that life would probably be better without him around? Perhaps he does — and the thought makes my blood run cold.

Chapter Ninety-One

'I've got to go away,' Charlie told Kyle as he blew out a stream of smoke. They were supposed to be helping his mum with the gardening again. They'd been to collect their spades from the Community Centre and were on their way back, but Kyle said he needed a fag break first. They were hiding in the stairwell in Bill Shankly House and his mum would kill him if she could see him – especially as he'd promised her that he'd be good from now on. But then she was taking him away and he didn't feel like being good any more.

His friend frowned and took the cigarette from him. 'Where to?'

'To Surrey.'

'Frig.' Taking a long drag of the cigarette, Kyle gazed thoughtfully out into the middle distance. 'Where's Surrey?'

'I don't know,' Charlie admitted. 'But it sounds like it's a long way away.'

He was surprised that his mum wanted to move now that she'd made the estate look so nice. Why do all that hard work when all you wanted was to go away? It didn't make any sense. But then a lot of what grown-ups did made no sense at all.

'We'll never see each other again,' Kyle said. 'We can't learn to drive for another eight years and then we'll have forgotten about each other.'

'I know.' He didn't really know, but he could trust Kyle on these things. 'What car would you get?'

'I'll probably get a BMW. A black one.'

'I'd like an Aston Martin.' Like James Bond. That would get him back from Surrey quickly. 'We could MSN each other.'

'That's for girls,' Kyle said, pouring scorn on the idea. 'And this is all because your mum's marrying that posh fella?'

'Yeah.' Charlie scuffed his shoe along the concrete – even though he knew his mum would go ballistic about that too. He knew that his mum wanted to get him away from here and, if he told the truth, away from Kyle too. 'I want to stay here and live with Johnny, but she won't let me.'

Charlie was really pleased that they'd taken the paintings to the gallery. That had been a good thing, even though it had got him into a lot of trouble. Mum said he wasn't to worry about Johnny, that they'd still see him often. But a lot of stuff that grown-ups said didn't happen. They just pretended, to make you feel better.

'You could probably live at our house,' Kyle offered. 'My mum likes you. I think she likes you more than she likes me. She's says that I've been Nothing But Trouble From Day One.' Funny, but Charlie's mum said the exact same thing about Kyle too. Charlie had never found Kyle to be Nothing But Trouble – he thought his best mate was a lot of fun. And he knew stuff.

'So what shall we do?'

'We could run away together.' Kyle's eyes brightened at the thought. 'Just me and you. We could clear off – go somewhere that they'll never find us, and then they'd all be really worried.'

'But where would we go?' Charlie wanted to know. 'What would we do for money?'

'It's not a properly formed plan yet,' Kyle admitted. 'But I'd like to live by the seaside, wouldn't you?'

'Perhaps Surrey is by the seaside.'

Kyle looked a bit disappointed at the thought of that.

'We'd better go,' Charlie said. 'Otherwise they'll wonder where we are.'

'They'll wonder where *you* are,' Kyle corrected.

'Your mum and stepdad seem to like you now,' Charlie pointed out. 'They've been digging with us and everything.'

'Yeah,' Kyle conceded.

'Perhaps one day you might think of your stepdad like I think of Johnny.'

His friend wrinkled his nose, but he didn't laugh as Charlie thought he would. 'Might do,' he shrugged.

Then he passed Charlie the butt of the cigarette and Charlie took the last puff before he ground it out under his heel. 'You know,' he said to Kyle, 'I think that I won't smoke any more. I don't really like it.'

His mate looked horrified, but Charlie just laughed.

Charlie's mum said that he'd find better friends in Surrey – nicer friends. But he was sure that he'd never, ever find a friend like Kyle Crossman again.

Chapter Ninety-Two

'Mixed marriages never work,' Debs advises me. 'One man, one woman – can't be done. Whoever thought that one up should have been shot.'

And I was simply concerned that she thought our backgrounds were too different.

My friend and I are sitting in the newly-created garden behind Bill Shankly House. It's still a work in progress. The hoodies – Jason, Daniel and Mark – are currently getting lessons in how to lay paving slabs from Ted, Brian and Jim, the allotment guys. It's so gratifying to see how attentive and helpful the boys can be when they're occupied by something they're interested in. You never know, I could be seeing the blossoming of the next generation of allotment blokes, and it makes me smile to think of it.

The bench was put in this afternoon at the back of the garden on a small but perfectly-formed patio, but the rose arbour has yet to go over it. Already, I'm visualising a profusion of sweetly-scented blooms next summer. If only I were going to be here to see it. By the time that the roses are blooming and Mrs Kapur and Dora the Explorer are sitting beneath them, I'll be Lady of the Manor in the depths of Surrey. I should be excited by that, shouldn't I?

Debs and I are supposed to be arranging gravel around the slabs, but we're currently road-testing the bench, enjoying the last bursts of sunshine.

'I'm discussing this with you because I want reassurance,' I tell her.

'You shouldn't need reassurance,' my bezzie mate points out. 'If you're mad enough to get married, you should be absolutely dead certain.'

'I'm not,' I confess. At the moment, I'm having a fit of the wobbles every five minutes.

'And this is because you think Spencer's trying to sideline Charlie.'

'Yeah. He wants to send my son away to school.'

Debs shrugs. 'Sounds great to me.'

'You don't mean that.'

'I take it there's been no talk about Little Lord Fauntleroy trading in the Porsche for a Renault Espace when you up sticks and move to Outerbumblefuck?'

I shake my head. 'I still don't think that the reality that I actually have a child has quite permeated Spencer's brain.'

'Will it ever?'

Now it's my turn to shrug. 'Perhaps it will be better when we're all living together permanently.' Spencer can hardly pretend that Charlie doesn't exist then, right?

'The thing I find is that women marry because they believe men can change. Men marry because they believe women *never* change. Both are usually mistaken.'

This does nothing to cheer me up.

I cup my chin in my hands. 'I just think that I'd be completely bonkers to pass up this opportunity.'

'Do you love him?'

'I *adore* him! What's not to love? He's gorgeous, he's intelligent, he's funny . . .'

'He's loaded.'

'As a man he's ninety-nine per cent perfect.'

'That's a pretty high percentage. They don't come along very often.'

'No,' I agree. From the woman who's had two men in her life who have both been fabulous. I've messed everything up with Johnny, what if I now blow Spencer away? Am I then destined to remain a single mum for the rest of my life? Joining Debs on the depressing merry-go-round of dating dubious men? I'd rather stay single and celibate. 'There's just this one sticking point. If Spencer loved Charlie like Johnny does, then there wouldn't even be an issue.'

'But he doesn't,' Debs reminds me.

'No.' I sigh and massage my temples.

My friend rummages in her handbag. 'Did you see this? I brought it over for you from my sister's in case you hadn't seen it yet.'

Debs hands me the local paper. She's right, I haven't seen it. Sometimes – more often than not – we don't get our local rag because the paperboy can't be bothered to climb ten flights of stairs. And who can blame him?

On the front page there's a story about Johnny. 'Wow,' I say. 'They're calling him Liverpool's answer to Jackson Pollock.'

'Jackson Pillock, more like.' Debs is clearly unimpressed by Johnny's newfound success.

'They're going to have an exhibition of his paintings at the Tate Liverpool.'

'Whoopee-doo.'

Will I get an invite to the launch-party? Do they have launch-parties for painters? I'm sure they must. It will be all champagne and canapés. How soon will it be? Will I already be in Surrey by then? Will Dana be the one who's gracing Johnny's arm instead of me? This is such an exciting time in Johnny's life and I'm so disappointed, after all we've been through together, that I'm not alongside him supporting him, sharing it with him.

I haven't seen him yet today. He's still over at the Community Centre working away with Dana and, try as I might to deny it, there's a bit of a barrier between us now. I think it's her. Johnny probably lays the blame at Spencer's door. Whoever's fault it is, something's definitely changed between us. I wish in so many ways that things could go back to how they used to be – but when they were how they used to be, I was miserable. And they say that women are complicated . . .

'So what do I do?' I ask Debs again. Though why I'm relying on her for my relationship advice is beyond me. She's never been any use to me before and I don't suppose she will be now. I'd be better off asking Charlie's mate, Kyle. 'Do I go ahead with my wedding plans and hope that after we're married Spencer will suddenly turn into the model parent?'

'They do say that love is blind,' my friend says.

'Yeah,' I agree. 'I guess it's marriage that's the real eye-opener.'

Chapter Ninety-Three

The mural on the outside of the Community Centre was nearly finished. Johnny had painted various scenes depicting the regeneration of the estate and they seemed to be going down well with the Kirberly residents – particularly those who had starring roles.

Mrs Kapur and the three hoodies were captured in their gardening endeavours. Dora and Ronaldo tripped the light fantastic across the next panel. Ted, Brian and Jim, the old boys from the allotments, leaned on their painted spades caught in the throes of discussing their next move. It had certainly helped that Johnny's face had been plastered all over the local paper this week. Even with that one piece, it had turned him into something of a celebrity, with people coming up all day long to congratulate him on his success and admire the mural and telling him what a wonderful painter he was. None of it was doing any harm to his ego.

It was nice to be recognised for something at long last.

'You are wonderful,' Dana told him, after the last in a long line of well-wishers had just departed.

'It just feels odd,' Johnny said. 'Everyone suddenly seems to know who I am.'

'Now that it's sunk in, I feel we should go out to celebrate,' Dana suggested. 'My treat.'

'That'd be nice.'

'We'll do it tonight, when we've finished up here.'

'I'm just about done,' he told her, as he stood back and cast an appraising eye over his work. It wasn't half-bad. Maybe he simply saw it in a different light, now that he'd won the approval of those in the know. Whatever, he was pleased with the mural and even more pleased that it was nearly finished. Then he just had the inside to do and you'd hardly recognise the old place.

The estate was looking fantastic and that was all down to Sally. She'd been the one with the energy to get this all started. He was certainly going to miss her when she moved away to Surrey. Johnny could hardly contemplate that he wouldn't be able to just pop round and see her in Bill Shankly House any more. As for Charlie . . . he couldn't even go there. He was going to miss him like hell.

Mrs Kapur and the hoodies had done a wonderful job in the little garden behind Shankly House. Who'd have thought that the patch of scrubby wasteland filled with old tellies, microwaves and goodness knows what else would turn out to be such a pleasant sanctuary? The old boys from the allotments had also worked wonders with the parched patch of land around the Community Centre. It had all been dug over and, where the mural was completely dry, they'd started to plant up a lush line of green shrubs. It had to be said that Kyle's mum and his stepdad had worked wonders here alongside their boy and Charlie, efficiently organising everyone to get the job done. That was something he'd never expected to see.

Other residents had worked on clearing up the grass verges, collecting rubbish, and Dana had brought her colleagues in from the Council to take away some of the stuff that had been dumped round by the garages – old cookers, bent bikes, a broken buggy or two. It was unbelievable the difference that alone had made.

There were some scruffy swings, slides and stuff on the other side of the estate that had been steadily vandalised by the teenagers over the years until they were unusable. All that had changed too. Sally's group of volunteers had repainted all the metalwork, obliterating the graffiti. The equipment had been mended and a new, protective ground covering had been installed. Now the kids would actually be able to use it.

When this project was finished and he got back to his painting proper, he thought that he might paint some street scenes from round here to commemorate it. It had been so nice to hear the neighbours out together laughing and sharing a joke with each other. Virtually all of the estate had been involved in one way or another. He hoped that the sense of community spirit that they'd all rediscovered would continue long into the future. He, for one, would try to make sure that it did. Now that the Community Centre had been spruced up, they could organise more events that would help to keep them all bound together.

The course of his future might have changed, but Johnny knew that it still lay around here. It was only a shame that Sally wasn't sticking around to benefit from the fruits of her labours. The thought of his ex-girlfriend made his heart squeeze with sadness. She'd be sorely missed around here. And not just by him.

'Are you all right for a minute here, Dana?' he asked, calling across to where she was still bent over working.

'Sure,' she shouted back.

'I'm just going to go and have a word with Sally.'

Chapter Ninety-Four

Debs has left me on the bench. She's off for a wild night out tonight – her words, not mine. But I'm still sat here contemplating my future.

The sun's going down, but this corner of the garden is still pleasantly warm. All my old dears are going to love sitting out here and gossiping. Such a shame that I won't be here to join them.

'Care for some company?'

'Johnny,' I say with a start. 'Didn't hear you coming. I was miles away.'

My friend sits down beside me. 'In Surrey?'

'Somewhere like that,' I concede with a shrug.

'This is unrecognisable.' Johnny gapes in awe around the garden, which gives me a rush of pleasure. The hoodies are just packing their stuff away in the far corner. 'Those kids have worked wonders.'

'They've been brilliant,' I agree. 'I hope this is a turning-point for them. I want them to realise what they can achieve if they only put their minds to it.'

'I'm sure that this has helped them to see that. They should be eternally grateful to you.'

I laugh at that. 'But I'm sure they won't be.'

'You should be very proud of all this too,' Johnny says. 'I hope that you are.'

'Just a little bit,' I admit with a smile. 'Well, quite a lot really.'

He puts his arm round me and hugs me. 'Don't suppose that we'll get many more moments like this.'

'No.' And it makes me unutterably sad to think that we won't. 'It's been really nice working together.'

'Yeah,' Johnny agrees.

Then we sit and take in the evening air in silence for a few minutes, before I say, 'Hey, I saw you in the local paper. Debs showed it to me. You should be proud of that.'

Johnny flushes. 'Now I've got fame *and* fortune,' he says. Then he turns to look at me and his eyes are troubled. 'But you're still leaving.'

I nod. How can I begin to explain to Johnny the turmoil that's going through my brain right now? Though I've certainly got my doubts, I think that they're better left unspoken. Especially to Johnny. I wouldn't want him to get the wrong impression. Even though I'm not sure any more what the wrong impression actually is.

'Do you know when you're going?' he asks, breaking into my mental meanderings. His voice is gruff and I avoid looking at him.

'We've got to finalise that yet,' I say, staring out across the garden. What I mean is that Spencer and I haven't even discussed it. Would I want to leave straight away or would I rather have one last Christmas at Bill Shankly House for old time's sake? Or could our move to pastures new wait until next spring, so that at least I'll see some of the things that we've planted in the garden come into bud for the first time? I don't know, is the short answer. I'll have to ask Spencer what he's thinking. 'Whether it will be sooner or later, I'm not sure.'

'Can I ask a favour before you go?'

'Anything.'

'I'd like to take Charlie out for the day. I'd like to treat him for all that he's done for me.'

'That's really nice, Johnny.' I've managed to forgive my son for his criminal tendencies and put it down to a minor aberration. As long as he doesn't view this as a reward for bad behaviour — I'll have to make that very clear. Still, I know that Johnny always has the best intentions when it comes to Charlie. I rest my hand on his bare arm and am surprised to feel a pleasant tingle go through my palm. The skin that once was so familiar to me has now become strange and exciting. I brush away the thought. 'I'm sure he'd love it.'

'I thought me and Dana could take him to Alton Towers, something like that.'

'Dana?' My throat goes dry as I say her name.

'You wouldn't mind if she came with us? The hotel there's supposed to be nice with some themed rooms and stuff. I'd like us all to stay overnight then we can get into the park early.'

'With Dana?'

'Yeah,' Johnny says. 'She's a junkie for those white-knuckle rides.'

They make me want to puke.

'I don't know,' I say, chewing my fingernail even though it's full of grit. 'Charlie's going through a lot right now, I'm not sure that he could cope with going away with someone else new.'

What I really mean is that I don't want my son getting too cosy with Johnny's new lady when all is not well in the world with my new man in the kid department.

'Charlie loves Dana already,' my friend says proudly. And I wonder whether the wistful note in his voice means that Johnny feels the same way too. 'They get on like a house on fire. She's so great with kids.'

A pathetic wave of jealousy whips through me. With *my* kid, I think. Charlie's *my* kid! Why can't Spencer get on with him 'like a house on fire', eh? Why can't *I* be the one to go to Alton Towers with Johnny and *my* boy? Then, before I can think better of it, I blurt out, 'I could come instead. The three of us could go. You, me and Charlie. It'd be like old times.'

Johnny looks slightly taken aback at my outburst. 'Except it wouldn't,' he says softly. 'Besides . . .' He pauses for a moment, clearly looking for the right words. 'I've kind of already mentioned it to Dana.'

'Of course,' I say, tears suddenly forming behind my eyes. 'She's your new girlfriend. Of course you'll want to take her.'

A traitorous tear spills out of my eye.

'Why are you crying?'

'I don't know,' I snap. 'Probably because I want to go to bloody Alton Towers too.'

'But you hate white-knuckle rides,' Johnny says, quite reasonably.

And I know that I do, but pointing it out just doesn't make me feel any better.

Chapter Ninety-Five

I'm kneeling down planting some small but healthy lavender bushes around the patio. The idea is that, along with the roses, they'll give the area a lovely scent. Spencer's kneeling next to me, shirt sleeves rolled up, digging holes with a trowel. He looks perfectly contented.

And I should be delighted that he's here as he dashed over eager to continue with the garden as soon as he'd finished today's computer class. A class which I should have been at, but missed. Spencer hasn't taken me to task over it – maybe he assumed I hadn't gone along just because I was too busy with the regeneration project. Partly, that's true. But to be honest, I couldn't face sitting in that stuffy little room staring at a computer screen any longer. The course only has another week to run. Then it's done. Frankly, I've probably learned as much as I need to know for now. I wanted to be out here. I wanted some peace and quiet. I wanted to feel the sun on my face while it's still around. The project has progressed so well and we've had so many willing volunteers that it will soon be over, and part of me will be so sad to see it end. It feels as if a chapter in my life – a very fulfilling one – is coming to a close.

Next to me, Spencer is chatting away while I let his words wash over me. I'm only half-listening, if I'm honest.

'We could have the wedding on the lawn at Alderstone House,' he says. 'Get a huge marquee. We did the same for my parents' fortieth wedding anniversary. The caterers were wonderful. They'd be perfect. We also have a florist who's done the arrangements for the house for many years. We haven't discussed your ring yet, but my grandmother left her engagement ring to me. I've always hoped that my wife would wear it.'

At that, I tune back into the conversation. 'Your grandmother's ring?'

'Yes.'

Do I want to wear Spencer's granny's ring? Isn't that bad luck? 'I think I'd quite like to choose my own.'

'Oh.' Clearly, Spencer hadn't considered that. 'It really is beautiful.'

And it's second-hand. I've spent all of my life being a second-hand Rose; I'd like something sparkly and new and mine.

Come to think of it, do I actually want a huge wedding with a marquee and caterers recommended by Spencer's parents and the old family florist? Who would I invite? I'd love Mrs Kapur to be there, but would she be too frail to make the round trip? How would the posh Knights cope with the wanderings of Dora the Explorer?

Somehow I always thought that the register office in Liverpool city centre would get my business when I finally decided to tie the knot. Next Spencer will be telling me that he's sold the exclusive coverage rights to *Hello!* magazine or, more likely, *Horse & Hound*. All this talk is starting to give me palpitations. I grab a lavender plant and inhale deeply. That's supposed to calm you down, right?

'I thought Tuscany for the honeymoon,' Spencer continues happily as he digs. I pass him a tender lavender plant and he takes it from me and lovingly commits it to the earth. Pausing in my toil, I look up at him. This man does everything with such care, such precision. I love him for it.

'Where's Tuscany?'

He seems taken aback at that and turns to see if I'm joking. I'm not.

'Italy,' he supplies.

'Oh,' I say. 'Sounds nice.' But even to my ears my response sounds lacklustre.

'I thought we could find a cookery course or maybe a painting course. I've always wanted to devote some time to watercolours.'

That takes *me* aback. 'You paint?'

'Dabble,' Spencer insists modestly. 'Nowhere near as good as Johnny.'

'No.' I sit back on my heels. According to the *Liverpool Echo*, no one's as good as Johnny.

'Does that sound okay?'

They both sound too much like hard work to me. I cook every day as it is – can't quite see the attraction of doing it on honeymoon too. Isn't the idea of a holiday that someone cooks for you? Painting? Never had, or am likely to have, any desire to put brush to canvas. 'So what will we do with Charlie when we're cooking or painting?'

Spencer flushes. 'We could organise it for when he's in school.'

I lay down my trowel. 'I told you, he's not going away to school. He's going to be at home.'

'Then my parents could look after him,' he capitulates.

That makes me laugh – and not in a good way. 'They'll hate him. Why would I leave him with them? He doesn't even know them.'

'I'm sure they'll love him.'

I'm equally sure that they'll hate him. Like they hate me. Can you imagine them liking a scrotty, council-flat kid born on the wrong side of the sheets running amok in their stately home? No wonder that Spencer's so anxious to get rid of him to some swanky school where he'll probably have to wear a tailcoat and a top hat. Well, not my Charlie!

'I don't think that's an option,' I say firmly.

'What about Johnny?'

'I can't dump Charlie on Johnny every time we want to swan off together. It might be okay for a couple of days at a push, but you're probably thinking about a week.'

'Two,' he says weakly.

I shrug. 'It's not going to happen.'

'You never really mentioned Charlie's father,' Spencer points out. 'Doesn't he have access or visitation rights?'

'He's in Walton Prison for armed robbery for the foreseeable future.'

Spencer pales at that. I normally try to keep that quiet, but my future intended might as well know what he's dealing with. In fact, I take some sort of perverse delight in telling Spencer. Perhaps he has visions of Charlie's dad turning up at Alderstone House armed with a sawn-off shotgun. He doesn't need to know that the further away I can keep Charlie from his dad, the better.

'So don't be thinking that you can palm Charlie off on *him*,' I snap.

When I see quite how horrified he looks, I feel awful and add, 'He wasn't an armed robber when I was with him.' Just so he knows that my taste in men isn't truly appalling. Though, if I'm truthful, even back then I could see the potential.

Then I sigh inwardly. Am I doing the same thing here? Am I simply ignoring the alarm bells that are quietly but persistently ringing in my head? Okay, Spencer may not be giving off violent criminal vibes and he may be the perfect man on paper, but can we overcome the more obvious and ten-year-old glitch in our relationship? Is it surmountable?

'Is a honeymoon out of the question at all?' he wants to know.

'We could go to Disneyland or somewhere that has a water park and take Charlie with us.'

Now Spencer looks like he's about to faint. 'On honeymoon?'

'That's what being a family is all about,' I tell him. 'We do things together. One of us doesn't get left out all the time. We're not a couple, Spencer. We're a threesome.'

'I know,' Spencer replies earnestly with a sigh. 'I have to start to think differently. It will just take time.'

But I wonder how long. Hasn't he had just about long enough?

He can obviously sense my doubts as he abandons the lavender plants and comes to put his arms around me and hold me tight. 'Don't give up on me,' he says. 'Please. We'll work this out. I promise you.'

I want to believe him, I really do. But do you ever do that thing when the batteries on the remote control for the telly are going flat and you just keep pressing the buttons harder in the hope that, against all the odds, it will finally work? Isn't that exactly what I'm doing now?

Chapter Ninety-Six

I've worried about the weather for days. Normally, the British weather is about as reliable as some of the more dodgy men who Debs has dated. I had visions of it pouring down and turning our barbecue to celebrate the end of project All You Need Is Love into a complete washout. But my fears were unfounded. Today, the elements are behaving perfectly. There's just the right amount of brilliant blue sky, the right amount of sunshine. And, like Goldilocks's porridge, it's not too hot, not too cold. There's the right amount of breeze too, enough to keep the kids from over-heating, but not too much to risk the flames from the barbecue engulfing the newly-renovated Community Centre.

Johnny and Spencer are in control of the man-kitchen and there's much discussion going on about the heat of the coals and whether the chicken has been marinaded for long enough. They're smiling and laughing together and my heart flips as I watch them and I don't know why.

They might be concerned about the marinade, I'm more worried whether we've got enough chicken for everyone who's coming along today. I take a minute to stand and look around me. In some ways it really saddens me that the project is just about finished. Ted, Brian and Jim are currently helping Johnny's mum who is sitting in her wheel-chair at a fold-up table putting a few last pretty, flowering plants into two hanging baskets to grace the front of our lovely Community Centre. But, other than that, we're done.

All the residents who've been involved are coming along to our little celebration and there'll be a few bods from the Council too including Dana and Richard Selley, the man who helped us to set it all up in the first place.

Dana Barnes might be younger, prettier and more competent than me, but I can't deny that she's been a great help around here – she's really thrown herself into the project with great gusto. All the people

293

on the estate love her – including Johnny, it seems. She's thrown herself with great gusto at my ex-boyfriend too. I feel ridiculously jealous, but despite that, I still really like Dana. I've even agreed that they can take Charlie away for an overnight stay to Alton Towers – even though I'll spend all the time having a heart-attack, wondering what my only child is up to and whether he's lying tangled in the machinery of a white-knuckle ride.

Debs and I are standing behind the buffet tables which have been covered with red and white gingham cloths in convenient wipe-clean plastic. I'm trying to organise the bowls of salad that we've already prepared this morning in an attractive fashion. Super Sal, needless to say, has been up preparing food since dawn. My dear friend is buttering finger rolls. She's been unusually quiet all morning.

'Feeling a bit under the weather?' I ask.

She shakes her head. 'Just thinking.'

'Want to share?'

Debs pauses in her buttering. 'How can you leave all this behind?' she says. 'Now that you've done so much for the area?'

'I don't know,' I answer with a sigh. 'Everywhere's looking so wonderful.'

'You've done a great job, Sal.'

'We all have.'

'I haven't planted a single thing,' she reminds me.

'Yeah. But you've been there with the bacon butties and the tea and stuff whenever we've needed it.'

Debs huffs and I can tell that she's not really worried about her lack of horticultural involvement. 'What's this really about?' I ask.

'What am I going to do without you?' she complains. 'You've been my bezzie since school. Just think of all the things we've been through together.'

'No one can take that away from us.'

'It won't be the same. What if they put some miserable old goat in your flat or a family of fifty Romanians?'

'Or they might put some hunky young single guy in there.'

She tries a smile at that, but then bursts into tears.

'Oh, Debs.' I abandon my salad display and put my arms round her. 'Don't cry.' Then I cry too.

'I don't want you to go to Outerbumblefuck,' she sobs. 'None of us do. Mrs Kapur's so upset, but she's trying not to show it. How will she manage without you? Who'll lug her shopping upstairs for her if you don't do it? Who'll go and get her prescriptions when she's ill? Who'll keep an eye on Dora when she has her wandering days?'

'Maybe you could,' I suggest.

'You know what I'm like,' Debs counters with a sniff. 'I'm full of bloody good intentions, but I forget. I'm such a selfish fucker. I'm not like you – I couldn't run round after them all like you do. Dora would be halfway to John O'Groats before I'd even noticed she was missing. Or worse, Mrs Kapur could be lying dead in her flat for three days with Gandhi chewing her face off. You hold this place together, Sal. You take care of everyone.'

'Isn't it time that I took care of myself for a change?'

'No,' Debs says passionately. 'We want you to stay here and keep wiping our noses and our arses for us.'

We both laugh tearfully at that.

'I won't be far away.'

'It's miles away,' she points out. 'We both know that. When you become all posh and lah-di-dah in your new life you won't want to know us plebs.'

'Don't say that.'

'But it's true.'

I sweep my arm around, taking in the 1960s housing estate of Kirberly in all its sunwashed glory, the monolith of William Shankly House with its pretty secluded garden, the Community Centre resplendent with its new coat of Johnny's murals, and pride swells up inside me. 'This is the place I love. These are my people. This is me.'

The poignant lyrics of 'Ferry 'Cross the Mersey' ring in my ears.

Then a pang of guilt or longing or something hits me square in the chest and I wonder exactly why I'm thinking of leaving it all behind. I've spent so many years hating it round here, but now that push comes to shove, do I really want to leave all that I've ever known, all that I've grown up with, all that I've worked so very hard to revitalise?

Chapter Ninety-Seven

Mrs Kapur, in best sari, is sitting on a deckchair eating a vegetable kebab. She's giggling along with the hoodies who have clearly taken a shine to her. I'm so glad that the lads have turned up today. Jason, Daniel and Mark have all worked so hard and have really become part of our community during the process rather than being disaffected and hanging around on the edges causing trouble. I hope that now they've contributed to the regeneration of the area that they'll take a greater pride in where they live rather than trying to destroy it.

They've all brought their mums and dads along today; the latter haven't been involved in the project, but are now looking like they wish they had been. We've set up a rota to help maintain the estate and Jason's dad has already put himself down for some grass-cutting sessions. Daniel's mum is currently helping Debs with the buffet and his dad is hovering round the man-kitchen talking to Johnny and trying to make himself useful. Mark's mum and dad are sitting with Mrs Kapur, basking in the praise that she's heaping on their son and looking like they can't quite believe it. They've already said that they'll help run some activities in the evenings at the Community Centre to give the local kids something to do rather than practise their advanced vandalism.

We've draped some bunting round the Community Centre and have rigged up a sound system. Take That are presently making the party go with a swing. Dora's dancing round with Ronaldo, and is competing with Gary, Mark, Jason and Howard by singing 'I'm in Heaven' very loudly. Mary Jones, hanging baskets finished, now has Ringo curled up on her lap. She's beaming proudly and tapping her feet in time to the music. The atmosphere's great and I don't think there's been a street party round here since the Queen's Silver Jubilee in 1977. That's the last one everyone can remember, and I certainly wasn't around then. It seems like a really great idea though, and I wonder whether we could make the barbecue an annual event – a bit like the Ewings. Though I seem to remember that the Southfork shindig always ended in a punch-up and someone being thrown in the swimming pool.

My own tummy's rumbling, though I think it's more to do with nerves than with hunger. I'm so anxious that today will be a day to remember.

For a moment, Take That are turned down and Richard Selley, my nice man from the Council, takes the microphone.

'Before we all start to enjoy ourselves *too* much,' he says, raising his glass — hearty laughs at that, 'I'd just like to say a few words. The All You Need is Love project has been a model of how an urban regeneration should be run. You've all pulled together amazingly and have transformed Kirberly beyond recognition. You should all be very proud of your achievements.' Pause for approving applause. 'But I'm sure you'll agree with me that none of this would have been possible without the energy and the vision of Sally Freeman, the lady who started the ball rolling on this project. She's the one who set everything up, organised the planning and has been the key player in the execution of this.' Cheers now from the residents. I can feel myself blushing. 'So I'd ask you to raise a glass to Sally Freeman.' This is where he should add 'Single Mum and superwoman'. Glasses are charged all around. Mr Selley raises his glass. 'To Sally Freeman!'

The call is echoed by the residents. 'To Sally Freeman!'

Glancing over towards the barbecue, I see both Spencer and Johnny raising their glasses to me. The sound of jubilant cheers and clapping is ringing in my ears. I suppose I should stand up and say something momentous, but I'm too choked to do so. All these people are here, together, celebrating the revitalising of the estate just because of me. I've done this. Against the odds, I've bloody well gone and done it.

Johnny winks at me across the crowd. He smiles softly and mouths, 'To Sally Freeman.'

Chapter Ninety-Eight

So, it's back to the party. I find my glass and slog some more white wine into it. Now it's my turn to relax. I've done all that I can. Charlie runs up and barrels into me. 'I'm starving, Mum.'

'There's plenty of stuff on the barbecue – chicken and sausages,' I tell him. 'Haven't you had anything yet?'

My son shakes his head.

'Go and get something then.'

'Okay.' He runs off again, working his way towards the barbecue.

I watch as he goes, proud that he's turned out to be such a nice kid. Charlie rushes up to Johnny, who's busy flipping burgers. My ex-boyfriend turns when he hears Charlie's voice and I notice that his eyes light up when he sees my boy. I also notice that Spencer, right next to him, doesn't even turn a hair. Johnny slips a burger into a bun, piles on some fried onion, squirts some ketchup onto it, checking at each stage of the procedure that it's suitable to his customer's liking. Then he hands it over to Charlie and they both grin madly as Charlie bites into his burger. Johnny ruffles his hair, pulls him into a bear hug despite the fact that he's likely to end up covered in ketchup and they laugh together as they share a joke. Spencer concentrates on his chicken.

I sigh to myself and go over to the barbecue, hunger gnawing at my stomach. Spencer's already serving someone, so I turn towards Johnny instead.

'Would madam like a little bit of my sausage?' he asks saucily, as I approach.

'Yes,' I say. 'But not for me.'

I flick a glance towards Ringo, who's vacated Mary's lap in search of food and is now sitting at Johnny's feet, tail beating a hopeful rhythm on the pavement, a steady whine directed at the grilling sausages. 'You have a customer who was here before me.'

'He's had three sausages already,' Johnny says.

'One more won't hurt him.'

Johnny takes a serviette and wraps the end of a sausage in it. 'Careful,' he says. 'It's hot.'

'Ringo,' I call. 'Come on, boy.' Not surprisingly, the little dog follows me to the front of the Community Centre where I find a place on the kerb to sit down near the shrubs. I pat the pavement next to me, 'Sit.'

The little dog does as he's told. I break off a bit of the sausage and blow on it, because it's still too hot for him to eat. 'Don't want you burning your doggy tongue,' I tell him.

His tail wags harder and his bottom hovers above the ground as he shuffles forward expectantly.

'You know,' I say to my canine friend, 'I might not have always liked you, but I've always loved you.'

He cocks his head on one side and studies me.

'That may not strictly be true,' I concede. 'But I'll love you from now on, okay?'

Ringo gives a little bark. I'm not sure if that means that he understands, because he does seem a bit distracted by the promise of the sausage. I hold it out and nearly lose my fingers, such is his enthusiasm for the treat.

He gobbles it down without pause. So I break another bit off and give him that. Then, as we're sealing our doggy pact, I look up and am surprised to see a big black limousine pull up outside Bill Shankly House.

Chapter Ninety-Nine

S pencer comes up to me and says, 'We have a visitor.' Then he takes my hand and pulls me up. Ringo, realising that the private sausage party is now over, trots back to Johnny to see if he can blag any more pickings.

My boyfriend walks me across the street and then I see who's getting out of the posh car. It's Spencer's father. I feel my heart sink to my boots. He's wearing a navy pin-striped suit with a red tie, white hand-kerchief in the breast pocket. The sun – which has bestowed its rays on us all day so far – scuttles behind a cloud. He smiles when he sees us which, I have to admit, takes me aback – even more so than the fact that he's here in Kirberly in the first place.

'Son,' he says, as he shakes Spencer formally by the hand. Then he turns to me and nods. 'Miss Freeman.' Not a great way for my future father-in-law to address me. I wonder how they took the news of our impending engagement. There's been no formal announcement, as far as I'm aware. I'm sure if Spencer had hooked up with some titled debu-tante it would have been in *The Times* quicker than you could say 'wedding cake'. For that matter, because I've been so busy with the project, we haven't even had time to go shopping for my engagement ring.

The car moves off, turning heads as it progresses down the street.

'I wanted Father to come here,' Spencer says, 'to see all that you've achieved.'

Perhaps this is the second part of my interview to see whether I'm suitable material for running Alderstone House alongside his son.

Mr Knight turns a full circle. The expression on his face doesn't alter. 'Marvellous.' What he really means is that he can't quite imagine how awful it must have been here beforehand. I feel like dragging him the ten floors up to my flat just for spite.

'Come and see the garden Sally's created,' Spencer urges his father, and we all trail through to my new secret space. 'Before my fiancée got her hands on it, this place was full of old televisions, microwaves and goodness only knows what else.'

'Really,' Spencer's father says. He takes in my garden. My pride and joy. 'In time, I'm sure this will be very lovely.'

'It can't compare to your extensive grounds,' I say a bit too tartly, 'but it's a vast improvement on what it was.'

'I'm sure,' he says. 'Very well done, my dear.'

'Will you stay and join us at the barbecue?' Spencer asks. 'There are some very good kebabs.'

Mr Knight looks like he might pass out at the word 'kebab'. He makes a fuss of checking his watch. 'I have to be on my way, I'm afraid.'

Hi son looks disappointed and I wonder whether this is why Spencer has so much trouble connecting with my son when it's clear that his own dad is such a cold fish. Can't he tell that Spencer wants to show me off and show off all that he's been involved with? I don't think so. Would it hurt him to pretend that he gave a fuck? Clearly, it would.

'I'll get the car,' Spencer says, and disappears out of the garden, leaving me alone with his father.

Mr Knight turns to me. 'So I expect you think you've made yourself a very nice catch.'

'I think Spencer and I will be very happy together,' I say. 'Thank you for your kind wishes on our engagement.'

'You'll not marry into *my* family,' he warns.

'Do you really think so little of your son's judgement?'

'Yes,' Mr Knight says. 'Look at this place. No wonder you're so desperate to get out of it.'

Is that what Spencer's told him? *Am* I so desperate to get out of here that I'd consider marrying into a family who can't stand the sight of me? 'I don't know why you've come all this way just to be nasty.'

'Don't flatter yourself, young lady. I was up here on business anyway. There's no way I'd go out of my way for *this.*' He nods disdainfully at the garden. 'I just wanted to see for myself just what a mess Spencer has got himself into.'

'And now you know,' I reply. 'He's got himself into a "mess" with good, hardworking people who want nothing more than to improve their lot in life. We can't all be born with silver spoons in our mouths, Mr Knight. You were lucky. The rest of us have to graft for what little we've got.'

Mr Knight's eyes are beginning to pop out of his head, but I carry on regardless. 'Just because you have money it doesn't give you the right to come here and act like a stuck-up arsehole. This is important to us, and if you had any manners at all, you wouldn't be so damned rude. I've done this. All of it. With the help of some very good people. So don't you go looking down your snooty frigging nose at it.'

At that, Spencer appears. 'Your car's here, Father.'

'Thank you,' Mr Knight says tightly. 'Goodbye, Miss Freeman. This has all been very illuminating.' Then he marches out towards his waiting limo.

I fold my arms and glare after him. Wish I had my Super-Soaker to hand now. Wanker.

Spencer comes back to me a few moments later while I'm still standing fuming. Oblivious, he takes me in his arms and kisses me. 'I think my father really liked it here and all that you've done.' My lover smiles. 'But how could he not love you, when you're such a charmer?'

'Oh, Spencer,' I say. If only you knew the half of it.

Chapter One Hundred

I am woman. I am strong. I am invincible. I'm also very tired. Maybe it's time that I hung up my Superwoman cloak and let someone else have a go. Perhaps it's time to realise that I can't take on the whole world by myself and win.

I feel as if my energy levels are at an all-time low. A bucket full of Pro-Plus would come in very handy right now. Also, I guess there's a bit of comedown too. I've spent so long on a high while all this was going on that, now it's over, I'm not quite sure what I'm going to do with myself. Yesterday was a perfect end to it. Everything went so well – if you ignore the bit where I called my future father-in-law a stuck-up arsehole, of course. That was, however, the only blot on the landscape. Everyone said how much they enjoyed it and I'm sure they'll be talking about it round here for years.

'You look a bit weary, doll,' Mrs Kapur says, putting a hand on my arm.

I force a smile. 'It's been a *very* long few weeks.'

'But look at this, Sally love,' she says, nodding at the garden. 'It's bloody marvellous.'

And it is. I can't argue with my neighbour's assessment. The rose arbour complete with rambling rose is finished. Okay, so the rose is currently about two feet tall at the moment, but in a few years it will cover this shelter with beautiful, sweet-scented blooms. I can't wait to see that. Then I'm stopped short in my reverie as I wonder if I ever will.

Lavender plants surround the patio and line the path which mean-ders its way back towards the flats. In the corner of the garden there's a little shed which Ted wired up with power for us. Now it's complete with kettle and mugs that I bought from Save-It. Well, you didn't think we were planning on carrying trays of tea up and down ten flights of stairs whenever the lift's on the blink again, did you? Dora is currently doing the honours and she comes trotting out laden down with mugs of tea and some chocolate digestive biscuits.

Johnny's mum, Mary, is here too. I gave him a call to tell him to bring her over so that she could enjoy the garden along with us and get her out of the house. We all helped Mary out of her wheelchair and now she's sitting on the bench on the other side of Mrs Kapur. There's a pink flush to her cheeks that I haven't seen in years. 'This is like a little piece of heaven,' she says with a contented sigh.

'I'm going to make sure that you come out here every day when the weather's fine,' I tell her. 'Get you out of that damp house.'

'Are you going to come back from Surrey every morning then?' she asks. Which makes me shut up.

They all laugh at that.

'I'll have to get Johnny to do it,' she says. 'Or that nice young lady he's got.' I'm not sure whether that's a pointed comment for me or not, because Mary isn't normally like that, but somehow it wounds anyway.

Dora sets the tea down on the low wooden table that we managed to buy out of the last of the budget, then hands out the mugs. Even Mrs Kapur's house cat, Gandhi, has put in an appearance today. I don't think that I've ever seen him out of doors before. His permanent home, for as long as I can remember is curled up in the corner of Mrs K's sofa. But, now that he's risked the great outdoors, he's clearly enjoying the sunshine too. He's happily rolling in the gravel, covering himself in dust, tail flicking at the air, the centre of attention. It's a shame that autumn will soon be upon us as I feel that I could sit out here for ever, letting my mind go into freefall.

'This is the life,' Dora says, as she settles in a chair with her tea. 'What more could anyone want?'

'I can bring my knitting out here,' Mrs Kapur adds. 'What do you think, Mary, love?'

'I think that's a sound idea.'

And it humbles me to think that these women have been made so happy, just by giving them a bench and somewhere a little bit nice and private to sit.

'It'll be really funny without you here, our Sally,' Johnny's mum says, her voice taking on a wistful air.

At this moment, I couldn't agree with her more. A lump comes to my throat and I feel like lying down on our newly-turfed lawn and crying my eyes out.

Chapter One Hundred and One

'Be good for Johnny,' I instruct as I search for my handbag. 'Go to bed when he tells you to and don't be a nuisance.'

'He's never a nuisance,' Johnny insists.

'I'm never a nuisance,' Charlie echoes, offended.

'I won't be late,' I promise.

'You always say that,' my son says. 'And you're always late.'

'Not tonight.'

I hear Spencer's horn toot and I head to the front door. 'See you both later. Thanks for this, Johnny.' I kiss him on the cheek, keeping it deliberately brief.

Johnny follows me and closes the door to the living room behind him. 'Everything okay?'

'Fine,' I say.

'You look a bit stressed, distracted. Sure everything's all right?'

'Yeah.'

'I don't want to delay you,' Johnny says, 'but we haven't really had time to talk much over the last few weeks, what with the project taking over our lives and everything. How about we get together for a cuppa sometime, do a bit of a download?'

'I'd like that,' I say.

'Pop round to Mam's sometime,' he tells me. 'When you've got a minute to spare.'

I don't really like to admit to Johnny that I've got too many minutes to spare now that my computer course has finished and the garden project has ended. My days seem so empty now that Charlie has gone to school too and they're starting to stretch ahead of me. I feel like a fish out of water.

'You did a great job, Sal.' Johnny strokes his hand along my arm. 'What next?'

'I'm not really sure,' I confess.

We hear Spencer's horn toot again. 'You'd better be going.'

I give Johnny a hug and fly out of the door.

Spencer's waiting to open the car door for me and he kisses me, then I slide into the cocoon of the Porsche. As my fiancé pulls away from Bill Shankly House, the hoodies are sitting on the step of the Community Centre and they all wave at me as we pass. The next thing could be to get the Community Centre up and running with activities every night to entertain the good folk of the area. Make it somewhere that Jason, Daniel and Mark can go into all the time rather than just hanging around on its step. I must get on to Mark's mum and dad to get it organised.

'Thought we'd try out a new bar that's opened,' Spencer says, breaking into my thoughts. We head back into Liverpool. 'It's been getting good reviews.'

'Can we just go back to your place?'

He looks at me, puzzled. 'Certainly.'

'I don't feel like going out on the town tonight,' I tell him.

'You could have called me. I could have just come round to your place for a coffee.'

'There are things that we need to discuss.'

Spencer laughs at that. 'Tell me about it,' he says. 'There's an engagement party to organise. Then a wedding. We need to agree on a timescale. Perhaps I should start an Excel spreadsheet.'

I say nothing, because I'm not sure what I can say.

Minutes later we're pulling into the garage below Spencer's apartment and we take the lift to the Penthouse. 'We could give that hot tub a try-out,' he suggests, slipping his arms round my waist. 'Isn't it about time?'

Shaking my head, I say, 'Not tonight.'

'You're very quiet, Sally. Is everything okay?'

'No,' I say. 'No. It's not.'

A look of concern mars his oh-so handsome face. 'Is it something that I've done?'

'No. Not really.' I sigh out loud. 'Can we go up onto the roof? I'd like to look out over Liverpool.'

We climb the stairs in silence, Spencer holding my hand and leading me out onto the terrace. I lean on the stainless-steel balustrade and Spencer comes close behind me, hands on my shoulders. The slate-grey thread of the Mersey flows slowly past below us. The faint sound of music drifts out from one of the bars in the Albert Dock, but I can't make out the tune.

'What will you do with this place?'

I feel Spencer shrug. 'I'm only renting it,' he tells me. 'The lease expires shortly. I guess we'll have no need of it now. Unless you want me to keep it on for when we come back to visit?'

Turning to face Spencer, I ease myself out of his arms. This is best done when I can't feel the heat of his hands on my skin or breathe the wonderful scent of him. 'That won't be necessary,' I say. Tears come to my eyes. 'I won't be leaving Kirberly, Spencer. There'll be no engagement, no wedding, no move to Alderstone House.'

His face is bleak. 'Why?'

'My life is here,' I try to explain. 'My friends are here. People who love me. Who need me.'

'But I love you,' he says. 'I need you. I thought you were happy.'

'I love you.' It's breaking my heart to do this. 'But I can't be your wife.'

Spencer sits down heavily on the edge of one of the sun loungers, head in his hands.

I sit next to him. 'We're from different worlds, Spencer. We want different things for our future.'

'Is this about Charlie?'

'I don't want him to be sent away to school.'

'He can go to the local school,' Spencer says. 'The *worst* comprehensive we can find, if that's what you prefer. I'll do whatever you want.'

'I want you to love him,' I say quietly. 'Like I do. And I can't force that to happen.'

Spencer says nothing.

'I don't want Charlie to have a stepdad who merely tolerates him. I want you to love him like . . .'

'. . . Johnny does,' he finishes.

'I wasn't going to say that.'

'But it's true, isn't it? I've seen how Johnny and Charlie are together.' Spencer gives me a rueful smile. 'I'm not stupid, Sally. Johnny's great with kids. I'm completely useless. But I can change.'

I shake my head. 'There are other things too. I'm too tired to battle against your family's opposition. The odds are stacked against us. I have to recognise that.'

'But I love you,' Spencer says.

'Sometimes that isn't enough,' I tell him sadly.

'Do you still love Johnny?'

I pause. I shouldn't really be having to think about this, should I? But I can't deny that there's still a strong pull there. Seeing him tonight . . . well . . . let's just say that Johnny is one of the people that I would have found it hardest to leave behind. I realise that I haven't answered Spencer's question and I hang my head. 'I'm sorry.'

Spencer sighs. 'You don't have to say any more, Sally.'

'I want you to be happy, Spencer.' I take his hand and squeeze it tightly. Part of me doesn't ever want to let this man go either. 'But I don't think I'm the right person for you. Maybe I was right for now, but not for the future.'

'I'll be going away soon and I can't bear the thought of leaving you. You've been a breath of fresh air in my life. What will you do? You can't stay in that terrible flat. That's no life for Charlie either.'

For a moment I detect a glimmer of real concern for my son, but maybe it's too little too late.

'Don't worry about me,' I tell him. 'I have plans. Big plans.'

And I do. I'm just not sure what they are yet.

―――――

Chapter One Hundred and Two

'You could read me a story,' Charlie suggested as Johnny pulled the duvet over him.

'Aren't you a bit old for that now?' Johnny said as he sat on the edge of the little single bed. Ringo jumped up beside him, circled three times and then found himself a comfortable spot.

'It doesn't have to be a soft one,' Charlie countered. 'I've got loads of scary stories. There's one here about a monster who gets his head cut off and then his guts spill out all over the place.' He did a perfect mime of guts spilling out.

'Yeah, your mum would like that if I scared you half to death before you went to sleep.'

'I could find something a bit in between then.' The boy wriggled out from beneath his covers and padded over to his bookshelf.

'Okay,' Johnny agreed. It had been ages since he'd read the lad a bedtime story. When he'd lived here, it had always been his job because he enjoyed it so much. Now this made him realise just how much he missed the task. 'But nothing too long. It's ten o'clock already. If your mum comes home and you're still wide awake, we'll both be dead meat.'

'She'll not come home early.' Charlie fingered his row of books as he made his selection. Pulling the book out, he climbed back into bed. 'When she's with *him*, she forgets about everyone else.'

'That's not true,' Johnny chided. 'You'll always come first with her.'

'Then why's she taking me to Surrey when I don't want to go?'

'That one's a bit more difficult to answer.'

'You're not going to go out with each other ever again now, are you?'

Johnny shook his head, a lump forming in his throat. 'No.'

'I like Dana,' Charlie told him, 'but I wish you were still with my mum more. Then I wouldn't have to go away.'

The boy handed the book to Johnny. He scanned the cover. *Scary*

309

Stories To Make Your Hair Stand On End. It didn't seem long since he'd been happy with fairytales from the Brothers Grimm or *Watership Down* – but then nothing ever stayed the same. 'Which one do you want?'

'You choose.'

'Settle down then,' Johnny instructed. Charlie snuggled down, pulling the duvet round his ears. 'Eyes closed.'

Charlie let his long lashes rest on his cheeks. Ringo was already snoring.

Johnny looked round the boy's room. It badly needed decorating in here. The kid needed something more modern, more grown-up. Perhaps he'd offer to do it for Sally over the next few weeks. Then he remembered that they wouldn't be here for much longer and the drab, peeling wallpaper wouldn't be their problem any more.

'Come on, Johnny,' Charlie urged excitedly.

Johnny lay down next to him, resting against the headboard, and opened the book. Charlie inched further into his side as he started the story. Johnny had long since realised that if he injected too much drama into the reading of Charlie's bedtime stories that it left the boy wide-eyed and buzzing and even further away from sleep than when he started. The more he read, the duller his voice became and, consequently, the heavier the eyelids of his listener became. He had to force himself to do it, because – if he was honest – he wanted Charlie to stay awake as long as possible so that he could spend every last minute available with him. He felt pathetic for feeling like that, but he couldn't help it. Who would read Charlie his bedtime story when he moved to Surrey? Would this be the last ever time that anyone did it for the lad?

As Johnny read, Charlie slipped his thumb into his mouth and his breathing softened. 'I love you, Johnny,' he mumbled as he drifted into sleep.

Johnny stroked the boy's hair, a tear running down his cheek. 'And I love you too, our kid.'

Chapter One Hundred and Three

Spencer drops me outside Bill Shankly House. He twines his fingers in my hair and pulls me close. 'I love you,' he whispers, his voice thick with emotion. 'Please change your mind.'

'Don't make this harder than it already is.' I'm crying now. We hold each other tightly. 'I wish things could have worked out differently.'

Then before I *do* cave in completely and change my mind, I slip quickly out of the Porsche and run into the foyer of Bill Shankly House for sanctuary. I hear the roar of Spencer's car as it pulls away, taking him away from me, out of my life for ever. I lean my head against the cool bricks, the bricks that have been freshly-painted to obscure all the graffiti in the lobby that's been scrubbed and cleaned and disinfected to take away the smell of wee. Another job expertly completed by the hoodies — but then it was mainly Jason, Daniel and Mark who messed it up in the first place. That's what I call just deserts.

I look round me. What if I do end up spending the rest of my life here? Would that be so bad, now that we've painted and weeded and scrubbed away all the grottiness and decline? It may still be a long way from Alderstone House, but now I've got a feeling of pride about living here. Hope to goodness that it doesn't wear off anytime soon.

I sniff into a tissue that I find screwed up in the bottom of my handbag. I could take the lift back up to my flat, because — miracle upon miracle — it's actually working as the Council came to fix it a couple of days ago. But sometimes ten flights of stairs come in very handy. I've now got as long as it takes me to climb to the top to pull myself together.

By the time I put my key in the lock, I've stopped snivelling. I'm probably as blotchy as hell, but I'm past caring. All I want to do is lie down in my bed and die.

Johnny's watching television with the sound turned down low when I go into the living room. Of Charlie there's no sign, so I hope that means that he was tucked up in bed by nine as he should have been. Ringo trots over to me, wagging his tail, and I bend down to stroke him and take a few moments to rough his ears up, which makes his tail go even faster.

'Everything okay?'

Johnny nods. 'Yeah. No probs.'

'Want tea?'

He shakes his head. 'I'd better go and check on Mam.'

'Of course.' If I didn't know better I'd say that Johnny had been crying too. My ex stands up. 'Is everything all right with Dana?' I ask.

'Dana?' He nods, looking surprised that I've asked. 'Yeah. Everything's fine.'

'Do you love her?'

My ex-boyfriend, hands stuffed in pockets, takes a moment to think about it. 'Yeah,' he says eventually. 'I think I do.'

'I'm pleased,' I say, even though I'm not. 'I hope that you'll be very happy together.'

'We're not planning to get married or anything.'

'I know. But . . .'

'Sal?' Johnny frowns. 'Are you sure that everything's okay?'

'Yeah. Yeah. Fine.'

I can't tell him that I've ended my relationship with Spencer or I'll cry again and I don't want to cry while Johnny's here. He'll be kind and loving as he always is, and that will make me fall apart completely. I want to smile and wish him happiness with his new love even though inside I feel like I'm dying.

'Go on,' I tell him. 'Or your mam will be worried.'

'Call round tomorrow,' he says. 'Any time. I should be at home.' Then he laughs. 'I'm at a bit of a loose end now that the project's finished.'

'I would have thought that you'd have lots of important artworks to create.'

'That still doesn't seem real,' he admits.

'I'm sure it will do soon enough.'

He picks his jacket up off the sofa and slings it over his shoulder. Then he kisses me gently on the cheek and I feel the warmth of his lips brand my skin.

'See you tomorrow,' I say, and the words create a small pocket of happiness in my misery. I'll be seeing Johnny tomorrow. And every day after that. Even though Johnny now has someone else to love, I feel happy that he'll still be around in my life, living just down the road. And I know someone else who'll be even more pleased.

Chapter One Hundred and Four

Charlie's still in bed, and if I don't wake him up in a minute, he'll be late for school. I hardly slept a wink last night worrying about whether I'd done the right thing or not. Am I crazy to pass up this opportunity? Could Spencer and I have worked through our difficulties and differences in time? Will I regret this decision for the rest of my life?

I pad through to the hall as I hear the post drop through the door. There's an official-looking envelope on the mat – which I hate because they're invariably bills or bad news and I don't think that I could cope with any more bad news today. It's come to something when I'm actually wishing that it's just a bill.

As I pick it up, a groggy Charlie wanders out of his bedroom, raises his hand in a cursory wave and mumbles, 'Hi, Mum,' before disappearing into the bathroom.

'Hi, Charlie.' I wave back at the bathroom door. Looks like I'd better get cracking in the kitchen then.

I chuck some bowls and a couple of boxes of cereal on the table, whack a few sandwiches together and stuff them in Charlie's ice-cream carton lunchbox and get the kettle on. Then, reluctantly, I turn my attention to my letter and sit down at the table while I open it.

I'm still in a state of shock and holding the letter when Charlie, now in his uniform and looking scrubbed, comes in.

'What's wrong?' he says, frowning.

'Nothing.'

'Then why do you look funny?'

'We've been nominated for an award,' I tell him. 'For the regeneration project. Richard Selley from the Council has put us forward. "Excellence in a Community Project".'

'That's good, isn't it?'

'That's great! All our hard work has been recognised.' I don't care if we don't win, to be nominated is affirmation enough. Who am I kidding? I'm *desperate* to win! I've got to tell Johnny right away. He'll be so thrilled.

'Come and give your clever old mum a hug.'

My son comes to me and winds his arms round my neck. 'I love you, Mum,' he says. 'You are clever. Kyle says I should be very proud of you.'

'And Kyle is always right.'

'Kyle says you're a MILF.'

My eyebrows raise at that. 'Does he now? And do you know what that means?'

'Yeah,' Charlie says uncertainly. 'I think it's a Mum I'd Like To Be Friends With.'

'It's a bit more than that,' I say. 'I'll explain another day, but I don't want you using it again.'

My son shrugs. 'Okay.'

I hug Charlie to me.

'I wish we didn't have to go away,' he mutters. 'Especially now you're going to get an award and everything.'

'We haven't won it yet,' I remind him. 'We've just been nominated. But I do have some other news for you.' I pat the chair next to me and Charlie slides onto it. 'We're not going to Surrey. Spencer and I aren't going out any more. We're not going to get married.'

Charlie's face lights up. 'That's sound!'

'I thought you'd be pleased.' Glad that my son isn't too concerned about my own broken heart.

'And we really don't have to go to Surrey?'

'No,' I confirm. 'We'll be staying here.' I avoid looking around the flat in case it sends me into a tailspin. This is the right decision. I must hold firm with that thought.

'Can I tell Kyle?'

'Of course you can.'

'And Johnny?'

'Maybe I should tell Johnny.'

My son puts his arms round my neck again and kisses me. 'You're the best mum in the world,' he says cheerily.

'Thanks.' I breathe in the soapy smell of his skin and feel the dampness of his freshly-washed hair on my skin.

My son wriggles away from me. 'Can I have my breakfast now?'

'Yeah. Help yourself to cereal. I'll put some toast in.' I sigh to myself as I stand up. For a Single Mum and Superwoman, it doesn't take long to get back to business as usual.

Chapter One Hundred and Five

When I've seen Charlie off to school and made a cursory effort of tidying the flat, I head over to Johnny's mum's house. He'll probably still be there after giving Mary her breakfast.

However, it's Dana who opens the door, which takes me by surprise. 'Hi, Sally,' she says. 'What brings you here?'

'I wanted to see Johnny,' I tell her as she keeps me standing on the doorstep.

'He's not here. He got a phone call first thing and he's gone off to the television studio down by the Albert Dock. He's going to be interviewed for a programme called *Art North West*.'

'Johnny's going to be on telly?'

She nods. 'Tonight, apparently. That's why I'm here. I've got a couple of days off and Johnny called me straight away to come and see to Mary.'

Normally, he'd ask me to do that. It just goes to show how quickly I've been replaced in his affections.

'Is that our Sally?' Mary shouts from the living room. 'Don't keep her standing at the door.'

'Sorry,' Dana says, standing aside to let me in. 'I wasn't thinking.'

In the living room, Mary's in her usual place in the armchair in front of the telly. Ringo's curled up on her lap, asleep.

'Sally, love,' Mary says, as I go and give her a kiss. 'Nice to see you, girl. You'll stay for a cuppa?'

'Yeah. I'll put the kettle on.'

'I've got it,' Dana says. 'It's just about to boil.'

'Oh.' Little Miss Organised.

'Dana's going to take me over to the garden today,' Mary tells me. 'Aren't you, doll?'

A 'yes' comes from the kitchen. I was going to suggest that I did it, but instead I keep my mouth shut.

'I love sitting out there with Dora and Mrs Kapur. She's such a little love that Mrs K. I feel like it's given me a new lease of life.' Mary claps her hands together in glee. 'And now our Johnny's going to be famous too! Looks like everything's working out for the best.'

'Yeah.'

Dana comes out of the kitchen with the tea and hands it round. She sits down next to Mary while I occupy the sofa.

'I bet you don't know what to do with yourself this week,' Dana says. 'Now that all the excitement has died down.'

'It does feel a bit strange,' I admit. 'I feel as if I'm a spare part. My computer course has finished now too, so I could go out and start looking for a job.' Hopefully Spencer has taught me well.

'In an office?'

'I guess so,' I say. 'I'm not sure that I'm cut out for it, but I don't know what else I can do. I've never really worked. What have I got to offer anyone?'

'Start your own business,' Dana says. 'You've made a fantastic job of this project. Do something like that.'

I laugh. 'I couldn't.'

She shrugs at me. 'Why not?'

'I don't know.' She makes it sound so easy. 'Do you think I could?'

'There are loads of grants kicking around to get you up and running if you know where to ask,' Dana tells me. 'I can help you with that. A good friend works at the Business Link centre; she can give you a hand with the paperwork side of things and get you on some business workshops.'

'I really enjoyed working with Jason, Daniel and Mark,' I confide in her. 'Just doing something so simple as a bit of gardening has really transformed them. I wonder could I do something to help other kids like that?'

'I wouldn't mind them coming and doing up my back yard,' Mary chips in. 'It's a real mess out there, but I've never really been bothered about it until now. Makes me feel scruffy compared to the rest of the estate.'

Then a little light bulb pings on in my brain. 'What if I started a gardening company that used delinquent kids to do the gardens of disabled people? Do you think there'd be a need for that?'

Dana smiles at me. 'It sounds to me like you have a plan.'

I laugh. 'I think I do!'

317

'I'll be your very first customer,' Mary says.

'But then you won't be around here for much longer, will you?' Dana points out. 'Still, I'm sure you could do a similar thing in Surrey.'

For some reason, I decide to keep the latest development in my love-life quiet. I want to discuss it with Johnny myself. Which reminds me . . . 'I came to see Johnny to tell him some good news,' I say.

'Ah, the community project award,' Dana says.

That takes me aback. 'How do you know about it?'

She shrugs apologetically. 'I was in Richard Selley's office giving him an update and I'm afraid that he let it slip.'

'You're going to get an award for all the work you've been doing?' Mary asks, and claps.

'I hope so,' I tell Johnny's mum. 'We've been put forward for it. Now we've just got to wait and see if we win.'

Mary claps again. 'That's great news, girl!'

'I know. I can hardly believe it.' I allow myself a big grin. 'I can't wait to tell Johnny.'

'I've told him already,' Dana confesses. 'Well, I just couldn't keep it to myself, could I?'

Oh. 'No. I guess not.'

'Johnny's so pleased.'

'Good. I'm glad.' I thought he would have called me the minute he heard.

'He did go out of here in a bit of a rush,' Dana says, as if she's reading my mind. 'I'm sure he'll give you a ring later when he has a minute.'

'I'm sure he will.' But, to be honest, I'm not sure of anything any more.

Chapter One Hundred and Six

'Can we get you anything else, Mr Jones?'

'Er . . . no,' Johnny said. 'No, thanks. I'm sound.' He sipped at his glass of water, mouth dry.

'Champagne? Croissant?'

'No. No.' It wasn't yet eleven o'clock in the morning. He'd had champagne twice in his life. Cheap stuff from Save-It that probably wasn't even real champagne. He certainly hadn't drunk it before dinner-time and he wasn't about to start now, even though a glass or two might have helped to steady his nerves.

He was waiting in the Green Room of the North West Broadcasting Company waiting to be interviewed for their arts programme. The studios were posh, housed in an old tobacco warehouse now kitted out with everything steel and glass. The nearest he'd been to them was going past the window of the studio that backed out onto the dock where he'd given the obligatory wave in the hope that he could catch one of the cameras and see himself in the background when whatever programme they were filming was broadcast.

Today, he was *inside* the building. And that felt really good. Getting through security alone had taken a good ten minutes. He was being slotted in at short notice between an update on the building of the new Beatles-themed hotel which included a few soundbites from *the* Sir Paul McCartney, and a new Antony Gormley sculpture that had been cast in time to feature in Liverpool for the European City of Culture celebrations. Did he really deserve to be here? Paul was an iconic figure; Antony Gormley, one of the foremost artists in the UK. All Johnny had done was knock out a few paintings in his lock-up.

It was still a mystery to him as to how he'd managed to get here at all. If it wasn't for Charlie, his main ambition would be to sell a few canvases on one of the markets, or he'd have continued with his painting and decorating, transforming homes that had last been decorated in the 1970s by the magic of Dulux Hint of a Tint.

The buffet table in the hospitality suite was laden down with an array of drinks and an extensive spread of pastries. It was a shame that he couldn't eat a mouthful. His stomach was churning with nerves. He'd never been on telly before, had never imagined himself doing it. Now they were treating him like he was the next Damien Hirst. He'd even been given his own stick-thin woman called Helena to look after him. She was a bit scary. Every time he moved, she was there at his elbow. Really he would have liked to go to the toilet, but he didn't dare move. Helena might have wanted to go with him.

Johnny looked round the room, but he didn't recognise anyone else and he'd never learned or needed to learn the networking thing, so he stayed put and pretended to watch whatever it was that was going out on the big, widescreen telly that was the focal point of the room.

He wished that Sally had been here with him today. He'd wanted to call her, but he'd left in such a rush that there wasn't time. Now he wasn't sure whether he should use a mobile phone or not. Plus, what would he say? Why would she be interested in his successes? She was on her way now. She was on her way out of his life. Wasn't it time that he let Sally go?

He'd nearly called her this morning to come and look after his mam, but then Dana had phoned and she'd offered to do it instead. He knew that he should be pleased that Dana was so caring, but it still felt weird leaving his mam with her instead of Sal. Not that his mam seemed to mind; she'd really taken to Dana. Times must be changing if even Mary Jones had given up on him ever marrying Sally. Still, he could have done with Sally here. Just having her around would have made it a lot easier for him.

The host of the show swept into the Green Room with his entourage. Bob Gibson was a slightly overweight man with hair that was too long for a bloke of his age. He wore a trendy suit and had a big smile that wasn't entirely sincere.

Johnny was still wearing his mate's borrowed suit and he knew that he'd probably have to invest in one of his own soon if this sort of thing continued. It would be the first suit that he'd ever owned. Maybe Sal could come and help him pick one out – or Dana, of course.

Johnny knew that Bob Gibson was an influential mover and shaker on the local music and arts scene and that he'd been doing this show for years. The man knew everyone who was anyone.

'Johnny!' Bob Gibson gripped his hand and pumped it. 'Nice to meet you. Love the work.'

'Thanks,' Johnny said.

'Are they looking after you?' He turned his gaze on Helena, the stick-thin woman, who looked panicked.

'Yeah.'

Bob Gibson clapped him on the back. 'We'll start the show in about ten minutes. Just relax. We'll chew the fat. Look at some of your paintings. Talk about your inspiration, how you were discovered. All sound okay to you?'

'Fine.'

'Hang loose,' Bob Gibson advised.

Johnny shook his shoulders in an attempt to do just that. 'I'll try to.'

'By the way,' Bob Gibson said, 'I'm on the Arts Council committee for the new stadium. We're looking to have a mural on one of the car park walls. Big fucker. Would be seen right across the Mersey. I heard that's your kind of thing?'

'Yeah,' Johnny said. 'That's right up my street.'

'I'll put you forward,' Bob said. 'Local boy made good. We like that kind of thing.'

It seemed that a lot of people did.

'We're looking at about 250K,' Bob Gibson added as an afterthought. 'That in your ballpark?'

'Yeah,' Johnny managed. Did that mean that they were going to pay him two hundred and fifty thousand pounds just to do a mural? That couldn't possibly be right.

'I'm sure it will just go through on the nod,' Bob Gibson assured him. 'Leave it with me.'

It certainly looked like that was what he meant.

'Good. I want to grab you before they all start clamouring for you. You're going to be a very popular man from now on.' He winked at Johnny. 'We'll get that signed and sealed as soon as possible, then you can get started.'

Two hundred and fifty thousand quid for a mural. And to think he'd done Ronaldo's painting in his studio in exchange for a dance lesson.

While Johnny stood and gaped, speechlessly, Bob Gibson, the television host and the maker of dreams, pumped his hand again

Chapter One Hundred and Seven

'I can't believe that's our Johnny on the telly,' Debs says, as she swigs her glass of wine and puffs her smoke out of the window. 'Look at the state of him. What a fox!'

Johnny's sitting on the sofa on the *Art North West* programme being interviewed by Bob Gibson, who's been on our telly since time began. And Debs is right, he looks fantastic. He looks cool, assured, not a hint of nerves and I feel so proud of him that I think my heart might burst its way out of my blouse.

I've gathered the girls together in my flat to watch Johnny's performance, plus I wanted to tell them all my news too. Mrs Kapur's here, so is Dora. We've got through two bottles of wine already and a tub and a half of Pringles.

'He looks just like George Clooney,' Dora swoons.

I have to admit that there's more than a hint of the Cloonmeister about my ex. Who'd have thought. Johnny looks like a stranger sitting there talking eloquently about art, not like someone who used to share my life, my bed. Did I know him so little?

On screen, Johnny recounts the story of how his paintings came to be at the Tate Liverpool, giving Charlie all the credit. We all cheer at the mention of my son's name. Charlie's out playing football with Kyle, but I'm videoing the programme so that he can watch it later. We all clap Johnny when the interview finishes and I fill up everyone's glass again. We'll be having to carry Mrs Kapur back along the corridor at this rate.

'To Johnny,' I say, raising my glass.

'To Johnny,' my friends echo, and we slug back our wine in his honour.

'Wish you'd stuck with him now he's going to be a famous artist instead of Little Lord Fauntleroy?' Debs asks, sounding a bit slurry.

'Ah,' I say. 'I've something else that I wanted to tell you.'

They all wait with bated breath.

'It's all off with Spencer. No moving to Surrey. No big posh house. No wedding.'

'Oh, Sally,' Mrs Kapur says, tears springing to her eyes. 'What happened?'

'It wasn't right for me,' I explain. 'More importantly, it wasn't right for Charlie.'

'But Spencer seemed like such a lovely young man.'

'He is, but . . .' I shrug my shoulders. How can I begin now to tell them about all the doubts that I've had when I've kept them all to myself? 'Looks like we'll be staying here after all.'

'Well, I'm glad to hear that, doll. I was going to miss you. So was Gandhi. But are you sure you've done the right thing?'

'I hope so, Mrs K.'

'He wasn't right for you,' Debs says. 'I could tell all along.'

'Yeah,' I agree. 'He was a bloke.'

We laugh at that.

'It was bound to end in tears,' Debs tells me sagely, then adds, 'Can *I* have his number?'

'No. Get your own men,' I warn.

I wonder what Spencer will do now. Will he do as his father hopes and find himself a well-heeled and monied Felicity, Charlotte or Arabella? Will he forget about me, about his time at William Shankly House?

'I need to go to my bed,' Mrs Kapur says. 'I'm feeling a little bit dizzy.'

I finish my own wine. 'I'll help you back.'

'I'm off too.' Debs jumps down from the windowsill. 'I've got a date. Firefighter. Woo hoo! I can see if he's got a mate now that you're available again.'

'No, thanks. I've done double dating with you before. That way disaster lies. Besides, I think I'll give men a rest for a while,' I say. I haven't told my friends about my plans to set up my own business yet. Could I really do it? It's all right keeping a project going for a few weeks with someone else's money, but could I do it full-time with cash of my own? I don't know. I need more time to let the ideas formulate before I'm brave enough to go public. Until then, it's my own little secret.

Debs comes and hugs me. 'I'm sorry about Spencer.'

'Me too.'

'You know these things happen for a reason,' she says. 'It may not be a good reason, but it's a reason nevertheless.'

'Thank you. That's very comforting.'

Dora gathers her cardigan and handbag together, clearly limbering up to dance her way back to her flat. Looks like they're all abandoning me. Oh, good. Back to spending my nights in front of the telly so soon.

'Come on, Mrs K. We can't have you wandering round Kirberly drunk and disorderly.' Taking my neighbour's arm, I help her towards the door. It has to be said that she's a little bit unsteady on her feet – more so than usual. At least she'll sleep tonight though.

'Can you manage?' I ask as I open the front door.

'Ooo,' Mrs Kapur says in surprise. 'Hello, love.'

Then I look up and there's Johnny, still in his smart suit and holding a bottle of champagne.

Chapter One Hundred and Eight

Johnny helped me to put Mrs Kapur to bed. It's a good job that I had an extra pair of hands as she'd developed a fit of the giggles by the time we'd got her to her flat and was all over the place. A good time, I think, was had by all. When we finally cover her with her duvet, she's already sparko. I'd better get down to Save-It in the morning to buy some Resolve for her. That little lady's going to have one hell of a hangover tomorrow.

Now we're back in my flat and Johnny's in the kitchen opening the champagne. I'd hardly touched the stuff until a few weeks ago and now I feel as if I'm swimming in the flipping stuff. I don't spoil Johnny's treat by telling him that though. Also, I've had more than enough to drink already and I bet I'll be nicking some of the Resolve in the morning too.

I've got two of Spencer's champagne flutes in the cupboard, but I can't bring myself to use them. Somehow it just doesn't seem right. Instead, I rinse out two of the wine glasses and dry them with the tea towel. We take them through to the living room and settle into the sofa.

The cork pops and Johnny fills our glasses with bubbles.

'Wow,' I say. 'I think that this is probably the first time that we've drunk champagne together.'

He clinks his glass against mine. 'I thought we had a lot to celebrate.'

'Look at you,' I say. 'You'll be too posh for this place soon.'

'Like you?'

'Well . . . that's something that I wanted to tell you. But first, let's drink to your success.'

'To my success,' Johnny says, and we both swig our champagne.

'I've already had more than enough to drink,' I tell him. 'But I guess a couple more won't hurt.'

'Special occasion,' he says. 'It would be rude not to.' Then Johnny sighs. 'I got a big commission today, Sal. A really big one. It's not signed and sealed yet, and I probably won't believe it until the ink's dry and the cheque's cleared. But the Arts Council have offered me quarter of a million quid.'

That nearly makes me splutter my drink out. 'How much?'

'I know. I couldn't believe my own ears either.'

'What have you got to do for that?'

'Paint a mural on a car park.'

'Wow.' It's hard to take this in. How can Johnny sit there looking so unruffled? I'd be running round, waving my arms in the air and screaming like a banshee. 'I'm glad that we got you to do the Community Centre while you were cheap.'

We have a laugh at that.

I raise my glass again. 'No wonder you can afford to splash out on champagne.'

His eyes meet mine. 'I wish you could have been there with me.'

'Me too.' I want to reach up and stroke his cheek, but I don't. Johnny hasn't shaved since this morning and I know exactly how soft his stubble will feel. Pulling my attention back to the moment, I add, 'And there's the nomination for the award to drink to as well.'

We clink and swig again.

'That's great news,' Johnny says. 'I hope you win.'

'Me too,' I confess. What I really hope is that we blast the competition into the weeds!

'Here's to us,' Johnny says softly, and we swig in unison.

'To us,' I echo, and there's a sadness in my words. 'You did so well on the telly,' I chirp, trying to bring some lightness to the moment. 'It was as if you'd been doing it all your life.'

'Looks like both of our dreams are coming true.' He takes my fingers and toys with them. 'In some ways.'

Then he takes my glass and puts it down on the coffee-table along with his. Johnny leans forward and he kisses me, long and hard. His mouth tastes of champagne on mine.

'Oh, Sal,' he murmurs.

My body arches into his, fitting together so well just as it used to. Tears spring to my eyes; this feels so good, so familiar. It feels as if I'm coming home. Johnny's fingers find the buttons of my blouse and he starts to undo them as he covers my throat with hot kisses. I ease his shoulders out of his suit jacket and tug at his tie, fumbling to get the knot undone.

Then I hear a key in the lock and Charlie bowls in. 'Hiya!'

He stops dead in his tracks and watches wide-eyed as Johnny and I scramble to rearrange our clothing.

'Hiya.' Johnny's the first to find his voice.

I duck behind him, rapidly doing up my buttons, my face red with embarrassment.

Charlie shuffles uncomfortably in the doorway. 'How did it go on the telly?'

'Great,' Johnny said. 'I think it went well.'

'Sound. Can I watch it now?'

I smooth down my blouse. 'Maybe not just now,' I tell Charlie. 'Why don't you go to your room and get ready for bed. Johnny and I have got a few things to talk about.'

My son raises his eyebrows at that. 'Okay.' He turns to go, then changes his mind. 'Did you tell Johnny our news?'

'No,' I say. 'Not yet. But that's the very next thing on my list.'

'Cool,' Charlie says, and then disappears into his room.

When he's gone, Johnny puts his head in his hands. 'Sorry,' he says. 'Really sorry. Just got carried away by the moment.'

'It's okay.' I try a laugh. 'It will teach me to be more careful. I never thought that my ten-year-old son would catch me making out on the sofa. I always expected it to be the other way round.' Though not for a good few years yet, I hope.

'It's my fault,' Johnny insists. 'I shouldn't have done that. I love Dana. I love her a lot.'

Which kind of bursts my bubble. Did I hope that Johnny's passion meant that there was a chance of us getting back together? Yes, I admit that I probably did.

'And you're with Spencer. I don't know what I was thinking of.'

Now I force a smile. 'Blame it on the champagne.'

Johnny's eyes search my face.

'It's forgotten already,' I say flippantly.

He stands. 'Maybe it's time that I left.'

'We still have a lot of champagne to finish.'

'I think the moment's gone.'

Then I stand too and I put my arms around his neck and give him a long, lingering kiss. Johnny doesn't object. We hold each other tightly and I never want to let him go.

When we finally break apart, I say, 'For old time's sake.'

Johnny nods. We move away from each other until only our finger-tips are touching. There's a catch in Johnny's voice when he says, 'Dana will be worried about me.'

'Yeah.' I nod. 'You should go.'

He turns and I follow him to the door.

'Just one thing before you leave,' I say. 'Charlie and I aren't moving away.'

My ex-lover, my best friend, frowns at me.

'It's over with Spencer. I'll be stuck at Bill Shankly House for the foreseeable future.'

'Am I supposed to be happy about that?'

'I don't know. Are you?'

'Yeah.' Now there are tears in Johnny's eyes. He strokes my cheek. 'I never wanted you to go. I never wanted Charlie to go.'

My heart should feel light, but it feels like a lead weight. 'Well,' I say. 'Now we're staying.'

And now you're in love with Dana.

Chapter One Hundred and Nine

'She was kissing him,' Charlie confided. 'All over. It sounded all slurpy like someone eating a peach.'

Kyle wrinkled his nose and passed another Blackjack chew to Charlie. His lips and tongue were already black as they'd eaten a load.

'I think Johnny might have undone my mum's blouse,' Charlie said. 'Do you think that they might have been going to do It?'

Kyle shook his head. 'Nah. Too old. People their age don't do It.'

'They looked like they might.'

'Nah.'

'Your mum does It.'

'That's different,' Kyle said. 'She's not like your mum.'

'Oh.' Charlie thought about it a bit more. 'They were sort of lying on the sofa, all squashed up together.'

'When old people do It,' Kyle explained, 'they only do it in beds, so they couldn't have been going to do It.'

'Oh.' Charlie was glad that Kyle knew so much about these things otherwise he would never know what was going on. 'What other sweets have we got?'

Kyle delved into the bag. Now that they'd given up smoking they had more money for sweets, and you could buy an awful lot of sweets for the five pounds a week they'd spent on cigarettes. And sweets tasted much better than cigarettes anyway. It also meant that they could sit outside on the grass round the estate and they didn't have to hide away behind bins or the bike shed at school.

'We've got Fried Eggs, Swizzles, Flying Saucers, Fruit Salad chews, Fizzy cola bottles and Drumstick lollies.'

It was an excellent selection. Charlie pondered his choice. 'I'll have two cola bottles and a Flying Saucer.'

Kyle handed them over, licking his fingers as he did. 'What happened to the posh bloke with the Porsche?'

'Dunno,' Charlie said. 'Blown out of the water.' He made a series of exploding noises to illustrate his point.

'Huh.' Kyle stuffed in another Fried Egg.

Charlie turned over onto his stomach and kicked his feet at the air. He really liked it round here now that his mum and everyone else – including him and Kyle – had done it up. It looked cool. He chewed thoughtfully at his cola bottle. 'Do you think if my mum was kissing Johnny then they might get back together?'

'I don't know,' Kyle said with a mouthful of Swizzles. 'My mum kisses loads of blokes, but that doesn't mean anything.'

'I hope that they do go out again,' Charlie said. 'Now that we're not going to Surrey. Then everything would be perfect again.'

'I'm glad that you're not going to Surrey. I would have had to look for another best friend.'

'Me too.'

He punched Kyle and Kyle punched him back. Then they rolled on the grass, fighting. Charlie laughed out loud. He had a sound best friend, a big bag of sweets and his mum said he could get his own telly for his room for Christmas. Why would he ever want to live anywhere else?

Chapter One Hundred and Ten

Charlie's gone to school, but I'm still slobbing around in my dressing-gown having a hair mare and, as yet, am a slap-free zone. Actually, I might look like a slob, but I'm not strictly slobbing around. I'm on the computer tapping out some notes, trying to put a business plan together for my new gardening company, which I think I'm going to call GROW. I talked to Richard Selley – my nice man at the Council, who's turning out to be a very nice man indeed – and he is going to put me in touch with some of the agencies who work with disadvantaged kids.

The idea is that I recruit some youths like the hoodies to help do gardening for disabled or elderly people. The advantages are two-fold: the youths learn some skills to help them keep on the straight and narrow out in the big, bad world, and people who are in need of assistance get a helping hand. I had a meeting with Dana's friend yesterday at the Business Link Centre and she's given me some really helpful tips – told me how to apply for some funding and how to put my business plan together. Now the rest of it is up to me.

I hear a car pull up outside the flats and, being nosy, I glance out of the window. It's Spencer's Porsche. I see him get out, armed with an enormous bouquet, and then he heads inside Bill Shankly House.

It's too late now to go running round getting dressed and generally tarting myself up – although I do have the overwhelming urge to do so. Even now, now that it's over, my heart still lurches when I see him. Sometimes, I regret that the lift is working perfectly. This is one of those times. Spencer will be up here in just a minute, so not too long to panic.

I'm standing waiting at the front door when the lift opens and Spencer steps out.

'Hello,' he says, surprised that I'm already waiting for him. His usual cool disappears and, self-consciously, he proffers his flowers.

'They're beautiful.'

'If I was feeling particularly cheesy,' Spencer says, 'I'd tell you that they're not as beautiful as you.'

I give a glance at my tatty dressing-gown. 'Today, I wouldn't believe you.'

We laugh and that goes some way to breaking the tension.

'I've come to say goodbye,' Spencer tells me.

I swallow the lump that comes to my throat. 'One last cup of tea?'

'No, thanks,' he says, 'I can't stay for long.' But he follows me into the flat anyway.

'I'm going to miss you,' I tell him truthfully.

'I think I'll miss you more.'

His eyes are too sad and I can't bear to look at them. I turn away from his gaze and say, 'I can't thank you enough for all the things that you've done for me.' I make a gesture at the computer to remind him of one small thing in a sea of kindness.

'How's it going?'

'I'm hoping to set myself up in business,' I confide, knowing that it won't hurt to tell Spencer. 'I didn't think I was cut out for office work so I'm hoping to form a company using disadvantaged kids to do gardening for disabled people.' The more I say it, the more feasible it sounds.

Spencer looks surprised. 'Just like that?'

I shrug. 'Yeah.'

'I think you'll be great at it,' he says.

Then we stand in silence and after a moment Spencer sighs. 'I have to ask you one question. Are you and Johnny together again?'

'No.' I shake my head. 'He always has been and always will be one of my best friends.' I try to block the lingering memory of Johnny's last forbidden kiss and the taste of his lips. 'He's happy with Dana. Who knows – they may even tie the knot.'

Spencer looks relieved. 'I came here today with an ulterior motive,' he admits.

'Oh?'

'I want you to change your mind,' he says flatly. 'I still love you. I want you to come to Alderstone House with me and I want you to marry me.'

'I can't,' I tell him softly. 'I belong here. With Charlie. With all of my friends. When all's said and done, I don't want to be rattling round in a stately home in the middle of rolling fields. It's not me. I'm a city girl, born and bred, Spencer. I don't fit into your way of life. I've smog in my lungs, the smell of high rise in my hair. I love it here. This is my home. Mine and Charlie's.' I try for a laugh, but it won't come. 'I guess it's true what they say – you can try to take the girl out of Liverpool, but you can't take Liverpool out of the girl.'

'I could come here,' he says, his face deadly serious. 'The times I've had here with you have been among my happiest. I don't want that to end. I could come here and help you to bring up Charlie.' Tears spring to his eyes. 'I've realised that I'm going to miss him too.'

I'm so choked that I can't speak. If only Spencer had felt like that sooner.

'I've let the apartment go from the end of the month, but I could move in with you, find a proper job again. There must be work round here or in Manchester that I can do.'

'What about Alderstone?'

'My father would have to find someone else to run the estate.'

'You can't do that,' I tell him. 'It would never work. You'd only begin to resent me for holding you here. That's your destiny, Spencer. This is mine.'

I go to him and lay my head on his chest. Spencer wraps his arms round me and holds me tight.

'Go home,' I tell him. 'Find a great girl with the right pedigree, one who your parents love, settle down, have kids, send them off to boarding school and do what you're meant to do.'

'Put duty before love?'

'Sometimes it's the only way.'

He kisses my hair, holding me as if he's never going to let me go. And, despite my brave and sensible speech, I don't want him to.

Then Spencer breaks away from me and heads for the door without looking back. I sit in the window, dressing-gown wrapped around me, tears coursing down my cheeks.

A minute later and Spencer's climbing into his car; he glances up at me and I blow him a loving kiss that I want him to hold in his heart for ever. I stay where I am, wondering whether I'm completely mad in letting this man go, or whether I've really done the right thing. Then I watch as Spencer drives away and out of my life.

Chapter One Hundred and Eleven

We've all sat and clapped politely through a lot of presentations already. Next to me, Charlie sighs and I dig him in the ribs, making him sit up straight. The Council have hired a big hall in the city for the awards ceremony. It's decorated with red and white balloons, and flower arrangements grace the four corners of the room. There's a huge cake at the back that's forming the centrepiece of a sumptuous finger buffet that we're doubtless going to descend on when all the formalities are done.

I feel so nervous, as if I'm about to sit an exam. Thankfully, I'm surrounded by my good friends and neighbours who are here not only to support me, but because without their help and enthusiasm, the All You Need Is Love project to spruce up Kirberly would never have got off the ground. Mrs Kapur's here, along with Johnny's mum, who went out and had her hair done especially this morning – the first time she's done that in five years. Her lovely son must have bought her some new clothes too with his newfound wealth as she looks a million dollars. Dora the Explorer is on the other side of her with her new boyfriend, Ronaldo – who seems not to be quite as gay as we first thought. Charlie's sitting next to Kyle. Or should I say fidgeting. Despite having wriggle bottoms, they're both looking newly washed and very smart. Even more surprising, Kyle's mum, Janice, and his stepdad, Paul, are here too, and I have to admit that they've been a great help throughout the project and it looks like they'll continue to do their bit now that it's formally over. I only hope that it's helped to bring them closer together as a family and perhaps now they'll start to look after their boy a bit better.

The hoodies – minus their hoodies – are also here looking fresh-faced and glowing with pride. They're all got their mums and dads in tow and it's nice to see them all together. Ted, Brian and Jim, the old boys from the allotments, are here sporting neatly-knotted ties and their best jackets. Debs is tarted up to the nines for the occasion, but she looks desperate to slip out and have a ciggie already. I'm amazed that she managed to last the full length of the project, as gardening – or manual labour in any form, come to think of it – is not her forte. But she's been there for me, as always. I smile across at her and she catches my glance and then makes 'get on with it' motions with her hands, which makes me smile more.

Just behind me there's Johnny and his new love Dana Barnes with her colleague, Richard Selley. Johnny seems to have grown in stature since this whole art thing kicked off. He's holding himself that bit straighter, his chin higher, he's walking taller. His hair is nowhere near as messy as it usually is. He came in holding Dana's hand and looking like a man who'd found the meaning of contentment and I'm trying not to feel too weird about that.

The only face that's missing is Spencer's, and I feel that little bit lonelier inside without him here by my side. He's been back home in Surrey for a few weeks now and I've heard absolutely nothing from him – no texts, no emails, no late-night phone calls. And, call me fickle, but part of me wishes that he'd called me every day begging me to reconsider just so that I could talk to him.

We applaud again as a project for adult learners picks up an award. Then it's our turn. The award for the regeneration project which has most affected its community is about to be announced. Charlie slips his hand in mine, making sure that Kyle can't see it and I give it a squeeze.

The presenter is the woman who normally does the afternoon show on Radio Liverpool, Tina Murby. In her radio presenter's voice, she reads out the nominees. We're up against a primary school in Everton Valley that's installed an eco-friendly wildlife area in a corner of its playground, and an old rundown pub in Toxteth which has been transformed into a vibrant youth centre. But I take none of it in until it comes to our name.

'The All You Need Is Love project was funded by Urban Paradise and concentrated on regenerating the Kirberly housing estate, creating a new garden area, safer, upgraded play facilities and repair and redecoration of the Community Centre,' Tina says. 'Murals featuring the residents have been painted both inside and on the outside of the Centre by esteemed local artist, Johnny Jones. The scale of the project and the involvement of all members of the community over all age

335

groups particularly impressed the judges.' She takes a deep breath and beams at the audience. 'Therefore, I'm delighted to present the award to Sally Freeman whose vision brought this about and who has spearheaded the project.'

My friends and neighbours go wild, clapping and cheering. I sit there, mouth agape.

'Mum,' Charlie whispers in my ear as he nudges me. 'You've got to go to the front and get it.'

Somehow I manage to stand on unsteady legs. We've done it. We've won. We've bloody well won!

Turning, I see Johnny who's grinning and clapping. I fight the urge to grab him and hug him. He and I have done this together. Apart from producing my dear son, this is the biggest achievement of my life. I think there are tears in his eyes as there are in mine.

I go to the front and Tina Murby hands me the award. I'm shaking as I accept it. Holding up the glass plaque, I find my voice and say, 'I couldn't have done this without you. Your enthusiasm and hard work have carried this through. And now we live in a great place, the sort of place that we deserve. So this is for us. For all of us. And it's for me.'

Then I punch the air as all good Superheroes do.

Chapter One Hundred and Twelve

'Look at the pair of us,' Johnny says as we stand by the buffet. 'What a couple of swells.'

I laugh. 'I know. I can hardly believe it.'

Around us, our friends and neighbours fill their plates with sausage rolls, spicy samosas and spring rolls – except Debs who has cleared off outside to have a smoke and a swig of the vodka that she's got in her handbag.

The hall is filled with excited chatter as the award winners and their entourages celebrate their victories. I'm clutching my plaque to my chest, already wondering where I can put it in the flat so that it takes pride of place.

'You deserve it,' Johnny adds.

'*We* deserve it,' I correct. 'You know that this is yours as much as it is mine.'

'I've had enough adoration over the past few weeks to last me a lifetime.'

'Yeah. Maybe it is my turn,' I tease.

'Dana says that you're looking to start a new business.'

'It was sort of her idea,' I admit. She might have nicked my old boyfriend, but I do have a lot to thank her for. 'I'm just putting my ideas together, formulating a cunning plan.'

'I hope it goes well,' Johnny tells me.

'What about you?'

'I got the commission for a mural on the new stadium and there are more coming in practically every day.' He looks like he can't quite believe his luck.

'You're in demand. As you should be.'

Johnny nods. 'Life will be very different from now on.'

'I'm really pleased for you.'

'We could have had this together,' he points out.

'And now you're with Dana,' I remind him. 'And you're happy.'

Our eyes meet. Johnny lowers his voice. 'That doesn't stop me from wanting to hold you or telling you that you look fabulous today.'

Debs had persuaded me to indulge in another Kirberly market purchase which I don't have the money for. Looks like it was worth it. 'Thanks, Johnny.'

'I'm so proud of you, Sally Freeman.'

'I'm proud of myself.'

Then, throwing caution to the wind, Johnny takes me in his arms and we hug each other tightly. As always, it feels so good. Why is it that whenever I'm with this man I feel more myself than I do when I'm alone?

Charlie bowls up with a plate loaded with all kinds of things that he's not normally allowed.

'This is great, Mum,' he says, already turning hyper and that's before he's had the red and white cake. My son's going to be bouncing off the walls come bedtime. 'I've never won anything before.'

'You've been fantastic,' I tell him. Taking his plate, I put it down and then I pull him into our hug. Johnny ruffles his hair and my son glows as he says, 'You're a top kid.'

'The only thing that would make it better,' Charlie says with a wistful sigh, 'is if we could all be a family again.'

Johnny and I exchange a regretful glance over his head. It looks like that's one area where my son will be disappointed.

Chapter One Hundred and Thirteen

I've had two letters today. One from Spencer and one from the Council. I don't know which to tell you about first.

I'm sitting in the garden behind Bill Shankly House with both of them open on the bench next to me. I've been into the shed and have made myself a cup of tea which I'm now nursing to me. All the digestives have gone and I'll need to go to Save-It later to get some more as I can't have my outdoor ladies' club going without. I'm going over to get Johnny's mum in a little while and then collect Mrs Kapur from her appointment with the chiropodist and bring them both back here. If the weather holds we might even have some sandwiches out here for our lunch.

The temperatures are cooler now as it's slowly chilling down towards winter, but it's still pleasant enough to sit out in the middle of the day if they keep their coats on. The ladies have decided that they want to continue meeting every day and will adjourn to the Community Centre when the weather becomes too cold. But they'll all be back out here as soon as they can next spring, I'm sure of it.

I need to water the plants later and do just a bit of tidying up. I've put some bird-feeders out and have filled them with nuts. Blue tits and brightly-coloured finches of some sort twitter round competing for the food and it's the first time I've seen birds, other than a few scraggy sparrows, round here in a long while. Perhaps that's also why Mrs Kapur's cat, Gandhi, is spending so much time out here.

I pick up the letters again. I'm not sure which is the most shocking. Letter number one is from the Council.

Dear Ms Freeman, it starts. Then it goes on to lots of formal blah, blah, blah. But this is the gist. Due to our success with the regeneration project, William Shankly House has been earmarked for a complete renovation starting in six months' time. All the residents of said crumbling highrise block are going to be getting new kitchens, new bathrooms and new electrics. All the leaking radiators will be replaced and posh new double-glazed windows will keep out the cold. The block itself will be completely revamped. The rust and rain-streaked pebbledash is going to be given a new coat of paint and the faded, peeling boards under-neath our windows will be replaced with smart hardwood panels. We're also going to have a new front door and secure entry system. Wonder if we can manage to wangle Mrs Kapur a move to a flat on the ground floor as well? The other highrise blocks are going to be given similarly grand and much-needed makeovers too. All the council houses are being upgraded – which means that Johnny's mum's home will be on the list for a makeover. She'll like that – even though her son could probably buy the place ten times over now. The rows of grey, dilapidated pre-fabs are going to be knocked flat, and smart new homes put up in their place. Kirberly's going to look like flipping Mayfair!

What do you make of that? I can hardly believe our luck. Finally, I'm going to have a home that I can be proud of too. I just wanted to lie down and blub with joy when I read it.

The next letter is just as unexpected. It's the first time that I've seen Spencer's handwriting and I let my fingers trace the fine script, the elegantly-penned words.

My darling Sally,

I'm settled back at Alderstone House now and, needless to say, am missing you desperately. There'll always be a void in my life without you and a sorrowful regret for the chance that I missed. However, you've made your decision and I know that you won't be swayed, no matter what I say. I'll always be here for you should you ever need me. All you have to do is call. To prove my commitment to your future happiness, I've enclosed a cheque to help you get your new business off the ground. If you can't accept the money as a gift – and I do hope that you will – then please view it as a long-term loan.

Wishing you every success and much happiness in your future. Give my love to Charlie.

You're always in my heart. Spencer xx

How can I read that without wanting to cry? I take the cheque out of the envelope and study it once more. Spencer has sent me a hundred thousand pounds. That will start my business, employ a dozen dis-advantaged kids and make a lot of disabled people very happy. I *will* keep the money and I'll make sure that Spencer gets an excellent return on his investment. That may not be in cold, hard cash, but I'll try to make his money work really hard for him in improving the lives of people who need it most.

I fold the letters and slip them into my jeans pocket, just as the garden gate opens and Johnny comes in.

'Is there enough tea in the pot for two?'

'We don't have anything as glamorous as a pot,' I tell him. 'But I can whizz a tea bag about in a mug for you.'

'Sit there,' he says. 'You look a bit weary.' He chucks me under the chin. 'I'll make it myself.'

He disappears into the shed while I continue to contemplate my good fortune. Minutes later, he reappears bearing a mug of tea. My ex sits down beside me and we're silent in the sunshine.

'I've had a funny morning,' I say after a while.

'It's not eleven o'clock yet.'

'Still,' I say, 'it's been very funny.' Johnny waits while I form my news into sentences in my brain, still not quite believing them. 'The Council are going to do up Bill Shankly House and Spencer's sent me a whacking great cheque to start my business.'

'That sounds funny in a good way,' Johnny notes.

'Yeah,' I agree. 'But funny nevertheless.'

'Do you think you can cope with one more piece of news?'

'Is it good?'

'Depends where you're standing, I think.' He stares out over the garden and now it's my turn to wait. 'Dana and I have split up.'

'Oh.' That's not what I expected. 'I thought you were in love with her.'

Johnny shrugs. 'She's a wonderful woman,' he says, as he fiddles with the handle of his mug. 'But she's just not you.'

I don't know what to say to that. So I say nothing.

'I love you, Sal.' My best friend reaches for my hand and tucks it into his. 'What Charlie said the other day, about everything being perfect if we could be a family . . .' Johnny turns to me. 'Well, I kind of agree with him.'

Hot tears spring fresh to my eyes and I find my voice again, 'Me too.'

'Let's make your son a happy kid then.'

A tear rolls down my cheek. 'Okay.'

Johnny slips his arm round my shoulders and pulls me into him. 'So now what do we do?'

'You could move your stuff back into the flat,' I tell him.

'We could buy a big house now,' he says. 'Move away from here as you've always wanted to. Have a fresh start. We could go somewhere posh. Formby, Southport, Ormskirk. Wherever you like.'

'What about your mum?'

'We could get a place with a little annexe. Take Mam with us.'

I think of how Mary has thrived now that she has this little garden to come to and her new circle of friends. I think of how much Charlie loves it here and how all that it will take to keep him happy is a 15-inch LCD telly and having Johnny back in his life. I think of how proud I am for turning this place around and making it somewhere fit to live for me and my boy. I think that every day I can look out of my soon-to-be newly-renovated flat and see Johnny's murals brightening up the Community Centre, brightening up my life. I might even get him to paint my name back on my own banner which still has a vacant space.

'Let's not rush into things,' I suggest. 'We'll stay here for a little while longer.'

Johnny smiles at me and I lean into him, putting my head against his chest and curling my feet up on the bench. We snuggle up together. There's birdsong on the air. The flowers turn their faces to catch the sun.

There's a comfort in the fact that I now know that I'm going to be here to see this perfect little space bloom and grow. I hope that the garden and I continue to flourish together. I hope that Johnny, Charlie and I will have a long and happy life as a family. And that Sally Freeman, Single Mum and Superwoman, will one day soon become a content, successful and married Superhero.